Cover Poster: "Beat the Whites with the Red Wedge" by Lazar Markovich Lissitzky, a 1919 lithographic poster from the Russian Civil War.

Beck & Branch Publishers
New York, NY
ISBN 979-8-9866069-6-5

LIVE NOT BY LIES

A NOVEL

PATRICK COFFEY

BECK AND BRANCH PUBLISHERS

To Ellen

PREFACE

ON FEBRUARY 12, 1974, Alexander Solzhenitsyn was arrested; on the following day, he was expelled from the Soviet Union. On the day of his arrest, he released an essay, "Live Not by Lies." Of Lenin, Trotsky, Stalin, and the others who had led the Revolution and killed millions in its name, he wrote, "Today, when all the axes have hewn what they hacked, when all that was sown has borne fruit, we can see how lost, how drugged were those conceited youths who sought, through terror, bloody uprising, and civil war, to make the country just and content."

The foundation underlying the edifice of the Soviet Union, Solzhenitsyn wrote, was lies. Over the years since the 1917 Revolution, those who denied those lies had been imprisoned, executed, sent to slave labor camps, starved to death, and drugged in psychiatric hospitals. Solzhenitsyn knew that not everyone would have the courage to follow that path. But he encouraged his fellow citizens not to believe the lies, not to repeat them, not to teach them to their children. There would be costs even to that, he admitted: a missed promotion, a bad apartment, a university admission denied. But lies were soul-killing, and some price must be paid to live as a human: "We are not called upon to step out onto the square and shout out the truth," he wrote, "to say out loud what we think – this is scary, we are not ready. But let us at least refuse to say what we do not think!"

This is a novel, a story of two families at the center of those lies.

TIMELINE

1878		Stalin born.
1879		Trotsky born.
1882		Boris Anokhin born.
1899		Leonid Eitingon born.
1902		Trotsky is exiled to Siberia, abandons his wife and daughters to escape. Meets and marries Natalia Sedova.
1904-05		Russia defeated in war with Japan.
1905		Uprising in Russia fails. Trotsky exiled to Siberia, escapes again.
1914	September	World War I begins.
1917	March 15	Tsar abdicates. Provisional Government headed first by Prince Lvov, then by Kerensky.
1917	November 7	Communist Revolution – Bolsheviks seize power, overthrow Provisional Government, Civil War between Reds and Whites begins.
1918	March 3	Russia leaves World War I.
1918	July 16-17	Murder of Tsar Nicholas Romanov and his family.
1918-20		Civil War ends in Bolshevik victory under Red Army leadership by Trotsky; "Red Terror" grain confiscation.
1920		Boris Anokhin and family move to Harbin.
1920		Zoya Zarubina and Irina Anokhina born.
1920		War between the Red Army and Poland, subject of Isaac Babel's RED CAVALRY.
1923		Solovki prison camp established, the beginning of the Gulag.
1924		Lenin dies. Stalin, Zinoviev, Kamenev form triumvirate to isolate Trotsky.
1925		Kamenev and Zinoviev join Trotsky in the "United Opposition" to Stalin, who joins with Bukharin.
1925-27		Stalin turns on Bukharin, then takes individual power.
1925		Vassily Zarubin posted to Harbin with his wife Olga and daughter Zoya; Zarubin is reposted leaving his family in Harbin. Leonid Eitingon takes his place.

1926		Anokhin family leaves Harbin; Boris Anokhin is arrested, then sent by Soviet secret service to Istanbul.
1927-29		Trotsky sent in internal exile to Alma Ata.
1929-33		Trotsky expelled from Soviet Union, exiled to Istanbul.
1929-31		Eitingon and his family posted to Istanbul, leave abruptly after fire at Trotsky's house.
1931-33		Construction of the White Sea Canal.
1932-33		Collectivization campaign with intentional starvation of millions, especially in Ukraine.
1933-37		Trotsky in exile in Paris, then Norway.
1934	December 1	Kirov assassinated.
1936-39		Spanish Civil War.
1936-38		Great Purges in Soviet Union managed first by Yagoda, then by Yezhov as heads of the NKVD.
1937		Trotsky offered asylum in Mexico.
1939		Leonid Eitingon sent to Mexico with instructions to kill Trotsky.
1940	May 24	Failed attempt to kill Trotsky led by David Siqueiros.
1940		Zoya's first marriage.
1940	August 20	Trotsky killed by Ramón Mercader.
1941	June 2	Zoya's daughter, Tatiana, born.
1941	June 22	Germany invades the Soviet Union.
1941	June 25	Finland invades the Soviet Union.
1941	December 5	Finnish troops take Medvezhyegorsk.
1943	November	Tehran Conference, Zoya interprets.
1944	June 20	Red Army recaptures Medvezhyegorsk.
1945	February	Yalta Conference, Zoya interprets.
1945		Zoya translates stolen American atomic bomb documents.
1945	May 9	Victory Day over Germany in the Soviet Union.
1945	July	Potsdam Conference, Zoya interprets.
1945	August	American atomic bombings of Hiroshima and Nagasaki.
1946		Nuremberg trials of Nazi leadership, Zoya interprets.
1949	August	Soviet atomic bomb tested successfully.
1951		Leonid Eitingon arrested and imprisoned.

1953	March	Stalin dies, Beria frees Leonid Eitingon.
1953	December	Leonid Eitingon arrested and then imprisoned again when Beria is executed.
1960		Ramón Mercader freed from Mexican prison, moves to Moscow.
1961	April 12	Yuri Gagarin sent into orbit, first man in space.
1964		Khrushchev deposed; Leonid Eitingon freed but not rehabilitated.
1968	May	Sakharov publishes his first dissident essay.
1968	August 21	Soviet invasion of Czechoslovakia.
1975		Ramón Mercader moves to Cuba.
1978	October 18	Ramón Mercader dies.
1981	May 3	Leonid Eitingon dies.
1985	March 10	Gorbachev becomes General Secretary of the Communist Party of the Soviet Union.
1986	December 19	Sakharov freed from internal exile.
1991	December 25	Soviet Union dissolved.

MOSCOW, DECEMBER 25, 1991

Christmas morning in the West. Not here though, not until January 7. But because we are a generous people, today we'll give America the Christmas present it has always wanted – our nation. This is the last day for the Soviet Union.

I'm on that cusp between sleep and waking, still caught in my dream of Yuri Gagarin, the first man in space. Yuri and I sat side by side on an upholstered green divan in the parlor of his Vostok-1 spacecraft, gazing through the window and marveling at the universe's splendor. I poured tea, and he complimented me on a mauve party dress that I wore on my twelfth birthday. I try to grasp at the dream's tendrils, but it's slipping away. Quite a dream, especially the roomy parlor in Yuri's space capsule, which fit him as snugly as his greatcoat.

The date that Yuri flew – April 12, 1961 – might have been the happiest day in our Soviet life. Not the proudest day. That was of course May 9, 1945, Victory Day over the Nazis. But on Victory Day we all grieved for our dead even as we celebrated. Yuri's flight, however, brought us nothing but joy, and we all flew with him. "Yuri" was all the name he needed – a first name like a favorite brother. I interpreted for Yuri on his foreign press tour, and we often dined together. Whenever we entered a restaurant, people would stare; I was almost a head taller than Yuri. He was a gentle man with a wonderful smile, and our nation gave him its highest award, Hero of the Soviet Union. We loved him, and we wept when he died piloting an experimental plane seven years later, a bad omen for Communism. Four months later we invaded Czechoslovakia.

I had another friend who wore the Hero of the Soviet Union medal, Ramón Mercader, who slammed an ice-axe into Leon Trotsky's skull. Like Yuri, Ramón risked his life for Communism. He did what we asked of him, and it cost him twenty years in a Mexican prison. He lived in Moscow after his release, where he became a part of my family, almost a stepbrother; my stepfather Leonid had directed him in Trotsky's murder, and he and Ramón were as close as father and son. Both Yuri and Ramón were Soviet heroes, but we treated them differently. Our leaders lined up to have their pictures taken with Yuri, but they shunned Ramón. They were embarrassed by the cruelty of what they had ordered him to do, so they pinned a medal on his chest and crossed the room at receptions to avoid him.

I awoke on my own today, but my clock radio has just switched on with the morning news. One of Yuri's successors, Cosmonaut Sergei Krikalev, is now orbiting the earth. Good luck to him. If he manages to return, he will find the nation that launched him has disappeared.

Time to get up, time for tea and toast and television. I'll spend the day in my dressing gown, going through old family photos and my typescripts of Leonid's stories while I watch my country dissolve. We Communists always talked about "the road to socialism," and demonstrators on my television carry a banner, "75 Years on the Road to Nowhere." There's truth in that banner, but it wasn't that simple. Our history had its excesses: execution of the tsar and his family, Red Terror during the Civil War, starvation of millions of Ukrainian peasants, the Great Purges, forced resettlements of whole nationalities, the invasion of Czechoslovakia, the Chernobyl disaster, and the Gulag, to name a few. All those stories, once denied, are now common knowledge in my disappearing country. But we also had our successes: we overthrew the tyrannical tsar; we turned our backward peasant nation into an industrial power; and 27 million of us gave our lives to save Europe from the Hitlerites. And yes, we sent Yuri into space. Like citizens of every nation, we celebrated our triumphs and excused our crimes.

I have lived as a Soviet citizen for 71 years. Tomorrow, I will be only a Russian. My lifespan almost matches my country's. I was born three years after the 1917 Revolution, and I'll soon be in the ground. And my story is as tangled as my country's: I am the daughter of one secret-police general and the stepdaughter of another; a former star athlete; a linguist; a mother; the translator of America's atomic bomb secrets; an interpreter for Stalin, Churchill, Roosevelt, and Truman; an activist for peace and women's rights; and the financial support of ten family members.

And a once-proud Communist. To be a Communist is unpopular now, and I don't believe in it the way I once did. My disillusionment was step-by-step: the arrest of my friend's parents, my friendship with Anna Akhmatova and Andrei Sakharov, Leonid's imprisonments, our invasions of Czechoslovakia and Afghanistan, the long stagnation under Brezhnev. Sometimes I thought there was hope for us – our victory over the Nazis, Khrushchev's repudiation of Stalin's crimes, Yuri's flight, Gorbachev's too-late attempt to start anew. In the end, however, "75 Years on the Road to Nowhere" pretty much sums things up. And that road was hard. The Revolution wrecked many lives, and people in my family – myself included – stand among both the wrecked and the wreckers.

I was a coward. I could have spoken out, as Sakharov and others did. Instead, I took what the Soviet state offered me and kept my head down when it threatened me.

I'm drowsy again, dozing in my armchair, drifting in and out of sleep. Remembering is like wandering through the halls of an abandoned building that I might have once known, perhaps a school or museum. Rubbish that might have some significance litters the floors. I hear steps and voices in the distance; many doors are open, but some closed doors frighten me. I turn away from those and stumble through the corridors, only to find I've somehow entered an avoided room from another direction.

I want to believe my memories, but they're unreliable. I forget things that disturb me, and I remember things that may never have been – stories (perhaps lies) that I've been told, things I've imagined or dreamed. My first memories are of Papa and Mama and Irina in China....

1

HARBIN, 1925

The day I met Irina. I was five years old. Papa had brought Mama and me to Harbin, and we'd been living in the fancy hotel for only a few days. When I told Papa that living there made me feel like a princess, he said that princesses were not part of Communism, but that he thought of me as a ballerina.

I'd watched a wedding that morning. Mama kept trying to drag me away, but I wouldn't move. That afternoon, I stood exactly in the center at the top of the hotel's grand staircase. Like that morning's bride, I pointed my toes ballerina-fashion and descended. I held my imaginary bouquet chest-high with both hands, and I stepped carefully; a bride shouldn't look down. I turned my head left then right and smiled at my guests.

A waiter carrying a tray of empty glasses started up my stairs. He stepped out of sight for a moment on the landing just below and when I reached the landing – like magic – he'd vanished! But then, I saw a thin crack in the marble wall, the edge of a wooden panel, artfully painted to match the stone! No knob, but when I pushed, the panel clicked open onto a narrow staircase. A secret passage! I knew I shouldn't, but I stepped in and pulled the panel behind me. The air was steamy, and I heard women's voices – one singing a love song – from below. I descended with a hand on the wall until the staircase opened into a large room, where women washed and ironed bedsheets and towels. They glanced at me, but no one stopped working or called out. Three dark corridors, dimly lit by bare electric bulbs, led from the laundry room. My heart was pounding, but I wanted to be an explorer like Vitus Bering, and explorers were brave. I chose the corridor to my right. Some doors stood open, and I soon understood where I was. Our waitress from last night's dinner sat in a chair and sewed, so the hotel's workers lived in my secret passage! But their rooms were dark and small, nothing like where I lived on the top floor with Papa and Mama.

The corridor made a turn to the left past a small alcove in the hallway. A girl with long brown hair sat cross-legged on the floor, where she was building an irregular structure from ragged butt-ends of scrap lumber. She smiled at me and said,

"Want to play blocks? I'm Irina."

I had left all my playmates behind in Moscow, so of course I wanted to play. I dropped to the floor beside her.

"Careful about splinters," Irina warned.

We'd been playing for about an hour when Irina's mother returned from shopping. She smiled at us, but even at age five I could see that my presence made her nervous. She asked my name, and when she learned that I was a guest at the hotel, she said it was time for me to go. I retraced my steps through the secret passage.

Mama was frantic, as I knew she would be, and telling her about a secret passage only made things worse. She told me never to go there again, but I cried and pleaded that I had no friends, and the next morning she agreed to meet Irina and her mother. I led her to the secret door; she looked over her shoulder to make sure no one was watching and stepped through. I didn't understand the conversation between Mama and Irina's mother, who was worried about rules concerning social contact with a hotel guest. But Mama told Irina's mother that it would be all right, and she left me there to play.

All was fine for a week, and then I received my first lesson in the separation of classes. I took Irina to the lobby, where we danced before the tall, gilt-framed mirrors. The hotel's concierge rushed from behind his desk and crossed the lobby in long strides. He seized Irina's arm and hissed, "You don't belong here!"

Without speaking to each other, Irina and I ran in opposite directions to our mothers. When Papa came home, Mama sent him to the concierge, and Papa returned smiling a few minutes later.

"Everything is fine," he told me. "You girls can play where you like."

Mama asked him what he had said.

"I used both the stick and the carrot. I told him I could have him fired, and I slipped him some cash." Papa always seemed able to fix things.

When Irina and I first met, I was the rich girl who lived on the top floor while Irina was the poor girl who lived in the basement, and my papa was an important diplomat while Irina's father was a doorman. But Irina had things that mattered. Irina's mother made us cookies, her grandmother taught us to embroider, and Irina's papa was there whenever he worked the night or evening shift. In good weather he'd take us to the park or to the river, and in bad weather he'd read us stories. Irina's family welcomed us in ways that mine didn't, so we mostly played in the corridor outside her door.

HARBIN, 1925

Like an icepick, the winter wind always stabbed at the same spot, precisely half an inch above the bridge of Boris Anokhin's nose. He pressed his gloved thumb there, but relief was only temporary. A monsoon over the Sea of Japan had formed the wind and pushed it toward the Korean mountains, which had shredded it and dumped it into the broad Chinese plain, where it reformed and gathered speed. By the time the wind reached Harbin and stung Anokhin's forehead, it was relentless.

Anokhin waved two gloved fingers, and a pair of bellboys scurried from the Hotel Moderne's baggage door and wrestled a steamer trunk from the roof of a horse-drawn sleigh-taxi. Anokhin glanced at the hotel clock. Not yet four o'clock, and the pale January sun was all but gone. In another fifteen minutes, he would trade places with the inside doorman and be warm. Until then, his job was to welcome arriving guests, summon taxis, and ignore the cold. He sniffed. The air was moister and a little warmer; after four years standing in the same spot, he could smell snow's onset. His shift was to end at six, but if it snowed, he would be up all night supervising the Chinese workers as they cleared and salted the sidewalks and hotel entrances. He blew into his cupped glove, deflecting his exhalation upward to melt the ice crystals that had closed his nostrils. He wasn't permitted to flip his collar, but he pulled it higher and tighter. When he'd taken the doorman's job, he'd despised the mock military uniform that the hotel made him wear. But although the blue greatcoat's gold braid and brass buttons still embarrassed him, he had come to appreciate its warmth. Each evening, his mother examined his jacket, his greatcoat, and his hat. She sponged and brushed, pressed a sharp crease into his trousers, polished his boots and brass buttons, and combed the braid of his epaulets. He'd never had a complaint from the hotel's manager at the morning inspection.

Anokhin came from a family of soldiers. His great-grandfather had commanded an artillery battery in the Raevsky redoubt at Borodino in 1812. When his gunners fell in the ferocious French attack, he loaded the cannons himself. He fought for four hours, and his corpse bore witness to his heroism: nine bayonet wounds and hands burned raw from loading the red-hot guns. Marshall Kutuzov pinned the Order of St. George on his chest and kissed his cheeks as he lay in his coffin. Anokhin's grandfather, father, and uncles all followed in the tsar's service, so his future had been predetermined. After seven years at the Page Corps, Russia's premier military school, he was commissioned a sub-lieutenant in the 85th "Vyborksky" Infantry Regiment in 1904. But he found no glory, only defeats: first in the war against Japan, then in the Great War against the Germans, and then in the final disaster, the Civil War against the Reds, when he'd fought in Kolchak's White Army as a colonel in command of a thousand men. After the White collapse in 1920, he fled to Harbin and sent for his wife, Anna, and his mother, Lydia Antonova. Now, after five years, he was grateful for his small salary and tips.

The massive, Italianate, three-story Hotel Moderne might have dropped in from Paris. It filled an entire block on Kitaiskaia Street, a boulevard so wide that in the blowing snow, Anokhin couldn't even make out the fashionable shops across the street. But on a clear summer day, guests climbed the hotel's cupola for Harbin's best views. To the north, the railway bridge crossed the Songhua River, and to the south, the green onion domes and Cyrillic crosses of St. Sophia's cathedral gleamed in the sun, prompting comparisons to St. Basil's in Red Square.

But Anokhin saw Harbin for the fraud that it was. The city imitated an ancient Russian metropolis, but it was less than thirty years old, thrown together by Russia's *nouveau-riche*. St. Sophia's new marble and gilt were pretentious replacements for the polished wood of St. Nicholas's, the modest Harbin cathedral built only a few years earlier. Harbin's leading citizens had contributed to St. Sophia's building fund, but they'd made sure their donations were noted and published. Not to be outdone, Harbin's Jews had financed two giant synagogues. Anokhin despised the businessmen, both Christian and Jewish. They cared only for money and show, and they'd made Harbin into a *faux* Moscow. Sometimes he thought that the Reds had the right idea about capitalists, although he never said that to his White acquaintances.

Harbin's fraud, however, went beyond its ostentation. The city was not even *in* Russia. The map made it clear. Harbin was in China, although one could go days hearing nothing but Russian and Yiddish in its streets. In 1896, Russia had strong-armed China into leasing a 500-mile belt across Manchuria so that it could shorten the railroad route to its Pacific port, Vladivostok. Harbin, a small Chinese village in the center of the shortcut, became a boomtown, first during the railroad's construction and then in its administration. Everyone who came to Harbin seemed to grow rich, at least for a time – everyone but the Chinese day-laborers who lived in hovels across the river.

In October 1917, the Bolsheviks seized power in St. Petersburg and Moscow, and everything changed. The Whites – a hodgepodge alliance of businessmen, nobles, clergy, army officers, and liberals – resisted the Reds, and the Russian Empire fractured into civil war. At first, the Whites won victory after victory. The Western nations supported them, and most of the tsar's Russian officers joined the White cause, Anokhin among them. He was still angry at the incompetence of Kolchak and the other White generals, who never tried to win popular support or to organize a unified command. By late 1919 the Reds were winning on all fronts, and White émigrés fled Russia, 200,000 of them to Harbin. At first, Harbin prospered. The refugees brought money and spent it; their imperial medals gleamed on their uniforms as they dined and danced; they boated and skated on Harbin's Songhua River as if it were St. Petersburg's Neva, as if the Revolution had never happened. Soon, they were certain, the Bolsheviks would collapse. Soon the Russian people would come to their senses and invite the Whites home. Anokhin, who'd been through the worst of the Civil War, had no illusions; the Russian peasants and workers might dislike the Reds, but they hated the Whites.

In 1920 China recognized the Soviet government, a disaster for White refugees because it made their Imperial Russian passports worthless and gave the Reds full control of the railway. By 1925, most émigrés' money was running out, and people made do. Countesses worked as seamstresses or prostitutes, and military officers, like Colonel Anokhin, became waiters or doormen.

Vigilance was essential for both a combat officer and for a doorman, and Anokhin regularly scanned the approaches to the hotel. He turned to his left and saw a hotel resident, Vassily Zarubin, stepping quickly along Kitaiskaia Street, gold spectacles on his round face. Zarubin twisted away from the frigid wind as he walked, and one of his gloved hands pressed his hat to his head while the other gripped his briefcase.

Anokhin opened the hotel's massive door and bowed slightly, "Good afternoon, Vassily Mikhailovich." A doorman's job was to be courteous to all guests, even to Reds like Zarubin, who were now living in the hotel side-by-side with those White émigrés who still had money. Passions had subsided. There had been surprisingly few incidents, especially considering the atrocities inflicted and suffered by both sides in the Civil War. An occasional fistfight in the hotel bar after the tenth drunken chorus of *The Internationale* by the Reds or of *God Save the Tsar* by the Whites, but nothing worse.

Anokhin knew that Zarubin was a diplomat at Harbin's Soviet consulate. Zarubin was not the worst of the Reds. He'd given oranges to the staff at Christmas, and when an elderly White princess fainted in the lobby, Zarubin lifted her to a chair and called for the hotel doctor. In another life, Anokhin thought, he and Zarubin might have been friends. True, the man had been his enemy in the Civil War, but he had at least risked his life for what he believed, and he carried his short, muscular body the way a soldier would. And Zarubin's daughter, Zoya, was his daughter Irina's best friend. The war was over. Perhaps Zarubin could help his family return to Russia.

HARBIN, 1925

I pulled the duvet up to my chin and pressed my cheek into my pillow, and the scent of bleach and laundry soap soothed me. I ran my finger along the red and blue flowers that my grandmother had embroidered on the pillowcase. I was five and could read, but I liked it better when Papa read my bedtime story. Sometimes I let him read others, but the rooster Golden Comb was my favorite. As he turned to the book's final page, I joined him in chanting the ending: "The cat and the thrush picked up their friend, Golden Comb, and took him home. They lived happily ever after. The End." Papa closed the book and sang the lullaby he sang every night.

Sleep sweetly, softly, my dear baby,
Bayu-bayu, hush-a-bye.
The quiet moon shines down upon you,
Bayu-bayu, hush-a-bye.
I'll sing you songs and tell you stories,
Bayu-bayu, hush-a-bye

On other nights, that was when the lights went out. But that night he kissed me and said that he must go to Moscow, that my mother and I would stay in Harbin for a short time and then follow. I tried to climb into his lap, but he gently pushed me back under the duvet. He said that the Party needed him, and there was no arguing with the Party.

"But what about helping people get home?" I asked.

"Others will help them," he said. "I'll be gone when you wake up, but we'll be together soon."

I didn't see him for two years, and by that time Mama was with Leonid.

❖ ❖ ❖

As I sit in my dressing gown this morning, 66 years later, I still understand only some of it. I was five years old in 1925 when my father, Vassily Zarubin, left us. He was a Chekist, a Soviet secret police officer. My mother, Olga, had gone with him to his new posting at the Soviet consulate in Harbin, where he was operating under diplomatic cover as second secretary. When I asked Papa what he did at work, he told me that thousands of Russians had fled to Harbin during the Civil War, and it was his job to help them go home. That was one way of looking at it, a version suitable for a small child. The Reds had defeated the Whites five years earlier, and 200,000 White refugees had fled to Harbin. Many were now destitute; they had run through their money and sold their jewelry and paintings. They were homesick, and my father offered passports and train passage to return to Russia. All was forgiven, he told them.

I have since learned this much: In Russia, nothing is ever forgiven. He indeed sent Whites home, where some, especially army officers and political leaders, were either imprisoned or shot immediately. Others might be offered a choice: prison, or a return to exile in one of the White communities in Paris, Berlin, Vienna, Istanbul, Shanghai, San Francisco or New York. There the Cheka would pay them a miserable stipend, and they would live as Judas goats, accepting any task the Cheka assigned them – perhaps informing on some deluded counter-revolutionary who, against all hope, planned an anti-Bolshevik uprising (Cheka assassins would murder him), or perhaps arranging false papers for a White general desperate to see his dying mother in Petersburg (the Cheka would seize him when he crossed the border).

But at age five, I knew none of that. After my father left, I pestered Mama about leaving for Moscow to join Papa, and her answer was always the same: it won't be long now, but we must wait for our travel documents. I mailed letters and drawings to Papa almost every day, but he wrote back only occasionally, and then with notes that didn't say much – not where he was or what he was doing – just, "I miss you both."

Two months after Papa left, I was playing dolls in the hallway outside our rooms with my friend Irina. Mama gave a sharp cry behind the closed bedroom door. When I entered, she pushed a letter into her sleeve and turned away wiping tears. Before I could speak, she gave a sing-song answer to a question that I hadn't even asked: "Everything is all right, don't worry, when the papers arrive we'll go to Moscow."

Twenty years later, she explained the letter: It had been signed only "A Friend" and warned that Papa had another woman in Moscow.

"And you believed it?" I asked her. She just shrugged.

Then Leonid arrived to take Papa's place, both at the embassy and in Mama's heart. I was playing with Irina in the hotel lobby when a friend of Papa's called out, "Zoya, meet your new Uncle Leonid, your father's friend! He's just arrived from Moscow and will live here too!"

Years later, Mama told me that it had been love at first sight, that she'd loved Leonid forever after, even when he was unfaithful. During the months that he was seducing Mama, Leonid was careful with me. He played with me and held me on his lap, but he left it to Mama to read bedtime stories and sing lullabies. Even later, after he married Mama, he never let me call him Papa. You already have a Papa," he would say, "a very good Papa."

Uncle Leonid visited our hotel room most evenings. He played his balalaika and sang, and he played *birulki* with me, a game like American pick-up sticks. Even then, I understood that he let me win most of the time. He would use his hook to pull a piece out, slip so that he knocked over another piece, slap his leg and pretend to be angry with himself. He would win just often enough so that I enjoyed my triumphs. I loved it. He seemed impossibly tall, with wavy black hair that smelled of rosewater, rough cheeks that smelled of soap, and wool suits that smelled of him. He took me with him to the market and even on train trips.

Once, the two of us sat alone on the green plush of a first-class train compartment. I was showing my doll Nastya the changing leaves of the birch trees that rolled past the train window, and Uncle Leonid was reading his newspaper. I heard nothing, but he suddenly stood with his finger to his lips. Without a word, he took Nastya from me, lifted her skirts, took a paper from his pocket, stuffed it into a slit in her body that I hadn't even known was there, and pushed the doll back into my arms. He bent to my ear and whispered, "When they enter, cry and don't stop."

At that moment a Chinese policeman flung the compartment door open, and two other policemen were standing behind him. Because I had a Chinese *amah*, I understood what they shouted, "Stand up!"

I hugged Nastya and began to whimper, softly at first, then louder. I stretched my arm to Uncle Leonid, and a policeman pulled me back. They braced Leonid against the window, felt his body for a gun, then gestured that he should remove his clothes. While the first policeman inspected his papers with a magnifying glass, another policeman went through the clothes Leonid had thrown onto the seat, emptied all the pockets, felt along the seams, slit the threads that held his jacket lining, examined his shoes by lifting the insoles and then prying open the soles and heels. I bawled, twisted in the policeman's grasp, pressed Nastya to my face.

The third policeman pulled our suitcase from the rack. He rifled through our clothing, slit the suitcase's silk lining and looked behind it, and he measured the suitcase's inner and outer depth for a false bottom. Then he thrust his hand behind the seat cushions, and he lay on his back to probe the springs below the seats. Finally, the policeman who had shouted "Stand up!" waved the other two out, and I let my screams subside into sobs. The policeman gave a quick bow to Leonid, who was standing in his underwear, and left.

Leonid put his finger to his lips and smiled at me as he dressed. He took me to the dining car for a vanilla ice.

❖❖❖

A fat envelope with passports and tickets arrived at last; I jumped and clapped, crying, "We're going to live with Papa!"

But that night I peeked between the panels of the painted Chinese screen that separated my bed from the rest of the hotel room. Leonid usually left after I'd gone to bed, but that night he was still there. He and Mama weren't shouting but whispering, and both were angry and upset. Mama's back blocked most of my view, but I could see Leonid's face. He told her that he'd been transferred to Beijing, and he asked – no, he *insisted* – that Mama and I go with him. Mama wept, crying no no no, but she threw her arms around Leonid's neck, and I saw Leonid's expression: a smile, but not a nice smile.

It was the smile of a man in control, a smile that I've seen more than once. As I flip through old family photos, I've just found one of Leonid raising his glass in a toast at my half-sister Svetlana's tenth birthday dinner, when I was sixteen. It was the first time I'd been allowed a small glass of vodka. It looked like water, and the rest of the family and guests just threw theirs back, so I did too, but I sputtered and coughed. Everyone laughed, Leonid loudest of all. I looked at him and suddenly remembered his smirk when he'd embraced Mama that night. I excused myself, saying the vodka had burned my throat. I lay on my bed and calculated backwards from Svetlana's birthdate. Mama was pregnant when she agreed to go with Leonid. Did she go with Leonid because she loved him or because she couldn't face Papa? Why didn't she have an abortion? Did Papa really have another woman? Who had betrayed whom? Why did I feel guilty, as though I had abandoned my father? I've sometimes thought it might all have been at the orders of the Cheka, who liked to pair agents as couples. Perhaps they'd ordered Mama paired with Leonid. Or perhaps they paired Papa with the woman he later married, my stepmother Lisa. I've never had an answer, and I never will; all I have are fragmented memories. Mama and Papa both died in the early 1970s, Leonid ten years ago. And Leonid wouldn't have told me much even if he were alive. Mama was only one of his many wives, and he never cared about any of his love stories.

MOSCOW, 1980

"Zoya! Zoya! I'm down to four packs of cigarettes!"

I called out, "I'm behind you, Uncle Leonid," but he didn't hear me. He'd been dozing when I'd left for the shops, and I must have woken him when I returned and opened the door. He didn't even know I'd been gone, and he wasn't wearing his hearing aid. "Ministry of Health trash" was what he called it, claiming he didn't need it anyway. The vanity of old men! When a man is eighty, who would notice an electrical box clipped to his belt or a wire that snaked from his shirt collar to his ear? He only wore the hearing aid for television football matches. I closed the apartment door firmly but not with a slam, watching him as I did so. No, he hadn't heard that either.

Leonid pulled off his reading glasses and struggled out of his chair, spilling *Pravda* onto the floor. He bent halfway to retrieve it and then stopped; Brezhnev, his suit jacket sagging with medals, glared up at him from the front page. Brezhnev had been General Secretary 16 years, and he looked old even in his airbrushed newspaper photos.

"Look at those eyebrows," Leonid muttered to himself, "like black beetles stuck onto his forehead. Why doesn't his barber trim them?" He planted his right foot on Brezhnev's face and shuffled into the kitchen, still calling, "Zoya!"

"Uncle Leonid, what is it?" I hadn't shouted, but he jumped. I folded the scattered newspaper and set it on the table.

"Cigarettes!" he said, "I'm almost out."

"I bought six packs, and Svetlana will bring more on Saturday."

I didn't argue with him about how much he smoked. He was irritable on the best of days, and without cigarettes he was unbearable. At least he didn't drink the way most pensioners did. He'd first gone to prison in 1951, a handsome man in his early fifties, a major general in the NKVD. He was freed in 1953 after Stalin's death and then imprisoned again after Beria's overthrow a few months later. When he was released for good after another eleven years, all his teeth were brown or missing, and his limp was much worse. They gave him only a soldier's pension of twelve rubles fifty kopecks a month, exactly the price of ten packs of cigarettes. He would go through those in three days. And they dumped him in a single room in a communal apartment that housed six families.

But Alexander Shelepin, who had been KGB director, remembered Leonid. He arranged a small flat and a job as a translator for him. Leonid later moved to one of the new high-rise boxes that ringed Moscow, where I visited him every week.

I looked around. The building was only two years old, but you would think it had been through the war. Perhaps the foundation had settled, or the prefabricated concrete panel that formed the wall hadn't been correctly attached, because the plaster was cracked and not all the windows shut or opened properly. And no one took care of the common spaces in any of these buildings. The hallways were littered with trash, and the elevators could be out for days. It was not much of an apartment, but it had its own bathroom, important for an old man up six times every night. He was failing, but who would have thought he would have made it to 1980? His gaunt face sagged, he waddled, and he left the apartment only to play cards or dominoes with his few surviving friends – no, not friends, his acquaintances. Leonid preferred women as his friends.

I remembered only two close male friends: Ramón Mercader, who had killed Trotsky under Leonid's direction; and Pavel Sudoplatov, Leonid's last boss at the NKVD and his companion in prison. I'd liked and pitied Ramón, who left Moscow for Cuba five years earlier, where he'd died. Sudoplatov was another matter. He'd been my boss in the 1940s when I translated the American atomic bomb secrets, and I'd be happy never to see him again. He'd been a tyrant then, although as Leonid's stepdaughter, I'd suffered less than his other subordinates.

I hoisted my shopping bags to the kitchen table and opened the fridge to store the meat and milk, but I could feel Leonid's agitation behind me. I turned to look at him.

"I need to tell you things," he said, "things you don't know."

I didn't react; if I sighed, he'd get worse. Because we both had worked for the Soviet secret police – now called the KGB, in our time mostly the NKVD, before that the Cheka and the

GPU and a few other names – he sometimes confided in me, telling me things he wouldn't tell any of his women or biological children. He didn't tell me everything, of course, only heroic stories of operating behind German lines or driving a tank in the Spanish Civil War, but nothing about pistol shots to the back of the head in the Lubyanka cellars. And he shared no state secrets, not even fifty-year-old secrets. I'd been only an interpreter and translator for the NKVD, and generals didn't share secrets with underlings. No shameful stories and no secrets limited his repertoire. I was positive that he'd already told me all the tales he was willing to tell, many times, like all old men. I wanted to go home. But before I could say that, he blurted, "About Trotsky!"

"Uncle Leonid, you've told me about Trotsky."

He had spit out "Trotsky" as if it were a bone stuck in his throat. A little calmer now, he lowered himself into his chair and lit a papirosa, a cigarette with a built-in cardboard holder so that less harsh makhorka tobacco would be wasted in a discarded butt. Few foreigners smoked paparosi; a few affected European actors did, but they smoked for the show rather than for enjoyment. When I gave a papirosa to a Czech friend, he threw it away after a single drag. Between coughs, he said that it was like hanging his face over a trash fire. Leonid had entered Vladimir prison smoking expensive French cigarettes, but paparosi were all that the prison canteen offered. When he came out twelve years later, he found other tobacco tasteless.

"This Trotsky story you haven't heard," Leonid said.

"Not about Trotsky in Mexico?"

"Much earlier, 1920 in the Civil War. He wasn't the great Satan then; he led the Red Army, the second man to Lenin. That's when I met him. When the hicks in Gomel tried to expel me from the Party, Trotsky made me his aide. I rode with him on his armored train from one front to the next. I helped him decorate the brave and helped him send cowards and traitors to the firing squad. Trotsky saved the Revolution, and he saved me."

Leonid had never said anything to me about being Trotsky's aide, and I was sure he'd never spoken about it to anyone else. Could he have invented this just now? He was erratic, but he wasn't demented. Still, it was hard to believe. Everyone associated with Trotsky – political allies, supporters, family, friends, secretaries, even his cooks – had been arrested no later than 1938. If Leonid had been Trotsky's aide during the Civil War, he wouldn't have become an NKVD major general, and he wouldn't have been awarded the Order of Lenin. He'd be in a mass grave at Butovo.

"But you did eliminate Trotsky in Mexico?"

"Sure, twenty years later. You know the story. Not with my own hand, but I recruited Ramón, I trained him, and I waited at the wheel of the getaway car while he slammed his axe into Trotsky's head."

The papirosa's ash cascaded down Leonid's shirt. None of it made sense. I started to speak, but I couldn't. A hundred clashing questions jammed the passage from my mind to my voice.

"Why did I kill him?" Leonid said. "You of all people should understand. It was my duty."

I wasn't ready to listen then. Leonid was lying or was crazy or his story was true. In any case, it would take hours, and I had to be home for dinner with my daughter, Tatiana, and her husband. The Civil War was sixty years past, so Leonid could wait until my next visit. But I wanted to hear what he had to say. And I knew, as he did, that his time was short.

I returned to Leonid the next Thursday. An hour on the crowded metro, then a bus, then up five flights of stairs on swollen ankles because his elevator was out again. He was eighty, I was sixty, and things weren't getting easier for either of us. I found him waiting at the kitchen table, shaved and dressed. He'd placed a notepad and pencils, clearly meant for me, in front of the chair across from him. He seemed calm, which would make the day easier.

"Please sit," he told me. "Let's get to work. Write it all down."

Yevgenia, his latest wife, stepped from the bedroom. She was almost certainly the last of the wives, and the worst. Pretty in a doll-like way, she was useless and demanding, always asking for things: Zoya, can you get us a new fridge, Zoya can

you get us a color television? And the way she'd decorated
the apartment! An Asiatic carpet on the floor, another cover-
ing the sofa, another on the wall, so that the patterns and colors ran together and clashed. She'd crammed everything she
owned into the flat. China cabinets, armoires, and bureaus
lined the walls and left only a narrow footpath. A fringed or-
ange lampshade hung over the dining table.

"Hello, Zoya, so nice that you could come," Yevgenia said.
"I'd love to talk, but I have an appointment to have my hair
done."

"Find something to do after that," Leonid told her. "Zoya
and I have confidential work."

Yevgenia pouted and left without a word.

I settled myself at the table. Leonid wanted something
from me, something I didn't understand. I wanted to probe,
but as I had done so many times with him, I let it go. Maybe if
I listened to one more story, some of my questions would be
answered.

"So, tell me about Trotsky," I said.

"We'll get to Trotsky, but not yet. Either I die with my stories, or I tell them now, and you're the only one I trust. We'll
start with the shtetl. I want you to use your shorthand. You did
it in English for Churchill and Roosevelt; do it in Russian for
me."

I'd been a translator at the Tehran, Potsdam, and Yalta
Conferences during the war, and I knew how Leonid bragged
about me.

He wanted to start with the shtetl? He'd told me almost
nothing about his Jewish boyhood, and I'd never really asked.
Leonid was Jewish, I wasn't, and it was all a long time ago.

"You always told me none of that mattered," I said, "that
after the Revolution there was no longer Jew or Gentile. But if
that's where you want to start, tell me about it."

"I've never told you about Shklov?"

"That's the shtetl where you were born?"

My interruptions irritated Leonid, and his reply was short.

"Born in Byelorussia in Shklov in 1899, left in 1917. The German invaders rolled into Shklov in 1941 and machine-gunned
all the Jews. A thorough people, the Germans."

That was a typical Leonid explanation. They spoke of the

Holocaust in the West, but Leonid never thought of the fate of the Jews as anything special. Of course, he said, the Jews suffered during the war, but so did everyone. The Germans killed three million Soviet Jews, but they also killed twenty-four million other Soviet citizens. If anyone brought up the Jews and Auschwitz, he would quote the Party's response, "Don't divide the dead."

Leonid had spent the week rehearsing his story, and I fell right back into my shorthand, so we were moving along.

"My father Isaak was a bookkeeper at the paper factory, and he named me Nahum," Leonid said. "He was considered handsome, and he's where I got my looks. We weren't rich, but we were comfortable. You know my two sisters, Sonia and Sima, and my younger brother Isaak. The Shklov shtetl wasn't Hasidic, but it had three synagogues. My father was a freethinker, always spouting Spinoza, but he dragged us all to synagogue every Saturday to impress his bosses at the paper factory. Shklov was 7,000 people, maybe four-fifths of them Jews, and its size made it safe compared with most shtetls. Every few years, refugees from pogroms elsewhere streamed into town telling terrible stories. A lucky Jew had gotten only a beating, but the goys killed men in front of their families, raped women and children, burned homes and barns, stole property and livestock. But no pogroms in Shklov, because there were too many of us. We would have resisted."

So maybe Leonid had a little Jewish feeling after all.

"In 1905, when I was six, Russia came close to revolution; you learned about it in school I'm sure, the film *Battleship Potemkin* and all that. The government incited pogroms that year. They thought that if people could beat Jews, they might be too busy to rebel. After the 1905 revolution failed, Trotsky was put on trial, and he produced documents that proved the government was behind the pogroms."

I must have looked surprised, because Leonid smiled.

"Right, the way you were taught, Trotsky has been written out of history. But more than anyone else, he *was* the 1905 story. He was President of the Petrograd Soviet and led the workers' strike, and the tsar's judges sent him to Siberia for it. Lenin only watched from the sidelines in 1905.

"Anyway, we didn't have a pogrom in Shklov that year, but

the government posted an army detachment there to keep
a lid on things. My father kept the books for an inn near our
house. I was with him, and we were walking up the steps to
the inn's porch when two drunk Cossacks – big mustaches,
long overcoats, tall fur hats cocked to one side – pushed the
door open. My father started to step aside, but one Cossack
raised his boot, shouted, 'Out of the way, yid!' and kicked him
square in the chest. He tumbled backward down the steps,
and the Cossacks left laughing."

A horrible thing for a boy to see. I reached for Leonid's
hand, but he pulled it back and continued.

"I was only six, so I didn't understand much, but I'd heard
that the tsar had sent the Cossacks, so from that day I hated
the tsar. When I said as much at supper one night, my parents
turned pale and shushed me. At school, the teacher told us
that the tsar loved and protected the Jews; I kept my mouth
shut, although I knew that was crap. When I was older, I told
myself, I'd kill the tsar.

"The workers at my father's paper factory went on strike
when I was nine, and the factory's owner hired scabs and
goons and called in police and the local army garrison. The
soldiers shot three workers at the factory gates, one of them
my best friend's father. At supper that night, my papa said
that the deaths were regrettable, but that the strikers had
brought it on themselves. I left the table in tears. My mother,
as usual, was silent.

"Papa died from a bleeding ulcer while he was on a business trip to Petrograd. I was eleven, and we moved in with his
father who paid my tuition at the local school. But I was a trou-
blemaker, a bigmouth. My friends and I would skip school
and buy vodka and tobacco, or we'd steal them if we had no
money. My mother died when I was fifteen, my grandfather
the next year, and I was suddenly poor and on my own. My
grandfather had given up on me. When he died, he left me
nothing."

I started to ask Leonid about his mother, but he cut me off.

"That's enough of my family and the shtetl. Let's get to the
important parts. Are you getting all this down?"

I nodded. That was all I was to hear, Leonid's entire family
history in two pages. Childhood – his, mine, his children's –

had never seemed to matter to him. But now, in his last years, he had started to talk, but he'd cut his story short when he began to reveal himself. And I often do the same. Ignoring what's most painful is one way to survive.

He pulled his shoulders back, sat straighter and continued:

"It was 1916. I cleaned lavatories, dug sand for a concrete factory, and washed gravestones. Later, that would help me call myself a proletarian and not the son of a bookkeeper. I became a Socialist Revolutionary, the biggest mistake of my life. I should have joined the Bolsheviks, but what did I know? I was sixteen, and I didn't know any Bolsheviks in Shklov.

"We SRs believed in direct action. We'd kill the tsar if we could, but we'd settle for killing his ministers. We thought that the Bolsheviks and Mensheviks – the two wings of the Social Democrats – had no balls, that all they did was argue about Marx. We were right about the Mensheviks, who said the revolution would have to wait fifty years, but wrong about the Bolsheviks. Lenin wanted revolution *now*. Again, what did I know? I thought shooting the tsar would fix things, which was why I called myself an SR.

"Then out of nowhere came the February Revolution, and in a matter of days, no more tsar. At first Prince Lvov was head of the Provisional Government, then Kerensky. They wanted to turn Russia into America, which any fool could see wouldn't work. But they did repeal the law that kept the Jews on the shtetls, and I saw my chance. I changed my name from Nahum Isaakovich to Leonid Alexandrovitch, a very Russian first name and patronymic, and I hopped the first train to Petrograd. I didn't want to be a Jew, somebody who got kicked down the steps. If people were going to be kicked, I wanted to be on the other end of the boot. Maybe I should have changed my last name from Eitingon, also Jewish, to something Russian like Dmitriyev. I'm not ashamed to be a Jew, but life's easier if you're not. Leonid, Nahum, Eitingon, Dmitriyev...what's the difference? I've worked under a hundred trade-names, some I don't even remember. I'm eighty, and I don't care what people call me."

Yevgenia's key was in the door; she hadn't heeded Leonid's instructions to stay out for the day.

"That's *your* story," I told him, "but you said you would tell me about Trotsky."

"We'll start on Trotsky next week. He and I have the same story – the Revolution."

HARBIN, 1925

Lydia Antonova nodded off. Her embroidery ring fell from her hand, made three slow revolutions across the floor, and, brought up short by its trailing thread, toppled with a rattle. She startled for a moment, her double chin lifted, then she nodded back into sleep. Four people – Boris Anokhin, his wife Anna, his daughter Irina, and his mother, Lydia Antonova – occupied a single room in the Hotel Moderne's basement, where they shared a bathroom and a kitchen with the families of three other doormen. Because the only light came from a foot-high window at the top of one wall, the room was dark even on the brightest days. The window gave only a view of the passing feet of pedestrians, but no one complained; the room was heated by the hotel's central furnace, and in Harbin's winter, warmth mattered more than light or ventilation.

Anna unrolled four sleeping pallets and released the curtain to divide the room in two. Boris and Anna slept on one side, Irina and her grandmother on the other. The curtain blocked sight but not sound, so when Boris and Anna made love, they did so as quietly as possible, and his mother pretended not to hear. But Irina was five now, and she'd cried out the other night when they'd awakened her. But they couldn't live elsewhere; the hotel insisted that its doormen live on the premises and be on call, and this single room was what the hotel provided.

Irina was asleep on the floor, her face pressed into the rug. Anokhin lifted her back onto her pallet and arranged her covers. He returned to his chair and whispered to his wife:

"What do you think, Anna?"

"I hate Harbin, Boris, and you do too. It's no place for Irina to grow up. And while *your* mother is here, my mother is in Moscow. I want to go home."

"Not easy to do. The Reds might shoot me."

"Their newspapers say it's all in the past, and anyway you fought for what you believed. You're a patriot. They should see that."

"Things happened, things they find difficult to forgive." Things he had never told her about. He remembered one White general, Kalmykov, whose Cossack soldiers routinely raped, looted, tortured, and murdered. Kalmykov took it as a compliment when someone compared him to Genghis Khan, and Anokhin had found it almost impossible to tolerate the man's presence at General Kolchak's staff meetings. But Anokhin knew that based on his own record, the Reds might view him as another Kalmykov. He hadn't obeyed the so-called laws of war either. No one had. He'd executed Red prisoners, just as the Red commanders had executed Whites. There were no prisoner-of-war camps, no transport, no spare food. But the Reds of course remembered only what *they* had suffered. So, no, he couldn't return to Russia as a White colonel.

"Then we just stay here, just exist?" Anna said a little too loudly, and Irina stirred. "What about Paris or Constantinople?"

"You think that would be better? They don't want us either, and here I at least have work. And how would we get there without papers?"

"What about that Red diplomat you talked about, Zarubin? Could he help?"

"Anna, I'm a White colonel! There's no going back."

"What if you weren't a colonel? What if you were someone else? People get false papers all the time."

He leaned forward and clasped her hands. "I've considered that. Maybe."

He wasn't ready to tell her his plan, but he'd heard of an expert Chinese forger. Another doorman at the hotel, Golov, had been a corporal in the White army. The Reds executed White officers, but they sometimes forgave private soldiers. If Golov would sell him his old paybook, the forger could change the photograph and signature page, and Colonel Anokhin would be demoted to Corporal Golov. For the rest of his family, he would get Nansen passports – papers that the League of Nations issued for stateless refugees. In themselves, Nansen passports were almost worthless. Few countries recognized them, but paired with Golov's paybook, they would be better than nothing. Once he had all the papers in order, he would take them to Zarubin and watch his reaction. If he seemed suspicious, they would stay in Harbin. If not, they might risk it and go home to Russia.

But how best to approach Zarubin? He couldn't speak to

him at the hotel. A doorman who bothered a guest with a personal matter would be fired. He might hand Zarubin a letter at the door as he entered or left, but there was a risk to that too. What if Zarubin reported him to the hotel manager? No, he should just steel himself and visit Zarubin at the Soviet consulate.

❖❖❖

By the time Anokhin had arranged the forged paybook, Zarubin had departed, replaced by Leonid Eitingon, also a guest at the Moderne. Anokhin had watched Zarubin and thought him sympathetic, although he knew that might be wishful thinking. Eitingon, however, was less to Anokhin's liking: too good looking, too charming, a too-bright smile when Anokhin held the door for him. And the man's personal behavior was scandalous. Zarubin had left his wife and daughter behind in Harbin, and Eitingon spent most evenings in their room, even taking the daughter on overnight trips. There are few secrets from the staff in a hotel, and the chambermaids reported that Zarubin's wife often visited Eitingon in his room in the afternoons, and that the towels and sheets provided conclusive evidence of what occurred there. The Reds were godless, but even they should behave better than that.

But did he have a choice? Just as he, Anokhin, was the doorman at the Moderne, Eitingon was his doorman to Russia. On Thursday, his day off, Anokhin dressed in his best suit and took Golov's forged paybook and three snot-green Nansen passports to the Russian consulate, located next door to the railway office. The consulate's shabbiness surprised him; the lobby was dark and in need of paint.

A Red Army soldier with a rifle stood inside the door, a clerk stamped papers at a wooden table, and a sour-faced bureaucrat in a soiled business suit sat behind a desk that held a telephone.

"May I help you?" the bureaucrat said without looking up.

"I am Russian. I wish to return home with my family. With whom should I speak?"

"You must speak with our Second Secretary. If I may have your papers, I will arrange an appointment."

Anokhin passed him the passports and Golov's paybook,

and the bureaucrat cranked the phone.

"Mr. Golov wishes to apply for Soviet passports for himself and his family."

The bureaucrat listened closely and nodded, then rang off, looking surprised at Eitingon's answer.

"Secretary Eitingon can see you now. Go up the stairs, first door on the right."

Anokhin hadn't expected things to move so quickly. He walked up the stairs slowly, rehearsing his military record as it appeared in Golov's paybook. He wasn't a good liar, and he wasn't confident that he could stand up to a close interrogation.

Eitingon waved him to a seat. Although the man passed him at the hotel door several times a day, Anokhin could see that he hadn't recognized him, but that was to be expected. People saw a doorman's uniform, not the man. Anokhin passed his papers across the desk, and Eitingon flipped through them and pushed them aside.

"I know this must be awkward for you," he said, "but I will try to make it less so. I assume you are not a Communist, so you need not call me 'comrade.' We will call each other 'citizen.' Citizen Golov, if you are allowed to return to the motherland, you must swear allegiance to the Soviet state and renounce all ties to counter-revolutionary organizations. Is that a problem?"

"No, Citizen Eitingon. For me, politics is over. I am Russian."

"Good. We are building a new world, and we welcome all who want to take part. You will be required to fill out a form explaining your military history. Soldiers of your rank may be amnestied, but if you fought under certain commands, we will have questions. Similarly, you will need to explain your activities since arriving in Harbin. Have you engaged in counter-revolutionary activities here?"

He could answer that honestly. "No, Citizen Eitingon. I'm just a doorman at your hotel."

Eitingon smiled. "I thought I recognized your face, and it bothered me that I couldn't place you. Since we are neighbors, I'll expedite your case. Bring the papers back tomorrow. If there are no problems, I'll have your passports ready in a week. Talk to the clerk downstairs about the details, the necessary photographs and fees. If you need money for the train tickets, the Soviet government will lend it to you. We welcome all men of good will, Citizen Golov."

Anokhin stood to leave, and as his suit jacket fell open, he smelled himself – two separate, familiar body odors that took him back to the battlefield, where those odors had been adulterated by smoke, blood, shit, and death. But today he smelled their essences clearly. If bottled as perfumes, he thought, the odors might be labeled "Despair" – the odor of a man certain he is about to die – and "Relief" – the odor of a man who has unexpectedly survived.

After Anokhin left, Eitingon pulled a sheet of paper from his drawer and uncapped his fountain pen. He wrote for a few minutes, then dropped the paper in his outbox, from which his aide would retrieve it. The sheet bore the heading "Instructions in the matter of Colonel Boris Anokhin."

MOSCOW, 1980

I'd nursed my daughter Tatiana through a stomach flu most of the week, but she was able to go to work on Thursday, the day I'd promised Leonid that I'd return for more of his stories. I wanted a day off and called him to reschedule, but he was insistent.

"This is important, Zoya," he said.

What was the hurry? But I'd spent years doing whatever Leonid demanded, and that was a habit not easily broken. I agreed.

When I arrived at his apartment, Yevgenia was nowhere to be seen. Leonid was impatient, although I was fifteen minutes early. He began as soon as I'd seated myself.

"When we left off, I'd just arrived in Petrograd from the Shklov shtetl. Petrograd was a mess in 1917. The tsar had abdicated, and Kerensky's Provisional Government was supposed to be in charge. But the workers listened only to the Petrograd Soviet, and then only when they felt like it. Trash was everywhere, and almost no streetlights. Long lines to buy anything with prices out of sight. No matter where you went, the whole city stank of piss. Half the workers were unemployed, and the other half were on strike. At one point, even the whores walked off the job.

"I watched strikers at an armament factory haul the owner out on a cart. They ran him to the canal, first let him see the shit floating in the water, then they tipped him in. When he tried to climb out, they stomped his hands and kicked at his face. They didn't kill him though; after an hour of fun, they let him drag himself home.

"I was supposed to register with the Petrograd police, but I wasn't that stupid. The war with the Germans was still on. Thousands of soldiers were deserting and just heading home, and the army was desperate for men. I had to watch out for conscription gangs in the streets. I was still 17, a month too young for the draft, but the police were grabbing anyone they could. I slept under bridges and in railroad stations, and the SRs fed me; I was tough, and they used me as an enforcer at their rallies. I had a leather sap filled with lead shot that just fit my palm. If anyone heckled an SR speaker, I would walk up behind him and give him a quick tap behind the ear. It didn't look like I'd even swung – maybe six inches of arc, nothing more – but he would drop to his knees.

"Petrograd was politics-crazy. Under the tsar, everything had been censored, but suddenly you could print or say anything you wanted. There were at least ten newspapers, one or more for every party, and people read them all. A real government was supposed to be elected by a Constituent Assembly that fall, and all the parties were trying to line up supporters. And that's where I first saw Trotsky.

"It was September, just before the October Revolution, and Kerensky had released Trotsky from prison, something I'm sure he regretted doing for the rest of his life. Trotsky was everywhere in Petrograd, racing from one rally to another. He spoke without notes, just his voice ringing out over the crowd's shouts and applause. He was the best orator I've ever heard. Lenin had forced the other Bolsheviks to bring Trotsky onto their Central Committee, although he had to twist some arms, including Stalin's, to get his way. 'Leninandtrotsky' became almost a single name, a name you heard everywhere. 'Leninandtrotsky say…' and 'What will Leninandtrotsky do?' Nobody in the streets even knew who Stalin was."

Leonid pushed himself up from his chair, opened the hall closet, and dragged a heavy suitcase from behind the coats. He undid the strap, and books, pamphlets, and papers spilled to the floor. The titles I saw frightened me: *The Revolution Betrayed* and *The Stalin School of Falsification*, with Trotsky's name as author on both.

"I remember it all," Leonid said. "I spent years studying Trotsky, and I read everything he wrote, every newspaper article about him or his followers."

"You shouldn't have these, Uncle Leonid," I said. "They don't imprison people for that sort of thing now, but you could still lose your pension."

"Not me. I'm the one who eliminated Trotsky, remember? I collected all this while I was after him. All authorized."

He rummaged through the books until he found a book with the title *My Life*, and he turned to an earmarked page.

"Trotsky spoke most evenings at the *Cirque Moderne*. I went every night. The Cirque was a dump, a shabby auditorium, badly lit by a few bare, blinding arc lamps, so every face was half brilliantly lit and half in black shadow. Here's what Trotsky had to say about speaking at the Cirque." Leonid began to read in a voice different from his own, a voice he must have remembered:

> My audience was composed of workers, soldiers, hard-working mothers, street urchins – the oppressed under-dogs of the capital. Every square inch was filled, every human body compressed to its limit. Young boys sat on their fathers' shoulders, infants were at their mothers' breasts. I made my way to the platform through a narrow human trench, sometimes I was borne overhead. The air, tense with breathing, exploded with shouts. Around and above me were densely compressed elbows, chests, heads. Whenever I made a sweeping gesture, I always brushed someone, and a grateful movement in response would let me understand that I should not worry, should not break off, but should continue. No speaker could resist the electric tension of that impassioned human throng. At times, it appears I felt with my lips the insistent searching of this crowd that had fused into a whole. It wanted to know, to understand, to find its way. Then all the arguments and words I had thought out in advance would break and recede, and other words, other arguments, utterly unexpected by me but needed by these people, would emerge in full array from my sub-consciousness. I felt as if I were listening to some other speaker, trying to keep pace with his ideas, afraid that, like a somnambulist, he might lurch from the platform at the sound of my conscious reasoning.

I tried to remember what I'd been taught at school about Trotsky. He'd led the Left Opposition that had tried to split the Party. He'd been cast out of the Party into foreign exile, after which he'd colluded with the Japanese, the Nazis, and the American capitalists until he was killed by a disappointed follower. Perhaps not a complete or reliable account.

"What did he look like?" I asked.

"Back then? Medium-tall, broad-shouldered, bushy dark

brown hair, wide mustache, small goatee. Most speakers showed up at the Cirque in a rumpled cheap suit or in what they thought was proletarian style – scuffed boots, a workman's cap and jacket. Trotsky dressed like a banker, with brilliantly shined shoes, a pressed business suit with a red cravat and boutonniere, and gold-framed eyeglasses. He said he dressed that way to show respect for his audience; maybe so, or maybe he just liked the outfit. When I knew him on his train, he was very particular about his tight-fitting, red-dyed leather coat and his polished black riding boots. He could move a crowd like nobody else. On the eve of the Bolshevik uprising, he addressed a huge rally at the Peoples' House."

Leonid stood, raised his fist, and declaimed: "'Repeat after me: 'I swear that with all my might and power of sacrifice, I will support the revolution to the end, the revolution that will bring the people peace, land, and bread. Raise your hand if you so swear.' Every voice roared out and every hand went up, mine included, although I was still an SR, not a Bolshevik, and we SRs opposed an immediate revolution. But I couldn't help myself."

I laughed. I'd wanted to raise my hand too when Leonid had recited the oath.

Leonid sat back in his chair and looked up at the ceiling, hands in his lap, fingertips pressed against each other.

"'Peace, land, and bread,' that's what Trotsky promised us: the Bolshevik slogan, maybe the best slogan ever. Four words, but it was what everybody wanted, what Kerensky wasn't giving us. Peace – two million dead in the German war, yet Kerensky forced Russia to fight on. Land – the peasants weren't waiting for Kerensky; they were burning country manors and seizing landlords' fields. And bread – food was so scarce that the cities starved, and gangs of hungry orphans ran in the streets.

"'Peace, land, and bread.' That slogan would bring us Bolsheviks to power, but we delivered none of it. Peace – five more years of war, first the end of the German War and then right into the Civil War with another four million dead. Land – we sent any peasant we called a kulak to labor camps in Siberia, and we seized every other peasant's land for collective farms. And bread – six million would starve in famines that didn't have to be."

Leonid lowered his gaze from the ceiling and looked straight at me. "I had a lot to do with all that."

I'd always thought Leonid was a good Communist. But he seemed to admire Trotsky. Had Leonid been a Trotskyist, the worst thing you could call a Communist? In 1957, Khrushchev had rehabilitated many of the Old Bolsheviks whom Stalin had executed in the 1930s, but not Trotsky. Never Trotsky. Leonid was speaking again, and I had to keep up with my shorthand.

"I was only a bystander for the 1917 Revolution," Leonid said, "an enforcer for the SRs, not the Bolsheviks. I knew nothing; I just stumbled through Petrograd hitting hecklers with my leather sap."

Leonid picked a book from the floor. "But Trotsky later told me the inside story of the Revolution when I was with him on his train, and he told it later in this book, *My Life*. Maybe he slanted the story his way, but I think it's close to the truth. Whatever his other failings, he wasn't a liar.

"Lenin had been hiding in Finland to avoid arrest and snuck into Petrograd for a Bolshevik Central Committee meeting. He pushed for an immediate uprising against Kerensky, and both Trotsky and Stalin backed him. Two Committee members, Zinoviev and Kamenev, argued that it was too soon, that any uprising was bound to fail. (Stalin would make them pay with their lives almost twenty years later. Pay for that and for other times they'd opposed him.) Lenin won the vote, and the revolution was on. Lenin assigned the planning to the military committee of the Petrograd Soviet, of which Trotsky was president, then took the train for Finland and left Trotsky in charge.

"Trotsky somehow managed to keep everything secret. His first job was to get the local military behind him. He promised the Petrograd garrisons an end to the war, and they agreed not to obey any orders that Trotsky's military committee hadn't countersigned. When Kerensky tried to ban the Bolshevik newspaper, Trotsky sent armed men to defend the print shop.

"Lenin arrived from Finland on the eve of the Revolution. He disguised himself – shaved his beard, wore a wig and a head bandage – and snuck into the Bolshevik headquarters.

He was sure that he would find that the planning had been bungled, but Trotsky had everything under control. He'd assigned combat roles to each Central Committee member: Dzerzhinsky to the post office and telegraph, Bubnov to the railways, Miliutin to the food warehouses, Nogin and Lomov to Moscow, Sverdlov to watch Kerensky's moves, Kamenev and Berzin to watch the SRs. All the Committee members had jobs except Stalin. Nobody could find Stalin. Trotsky later called him 'the man who missed the Revolution.' Not a wise thing to say, as things would turn out.

"Trotsky prepared so well that the Revolution succeeded almost bloodlessly. You've seen Eisenstein's film *October*, where he made storming the Winter Palace into a fierce battle? It makes for a more exciting movie, but it didn't happen that way. Kerensky and his lackeys just gave up, and most of them headed for Berlin or Paris.

"A month later, White armies began forming. The White generals claimed they wanted to restore the tsar – not to restore Kerensky, because nobody cared about him – but most of them were just out to be top dog themselves. It was the Reds against the Whites, the Civil War.

"Right after the October Revolution, I abandoned the SRs and told anyone who'd listen that I was a Bolshevik. Trotsky's speeches had convinced me. Besides, every boy wants to be on the winning team. I wasn't a Party member yet, but I did whatever the Party wanted done. In 1918, food was short for the troops and the workers in the cities, and the Party assigned me to the supplies squad. Our job was to 'requisition' food from the peasants, especially from the rich peasants, the kulaks. That meant taking food by force, as no peasant gave up grain or livestock if you just asked nicely. And when they resisted, we 'suppressed kulak sabotage.'

"Our squad leader, Avdeyev, showed us how to requisition. My first day on the job, we rode into a village on horseback and searched house by house. The larders were almost bare, we found maybe two hundred kilos of wheat in the whole village, no cattle, three pigs, a few chickens, and a scrawny horse or two. We forced the men into the church at bayonet point, and Avdeyev explained things to them, told them that the workers and our soldiers fighting against the

Whites needed food, that he knew they were hiding grain and livestock, but he would forgive them if they showed him everything. No one spoke for a long time, and then one kulak couldn't take the silence.

"'Gospudin, what you've seen is all we have. The harvest was bad, and the Whites took what was left...'

"Avdeyev drew his Mauser, stepped to the kulak, and without a word shot him in the face; he dropped like a stone. Avdeyev turned to the others: 'Where is everything?'

"Like magic, hidden cellars opened, and the women went to the forests for the livestock. We made the peasants load their carts with grain, with caged chickens and pigs, made them hitch their horses to the carts, then drive the carts and their cattle to the railroad. We left them seed grain and enough food so they could get through the winter, which was more than Soviet requisitioners would do in the Ukraine ten years later, when whole villages would starve and die.

"The next village, Avdeyev told me, would be my turn. I didn't sleep well the night before. I knew it was a test; if I failed, there would be no place for me in the Revolution. I steeled myself, and I gave the speech exactly as Avdeyev had, and I shot the kulak exactly as he had, without flinching.

"I remember that kulak's face well, and maybe the next four or five, but after that they're all the same, just class enemies. Shooting and bayoneting didn't bother me much. I liked the comradeship with the other Bolsheviks. I felt important. And, as our superiors told us, it was our duty."

He stopped speaking and stared off into space, lips still moving but no sound.

❖❖❖

Horrible, but I wasn't surprised. Even though Leonid had never told me *his* stories, I'd known of such things even as a young girl. At age fifteen, I became aware of the larger world, both its beauty and its dangers. I visited art museums, and I read Pushkin, Turgenev, Tolstoy, anything I could get my hands on. I found Leonid's copy of Isaac Babel's *Red Cavalry* in a closet, and Babel described the brutality of the Civil War. I remember – it was a Sunday afternoon, just after the celebration of the 1938 October Revolution – and I was reading

Red Cavalry in an armchair in the living room. When Leonid saw the book, he snatched it from me and warned me not to speak of it to my teachers and friends. He may have burned it – at least I never saw it again. Much later, I learned that the book was published in 1926 but soon removed from bookstores and libraries.

I didn't ask Leonid why I shouldn't talk about *Red Cavalry* with my teachers and friends; I already knew the answer; everybody knew but nobody talked about it. The purges had begun, and traitors and spies were being arrested from our apartment building every night. I obeyed Leonid with one exception: I'd already shared the book with my soulmate and best friend Vera, and she was as horrified and transfixed as I was by Babel's stories. I did pass Leonid's warning on to Vera, and she agreed to keep her mouth shut.

Isaac Babel and Anna Akhmatova were the two writers Vera and I loved best. Babel would be executed four years later, and Akhmatova's son was held in the Gulag for years as a hostage against her speaking out, although we didn't know that then. But looking back, I mark the day that Leonid grabbed *Red Cavalry* from my hands as the beginning of my doubts about Communism. What could be wrong with Babel?

HARBIN, 1926

Anna waited for Boris to return from the Soviet consulate, twisting her handkerchief until her fingers ached. She heard his steps in the hall and rushed to the door. As she helped him out of his coat, she asked as calmly as she could, "Did it go well?"

Anokhin removed the passports and visas from his briefcase. "No problems. I paid the clerk at the consulate three rubles, and he stamped our papers. That was it. Then I went next door to the railway office and bought the tickets. We leave two weeks from Monday."

"You bought tickets in soft class?"

He nodded yes, but her nagging irritated him. Now that the Communists were running the railroad, there were only two ticket classes: hard and soft. He'd wanted to economize by going hard class, but Anna had argued that his mother was too old to spend fourteen days on a bench. She was right, but the soft-class tickets emptied their savings. They would have enough money for food as they traveled, but they would arrive in Moscow almost penniless. He'd considered accepting Eitingon's offer of a government loan to buy the tickets, but he wanted as few interactions with the Reds as possible.

"I'll give notice at the hotel tomorrow," he told her. "The manager won't care – he'll have ten people fighting for the job."

Anokhin had worried about what to say at work. If he left with no warning, just abandoned his job and room, the hotel might make inquiries with the police. It would be better to have an innocuous story about his departure, that he was moving his family to Shanghai. Then, using Golov's papers, they would travel to Moscow. The Cheka must have better things to do than keep track of doormen in China.

Anna packed. She couldn't risk telling Irina they were leaving – a five-year-old wasn't to be trusted with secrets. So she told her that she was "spring cleaning," even though it was January. The train's baggage allowance for all four of them was 140 pounds. Not much for an entire life. She piled the things that mattered most to one side of the room –

photographs, family silver, fine china from her grandmother, Boris's medals and commendations, Irina's two favorite dolls, their best and warmest clothing, the tablecloths her mother had embroidered. She wouldn't pack her jewelry, that she'd carry on her body. She piled their everyday dishes, cooking pots, and the books they would never read again on the room's other side. Undecided items went in the middle. She judged those one by one, as God would separate the saved from the damned on Judgement Day.

The day before they were to leave, she stood before all the rejects in the cold of the open-air market. She looked around; her neighbors were also selling. Harbin was a buyer's market for used household goods. She stood for six hours and took what she could get. Not much.

MOSCOW, 1980

Leonid's brutal stories disturbed me, so I did what I often did; I buried myself in work so I wouldn't have to think too much. I was working on a Russian translation of John Dos Passos' *U.S.A.* trilogy, a monumental work about America's suppression of socialism. Whenever Leonid shooting peasants crept into my thoughts, I pushed him away and concentrated on Eugene Debs, Woodrow Wilson, and the Wobblies.

I returned the next week to hear worse, much worse from Leonid.

"We left off with Avdeyev teaching me how to requisition," he began. "I was a good pupil, and I was invited to join the Party and the Cheka. Our job was to defend the Revolution (which meant the Party) against its enemies by all means – enemies as defined by the Party, means as directed by the Party.

"My next job was the same as my old job with the supplies squad, but in a bigger territory and with a promotion. I was a squad leader, the new Avdeyev, and the Cheka gave me a leather coat. A directive would come to me by telegraph or messenger, and I would call my men together and explain our mission. We were extracting food the peasants didn't want to give us, I told them. It was easy to see how true that was. By the time we entered a village, they'd already slaughtered all the livestock. They sold the meat, sold the leather, and they stuffed themselves before we arrived. Someone later wrote that they gorged on so much meat that they vomited constantly and waddled like walking barns, which wasn't much of an exaggeration; you could smell meat in their latrines or on their greasy skin.

"Catching them out was easy – bones in the trash pits, cow-shit on their boots. My men beat kulaks, ripped up the floorboards, smashed the furniture. If the kulaks didn't produce, we administered the remedy – a bullet in the back of a random kulak skull. As a French general said earlier, shooting a few 'encouraged the others.' It was Red Terror, but I practiced it as efficiently as possible. We usually shot at most one or two in each village."

My face must have shown my revulsion.

Leonid leaned forward, his voice louder. "I have no regrets; it was the only way to save the Revolution. Do you understand those times?"

I didn't trust my voice, so I said nothing.

"Everything was falling apart by summer 1918," he said. "The Whites controlled most of the Trans-Siberian Railroad and had pushed us out of Siberia. In July, I was sent to Yekaterinburg, where we held the tsar and his family as prisoners. Yakov Yurovsky led the Cheka there. He was strict with incompetents, and I made sure I never disappointed him.

"Yurovsky had taken charge of the tsar and his family and their servants in early July, just before I got there. The former commandant had been allowing rich food to be sent in so that he could steal most of it. Yurovsky put the family on soldiers' rations.

"We couldn't hold Yekaterinburg against the Whites, and we couldn't let the Whites capture the Romanovs. Yurovsky received a telegram from the top. Sverdlov's signature was on it, but that meant it came from Lenin too: Execute every one of them, all of their servants, and make sure the bodies are hidden. No surviving witnesses. Yurovsky handpicked a dozen men he considered reliable, me included, and called us together. He read the telegram and asked if we would be able to do this, and three Latvians said they couldn't. He let them go and replaced them. He then loaded twelve revolvers and laid out a plan. Each of us was assigned specific people to shoot; he wanted it all organized. I did my job, but the others fucked it up. It was a bloodbath."

Leonid was cursing, I thought, something he didn't often do when he spoke to me. He seemed uncomfortable telling me this.

"Alexei, the tsar's hemophiliac son," he continued, "had a playmate, the Romanovs' cook's assistant, Sednev. Yurovsky thought Sednev didn't deserve to die, so he sent him away. Maybe that wasn't according to his orders, but that's what he did. Sednev's leaving made the Romanovs nervous, but Yurovsky told them the boy's uncle had arrived for a visit, and they calmed down.

"We were waiting for a truck that was supposed to arrive at eleven that night to haul away the bodies, but Yermakov, a fuckup who had been put in charge of the truck and the burial, didn't show up until half past one. He was drunk and so were his men, and he brought a flatbed truck rather than a closed van.

"The twelve of us were waiting and growing nervous, just like soldiers do before a battle that starts late. Once the truck arrived, Yurovsky ordered the family's doctor to wake the Romanovs up and tell them to get dressed. He told them that there was shooting nearby, that trucks would soon come to move them, that they would wait in the basement where it was safer.

"They took forever to get dressed. Yurovsky had told the doctor that they should bring nothing with them, but they brought pillows, bags, even a small dog. Yurovsky didn't make a fuss about anything but the dog, which he took from them, and we led them down to the basement. But he should have checked the route to the basement. There was a full moon, it was the middle of summer, and the sky was already brightening as we passed the basement's outside wall, where some soldier had drawn a charcoal cartoon of Rasputin and the empress. Rasputin was grinning like a maniac, his greasy hair plastered to his skull, his straggling beard spread over the cassock that he'd pulled up to expose an enormous organ that he was shoving between the empress's fat thighs. She was bent double, her petticoats pushed up, a stunned expression on her face as he took her from behind. It was an excellent likeness of her, I thought. The Romanov family walked right by without a glance. They either didn't see it or more likely pretended not to.

"The tsar was carrying Alexei, and the empress complained that there were no chairs. Yurovsky had a couple brought in. Alexei sat in one near the left corner of the room, the empress over near the right corner, the tsar stood next to Alexei. The rest lined up like it was a family portrait. The twelve of us were just outside, revolvers ready. I could see everything through a window.

"Yurovsky read the order aloud, just as Sverdlov had ordered him to do: 'Nikolai Alexandrovitch, in view of the fact that your relatives are continuing their attack on Soviet Russia, the Ural Executive Committee has decided to execute you.'

"The tsar had been speaking to the empress. He jerked his head toward Yurovsky and blurted, 'What? What?'

"Yurovsky shot him in the heart, killed him with a single shot. He'd told us to aim for the heart, that there would be less blood that way.

"That was the signal for the twelve of us to come in one after the other through the doorway, each to shoot his assigned person. I did my part. But the rest were too worked up. Either two of them would try to enter at once and jam the doorway, or they would shoot without aiming and empty their revolvers, or they would shoot the wrong person. One soldier shot from outside the doorway, and his bullet whistled past my face.

"The empress and her daughter Olga were crossing themselves when the bullets hit them. Alexei was still alive, sitting dazed in his chair, so Yurovsky shot him again. We were choking with the smoke, and Yurovsky ordered the doors opened. He told us to finish off survivors using bayonets because, with the doors open, shots would be heard outside. Three of the girls had pounds of diamonds sewn in their bodices, which had protected them from the bullets, but our bayonets pushed through. Some soldiers were trying to steal the jewels, so Yurovsky told them he would shoot them too, which put a stop to that. We carried the bodies out to Yermakov's flatbed truck and tied a tarp over them.

"It wasn't Yurovsky's job to bury them; that was supposed to be handled by Yermakov, the asshole who'd already pissed us off by showing up two hours late with the wrong truck. It's a good thing Yurovsky didn't leave the job to him. If Yurovsky hadn't climbed onto the truck too, the Whites would have had the bodies for sure. He ordered me and two of the others to join him on the truck. The plan was to dump the bodies in an old mine, but we were met on the way by a crowd of people on horseback and in carriages. Yermakov had told them to meet him just in case he needed help. They wanted to see the execution and were disappointed when they found that everyone was already dead, so they left.

"The road was marshy, and the truck sank past its axles into the mud. We pulled a few bodies off to lighten the load as we pushed, and we left them in a ditch for only a minute.

Once we got the truck moving, I looked back and saw peasants in a field on the right, where they were stretching out the girls' blouses. They'd found more jewels. Yurovsky did the best he could to get the jewels back, but I'm sure we missed some. We stripped the bodies to the skin and gathered the rags into a bundle that we could search later.

"When we got near the mine, we found dozens of peasants waiting for the big show. Bigmouth Yermakov had fucked us again. Yurovsky told us to disperse the peasants and to shoot any who wouldn't go. They all left.

"By then it was broad daylight, which hadn't been in the plan. We pulled the tarp off the bodies, and buzzing flies rose in clouds. If we didn't bury them soon, there'd be maggots. The Romanovs were all naked now after we'd stripped them, the princesses' eyes wide open, the bullet wounds mostly clotted and black. The bodies had stiffened so that arms and legs were twisted together, and it was hard to untangle them as we took them off the truck. Yermakov's men dumped the bodies in the mine, but there was only a foot or two of water there, and any passerby would have spotted or smelled them. The useless mine had been Yermakov's choice. I could see Yurovsky was thinking of shooting Yermakov, but that would have meant dealing with yet another body. He ordered us to fish the bodies out of the mine, put them back on the truck, and tie the tarp over them again. Someone said there was a deeper mine a few miles off, so we headed for it, and then the truck broke down completely. It wouldn't start. Yurovsky had us pull two of the smaller bodies, Alexei's and Demidova's, off the truck for a test. We poured petrol over them and burned them in the ditch. The flames only charred them though, and they were still identifiable.

"Yurovsky took me with him, and we walked two miles into town. We took a car from the director of the state bank, requisitioned sulfuric acid and shovels, and drove back. The car wasn't big enough to carry all the bodies, but some peasants on horses showed up on the road with two horse-drawn carts. The bodies were getting ripe in the summer sun, and I could tell that the peasants wondered about the smell under the tarp. We commandeered their horses and carts and sent them on their way on foot. Yurovsky climbed onto a horse, and it rolled over and smashed his foot. The entire day was a comedy.

"By the time Yurovsky had wrapped his foot, it was night again – we'd been working for twenty-four hours without food or rest. But without a moon, we thought, no one could see us, so Yurovsky ordered us to dig a pit where the soil was all clay near the road. But after the moon rose, we realized that one of Yermakov's many friends was watching us from a distance. We would have to move and dig somewhere else, which caused a lot of complaining among Yermakov's men – I kept my mouth shut. Yurovsky had us fill the hole with the dug-up dirt, and it was obvious where it had been dug up; he sent one of the carts to the depot for railroad ties so that we could cover the next hole, which we hoped would be the last. We headed off in the other cart with the bodies under the tarp. Moving was slower than it had been with the truck, but when the cart got stuck in the mud, we at least had horses to free it. About midnight we dug a second pit. We dumped the bodies there, poured acid on them, shoveled the dirt in, and covered it all with railway ties. We finished just before dawn.

"Yurovsky left Yermakov and his men with the cart and horses. He ordered the three of us who were his men into the car, and we drove back to the basement. Blood was smeared in long streaks where the bodies had been dragged, elsewhere blood was caked or still pooled. Bullet holes in all the walls. We didn't leave the Whites any Romanov bones as relics, but we did leave them a message, again on Sverdlov's instructions. Yurovsky didn't know the western alphabet, so he told me what Sverdlov had told him to write, and I scrawled this on the wall in German: 'Belsatzar was, in this same night, killed by his slaves.' Sverdlov was an admirer of Heine, and that's taken from one of Heine's poems. The joke in this was that Heine had written 'Balthazar' and Sverdlov had changed it to 'Belsatzar,' inserting the tsar's title. A lot of work for a poor joke, in my opinion."

Leonid closed his eyes and leaned back in his chair. I'd been wrong that he'd wanted to avoid the story. His face showed only pride in a job well done.

Neither of us spoke for a long time, and then I asked, "Have you told anyone else this?"

"I was ordered not to, so of course not."

I forced myself to look at him. "Who did you shoot?"

Leonid didn't want to answer that. He drew himself up after a few moments and said, "The Grand Duchess Anastasia."

"Did you look her in the eye?"

"I looked at her heart, where I aimed. And I aimed well."

"How old was she?"

"Seventeen, I believe. A year younger than me."

"How could you?"

Leonid exploded. "So, you criticize us for what we did at Yekaterinburg? Are you one of those Communists who refused to shake Ramón's hand after he killed Trotsky? One of those who turned his back on Yurovsky because he executed the Romanovs? You think it was done too crudely? All of you are cowards. You draw fine distinctions, you say, oh, maybe you had to execute the tsar, who had the blood of millions on his hands, and maybe the empress, the cunt who'd egged him on, but not the doctor and the maids, not Alexei and his sisters, not the innocents who'd never hurt anyone. I say fuck that, they were all class enemies. Think of the workers' and peasants' children who died in the Civil War. Why should the tsar's children be spared? Any Communist who says different is a hypocrite. Ramón and Yurovsky did what needed to be done, and yes, so did I. I'm proud of it. No one wants to shake hands with sewer workers, either, and that's what we Chekists were: we were the Revolution's shit-shovelers. Without us, the Revolution would have died of cholera."

Leonid glared at me, daring me to argue. I stared back without expression. Listening to his horrible stories exhausted me, and I wasn't sure I could continue. Even if his story were true, if it was his and the Revolution's history, it might be better left untold.

❖❖❖

The bus ride home that afternoon was a blur; I couldn't stop thinking of Leonid shooting that poor girl. Maybe he was right, only hypocrites shun people like him, people whose secret work allowed the rest of us to preserve our illusions. But it wasn't only my stepfather who had lived wearing a mask. My father had too, and all the NKVD officers and Party officials

I'd grown up around. Perhaps I didn't want to pull the masks away.

I had nightmares all week – dreams of Leonid grinning in a leather coat, of children's corpses. I awoke terrified, but also furious. After a lifetime of secrecy, death was snapping at Leonid's heels, so he wanted to tell me his disgusting stories. He assumed I would not only listen but would faithfully record his every word. Was he simply bragging, or was he justifying his life, or was he searching for absolution? And how much of it was I to believe?

But I decided to listen and record. His story was more than a family story. It was the Revolution's story, and I was a child of the Revolution. I would continue, I thought, but I'd transcribe his accounts with my professional ear and keep them far away from me.

HARBIN, 1926

Anokhin's family waited seven hours at the station. If the train was this late after the first leg from Vladivostok, Anokhin thought, what did that mean for the rest of the journey?

"This always happens, Gospudin," a porter told him. "They never explain, but the train from Vladivostok is always late."

The porter was old and stooped, but he knew his job. He'd found four seats for them in the waiting room near the tiled stove, and when others tried to shove in front of them, he'd shouted them away. And he had a plan.

"When the train arrives," he advised, "please let me handle things, Gospudin. Passengers will not be allowed to board immediately. The train's conductor and his assistants will all congregate and confer with the station agent. They have nothing to say to each other, but there is a reason for the meeting; it allows time for the selling of places. You must pay if you want a coupé – a four-person compartment for all of you – and it's us, the porters, who are the conductors' agents. I'll take your luggage aboard and find an empty coupé, for which I must pay twenty rubles to the conductor. Another ten rubles for me, and you're sitting together the entire journey to Moscow. But a warning: if you leave the coupé unoccupied even for a moment, you'll return to find your luggage in the corridor and four fat drunks in your seats."

Perhaps the porter was lying, Anokhin thought, but it sounded like the truth. They needed to stay together. Mother wasn't well and was growing more confused, and Irina needed to be with Anna and with him. He tried to negotiate the price for the coupé, but the porter wouldn't bend. Anokhin gave him the thirty rubles.

The train, enveloped in white steam, finally pulled into Harbin nine hours late. A red star was emblazoned on the locomotive's nose. Holes, regularly spaced every few inches along the locomotive's sides, showed where armor plate had once been bolted. This, Anokhin could see, had been a military locomotive during the Civil War, perhaps part of Trotsky's famous train, perhaps part of one of the White trains, perhaps, at different times, both.

Irina was dozing on her grandmother's lap when the train

arrived, but she woke at once and pulled on her coat. The crowd pressed toward the train but just as the porter had predicted, a guard blocked the entrance to the platform.

"Watch for me, I'll wave from the window of your coupé," the porter told Anokhin.

Old and stooped as he was, he lifted their baggage as if it weighed nothing and slipped past the guard at the door. He exchanged nods with the conductor at the door of a soft car and soon appeared in a window, waving to Anokhin. Fifteen minutes later, those passengers who hadn't understood the system were permitted to fight for unassigned seats.

When Anokhin and his family boarded, they found their porter blocking the door to their coupé and holding a "Reserved" sign.

"As promised, four seats together, two at floor level, two raised," the porter said. "The seats fold into beds at night. Your bedding is in the cupboard."

The porter waited for a further tip, but Anokhin outlasted him – thirty rubles was enough.

All four of them removed coats, hats, and mittens as quickly as possible. The compartment was unbelievably hot, ten degrees of frost outside but an oven within the train. Anokhin strained to crack the window, but it wouldn't budge. Anna pointed to a small, infuriating sign "Windows do not open." Anokhin boosted Irina into one of the upper seats and climbed into the other, leaving the lower two for Anna and his mother. It was even hotter near the ceiling, and Anokhin wiped sweat from his eyes.

The train whistled to announce its departure, and Irina, perched high in the air, clapped in excitement. "It's like our own little house!"

Anna sliced sausage and bread, and Anokhin went to fetch tea from the car's samovar. The excitement soon wore off, and they all dozed in the heat. When it was time to unfold the beds for sleep, Anna worried about Irina falling out of the high bunk and swapped places with her. Anokhin slept badly, and not only because of the heat. Tomorrow they would enter Russia, where the border guards would inspect their papers.

Late the next afternoon, a signpost on a bleak plain

announced the Chinese-Russian border, but there was nothing to see, and the train did not stop. Anokhin hailed the conductor, who told him that the border inspection would be at Chita, still five hours away, where everyone would disembark with all luggage.

"If you like," he said, "I can make sure that no one takes your seats."

Anokhin saw no alternative; he gave the conductor another two rubles.

At Chita, porters swarmed the train.

"Only one ruble, Gospudin!" one cried. "I will protect your luggage and will return it to this very car!"

Anokhin glanced at the conductor, who nodded that the man was honest. Anokhin stepped from the overheated car, and the sweat on his face and hair crystallized. He brushed away the rime and led his family into the station, where a porter had secured a place in the baggage line.

"At least two hours before your turn," he told Anokhin. "I will stay here while you dine in the buffet."

The buffet doors opened outward, and a crush of travelers pressed against them trying to squeeze inside. Anokhin lifted Irina to his shoulders, his mother hooked her hand on his belt, and Anna followed behind as he shouldered their way through the crowd. The buffet was a narrow white room with a communal dining table that stretched down the center. On the right, men struggled for space and attention at a bar where vodka was poured at twenty kopecks a glass.

Anokhin wanted vodka, but first he needed to settle his family. When two seated soldiers stood up, he spread his arms wide to block others and seated his mother and Anna, with Irina on Anna's lap. He would eat at the bar. It was a fixed meal, and the waiters first delivered cabbage soup, then bowls holding great slabs of unidentifiable brown meat floating in fat. The patrons stuffed themselves without speaking.

Irina protested that she wasn't hungry, but her mother insisted: "Eat, this may be the last hot meal for days."

Anokhin's mother only picked at her food.

He pushed his way to the bar and downed three quick shots of vodka; perhaps being a little drunk might relax him for the interview with the border guards.

But the interview was nothing. The guard started to inspect his family's papers and luggage, but when he saw Eitingon's signature on Anokhin's visa, he waved them through. They were home in Russia, although still nine days from Moscow.

A day passed as the train climbed through low mountains. The car's heat and the monotonous clicking of the wheels over the rail junctions hypnotized them, and they rarely spoke. Occasionally one of them scraped a hole in the ice that formed on the window, but the view was unchanging; the pine forests were so close to the tracks that only the highest mountains were visible above them. There was one recurring sight. Every few kilometers, the train passed a hut where a track guardian and his family lived. The guardian's job was to inspect and repair his section of track, to clear mud and branches, to shovel snow in the winter, to scythe the verges in the summer, and to stand at attention and salute as each train passed. Irina waved at the guardians, but they never waved back. She stopped waving.

Anokhin awoke at first light to his mother's whistling as she snored. The locomotive's engine was silent, and he had the feeling that they'd been stopped for some time. The train lurched forward, and he scraped the frost from the window to see the name of the station they were leaving – Ulan-Ude – a signpost he remembered. They were approaching Lake Baikal, and the car swayed as the train navigated the sharp curves that had been cut into the cliffs that surrounded the lake. He'd crossed Baikal twice before, by boat in 1904 and on foot across the ice in 1919.

His first crossing was the beginning of his disillusionment with the army and the tsar. His father and mother had come to St. Petersburg for his graduation ceremony from the Page Corps. The commandant pinned the cadets' straps – gold, with two red stripes and two small stars – onto their shoulders and accepted their salutes. They now were commissioned officers in the tsar's army, although at the lowest rank – *podporuchiki*, or sub-lieutenants. Four hours later, Anokhin and his entire graduating class boarded a train waiting at Moskovosky Station. The young officers were jubilant. There was still time, they thought, to share in the glory of certain victory over the primitive Japanese. They were told that they would join their regiments in Mukden; what they were not told was that the Russian army had retreated to Mukden after a defeat at Liaoyang.

The sub-lieutenants crowded into sleeper cars with three men for every bunk; each man owned the bunk for eight hours and otherwise sat on the floor. There they gambled, sang military songs, and lied about women. Anokhin spent the long train ride writing love letters to Anna, whom he'd met at a ball in Moscow the previous summer. He'd been smitten on the spot, and she'd welcomed his visits to her home, but they had progressed no further than reading Pushkin and Gogol to each other. His first letters to her from the train were formal; he addressed her as "My dear Anna Mikhailovna." But by the journey's end, he wrote "Dearest Anna," although he feared his love was not returned.

Whenever the train stopped for water or coal, the sub-lieutenants burst through the doors for football games in the railway's narrow verges. The ordinary soldiers, who traveled forty men to a baggage car, had it much worse. The railroad, thrown together in three years at Tsar Alexander's insistence, was a mess. The track's ballast was poor, the rails were too light, the ties were too few, and the curves were too sharp. Frequent derailments and equipment failures, including burst boilers, meant waiting a day or more for a replacement locomotive. Rations were issued only at stations, so waiting for repairs meant that food was short for the officers and was missing entirely for the ordinary soldiers. There was a single track along the entire route, so their train was often shunted aside for hours for a westbound train. They waited several times to allow a train flying a general's flag to pass. And they often waited for what seemed to be no reason at all.

By the time the train reached the lake at Port Baikal, where the tracks ended, the young officers' euphoria had evaporated. Anokhin stepped from the train into a vista of acres of supplies waiting for transport: field guns, cases of rifles and ammunition, bales of blankets for the coming winter. He approached a grizzled sergeant who was directing a work gang that had begun unloading their train. The soldiers tossed everything into disorganized piles.

"What's all this?"

"Fucked up, is what this is, sir. The only way across the lake is by boat, and everything you see here is waiting for that boat. So are the men. We have one boat that carries twenty-five railcars, and it can make two trips a day. The trains bring two hundred new cars full of supplies and men every day, so it all keeps piling up. The lake will start to freeze in a week or two, but the boat has an icebreaker prow, so it will be able to keep moving cars for a while. Once the lake freezes solid, we can only cross by foot and sledge, and that's hell. Forty miles in blasting, frigid wind. We lost a thousand men to the cold last winter. They tried a temporary railroad across the ice, but the locomotive broke through and went to the bottom. You won't see many volunteers if they try that again."

"How long before the railway goes around the lake and we won't need the boat?"

"The official story is that the railroad's finished. The schedule was for some time next year, but they brought in thousands of workers to hurry it up. They ran the test train yesterday. Moving at a walking pace, it derailed ten times. The tracks are for shit. They built one of the tunnels too low, and it ripped off all the chimney ventilators before they could stop the train. For now, the boat's the only way across."

Even Anokhin's elementary military training had taught him this much: an army's supply lines were critical. Russia's troops were fighting five thousand miles from Moscow, and their only supply link was this single-track, badly engineered, unfinished railway. Japan's army was fighting at a tenth that distance from its home base. It would have meant a court-martial to ask the obvious question directly, but what had the tsar and his generals been thinking when they went to war?

After three weeks, Anokhin's turn came to cross the lake by boat. The rest of the journey was tedious but uneventful. He arrived in Mukden on Christmas Day, 1905, five days after General Stessel had surrendered Port Arthur, Russia's only year-round Pacific naval base, to the Japanese. At the officer's mess, everyone was drunk and cursing, demanding that the traitor Stessel be hung.

Anokhin reported to his company commander, who seemed a good sort. He told Anokhin to sit, then poured brandy and explained the situation. The army, commanded by General Kuropatkin, faced a long Japanese line a few kilometers to the south. Both sides had dug in months earlier, because the cold and snow made operations almost impossible.

"But Kuropatkin has a surprise planned for the Japs," the captain told Anokhin. "We'll attack at Sandepu in four days, crack the enemy line and snatch victory from the proverbial jaws of defeat. Draw winter clothing and make sure your platoon is ready. Inspect every rifle, bayonet, and cartridge case. Our soldiers are illiterate *muzhiks*, and if you let them, they'll stumble into battle with their rifles packed with mud."

Anokhin wore a high fur hat, and he led his platoon into battle without any idea of what was happening. He followed orders, or if orders didn't arrive, he had his men follow the units adjoining theirs. His platoon charged, moved left and right along the front, and finally fell back in the general retreat. Several of his men were shot, and he didn't even know from where the fire had come. The generals all blamed each other in the press. Anokhin's captain congratulated him on his performance.

But Sandepu was only a rehearsal for the final defeat. Six weeks later, the Japanese almost encircled the Russian army. Kuropatkin managed to retreat, but with 90,000 casualties. A third of Anokhin's platoon was killed, and he took a bullet through his thigh, for which he was awarded the "For Zeal" medal. The medal didn't seem much of a distinction – half the junior officers showed it at the neck of their tunics. Two months later, the Japanese annihilated the Russian fleet. The war was over, but the remnants of the Russian army sat for three months until the peace treaty was signed.

Anna's letters arrived in a batch, hundreds of them, one for each day since he'd left. She loved him too.

He'd seen nothing worthwhile in any of it. "Stupidity and mismanagement," he told his father upon his return. "Our generals were a century behind the times, ready to fight Napoleon again, while the Japanese had modern weapons and tactics. We outnumbered them in every battle and still lost. I'm resigning my commission."

His father wouldn't hear of it. Abandoning the army would be a betrayal of Anokhin's duty to the tsar and to his ancestors. He stayed.

His second trip across the lake had been much worse. By late 1919, the Civil War was going badly for the Whites. The Reds broke through in the Urals and pursued Kolchak's White army, including Anokhin's brigade, eastward along the railroad. The terrain was all flat steppes with nowhere to establish a defensive line. The Czechs captured and executed Kolchak in October, leaving General Kappel to command the army's remnants. He led the Whites' retreat until they found themselves wedged against Lake Baikal.

Kappel called a staff meeting. "As the Reds control the railway," he said, "our only route is on foot, across the ice."

Anokhin had remembered the sergeant's warning from fifteen years earlier about the hellish winter journey across the lake, but they had no choice.

It was worse than hell. When the Russian army had sent its soldiers across the ice in 1904, they'd placed warming huts every three miles to offer hot food and overnight rest. Kappel's men had none of that – forty miles, thirty degrees below zero, and no shelter from the February winds that swept unhindered across the lake. Men dropped onto the ice, and their comrades left them where they'd fallen because there was nothing else to do. General Kappel died from pneumonia, and Anokhin lost three toes to frostbite. He received another medal for it, the Order of the Great Siberian Ice March, an ice-white crown of thorns with a crossed sword. What a joke! In the throes of the White Army's final defeats, some idiot staff officer had found time to design, manufacture, and award a new decoration. He'd never worn the medal, but he supposed Anna had packed it.

The train was climbing now, almost to the lake, and he was at last drifting back to sleep. Had his life meant nothing? If Irina ever asks about my life as a soldier, he thought, I'll tell her that it prepared me to be a doorman.

❖❖❖

Anna and Irina woke, and Anna passed round a breakfast of bread and cheese. The train stopped at Mysovsk at noon and began its swing around Lake Baikal. Irina couldn't sit still; she perched on the edge of her seat, then ran first to her mother's lap, then to her father's, to press her face against the window. The wind had swept the snow from the frozen lake, and the ice, four feet thick, was as transparent as glass. The lake was a mile deep, its water unclouded and deepest blue. The clouds sped past the sun, first hiding and then illuminating long fractures in the ice like a jeweler's cuts in a sapphire that stretched forever. The cliffs dropped straight into the lake, and the train ran inches from the edges of a shelf dynamited into the rock face.

Anokhin wrapped his arm around Irina's waist. "If you were a bird," he told her, "you could fly in a straight line forty miles across the lake, but the track is four times that distance, and the train runs so slowly around the switchbacks that it will take an entire day."

At first, Irina counted the bridges and tunnels but soon gave up. She wanted to wake her grandmother so that she could see the lake too, but Anna shushed her, "Quiet, let her rest."

After an hour, even the beauty of the lake couldn't keep Irina in her seat. Anokhin gave her permission to play in the corridor with other children. Lydia Antonova was still asleep, so he and Anna had a rare chance to speak privately.

"I've been thinking about the other times I've crossed the lake," he said.

"I've had the same thoughts," Anna said, "about my trip across the lake. It was spring, five years ago, when I brought your mother to Harbin, and the ice was breaking up. She didn't want to leave Russia, and she wept the entire trip. I was so frustrated with her. What were we supposed to do? We couldn't stay in Moscow without you."

"I hated Harbin, hated my job," he said, "but at least I had you there."

They'd waited to marry until 1913 when he was promoted to captain. Then they'd had only a year together before his regiment moved to the front against the German army in September 1914. After that, they'd spent only the odd week together during the next six years. After the Reds took power, Trotsky had signed a shameful surrender to the Germans. When the Civil War began, Anokhin joined the Whites. He'd sent for Anna after the final White collapse. She'd asked no questions – not where will we live, or what will you do? She sold a necklace to buy train tickets for herself and his mother and joined him in Harbin. Irina was conceived the night she arrived.

Anokhin's mother's breathing was shallow and rapid, and her face was flushed.

"She's been sleeping too long," Anna said. She stroked the old woman's face, gently at first, then more vigorously. "Boris, she won't wake up!"

HARBIN, 1926

My mornings in the Hotel Moderne were all the same: porridge for breakfast, kiss Mama, open the secret passage, down into the basement to find Irina. But that morning was different. Irina's door was ajar – she was gone, her family was gone. All that remained were a few abandoned furnishings and cracked dishes that had been pushed into a corner.

I ran back to our rooms crying, "Where's Irina? Where's Irina?"

At first Mama couldn't understand me, and then she said she knew nothing. Leonid, I would discover sixty years later, knew everything but pretended ignorance. He promised me that he'd look into it. Two weeks later, he came home with an official-looking telegram from the Soviet consulate in Shanghai saying Irina's father was working as a doorman at a hotel there.

I cried for days, missing Irina, missing my papa. People I loved just disappeared. I never felt safe after that.

Leonid moved us to Beijing, to three rooms in the Soviet compound. There was no Russian school, so I attended the American school and learned English the way a child does, intuitively and without an accent.

I opened the bathroom door one day to find Mama naked, clipping her toenails with one foot on the tub's rim.

"Wait!" she gasped and almost fell as she tried to simultaneously turn away and stand. The nail clipper clattered to the floor. With her back to me, she said, "I'll be out in a minute. Wait in your room."

I didn't move. I'd seen a swollen sphere jutting from her belly.

"Is it a baby?"

After a long hesitation, "Yes."

"Is Uncle Leonid the papa?"

"Yes."

I wasn't surprised. I knew babies had something to do with bed, and Mama and Leonid had been sharing a bed since our move to Beijing, and that had been the end of talk of joining Papa in Moscow. I asked about Papa, and Mama said that we were with Leonid now.

When I cried, she snapped, "Stop that! Crying won't change anything!"

The baby was born two months early, while Leonid was off on one of his unexplained trips. I came home from the American school with my books and a crayon drawing of the complicated American flag. As I touched the doorknob, I heard Mama inside; she was crying and saying bad words. I pushed the door open.

Sweaty and pale, she held tight to the mantle, faced me with a fake smile, and asked, "How was school?"

"What's wrong, Mama?"

"I think the baby's coming."

She tried to sit and look at my drawing, but she couldn't stop pacing. Every few minutes she would lean against the wall or the nearest table with a tight face. More weeping and cursing; she muttered "Not yet" and "Oh God" and "Where's Leonid?"

Then water suddenly soaked her dress and stockings and the rug. "Go quickly," she said. "Fetch the doctor."

I did. I wasn't allowed to stay with Mama, and she had no women friends in Beijing, but someone arranged for an old woman to care of me. The woman had a purple wet tumor like a spider on her face. She told me to call her "Auntie," but I refused to call her anything at all. Where was Mama, where was Uncle Leonid? After three days, the woman told me that I had a new sister, but that she would die because she had been born too soon.

After a week, I was allowed to see Mama. When I was taken to the hospital, Mama said, "Come hold your sister Svetlana."

I wouldn't touch her. She was so small, and I was afraid I'd hurt her. Leonid returned with flowers and spent an hour with Mama each evening, but he didn't hold Svetlana, who needed round-the-clock nursing by a Chinese *amah*. Mama didn't speak a word of Chinese, but I had learned enough to interpret between her and the *amah*. Despite what the witch with the growth on her face had told me, Svetlana lived.

I gave up crying and became mischievous, which irritated Mama and amused Leonid. On a dare from a boy, I rode my bicycle along the top of the wall that separated the Soviet and American compounds. When I looked down to wave at the boy, I fell off into a rose bush on the American side. I went right over the handlebars, face down in the soft earth with the wind knocked out of me. The Americans picked me up, bandaged my scratches, and delivered me to the front gate of the Soviet compound. At dinner, Leonid announced that I'd set off a diplomatic incident, which scared me until I saw the adults stifling laughter.

And then Chinese soldiers smashed the gate of the Soviet compound and stormed into our apartment. I remember them screaming in almost unintelligible Russian, "Nobody move! Nobody move!"

Some of the women tried to burn documents, but the soldiers had a fire pump and doused the flames. I'd always thought of water as soft, but the spray from those hoses stung.

As Mama and the other women led us through the streets from the compound to the Soviet embassy – Mama carrying Svetlana and holding my hand – I heard gunfire and choked on smoke.

Leonid was at the embassy. He held Mama and tried to calm her. "Don't worry, they won't come in here. This is Soviet territory."

She wasn't reassured.

Then he pulled me aside. I could tell that he didn't want Mama to hear what he was about to say.

"Zoya," he told me, "I need you to do something very brave. Go back to our apartment, go to my bureau, and under my shirts you'll find something wrapped in yellow oilcloth. I need you to bring it to me, but don't look."

I did it. I walked alone for what seemed forever. Now there were bodies in the streets, and I saw a man running and then a soldier shot him in the back and he fell. I kept walking – no one noticed a seven-year-old girl.

I entered the compound and waded through the firehose puddles. Soldiers were still rummaging through the papers, but our apartment was empty, although people were shouting outside the window. I opened Leonid's drawer, and under his shirts found a yellow oilcloth. I lifted the cloth and looked; it was his revolver. I wrapped the cloth tighter and carried it back to him. He told me how well I'd done, that I was a true Bolshevik, but not to tell Mama. I had bad dreams: sometimes the man was shot, sometimes I was shot. But I didn't tell Mama, not even about the dreams.

Leonid sent us to Moscow, but he didn't go with us. He just put us in an embassy car and told the Chinese driver to take us through the jammed streets to the port at Tianjin. Chinese soldiers banged on the car's doors with their rifle butts and spit at the windows. It was four hours before we got to the ship. I remember that because, whenever Mama and Leonid fought after that, she would shout "Four hours!" at him.

At the port, Russian sailors led us aboard a Soviet freighter bound for Vladivostok, the end of the Trans-Siberian railroad. The freighter had no passenger accommodations, but the captain ordered the first and second mates to give us their cabin for the two-week voyage. The creak of swinging hammocks and the smells of unwashed men and of Mama's vomit are still with me. Then a ten-day train trip across Russia to Moscow, where a car took us to the Metropol hotel. No Leonid, and no Papa.

"Where's Papa?" I pestered Mama, "Is he here in Moscow?" She slapped me when I asked once too often.

Leonid appeared a month later, and the four of us moved to a two-room suite with a telephone in the Metropol. Leonid left early each morning and returned late at night if at all, and he sometimes disappeared for days without explanation. We left the room only for starchy meals in the hotel restaurant.

The phone rang often. Mama would pick up the receiver, I'd hear Papa's voice say "Olga?" and then she would slam it down. When I tried to answer the phone, Mama grabbed my arm and shouted at me.

It was Leonid, not Mama, who finally took me to Papa. He packed my nightgown and clothes into an old briefcase and led me out the door while Mama sobbed. We walked no more than three blocks to a three-story grey building with a high door.

"This was a banker's house before the Revolution," Leonid said. "One bourgeois family lived in twenty rooms here. But now it's home for many citizens, including your father."

I gripped his hand as he led me up a marble staircase to the second floor.

"The Party has given your father a very nice apartment

– you'll see," he told me, "two rooms and a window. Many families in this building are living four people or more in a single room."

If Uncle Leonid knew all that, he must have visited Papa here. Had Mama been here too?

Leonid knocked on a door at the end of the hall, and Papa answered immediately. He picked me up, tousled my hair and kissed me as if he'd never been gone. He shook hands with Leonid and offered him tea, but Leonid said no, it was my day to be with my father. But the two of them were friends, laughing and smiling. Papa liked Leonid, and Leonid liked Papa. It was only Mama who didn't like Papa, and I didn't know whether Papa liked Mama.

"I have a wonderful day planned," Papa told me. "We'll hunt mushrooms. I have a book that tells which ones are good to eat."

We took the metro to Sokolniki Park, where we rode the Ferris wheel and looked out at the Kremlin and ate ice cream. We wandered through the nature reserve.

"Not many mushrooms left," Papa said. "They've been picked over. But enough so you and your mother can pickle a jarful."

I asked Papa where he'd been, and he answered, "Everywhere. On Party business."

That night I found a woman's dress in the closet, and I asked him if he had a new wife.

"I did for a time," he said, "but no more."

"Will you come back and live with me and Mama?"

"You are both with Uncle Leonid now. He's a good man."

I brought the mushrooms home the next night. Mama said nothing, but the next morning, they had disappeared.

"Poisonous," she said. "Your father knows nothing about mushrooms."

Mama eventually relaxed, and as divorces go, I suppose she and Papa had a good one. They never bad-mouthed one another, and I got on with Leonid. He loved me more than he loved his own daughter Svetlana, who disappointed him with her timidity. I didn't know Papa as well as I came to know Leonid, but looking back, the two of them were alike in many ways. They gave their lives and their families' lives to the Party. Both fought with the Red Army in the Civil War, both served in the NKVD's foreign services, both were major generals, both were awarded the Order of Lenin (Papa twice, Leonid only once, and his was taken away). And both were cast out of the NKVD, although Papa wasn't sent to prison as Leonid was.

After a few months in Moscow, when I was seven, Leonid took us back to China, where we lived until I was nine. Then we went to Turkey for two years, so I didn't see much of Papa until I was eleven, in 1931. But then he taught me to swim and encouraged me as an athlete – not something that interested Leonid. Papa played the balalaika and the piano, he sang, and even at age fifty he amazed my friends by doing full handstands in his general's uniform. But like Leonid, he was somewhere else for most of my childhood. He married Lisa, another NKVD agent, in the late 1920s. Lisa was beautiful and elegant, but she had no interest in being a stepmother. Papa and Lisa moved from one posting to another – to Finland, Denmark, France, and Germany before the war, and then to the United States during the war. I never knew where they were or where Leonid was, except when he took us to China and Turkey as his cover, and even then he gave no explanation. Everything was a secret.

Whenever Papa and Leonid were in Moscow at the same time, my two families were often together, for picnics and dacha visits during the summers, for dinners in one or the other apartment in the winters. In those moments, I could almost believe we were a normal family. Perhaps a few harsh words from Mama after she had a drink too many, but the splits were always repaired. Mama had no reason for jealousy, because Lisa was not the woman she blamed for breaking up her marriage, if such a woman even existed.

In 1968, Papa and Lisa rented a cabin, deep in the woods outside Moscow. Lisa telephoned me in a panic – Papa had collapsed and was unconscious. I still marvel at Lisa's incompetence. The woman had lived as a secret agent in enemy countries, but she called her stepdaughter in Moscow for help when her husband collapsed next to her?

One thing that I had learned from Leonid and Papa was to step forward in a crisis. I was teaching at the time, and I recruited ten of my language students and sent them with a stretcher to the cabin, told them to carry him through the woods to the rail line. I didn't go with them. Just as a general doesn't advance with his troops but stays at the communications center, I was more effective on the telephone. I notified the rail scheduling office that the suburban train should stop when the students flagged the engineer, and I had an ambulance waiting at the first Moscow station. Papa lived another four years.

I've spent years considering how my family shaped my life. I think that Papa's and Leonid's unreliability made me both mistrustful of men and desirous of their attention. A bad combination. Mama's weakness, on the other hand, made me want to be strong but closed, so that I would never need to depend on men as she had. But what is the point of thinking like that? Our parents can blame their parents, and our children can blame us. Best just to get on with it, which is the Russian way.

MOSCOW, 1980

From Leonid the next week: "In late July 1918, after the tsar's execution, the Party sent me to Tsaritsyn. The Cheka was in a two-story building, with offices on the top floor and cells and interrogation rooms on the bottom. The Cheka head there was Alexander Chervyakov, a pig and a bully. Chervyakov had arrested hundreds of locals, all pretty much at random – mostly priests, shopkeepers, and tsarist officers who had come to Tsaritsyn hoping to enlist in the Red Army. The cells were crammed, and Chervyakov's solution to the overcrowding was to execute enough every day to make room for the next batch. I understood the necessity for Red Terror if we were to save the Revolution, but not the way Chervyakov was doing it – a Tsaritsyn Cheka trademark was cutting through bones with a handsaw during interrogations. I'd shot maybe twenty kulaks by the time I arrived in Tsaritsyn, but there had been a purpose to each. I shot them, and others delivered the food we needed. But there was no purpose to what the Tsaritsyn Cheka was doing. Why beat a priest to death in an interrogation? So that you can get the names of believers? It was all a waste of time. Chervyakov was a drunk and a thug, and I stayed out of his way and hoped for another posting.

"Before the Revolution, the Bolsheviks had promised that soldiers in the Red Army would elect their officers. Political commitment, not technical knowledge, was what counted, or so they said. A battle-hardened Communist private might make a good general even if he knew nothing more than firing his rifle and stabbing with his bayonet. Lenin put Trotsky in charge of the Red Army, and Trotsky soon found that all that talk about military democracy and equality was bullshit. He needed trained officers, and the only ones available had served the tsar. He got Lenin's approval to recruit them as 'military specialists.' Now, Trotsky was no fool about the military specialists; he doubted their reliability, so he paired them with Communist commissars, and he took their wives and children as hostages.

"We were losing the Civil War. The workers in Moscow and Petrograd were down to four ounces of bread a day. Tsaritsyn was in the middle of the Volga's wheat fields, and Lenin saw it as the key to the Reds' survival. He sent Stalin down as 'Director for Food Affairs.' Stalin already had a reputation. People called him 'bandit-in-chief,' although not to his face. In 1907, before the Revolution, he'd organized a daytime bank robbery in the town square of Tiflis. He wasn't there, but twenty gangsters, headed by his boyhood friend, Kamo, pitched hand grenades at the mounted Cossack bank guards, blew three of them to pieces, and killed three dozen civilians. Kamo then traveled to London and delivered 250,000 rubles to Lenin and a box of chocolate-covered nuts to Lenin's wife. When Lenin needed something done and didn't care about methods, he called Stalin.

"Stalin had arrived in Tsaritsyn with his new wife, Nadya, about a month before I got there. She was seventeen, a year younger than me. He didn't join the other administrators in the Hotel France but set himself up in a military railcar like a commander, although his orders from Lenin had nothing to do with the military situation. He telegraphed Lenin, 'Be assured, our hand will not tremble' and promised that he would 'pump out' the region of grain. And he did send carloads of wheat north, perhaps not as many as he'd promised, but better than before he arrived.

"Officially, Stalin had nothing to do with the Cheka, but when I went to my first Cheka meeting, he was the one giving the orders. Stalin was young then, not the way you remember him from the wartime conferences. But some things were the same. He was short, pockmarked, with a withered arm and a big mustache. He never said an unnecessary word. What struck me was the yellow cast to his eyes, like an animal's.

"Maybe ten of us junior Chekists were at that meeting, and Chervyakov was going around the table assigning interrogations to each of us. Stalin would add instructions: tell this prisoner we know that he spies for Denikin and we'll shoot his daughter unless he identifies other spies; beat that one until he implicates so-and-so. And he would fix the man he spoke to with an unblinking gaze. When my turn came, I did what I had done when Avdeyev had made me shoot my first kulak, I steeled myself not to flinch. After what seemed an hour but was only seconds, Stalin turned from me to the next man. I watched him make notes as he addressed each of us. He was recording the names of those who looked away. He never trusted a man who couldn't look him in the eye.

"Stalin was a Georgian, and there was a young Georgian among the Chekists, Lavrenty Beria, same age as me. Stalin formed a bond with him in a way that he didn't with the rest of us, not that I was looking for anything like that. For me, Stalin was someone to stay away from. When the meeting ended, we all headed down the stairs for our interrogations. I got to work, but Beria was positively eager."

I stopped writing; I wasn't sure I could bear listening to Leonid describe how he and Beria had tortured some poor soul. But Leonid spared me the details:

"I shared only one interrogation with Beria, and all I'll say is that he was enthusiastic and had no problems with Chervyakov's methods. Beria had a lot going for him: he was a Georgian, he was able and ruthless, and he bonded with Stalin. That's why he would be head of the NKVD in 1938, when I was only a colonel. And why he was shot in 1953, while I'm still here.

"Tsaritsyn's military situation was bad when I got there. We Reds faced two White armies. Trotsky had appointed General Snaersev, a former tsarist staff officer, as military commander. Snaersev was recruiting as many other ex-tsarist officers as he could find and making them military specialists. He had them training a mob of 20,000 conscripts and volunteers, trying to turn them into an army. But Chervyakov wasn't buying Trotsky's military-specialist program; if he caught ex-tsarist officers before they got to Snaersev, he arrested them.

"Stalin wasn't satisfied with running the food transport and the Cheka. He wanted everything, and he cabled Lenin, 'For the good of the cause, I need military powers. Without formalities, I will dismiss military commanders who are damaging the cause. The absence of a paper from Trotsky will not stop me.'

"Lenin needed the food Stalin was sending, so he didn't argue. Stalin locked up Snaersev and his military specialists and put his own man, Voroshilov, in charge. Voroshilov was the opposite of a specialist. He'd left school at age eight and had six months of military experience. He and Stalin shuffled troops around and launched an offensive that failed at once.

Worse yet, they pulled troops away from the rail line north to Moscow, and the Whites cut the line. For some time, Tsaritsyn couldn't send Lenin food. Stalin cabled Lenin and blamed Snaersev.

"Stalin kept conscripting more peasants, but without any military specialists to train them, they were only a mob. He had 100,000 men, the Whites had a fifth that number in their two armies, and yet Tsaritsyn was in danger of falling. That's when I was ordered to Sviyazhsk and left Tsaritsyn. But I can tell you how things turned out there. Trotsky and Stalin continued to squabble, and Lenin finally backed Trotsky. Stalin left, Trotsky arrived soon thereafter, and the city was saved, not by Stalin or by Trotsky, but by 15,000 fresh Red troops who broke into the Whites' rear. Stalin had meanwhile returned to Moscow, where he appeared before the Central Committee and took credit for the victory.

"In a tribute to that victory, in 1925, the Party would give Tsaritsyn a new name – Stalingrad. I know, I still haven't gotten to meeting "Trotsky. Next week, I promise."

I closed my notebook and put it in my bag. I wanted to ask Leonid, "Were you always this contemptuous of Stalin?" but there was no point. I knew the answer. In 1919, Leonid might well have been contemptuous of Stalin and have admired Trotsky, and in what he was telling me now, he was speaking from that time. But after Stalin took power, after Stalin *was* the Party, Leonid never looked back. Friends and family were always secondary to him. Leonid's had two loyalties: to the Party and to himself.

MOSCOW, 1980

Once again, Leonid was impatient when I arrived. He didn't even greet me, just waved me to my chair. I've heard it said – and it's true – your family treats you more rudely than strangers ever would. He'd asked for my help; so why was I was putting up with his discourtesy? If someone had hired me to take dictation and had treated me as he did, I would have walked out the door. And yet I kept returning to transcribe his horrible stories.

He gave me only a moment before he began, "Today, Trotsky and I will finally meet, I promise you. I was telling you about Tsaritsyn last time. In August 1918, I was ordered from there to Sviyazhsk, where the Red Army had regrouped after the fall of Kazan. Whites attacked our train near Samara. They felled trees to block the line, and they raked the train with machine-gun fire. We had a company of infantry on board. I was riding in a baggage car near the front of the train, and I jumped off on the opposite side from the attack and ran back to join the soldiers. I had only my Mauser pistol, no rifle. Before I could get there, the White cavalry charged. I took a saber cut in the back of my left thigh. I crawled under the train and took a few shots at the riders, but I doubt I hit anyone. A pistol's not much good against a moving target at a distance.

"The skirmish went on for an hour or so. Then the Whites left. They didn't have enough men to take the train. Our soldiers cleared the trees from the tracks while the medics bandaged my wound and helped me back on the train, and we proceeded to Sviyazhsk. It was another three days before we arrived. I tried to walk from the train, but my leg was hopeless. Two soldiers carried me to the hospital on a stretcher.

"The wound smelled bad, and I knew what that meant. Red Army field hospitals always had a pile of arms and legs outside the back door. The doctor said I had gangrene and that if he didn't take the leg, I'd die. I threw back the sheet and showed him my Mauser, told him I'd shoot him if he tried.

"He shrugged, 'Suit yourself,' and left.

"I was on my own. The doctors and nurses would have nothing to do with me after I pulled the gun. I scraped the wound, let maggots breed and eat the rotten parts, changed my bandages every day, and bathed the wound with alcohol and iodine. I began to recover.

"Traitors in our ranks were feeding the enemy our locations, so the Whites' artillery was smashing our positions. Our troops' morale was bad; we were a beaten mob, nothing more. And as new troops arrived, they took on defeatist attitudes. But then Trotsky showed up with his armored train, which everybody was talking about. I wanted to meet the train, but I couldn't walk.

"Trotsky turned things around. He issued a general order: 'I give warning that if any unit retreats without orders, the first to be shot will be the commissar of that unit, and after that the commander. Brave and gallant soldiers will be appointed in their places. This I solemnly swear in the presence of the entire Red Army.' And he meant it. He shot a hundred traitors and cowards at once, starting at the top. It only took a month to restore discipline, and the Whites broke and fled. We had Kazan back.

"On the day that our troops entered Kazan, I received a letter from the Provincial Review Office in Gomel. They were revoking my Party membership because of my 'bourgeois background,' my 'lack of proletarian psychology and discipline,' and my 'commissar-like attitudes.' That was what fat-assed bureaucrats in the rear said to me, a fighting Chekist at the front.

"Trotsky visited the hospital after the victory in Kazan. I had almost recovered by then. The wound hasn't bothered me much in later life; I limp a little, but women seem to find that attractive. Anyway, Trotsky stopped at my bed. He took an interest in me, maybe because he noticed my Cheka uniform tabs or maybe because he saw a Jew like him, although we never discussed our Jewishness. I started to stand at attention, but he waved me back to the bed. He wore a long, tight, red-dyed leather coat. His aide, smartly uniformed with close-cropped blonde hair in the German *Junker* officer fashion, brought a chair for him.

"Trotsky must have talked to me for an hour. He asked if I found the Red Terror difficult, meaning did it bother me to shoot grain-hoarding kulaks, White bandits, and deserters.

I told him no, that I took no pleasure in killing them, but I knew it was as necessary as shooting rabid dogs. He liked that, and he laughed when I told him the story of the doctor and my leg. And then I took a risk: I told him that I was being expelled from the Party and asked for his help. His face darkened, and he told me not to worry, he would fix it. Then he asked if I wanted to be his aide. I glanced at the current aide, the blonde standing by the wall, who now looked as if he'd been punched in the stomach. I said that I would be honored; I stood up, gathered my things, and I limped behind Trotsky to his train. I never saw the blonde aide again, and we never spoke of him.

"Trotsky's train went wherever things were hot; he calculated that he covered 105,000 kilometers in two and a half years of war. The train was jet black, and the thick armor plating on the engines and machine-gun cars was so heavy that we needed two engines, one of which was always under steam so that we could race quickly to a new trouble spot (or retreat quickly in the face of a White advance). We had a library, a print-shop, an electric generator, a radio station, a telegraph room, an automobile, a washroom with an adjoining private bath, and a conference room. A hundred shock troops called the 'Red 100' barracked in two cars, ready to repel attacks against the train or to be thrown into the breach at a decisive moment in a battle.

"A military aide usually carries orders or questions to other commanders and then returns with reports. My job was different. The train carried us directly to commanders who met us nervously on the platform, or we drove from the rail line to the front in our automobile. That meant that I didn't carry orders, and I had little contact with officers other than the few on the train. I was disappointed about that. I'd hoped that being aide to the Red Army commander would have been the start of my road to the top. But I was lucky, because if my name had been tied to Trotsky's, I would have been executed fifty years ago. I later got some help removing records from my file.

"Officially I was Trotsky's aide, but I was really his supply officer. At each battle, the train's engineer would bring us as close to the front as possible. If things were quiet, Trotsky climbed to the roof of his car and addressed the cheering soldiers who crowded close on both sides. Then he reviewed the troops with the commanders. He insisted on going behind the scenes. He inspected everywhere – the kitchens, the commissary, the armory, the clothing depot. He wanted to see how things really were. Then he met with as many of the commanders, senior sergeants, and commissars as could be crammed into the conference car. He demanded situation reports be given there, because he wanted to hear from everyone, not just bullshit from the senior officers.

"Everyone, of course, needed more of everything – men, equipment, and arms – desperately and immediately. Trotsky knew what was possible down to the last man, boot, and rifle. Based on the military situations at that front and elsewhere, he decided what he had to give. My job was to write the orders, get his signature, telegraph the orders in his name, and then follow up to ensure that it all happened. Three hours sleep was a good night for me.

"For Trotsky, morale was as important as supply, and there were two parts to morale. First, Trotsky promoted successful commanders and commissars in front of their troops, and he commended those who had not broken even in defeat. Our train carried cartons of medals, and Trotsky personally pinned these on as many brave chests as possible. We also carried warm stockings, underwear, boots, fur hats and gloves, which he gave to those soldiers who had shown bravery. In winter, those were as important as medals.

"The other side of morale was dealing with cowards and traitors. He stationed Chekist machine gunners behind our front lines, and they shot deserters who fled from battle. Those who were caught sneaking off without waiting for battle would meet a firing squad drawn from their own units, with different men assigned for each execution. Rotating the firing squads broadened the experience, so that every soldier understood what happened to cowards.

"That was the fate of deserters who broke their revolutionary oath. There was another class of men, shirkers who'd run from the Soviet draft. Russia had a long tradition of running from the tsar's conscription. Trotsky believed it was just a matter of education, that once the shirkers understood the difference between Communism and the tsar, they could be turned into soldiers as good as any others. The Red Army was being built from scratch, built under fire. Our troops were peasants, or refugees from the Whites, or workers sent to the front by their unions. They showed up without uniforms, boots, rifles, or cartridges; they were completely untrained, and almost none of them wanted to be there.

"The war commissariat in Ryazan herded fifteen thousand shirkers into an open field, where Trotsky climbed onto a table and dismissed all the Cheka and Red Army guards, saying, 'You can go – there's no need for you here. These are brave men, and I need to talk to them alone.'

"He spoke for over an hour, and he explained our struggle. Then he did what he'd done in Petrograd in September 1917, when he'd inspired me to raise my hand to swear the Bolshevik oath. The shirkers all swore that same oath, and as far as I know, they turned out no worse than any other gang of peasant conscripts.

"As the train crossed the steppes from one battle to the next, Trotsky rose from his bed each morning with a new propaganda leaflet fully composed. His two secretaries – later died in the camps, good men both – waited for him in his study. His batman brought him his dressing gown and a cup of tea from the samovar, and Trotsky sent one of the secretaries to the library car for the books that he wanted, specifying what quotations he needed. As he sipped his tea, he either dictated to the other secretary without hesitation, or he wrote rapidly in pen, as fast as if he were taking dictation from someone else. The secretary typed a copy, ran it to the train's print-car for typesetting, proofread the result, put the proofs on Trotsky's desk for final edits, and returned the corrected proofs to the printers. The next morning, soldiers heaved bundles of Trotsky's latest pamphlet from the speeding train as we sped past army encampments and peasant villages. The train's printing press ate paper and ink the way Red Army soldiers ate kasha, and my job was to feed it, to telegraph ahead so that its next meal would be served up on the station platform."

"Did you know Trotsky as a man?" I asked. "Did he know you?"

"I admired him but was much too young to understand him. I was good at my job, and that's all he cared about. There was always too much to do, and he trusted my judgment about what was important, what was urgent – important and urgent aren't always the same. I think he saw me as a protégé. I'd left school at fifteen and hadn't read anything more complicated than a newspaper. He told me that an ignorant Chekist was a useless Chekist, and he had his secretaries tutor me. First, the Russian classics – Trotsky loved Pushkin and Tolstoy – and then Marx, Lenin, Engels, and his own writings. I was in and out of the train's library every day. He said I had to know the Revolution's enemies too, so I read Mensheviks like Plekhanov and Martov, read Adam Smith, Kant, and Nietzsche. But I never cared much about philosophy or economics. The Party had people who would decide all that for me, and bad things could happen to men who took too much interest in those subjects.

"But where Trotsky and his secretaries helped me most was with languages. I already spoke fluent Russian, Byelorussian, and Yiddish, and fair Polish and Ukrainian. The Revolution was for the entire world, Trotsky said, not just for Russia. He said that the German workers would rise next, so I studied German. My Yiddish helped there, and within two months I was reading *Das Kapital* in German. Then on to English, which I found easy to read, although I could never spell English properly. Engels was my text there. No Spanish or Turkish yet – I would learn those in Cheka language schools after I left Trotsky. The Cheka's teachers taught me how to speak without an accent, how to talk one way with bankers and another with dockworkers. I'm good at languages, as are you, Zoya. When I left Spain for Mexico, I spoke Catalan and two dialects of Spanish so well that it would take a good ear to know I was a foreigner."

❖❖❖

I thought about Leonid on my journey home. Trotsky was Communism's great betrayer, or so I and every Soviet schoolchild had been taught, and Leonid had been his wartime aide. Even now, sixty years later, Leonid spoke admiringly of the man, and yet he had orchestrated Trotsky's murder at Stalin's command. I realized I'd never known Leonid at all. What kind of man was he? How could he have gone to work every morning knowing that a newly discovered file documenting his connection to Trotsky would have meant his death sentence? How could he have murdered Trotsky, a man that he admired, maybe even loved? Or maybe Leonid was incapable of love, even for himself.

My feet were swollen when I arrived home, and Tatiana filled a basin for me with Epsom salts and hot water. Her husband was asleep on the sofa, likely drunk. He wasn't as bad as either of my husbands had been, but the best word I had to describe him was "useless." Had Tatiana inherited my predilection for doing whatever men wanted? It's not good to be critical of your children, but Tatiana had always seemed to me to be a bit lifeless. I know that Leonid saw her that way, and I'd always said that he didn't know her. But all she talked about was her boring husband, her clothes, her television shows. Leonid and the others who had made the Revolution may have been brutal thugs, but they had energy. My generation had less of that, and Tatiana's less still; I was a footnote to the Revolution, Tatiana not even that. Where was our country headed?

I was lonely, not so much for a man as for anyone who interested and inspired me. Tatiana and Leonid couldn't fill that role for different reasons. It's hard to make new friends as you grow old, but that's what I needed, a friend like I'd had in Irina or Vera.

TRANS-SIBERIAN RAILWAY, 1926

"Mama! Wake up!" Anokhin shouted, his lips only inches from his mother's drooping face. He squeezed her cheeks, and her eyelids fluttered.

Anna ran to summon the train's conductor, and a doctor, a young man wearing a tweed suit and carrying a leather bag, arrived a few minutes later. He loosened Lydia Antonova's clothing, lifted her eyelids and inspected her pupils, checked her heart, pulse, and temperature.

"I think she's had a stroke," he said. "In any case, it's serious. I can't help her. She needs a hospital."

The conductor stood by the compartment door. "Irkutsk is the next hospital," he said. "We arrive tomorrow at ten o'clock in the morning. I'll bring blankets. Call me if you need anything else."

Irina had been pushed into the corner and forgotten in the confusion. She said nothing until her mother looked her way. "Will Grandma die?"

"She's sick, Irina, so we'll take her to a hospital where the doctors will help her. But we can pray for her." Anna turned to the conductor. "Is there a priest on the train?"

As she spoke, she knew the answer. Not now, not under godless Communism. She began the Orthodox prayer for the sick that she'd learned as a child. Anokhin joined her, and within a few repetitions, Irina took it up as well. Even the conductor, although unwilling to pray aloud, knew the prayer and moved his lips.

O Merciful Lord, visit and heal Thy sick servant, Lydia Antonova, now lying on the bed of sickness and sorely afflicted, as Thou, O Savior, didst once raise Peter's wife's mother and the man sick of the palsy who was carried on his bed: for Thou alone hast borne the sickness and afflictions of our race, and with Thee nothing is impossible, for Thou art all-merciful.

Anokhin and Anna sat with his mother through the night. She choked when they tried to give her water, and as hot as the compartment was, her skin was dry.

The conductor stopped by each hour: "I've sent ahead to

have an ambulance waiting for the train at Irkutsk. Don't worry about your baggage; I'll have it stored with the stationmaster. Your tickets are good for a month. The train for Moscow comes through three days a week, Mondays, Wednesdays, and Fridays. The best hotel, so I've heard, is the Europa. But if you're tight for cash, cheap hotels are near the river docks."

"Thank you for your help," Anokhin said. "I'll look by the docks."

When the train pulled into Irkutsk, two men with a stretcher carried Lydia Antonova to an ambulance sleigh. Anna and Irina squeezed into the back, and Anokhin rode on top with the driver. The attendants carried his mother into the women's ward, a long, high-ceilinged white room with beds along both walls.

The head nurse stopped them. "You must wait while the doctor examines her."

The three of them sat in a cold, dismal room. All hospital waiting rooms were dismal, Anokhin thought. He'd been in this hospital during the Civil War, he remembered, retreating with Kolchak in 1919. The building had been filled with wounded, frostbitten soldiers.

The doctor – a young woman! – shook first Anna's hand and then Anokhin's and introduced herself.

"The doctor on the train was correct," she said. "She's had a stroke. There's not much we can do. We'll feed her intravenously and bathe her. Some do recover. We'll see."

When Anokhin asked about payment, the doctor answered as if insulted.

"That's all in the past, Comrade. Treatment is the right of every Soviet citizen."

The Hotel Moscow, the only cheap hotel with a room available, wasn't as accommodating as the hospital. Like the train, the overheated room had its windows locked tight. The entire hotel reeked of backed-up sewage.

Irina complained, "What a stink!" and her mother snapped, "If you don't like it, hold your nose," which brought Irina to tears.

The legs of an iron bed, the room's only furniture, rested in four kerosene-filled tin cans. "An old army trick," Anokhin said. "The kerosene stops the cockroaches."

The three of them would share the lumpy bed, Anna and Anokhin on the edges with Irina in the middle. They had only a few rubles left, and the food Anna had packed for the trip was finished. They had eaten only black bread for two days.

That night, Anokhin and Anna stood on opposite sides of the bed as Irina slept. Anna pulled her gold wedding ring from her hand and handed it to Anokhin. "Sell it," she said.

He went to a pawnshop the next morning, got fifty rubles for the ring, and returned with bread, sausage, cheese, and kvass. And then a miracle! When they arrived at the hospital, his mother was conscious. Anokhin couldn't understand her mumbling speech, but she recognized him.

"She needs to stay at least another week," the doctor told him. "I don't know whether she'll improve further, but she can't travel yet."

It was two weeks before she walked across the room with the help of a cane, dragging her right leg. When they returned to the train, they had lost their coupé. The conductor – by great luck the same conductor who had been helpful earlier – forced two miners to give up their seats for Lidya Ivanovna and Anna, who took Irina on her lap. Anokhin sat in the corridor until he grabbed a seat in another car two days later when the train stopped in Omsk.

Finally, almost a month after they had left Harbin, the train pulled into Moscow's Yaroslavskaya station. Anokhin, who was still sitting separately, had told Anna to wait for the other passengers to leave, that he would then come and help with his mother and the luggage.

He was pulling at a door between cars when a hand grasped his shoulder from behind, and a voice said, "I arrest you in the name of the Soviet people."

There was no point in struggling. The arresting officer stepped back, and two soldiers pushed Anokhin from the carriage to the platform. He said nothing. Perhaps they didn't know about his family, perhaps Anna wouldn't be stopped. But as the soldiers spun him around for the handcuffs, he saw. Three cars away, policemen had his mother in a wheelchair and Anna by her arm. He followed Anna's gaze. A thickset woman in a brown uniform bear-hugged Irina, who screamed and pounded her fists against the woman's encircling arms.

He heard Anna's long cry "No!" as the woman carried Irina through a door marked "Official Use Only."

MOSCOW, 1926

The matron slapped Irina's face. "You little brat!" she shouted. "No food until you speak!"

She yanked the bowl of kasha away. She had spent two days trying to jolly Irina into cooperation. She'd offered candy, toys, sympathy, and yet the girl just sat there.

Irina flinched reflexively at the slap, but she didn't cry. She stared at the matron and said nothing. If she started talking, she knew that she would be lost. She refused to cry in front of *them*, only at night with the blanket over her head. And she didn't care about the kasha. She wasn't going to eat anything *they* gave her.

The matron had collected herself enough to give it another try. "I'm sorry I hit you, Irina. You may be here for a while, and it's important that you eat."

"Where's my mama? My papa? Grandma?"

"Don't keep asking that. I've told you before: they are being questioned. They would want you to eat."

Irina said nothing.

The door opened just as the matron was about to slap her again. A man with a stethoscope beckoned to the matron, who went into the hall to speak with him. But the door was open a crack, and Irina could hear what he said to her.

"If she won't eat, we can't keep her here. She's not dying on my watch. Send her to the dormitory with her grandmother."

For the rest of her life, Irina would remember that day as her first victory over Communism.

❖❖❖

The black police van skidded along Moscow's icy streets, bouncing on cobblestones and dropping into sudden potholes. Ten prisoners rode in the back with their hands bound, and every unexpected turn flung them at each other and into the compartment's steel walls.

Fifteen years in the army had taught Anokhin to observe, to anticipate, then to act without hesitation. When the van slowed, he pushed his shackled hands between his knees and balanced in a squat on his toes. When the guards threw the van's doors open and bellowed "Out!" he was the first into the courtyard, standing to one side as the guards clubbed the slow movers. He looked upward; the building was eight stories high, and he heard city traffic. Most likely it was the Lubyanka, the central Moscow building he'd heard the Reds had turned into their secret police headquarters.

One after another, eight more vans dumped prisoners into the courtyard. Then, just as in the army, nothing happened for an hour; they stood in the sleet while the guards checked the paperwork and finally began a roll call.

"Anokhin!" the sergeant shouted.

He considered denying his identity, but that would only mean a pointless beating. They knew who he was.

"Here!" he replied.

A guard grabbed his arm and hustled him into the building, down two flights of stairs into a maze of corridors. The walls were painted dark green near the floor, light green four feet above that, and the hallways were lit by dim electric lights recessed into the ceiling behind wire screens. It was a shabby Soviet paint job, but the floors were intricately tiled. He was right – this was the Lubyanka – and the tiles were a remnant of the building's original purpose, the central office of an insurance company.

A silent guard shoved him along. As they neared each turn, the guard snapped his fingers and waited for an answering handclap. At the third corner, the handclap didn't come. The guard shoved Anokhin face-first into a small alcove, evidently designed for that purpose. Anokhin heard two men pass behind him. The guard yanked him back, and they proceeded. His first bit of prison knowledge: he was forbidden even to see the faces of other prisoners.

After six such turns, Anokhin's guard shoved him into a room that reeked of disinfectant. "Strip!"

Anokhin did as he was told, and two men with stiff brushes scrubbed him head to toe with kerosene, concentrating on his hair, genitals, and anus. When they'd finished, a third man tossed him a blanket and a faded grey prison uniform. "Dress!"

They took his picture from front and side views, fingerprinted him, then returned him to his silent guard, who resumed his finger-snapping route through the corridors to an open cell. The guard pushed him in and locked the door. Not much to see: a concrete cell with two steel bunks, a slop bucket, and a single electric ceiling light identical to the corridor lights. No window.

They left him alone for six days. At least that was his best guess, as his only calendar was the cart that collected his slop bucket (he could smell its approach far down the corridor) and the twice-daily silent delivery of a fist-sized hunk of bread and a cup of un-sugared, tepid tea, which he was forced to drink while the attendant waited for him to return the cup. After each meal, he forced himself through his army calisthenics. The electric light never dimmed, and a silent guard sometimes opened the door's viewing port and then shut it. Footsteps passed his door, but no voices. It would be best to blank his mind, but that seemed impossible. He huddled under his blanket and dozed but never really slept. Where were Irina, Anna, his mother? Had they been released? Was Irina in an orphanage?

On the seventh day, Anokhin was sitting on the bottom bunk when a guard opened the door and pushed another prisoner in. A criminal, obviously, with a scarred face and a broken nose, the edges of tattoos showing at the base of his neck.

"You're sitting on my bunk," the new man growled. "Move to the top."

The first test. If he gave in, there would be no end to the demands. Anokhin sat where he was and stared back.

After a minute, the criminal said, "OK, you were here first. I'm Yuri, but they call me Skull. You can call me what you like."

He climbed onto the top bunk and sprawled on his blanket. Anokhin smelled the kerosene on him.

"Boris Andreyovich Anokhin." No harm in giving him that much.

"You're some sort of political. What? A White? A spy? You're fucked whatever you are. It's better to be a thief and a murderer than a political. What did you do?"

"I don't know why I'm here."

"Bullshit. You know why you're here. But you're smart to

keep your mouth shut. I'm here because they caught me with a truck of stolen meat. They may shoot me for it, but what the fuck? Nothing I can do. You been interrogated yet?"

"No."

Skull leaned his head down from the top bunk and shook a box of matches. "Want to play match?"

Anything to pass the time. "Match" was pick-up-sticks played with matches, which Skull told him was the standard prison game.

"Cards and dominoes they can take away, but not matches. If they take away the matches, no one can smoke, and there would be riots. You've got nothing to gamble with, but I've seen prisoners play for big stakes – for stables of whores, or thousands of rubles."

They played for three hours, and Skull won every game.

"You been here six days with no interrogation?" Skull said. "You have family or friends on the outside? If you can pay, I can get messages out. It's cash on delivery; the one who receives the message pays. Or you get your knees broken if he doesn't pay."

"No thanks," Anokhin said.

He'd suspected as much, but he now knew that Skull was an informer. He hadn't told him that he'd been here six days. If that hadn't been enough to confirm his informer status, Skull became more insistent, wanted to know his family history, where he'd been in the war, every detail. Anokhin told him nothing.

On the next day, a guard summoned Anokhin for another walk through the maze. They climbed four flights of stairs, and sunlight filled the corridor as they exited the stairwell. Men in business suits and officers' uniforms passed, and the guard no longer shambled along but marched toward a mahogany door where he rapped once. When a voice called, "Enter," he pushed Anokhin inside.

Vassily Zarubin looked up from his paperwork and dismissed the guard with a wave.

"Sit down, please, Boris Andreyovich. Yes, we know each other. May I offer you a cigarette? I'll just be a minute."

Anokhin hadn't expected this. He accepted the cigarette and lit it from the box of matches at the edge of the desk.

Zarubin finished whatever he was working on and picked up a file, almost certainly *his* file.

"Colonel Anokhin," he began, "I'll go straight to the point. We've been watching you for the five years you've lived in Harbin. You haven't been involved in any counter-revolutionary activity, which is of course in your favor, so there is little to be gained from interrogating you. But you were a White colonel, you executed prisoners of war, and you've entered the Soviet Union using forged papers. Indisputably, those are crimes.

"You have a choice. One alternative is to refuse to cooperate with us. In that case, your guard will take you directly to the execution chamber, where you will be shot. Your wife and mother are also guilty of using forged entry papers, but that crime is not serious enough to merit death. They will be sent to a labor camp in Siberia for a five-year term. Your wife might survive that, but your mother will not. Your daughter Irina is of course guilty of nothing, so the Soviet state will care for her in an orphanage until she is eighteen."

Zarubin paused to let him imagine all that, then continued.

"You have another choice – to work for the Soviet Union as a confidential agent. You will move to Constantinople, now called Istanbul, where you will be a doorman again at the city's finest hotel, the Pera Palace. Your family will stay here in Moscow, where they will be assigned lodging and your wife will be given a job with pay sufficient to support your daughter and mother. Your job will be to do whatever we tell you. Istanbul is a nest of counterrevolutionaries, and you will report on any suspicious activity and on the comings and goings of all guests, especially Russian speakers. You will aid our security services directly when told to do so. You may, for example, be told to arrange for female or male prostitutes to be sent to guests' rooms, or to admit our people with listening equipment to rooms. If you can ingratiate yourself with any of your old comrades-in-arms, you will report what you hear. I repeat: You will do as you are told, and you will report whatever you see or hear. If you fail, your execution will be immediate, and your family will be dealt with as I have described."

"Will I see them again?"

"Perhaps. If you do well, we may allow you to visit. In return for your work for us, you will receive a stipend of thirty rubles a month."

"I'll do what you ask, but I don't want your money."

"You'll do what we order, and you'll take the money too. I imagine you'll want it paid directly to your wife."

Anokhin had no choice; he nodded his agreement and wondered whether Judas had tried to decline his thirty pieces of silver.

MOSCOW, 1980

"Pour yourself some tea if you want," Leonid grunted.

That was a small improvement on the previous week; at least he'd thought to make tea. I started to tell him about my daughter Tatiana's problems with her husband, but I could see he wasn't interested. He'd always been like that – ordinary people and their lives didn't matter. Just his life, and even that was of interest only because he knew that he was about to leave it. I picked up my pad and pencil, and he began.

"Trotsky would tell stories some nights on his train. We didn't converse; he had no patience for listening to others."

Just like Leonid, I thought.

"But he did love to talk, and his secretaries and I were his audience. I'll tell his stories the way he did. We'll start with Trotsky in 1902, when the tsar's government exiled him to Siberia the first time. That was the beginning of his serious political life. He was 23 years old. He wasn't called Leon Trotsky then, just Lev Davidovich Bronstein, one more Jewish revolutionary. But let's call him Trotsky, because it's impossible to call him anything else –"

"Wait," I said. "I thought you wanted to tell me about you and Trotsky. You were three years old in 1902."

"I'll get to that. But first you need to know Trotsky a little. Being sent to Siberia under the tsar was not as bad as it would be later under Communism. No big slave-labor camps. Exiles back then could bring their families with them – the idea was to put them somewhere they couldn't cause trouble."

Leonid was smiling, something I hadn't seen in a while.

"I remember a story Trotsky told us, about what he did every summer night in Siberia. He grabbed the broom and went for the cockroaches. His wife Shura – full name Alexandra Lvovna Sokolovskaya – wouldn't let him spread roach powder because of the babies. When he'd swept twenty or so roaches together, he broke into what Shura called his cockroach dance. He knew killing roaches that way was hopeless – thousands waited to take the place of each one he stomped – but every crunch brought satisfaction, a sharp snap he could feel through the sole of his boot. Even as his feet smashed Siberian roaches, his hand slapped Siberian mosquitoes on his neck and face.

"When he was sentenced, he'd worried about the cold, but he hadn't considered the insects. The lice were the most manageable. Every two months, the camp elders gathered the men in one hut and the women and children in another. The small children who'd been through it before knew what was coming and howled. The elders counted heads – one person missing and they would all be picking lice again in a week. Everyone threw clothing and combs into a barrel of kerosene, then stripped to the skin for a kerosene scrub followed by kerosene combing of body and head hair. That liquidated the lice, but the mosquitoes were more difficult. Netting over the beds and windows helped some, but the only real relief came in September when the mosquitoes died on their own. That left the roaches, who wouldn't die without a formal execution, scheduled for the first hard frost in November. The households split into two groups, and the first group threw its doors and windows open to the cold and moved in with a family from the second group. After four days, they would switch places, when group two opened its houses to the cold and moved in with group one. Twenty degrees of frost liquidated adult roaches, but nothing could kill their eggs. In February, three months later, the roaches were back, and the prisoners repeated the house switching with another temporary success. Then in April, both roaches and mosquitoes returned and were unstoppable.

"But Trotsky's time horizon was shorter than that. He planned to leave before the November frost. He told us he remembered looking across the bare wood floor, watching Shura nurse Nina. The older daughter, Zina, was asleep in her cradle. He told us that they'd been lucky to find a log cabin mortared tight against the winter winds, two floors with a good stove downstairs and small windows cut into the southern walls. Once Nina was asleep, Trotsky and Shura would climb the ladder each night to their bedroom, where they would read and discuss the latest Marxist essays, and he would write.

"Shura was thirty, eight years older than he was, the sister of a friend. They'd met at a lawn party when he was seventeen, a braggart with dreams of heroism. (Those were

Trotsky's words – he'd shaken his head and smiled when he told us that.)

"Shura explained Marx's demonstrations of inevitable historical process to him, and he laughed, saying, 'I can't believe a beautiful woman is interested in all that dry stuff!'

"She didn't take that as flattery. 'I can't imagine that a man who claims to be logical can be satisfied with vague idealism,' she told him.

"She converted him to Marxism, and maybe her looks had as much to do with that as her ideas. An older woman in bed can be very persuasive to a young man. Together with four friends at the university in Nikolayev, they organized the local workers. All of them were arrested, put in solitary for three months, and exiled to Siberia.

"It was all Jews in that Siberian camp on the Lena River. The police didn't want gentile prisoners corrupted by Jewish Marxist thought. But life wasn't so bad there. Trotsky wrote for a local journal. The censors were looser in Siberia than in Moscow or Petersburg, and his essays called for improved treatment of peasants, for better schools, even for better prison conditions. Nothing revolutionary, but at least he was writing, and Shura was a good editor.

"But he soon lost interest in Siberian journals. A friend mailed him some books by Tolstoy and Pushkin, and he felt lumps in the bindings. When he cut them open, he found the first issues of the Social Democratic magazine *Iskra* and Lenin's pamphlet 'What Is to Be Done?' Lenin argued that a vanguard of dedicated revolutionaries could lead Russia directly to socialism, skipping over the bourgeois capitalism that Marx had said would follow the collapse of Russia's feudalism. You've read Lenin, Zoya, so you know those writings. Exactly the line that he himself was taking, Trotsky thought! The revolution needed his pen, and he knew he wouldn't have freedom to write in Russia. Lenin was in London, so that's where he'd go. But he would have to leave before winter. Perhaps the children had been a mistake. Without them, Shura could go with him. But if they took the girls, their cries would give the game away. The children would stay here with Shura. He would tell her that night. He loved his family, but the revolution came before all else, and he would sacrifice more than she would.

She would have the children, while he would be alone. She was a revolutionary too, and she'd understand.

"They climbed the ladder, and he told her he was leaving.

"Her reply was: 'Go, a great future awaits you.' But he said she turned away when he tried to embrace her."

"She just told him to go?" I said. "He told her he was leaving her with their children, and that's all she had to say?"

"Well, that's the way he told the story," Leonid said, "but none of us believed it could have been that easy. Shura once asked Grigori Ziv, the closest thing Trotsky had to a friend, what he thought of Trotsky's love for her, for their children, and for his friends. Ziv thought for a moment and told her, 'He loves us all sincerely, but his love is like a peasant's love for his horse. He'll feed it and caress it, he'll undergo danger to protect it, his mind will even connect to the horse's mind. But when the horse becomes useless for work, without a thought he'll send it to the knacker's yard.'"

Leonid's ironic grin made me think of how Leonid had treated his family.

"And you, Uncle Leonid," I said, "what do you think of Trotsky leaving his family?"

"So, you blame Trotsky for abandoning his wife and babies with winter approaching? I don't. It's true that he took up with his second wife, Natalia, soon after he escaped. It's also true that he entertained a string of typists and switchboard girls in his bed on the armored train – I ushered them in and out of his carriage – while he was married to Natalia. And even in Mexico, when he was sixty, he took up with that gimpy painter Frida Kahlo and then chased after her sister as well. But a man is a man, and if we Bolsheviks had worried about marriage and family, we'd all still be living under the tsar. We sacrificed everything – including family – for the Revolution. I've had several wives myself, some I married more than once. Yevgenia has been in and out of the picture for years, as was Olga, your mother, a true revolutionary. Olga never blamed me."

I had heard Mama weeping many nights, but arguing with Leonid was pointless. On the bus ride home, I thought about the Old Bolsheviks. Trotsky, Leonid, my father. They were all bastards. None of them gave a shit about their families.

MOSCOW, 1980

When I arrived at Leonid's apartment the following Thursday, he started another rehearsed Trotsky story, but I stopped him.

"I spent the last week thinking about how Trotsky abandoned his family," I said. "All you Old Bolsheviks did it. My father left Mama and me in Harbin, and you had children by three different women and picked up a new 'wife' whenever you felt the need; Mama was just your Moscow wife. Every big-shot revolutionary wanted a woman to share his bed, to keep his house, to comfort him when he was down, wanted a family to show off at summer dacha parties. But the Revolution always came first. Bolsheviks were willing to sacrifice their own lives for the Revolution, so why shouldn't they sacrifice their families' lives? Besides, replacing a family was easy enough. Just start over wherever the Party sent you."

I was flushed and almost spitting by the end of that, and he was taken aback. Without answering me, he tried to start his Trotsky story again, but I shook my head.

"First we talk about how you used us," I said. "Remember the time on the train? When you hid your secret paper in my doll?"

Leonid smiled. "I was so proud of you. I told all the other Chekists about you. You were screaming so loud. None of those policemen even thought about ripping that doll out of your arms."

"But you used me, and I was only five! You took me on the train with you as your cover!"

"That was my plan. A man traveling with a child is much less suspicious. But you weren't at risk."

"If you had been arrested, what would have happened to me? And in Beijing when you sent me for your gun!"

Leonid blanked for a moment, then his face lit up.

"I'd forgotten that. You were too young to understand what was happening, but it was 1927, just before Stalin's final humiliation of Trotsky. Chiang Kai-shek was running the Chinese Kuomintang army, and Stalin backed him, called him the 'Red General,' had his picture carried in the May Day parades next to Lenin's and Marx's, and even sent money to Chiang to fund his fights against the warlords. Chiang was no more a Communist than Winston Churchill was. Stalin ordered the Chinese Communists to back Chiang. I was in Beijing then, and it was my job to make sure that they followed Stalin's orders. Lee Kyo, the local Communist military leader, spent an entire night pleading with me. Even I could see that he was right about what was coming, but I ordered him to surrender all his arms to Chiang."

I tapped my fingers as I waited for Leonid to finish. I was angry, and I didn't want this to turn into a shouting match. But Leonid, caught up in his memories, paid no attention to my impatience.

"Within a year," he said, "Lee Kyo was dead along with 300,000 other Communists. It started with a slaughter in Shanghai that April. Chiang's officers called morning assembly, then ordered 'Communists, step forward.' Taking that step meant death. They were led off ten at a time and machine-gunned. Trotsky was right about Chiang and Stalin was wrong, which only made Stalin more determined to get rid of Trotsky–"

"Stop!" I said. "You're giving me a history lesson, and I'm talking about how you put me in danger. I walked a mile from the embassy to the compound and back with your gun."

"Well, nothing happened, did it? And it wasn't a mile, not more than half that. You were a Bolshevik already, whether you knew it or not. And if they'd caught you with the gun, even Chiang wouldn't have put a seven-year-old in front of a firing squad. I would have gotten you released. Besides, I sent you and your mother back to Moscow the next day so you'd be safe. Now let's get to work."

I slapped the table. "That's all you have to say? 'Let's get to work?' What work is that, telling your self-important stories? Who is the audience for these stories, Leonid? Because if it's me, I'm no longer seven years old and I want some answers."

I picked up my bag and left.

MOSCOW, 1928

Irina waited until her grandmother began to snore in her armchair.

"Mama, it's been three years since Papa left. When will he come home?"

"Soon, I hope. We all miss him. But I've told you how important his work is for our government."

"What kind of important work?"

"It's a state secret, so I'm not sure."

"Where is he?"

"Another state secret, he can't tell us, sorry."

Irina was nine years old and was no longer willing to accept her mother's evasions. They received only one letter each month from Papa, and that never said much. Was her mother telling the truth? Maybe Papa was dead! But he wrote letters, so he must be alive. She hadn't forgotten the awful days after the train trip from Harbin. At school, they talked about how much better everyone's life was under Communism and how Comrade Stalin loved and cared for children, but before Communism, Papa was always with them, and now he was gone. She'd said that to Mama once, and she got angry and scared and told her never to say that again, especially in front of anyone else. Why couldn't Papa come home just for a little while?

"Mama, is Papa in prison?"

"Of course not!"

"Is Papa a Communist?"

Her mother paused for a moment before answering. "He loves our country."

Her grandma had shaken herself awake and mumbled "Is it time to go?" in a voice that only Irina and Mama could understand. The stroke on the train had left the right side of her face immobile, and she dragged her foot when she walked. Despite that, she took Irina for their "special time," every Sunday afternoon, tea and cherry cake at Sonya's Nightingale Cafe. Irina and Mama helped her up from the chair, helped her with her coat, and Grandma and Irina were out the door. Irina helped her down the stairs – Grandma gripped the handrail and did them facing backward, like descending a ladder

– and half an hour later they'd covered the three blocks to the café.

Irina held the café door open. Grandma was breathing harder than usual; each Sunday was more difficult for her.

"I'm so old," she wheezed. And with that, she fell like a cut tree.

Irina froze, but Sonya, the proprietor, ran to her side – she loosened Grandma's clothing, sent a customer into the street for a policeman, and told Irina to run to get her mother.

Irina sprinted down the street, up the stairs, turned the knob. The door was locked! Was Mama out? She banged on the door.

"Mama! Come quick! Grandma's hurt!"

She heard shuffling noises inside and a few seconds later her mother's voice: "Just a minute!"

It was a full minute before the door opened only a little and her mother squeezed out. But Irina had seen what her mother didn't want her to see – a man's coat hanging on the back of a chair at the kitchen table.

❖❖❖

"She's dying," the doctor said. "There's nothing to be done."

Irina and her mother had spent the night at her grandmother's bedside, listening to the labored, irregular rasp of her breath.

The government had begun a new anti-religion campaign that year, and priests were not allowed to visit hospitals. But Irina's mother obtained holy oil from one of the few remaining Moscow priests and diluted it with ordinary cooking oil to hide the scent of myrrh. They washed Grandma's body quite openly, and the head nurse thanked them for saving the nurses the trouble. Then they quickly anointed Grandma's forehead, hands, and feet during the nurses' shift change at dawn. They whispered a prayer for the dying, Irina repeating each line after her mother:

> *O my Lord Jesus Christ,*
> *I ardently beg Thee again and always:*
> *at the time of her departure, send her the resplendent Virgin,*
> *the most pure temple, the sacred treasury of Thy wealth,*

O my Christ, to strengthen her.
Send her at that time
the holy Forerunner and Baptist John,
the luminous stars - the Apostles -
the prophets and the martyrs,
the preachers and evangelists,
confessors, ascetics, and righteous,
that Thy creature may be glorified.

Irina knew that her grandmother was a believer, but her mother's memorized prayer surprised her. She worked for the Party, so how could she believe? Many things about her mother surprised her these days. Every child thinks his or her mother is beautiful, but Irina saw how men looked at her mother. They thought she was beautiful too.

"Mama, whose coat was on the chair?"

Her mother didn't answer right away. "That was my boss's coat. We were reviewing some files."

"Why was the door locked?"

"Force of habit, I guess. I didn't know I'd locked it."

"Why did you take so long to open the door?"

"Enough questions! Pray for your grandma!"

❖❖❖

Lydia Antonova died at dawn, and Irina spent the day at home with Mama lighting candles and praying. Mama couldn't go to church because she might lose her job if she were caught.

"Irina, I've told you many lies," she said. "I had to do so. You were too young to be able to live with the truth. But you're nine now, and I won't lie again. Like me, you'll need to pretend to believe all the lies they tell you at school. Next year you'll be a Pioneer, and you must sing all their songs and march in all the parades. If you don't, they'll come after me. Your father's not a Communist, and I'm not either, even if I pretend to be. I don't know where he is, and he's not allowed to tell us. He's working for them because if he doesn't, they'll hurt us. And the man whose coat you saw is my boss. I didn't lie about that. He was also my interrogator when we were arrested after the train ride, and he's not a bad man. He's whI have my job at the Lubyanka, and why you're not in an orphanage. Don't ask too many questions about him. I promise you – I love only your father."

MOSCOW, 1980

I picked up *1905*, one of the books that Leonid had lent me, Trotsky's autobiographical account of that year. It was three in the morning before I put it aside.

I had, of course, learned about the 1905 uprising in school. The way that I'd been taught, 1905 was a disorganized precursor of the 1917 Communist Revolution. More than 400,000 workers and peasants across the country had risen against the war in Japan and the hunger and oppression at home. But the time wasn't right, and the uprising failed. The old regime still had too much strength, and Lenin and the Bolsheviks were not yet strong enough. My history teacher never mentioned Trotsky's involvement in 1905. But in his book, Trotsky claimed that he was the one who'd united all factions within the Petrograd Soviet – Bolsheviks, Mensheviks, and Socialist Revolutionaries – and that he'd asked for Lenin's support, but that Lenin refused. When the tsar reneged on his promises for a democratic Duma and put Trotsky and the other leaders on trial, Trotsky wrote that he stood and faced the judges and waited until he saw fear in their eyes. Then he turned his back on them and spoke to the public and the press:

> The prosecution charges that the Soviet armed the workers for the struggle against 'the existing form of government.' I answer 'Yes, of course it did!' What we have is not a government but an automaton for mass murder, a machine that is tearing into parts the living body of our country. If you tell me that pogroms, murders, burnings, and rapes are 'the existing form of government' of the Russian Empire then yes, we were arming ourselves against it…The tsar and his lackeys had hoped that this trial would split the workers from the revolutionaries as Peter denied Christ. But they have failed. On one side is struggle, courage, truth, freedom; on the other, deviousness, baseness, slander, slavery. Citizens, make your choice!

Could this be true? When I visited Leonid the next week, I asked him.

"No doubt Trotsky exaggerated his contributions," Leonid said, "but more than anyone else, he was the man in charge in 1905."

I'd only made it halfway through the book. Trotsky might be a self-important braggart, but he interested me. I asked Leonid, "What happened to Trotsky after the court sent him to Siberia?"

"He escaped, of course. And I know that story well, as he told it to visitors many times on his train. He told it like a boys' adventure story – outsmarting the police, dashing 700 miles across Siberia in February on a sled pulled by reindeer and driven by a drunken Asiatic. And he was, as always, the hero. When he needed money after Stalin kicked him out, he published the story."

"What did Trotsky do between 1905 and the 1917 Revolution?" I asked.

Leonid smiled at that; I was finally asking for the stories he wanted to tell.

"Nothing worth mentioning, same as all the other Bolsheviks. The ones who were in prison or in Siberia rotted there. The ones who escaped to exile in the West, like Lenin and Trotsky, wrote revolutionary screeds and argued in cafes. And when the world war started, Trotsky was right about the consequences. When the tsar backed Serbia in 1914, he might just as well have shot his family himself. His empire was collapsing even in peacetime, and the war pushed it over the edge."

"In the time you spent with Trotsky on the train," I asked, "did you find him likable?"

Leonid snorted at that. "Nobody much liked any of the Old Bolsheviks, including the other Old Bolsheviks. Being liked wasn't what they were about. But that was especially true of Trotsky. He could bring a crowd of ten thousand to its feet, but he pissed off everyone who knew him. He would flip through his English vocabulary cards while others were speaking at Politburo meetings. He had allies and supporters, but never friends. He was always the smartest man in the room, and he made sure everyone knew it. The other top Party members drank together, screwed ballerinas together, had Black Sea dachas where they all took their families in the summer.

There they watched their children swim while Trotsky sat in his study and wrote yet another brilliant treatise. And he still wanted to be every story's hero. Lunacharsky, who knew all the Old Bolsheviks, wrote that Trotsky was the most capable except for Lenin. But he said that while Lenin never worried about how posterity would view him, Trotsky was always stepping back to look in the historical mirror, that he would have gladly given his life for the Revolution, but only if he could assemble a large audience to watch him do it."

MOSCOW, 1980

Four hours before I would leave for my next visit with Leonid, I woke wide-eyed, not from a nightmare, but from a dream of doubt. I ran through my languages. No word for "dream of doubt" in Russian, but perhaps *Zweifeltraum* in German; the Germans had a word for everything. How much of what Leonid had told me was true? Had he really been part of the Romanovs' murder? How could he have been Trotsky's aide and survived the purges? He claimed his Cheka file had been magically fixed? If he couldn't explain that, then there was no point in continuing to transcribe his inventions.

❖❖❖

I opened Leonid's door. As always, he was ready with this week's story. But before he could begin, I confronted him.

"How did your time with Trotsky disappear from your file?"

I thought he would be angry with me for doubting him, but no. His wrecked face twisted into a grin.

"I spent sixty years wondering the same thing, always expecting to be discovered, and I learned the answer only this year. Of course, I was never allowed to see my own personnel file – that's completely forbidden no matter what your rank. But I did someone a good turn in 1920, and it paid off.

"Trotsky's train stopped somewhere in the Ukraine, and I had a whole sheaf of orders that I needed transmitted. I sat with a fifteen-year-old telegraph operator for eighteen hours straight. I would modify orders, encode them where necessary, and hand them to him. He would send them out. He was fast – I had trouble keeping up with him. Anyway, we finished sending the orders, ate some kasha, drank a little tea, and about midnight stretched out on benches in the office to take a break before the replies would arrive. I woke to find two drunken sergeants pushing the boy around, kicking him in the ass, 'Hey pussyhole, polish my boots!' and 'The samovar fire is out, you little shit!' Abusing the boy was a regular game for them. They hadn't seen me – the back of the bench hid me as I'd slept. I stood up quietly and with my right hand grabbed one of the drunks from the back of his collar, pulled him backward and choked him. His friend started to go after me but stopped when he saw my captain's badges. I grabbed him with my left hand by the front of his shirt, pulled him forward and smashed their faces together.

"I twisted them to face the telegraph operator and explained things. 'While you two shit-heels have been sucking up vodka and chasing whores, this man (I didn't call him a boy, although he wasn't shaving yet) has worked for eighteen hours transmitting Commissar Trotsky's orders. Commissar Trotsky and I will return. If I hear you're still fucking things up for real soldiers, I'll have you before a firing squad.'

"I released them, and they left in a hurry. The boy was embarrassed but grateful. I asked him his name — Pavel Sudoplatov.

Sudoplatov! Leonid's one-time boss and prison-mate, who had been my boss in our atomic bomb project!

"That's where you met Sudoplatov?"

"Yes, and I didn't see him again for seven years. But he joined the Cheka too, and he remembered me. He was on night duty in the central file room in 1925, when Trotsky's downhill slide began. Controls weren't as tight then as they later became. He retrieved my file and removed everything from my time with Trotsky. That left a hole, but many records were sketchy during the Civil War."

"When did you learn this?"

"Pavel told me the story a few months ago, over drinks. He knows how to keep a secret, and it would have been his life, too, if anyone had known what he'd done, so he had no reason to tell me then. We were together through the Spanish Civil War, the Purges, the Great Patriotic War, and then prison. He never mentioned it."

Pavel Sudoplatov, an unpleasant man, had saved Leonid's life. That explained the bond between them, which I'd never understood.

"When did you leave Trotsky and the train?" I asked.

"In late April 1920, when four of us on the train came down with typhus. I've never been that sick before or after – fevers, chills, headaches. They put us off the train as quick as they could at an army hospital near Kiev. The other three died. I didn't."

I hadn't heard that story. Another near-death experience that Leonid had forgotten to mention. He was indomitable.

He continued: "The Whites were collapsing in the East and South, but the Ukrainian Whites had joined up with the Poles in the West. They'd been whipping us, but we turned things around that month. I had nothing to do with it. I just lay in my hospital bed, at first hallucinating, then slowly recovering.

"In late May, the Polish army retreated, and there was an argument in the Politburo about how far to go. Trotsky argued for pushing to Warsaw because he wanted a Polish Communist Republic as a bridge to spread the Revolution westward to Germany. Stalin was more cautious. He wanted to establish a defensive line against the Poles and then send troops south to the Crimea to finish off the Whites there. Lenin and the Politburo backed Trotsky.

"By the time I recovered, we were advancing west toward Poland so fast our supply lines couldn't keep up. I was posted to the First Cavalry, commanded by General Budyonny – you've seen pictures of him with his big mustache. In Russia in 1920, 'cavalry' meant 'Cossacks.' They had fought for the tsar, and after him for whoever paid: some for the Whites, some for the Poles, and some for us Reds. More bandits than soldiers, they rode and fought like nobody else, looted and raped in every village they took. And they despised Jews. Remember 'Out of the way, yid!' when Cossacks kicked my father down the steps in Shklov? Suddenly I was living with them. But I was a tough bastard, too, by then. I'd changed my name, and I didn't look that Jewish. And I wore Cheka chevrons, which meant I could put anybody who looked at me wrong up on charges, maybe in front of a firing squad. I didn't worry much about Jew-hating Cossacks."

There was that story again, Leonid's father being kicked down the stairs. That was at the center of his soul, I realized. The first time he'd told the story to me, he'd summed himself up in a few words: "If people were going to be kicked, I wanted to be on the other end of the boot."

My view of Leonid's loyalty was evolving. I'd know it wasn't to his family, but I realized that it wasn't even to the Party, although that was his claim. It was to himself. He would never be his father, a man kicked down the stairs. His choices and actions had kept him alive, and however I might judge them, they'd kept me alive too.

Leonid continued: "I didn't see any other Jews with the cavalry until a newspaper writer for a soldier's rag called *Red Cavalryman* showed up. I don't know what the editor was thinking when he gave that job to a Jew. The reporter called himself Kyrill Vasilievich Lyutov, as Russian a name as possible, but he wasn't fooling anyone. He looked like a cartoon of a Jewish peddler – short, flabby, balding, big nose, thick lips. I laughed when he told me his made-up name, but he could see I was a Jew too, and he told me his real name: Isaac Emmanuilovich Babel. He was from Odessa. We hit it off."

This was Leonid's story for today, I realized. Isaac Babel. I listened more closely.

"Babel's newspaper was only four pages long," Leonid said, "and his editor wanted nothing more than an occasional account of bravery and socialist idealism. But Babel took his assignment seriously. He'd been watching the war with a writer's eye, and he told me, 'This isn't a Marxist revolution, it's a Cossack rebellion.'

"He was right. But he wanted to get *inside* the Cossack mind, which for a Jew is not a comfortable place. The Cossacks organized their camps around their horses, each man with his saddle, bridle, greatcoat, saber, and rifle. They ate together, slept together, cooked together, and Babel would just drop his bedroll into the middle of them. When Babel first arrived, he couldn't ride worth a damn. He had bleeding saddle sores on his ass and thighs, and his horse did whatever it wanted. But he kept at it. After a month, he rode as well as I did – nothing like a Cossack of course, but well enough that they stopped mocking him. Eventually, they tolerated him and stopped calling him Jew-boy. They forgot him, which let him do what he wanted: observe and write.

"One of the Cossacks, named Prischepa, actually befriended Babel. Prischepa liked Jewish girls. He could have done what his comrades did – rape them – but he preferred willing partners. He saw Babel and me as his way to meet them, although both of us were pretending to be Russian. He had us take him visiting. I don't remember the village, but

Prischepa brought a sack of meal, and the three of us found ourselves in a house full of children and women. No one spoke of the missing men who had been killed in pogroms or conscripted into somebody's army. Prischepa wanted to eat fried potatoes, but it was Friday night, and making a fire is not allowed to Jews on the Sabbath.

He started cursing, 'Fucking yids, go dig potatoes, light the fucking fire.'

"They did. Prischepa was drinking vodka, stuffing himself with potatoes. Babel and I did the same. Prischepa was illiterate but fancied himself a Marxist, and he argued about the existence of God with a fourteen-year-old yeshiva student. The student's mother pulled at the boy's sleeve and shushed him. Prischepa was drinking fast, and he was filling the glass of a Jewish woman from Krementz who was wearing white stockings. She was good-looking, a little heavy but curvy, black hair, white skin. She was quite taken with Prischepa. Babel and I were looking at each other, hoping she wouldn't go off with him, because we knew he had syphilis. He passed out, and we got him out of there."

Leonid picked up a copy of Babel's *Red Cavalry* and opened to the first of many bookmarks. "Babel's book appeared in 1926, six years after I last saw him. He wrote without pity, spared no one. I was there for this, which Babel told exactly as it happened:

> Directly under my window several Cossacks were shooting an old Jew with a silvery beard for espionage. The old man was screaming and trying to tear himself free. Then Kudrya from the machine-gun detachment took the old man's head and put it under his arm. The Jew calmed down and stood with his legs apart. With his right hand Kudrya pulled out his dagger and carefully cut the old man's throat, without splashing any blood on himself. Then he knocked on the closed window frame. 'If anyone's interested,' he said, 'they can come and get him. He's all yours ....'

Without emotion, Leonid flipped to the second bookmark. "Another story I remember, also true. Babel and I were sitting by the fire. Our division commander, General Timoshenko, had been a peasant, and he told us how after the Revolution he'd gotten his hands on his landlord, a man who'd kept him in debt for years and had repeatedly raped his wife until she'd been driven mad. He'd dragged the landlord before his wife so she could watch what he did. Babel wrote it this way:

> And then I trampled on Nikitinsky, my master. I trampled on him for an hour or more than an hour, and during that time I got to know him and his life. Shooting – in my opinion – is just a way of getting rid of a fellow, to shoot him is to pardon him, and a vile compromise with yourself; with shooting you don't get to a man's soul, where it is in him and how it shows itself. But usually I don't spare myself, usually I trample my enemy for an hour or more than an hour, I want to find out about the life, what it's like with us ....

Leonid spoke as flatly as if he were reading a newspaper, and that made me understand Babel in a way I hadn't when I had read him as a girl. The horrors of the Civil War had nothing to do with Marxism or monarchy, with right or wrong. Just the worst of human behavior – gang rapes and offhand murder – on all sides. On the Red side, done in the name of proletarian liberation. All the contradictions of the Soviet Union were summed up in that book. How many crimes, I wondered, had Leonid committed? He claimed to have been there with Babel. I wasn't sure how much to believe.

"You were Babel's friend?" I asked.

"For only two months in 1920, but in war men become brothers in a day. When I met Babel, we were advancing on Lwov, as the Poles were still retreating. The two of us were stationed with a platoon of 26 men and one girl, Shura the nurse. She was sleeping with all of them on demand – not with me or Babel because she certainly had syphilis. She'd started off sleeping with the company commander, then went with a few others when he got tired of her. After that, she didn't have much choice. They all passed her around. She was half crazy, incoherent.

"I heard her tell one soldier, 'If your wife turns up I'll kill her.' She saw Babel as her savior and kept appealing to him. He asked me for advice, and I told him there was nothing he could do.

"The Polish war was going well when Babel arrived. Our General Timoshenko would stride through our camps in red leather riding britches. He was fearless. I saw him in the middle of a battle with his revolver in hand screaming, 'Go you bastards, if the Poles don't kill you I will!'

"But then our advance stalled, and he was demoted to brigade commander. Babel sent a report that was critical of Timoshenko's demotion, but his editor wouldn't publish it.

"We were still moving west with plans to encircle Warsaw; Budyonny's First Cavalry had orders to form the southern rim of the circle. Trotsky, the Red Army commissar, was behind the plan, but not Stalin, who was Budyonny's commissar, and he ordered Budyonny to hold back. Stalin wasn't interested in helping take Warsaw. He wanted the glory for himself for taking Lwov. Same insubordination as he had pulled at Tsaritsyn two years earlier. The circle couldn't close without Budyonny. Stalin eventually gave up on taking Lwov, so Budyonny's First Cavalry finally headed north. But it was too late. The Poles broke through and threatened to surround us, but the commander that Budyonny had demoted, Timoshenko, attacked the Polish rear and gave us an exit.

"Babel and I were at the railroad station as the Poles were closing in. Our infantry troops were filthy, hadn't eaten in days; everybody sick. They threw away their rifles and ran after the train, trying to climb aboard, some stumbling from leg wounds or with only one good arm. I made the train, Babel didn't. That was the last day I saw him."

"I remember *Red Cavalry* so well," I said. "I must have read it ten times. What happened to Babel?"

"Well, his book was a popular success, but General Budyonny called it a slander on the Red Army. He wanted Babel shot, but Stalin wouldn't have it. He was more tolerant of good writers than people give him credit for. Babel refused to write the usual socialist-realist crap, so didn't write anything, which made the hacks who ran the Writers Union unhappy. But his big mistake was socializing with NKVD heads, first Yagoda then Yezhov. It was the same thing he'd done with the

Cossacks, but much more dangerous. He was like a moth to the flame. A friend asked if he enjoyed touching death, and he said he just liked to have a sniff, to see what it smelled like. He wanted to understand men who could kill millions.

"How could a man as smart as Babel be so stupid? Being Yezhov's friend was like being Caligula's friend – you didn't want his friendship, you wanted him to forget you existed. After his arrest, Yezhov named Babel in his own confession. Babel was arrested in 1939, and like everyone else, he confessed to whatever they put before him and then named others. He accused Eisenstein, Mikhoels, and Ehrenburg, all great artists and fellow Jews, of conspiring with him in his treason. They were interrogated and released, but Babel was shot. All his unpublished work was destroyed, lost forever."

I told Leonid I wouldn't be back for two weeks. He was unhappy with that, but what could he do? America's President Carter had pressured 65 nations into boycotting the 1980 Moscow Olympics after we invaded Afghanistan, and I was put in charge of a letter-writing campaign to invite female athletes from those countries to come on their own and to compete under the Olympic flag. Aeroflot would fly them without cost, we told them, and Moscow families would host them. In the end, few came. Most of those who did were banned from future international competition by their national sports organizations.

I understood the disappointment of the athletes who couldn't compete. I'd hoped to represent the Soviet Union in track and field in the 1940 Olympics. The games were to have been held in Tokyo, but the war put an end to them. I dreamed of marching with the Soviet team under the hammer and sickle, of a medal draped around my neck while the band played the *Internationale*. Would I have won a medal? Maybe not, but that's the dream of every athlete. By 1948, I was too old to compete, and most of the athletes who might have come to Moscow in 1980 lost their only chance when President Carter imposed his petty boycott as punishment for our invasion of Afghanistan.

Carter didn't need to punish us; we punished ourselves

in Afghanistan. Brezhnev sent our troops in on December 24, 1979, perhaps hoping that the West would be too busy with Christmas to notice. I was dressing for work when I heard the news, and my first thought was this: Didn't we learn anything from America in Vietnam? We were sending our boys to die in a foreign country to support an unpopular puppet government. I couldn't say that publicly, nor could anyone else. But every Soviet citizen hates and fears war. We all remember the price we paid last time.

Soon legless veterans begged for coins and sang war songs: "My blood type is on my sleeve," and "Do you, Comrade, remember Afghanistan? Glows of fires, Muslim cries?" Like America's Vietnam, our war was fought by conscripts drawn from the poor, because parents' money or influence bought their son an exemption. Our government never announced casualty figures, but the zinc coffins and mutilated soldiers couldn't be ignored. Gorbachev finally called it quits after nine years of useless carnage, although he never spoke of the stupidity of the invasion. After our troops left, the Taliban hanged the president of our puppet government from a Kabul stoplight.

ISTANBUL, 1929

Boris Anokhin pulled at the top button of his doorman's coat. His attempt to ventilate his dripping armpits, repeated every few minutes, was futile. He wasn't permitted to unbutton the coat, but removing his hat for a moment and wiping his brow was tolerated – at least the manager hadn't objected. July in Istanbul was hot and muggy, and the summer air was still. His Pera Palace uniform was an improvement over the military caricature he'd been forced to wear in Harbin; this coat was more like a glorified tram conductor's than a *faux* field marshal's. And Istanbul's weather was better than Harbin's. Harbin had been hot in the summers too, and its winters had been hell, while Istanbul's winters were damp but mild. If only he had his family with him, life would be fine. But Anna and Irina were hostages in Moscow, and his only contact with them was a single letter exchanged each month through his NKVD controller, who read and censored their communications both ways. He and Anna could speak intimately only through allusions – "that night in May, in Odessa" or "our simple pleasures."

The Pera Palace was even gaudier than Harbin's Hotel Moderne. It was a square, six-story building in Istanbul's Pera neighborhood, decorated with red velvet draperies and gilt furniture, all marble inlay and filigreed screens. He would have preferred to work at the southwest entrance to the hotel, which offered a view of the ships on the Golden Horn and the mosques. But his NKVD controller insisted that he work on the opposite side, facing Pera's clubs and brothels. Anokhin understood the reasoning. It was surprising what White Russian drunks would say as they passed through a door held by an anonymous doorman. But he was effective as an eavesdropper only with Russians – he spoke no other languages. Istanbul was a city of Turks, but also of Jews, Russians, and a few remaining Greeks and Armenians. And because it was the terminus of the Orient Express Railway, tourists speaking English, French, German, Italian, and languages that he couldn't even identify streamed through his door. He spoke a pidgin Turkish, but he'd learned only a few phrases in other languages: "Welcome to the Pera Palace," "Good morning, sir!", "May I get you a taxi?" He was past forty and too old to learn new languages. That should have made him unsuitable as a doorman, but the NKVD paid his manager to hire and keep him. In Istanbul, money could do anything.

Anokhin was desperately alone, separated from his family and with no White Russian friends because he was a known Red informant. He sometimes had a drink with a Russian-speaking Finn who cooked at the hotel, but he wasn't sure that he could trust him. Perhaps he worked for the NKVD too. His life had no purpose, and he found sexual entrapment of hotel guests degrading beyond belief. Two weeks earlier, he'd spent two hours preparing one such session with a whore and her pimp. When the pimp went to the toilet, she'd winked at him, said she found him attractive, and that she'd give him a free night; he was so lonely that he'd almost accepted.

The muezzin's sunset call to prayer signaled the end of his shift. He went to his room in the hotel basement, where he hung his soggy uniform and waited for a turn at the communal shower. At eight o'clock, he left the hotel for his weekly meeting with his NKVD controller. He walked down Istikal Avenue toward the Galata Bridge. The rose and purple remnants of the sunset formed a backdrop for the massive domes of the mosques on the opposite side of the Golden Horn, and the evening star kissed the spire of the Galata Tower. He passed shops and restaurants of every nationality. Anna would love Istanbul, he thought, but that was not to be.

He crossed the bridge, bought two kebabs and a newspaper, and found an empty park bench in a small public square near the Yeni mosque. He pretended to read his Turkish newspaper. A young couple, the man in a black suit, the wife with her face veiled, shared the bench beside him for a time. When they left, his controller took their place and fed peanuts to the pigeons. Neither he nor Anokhin looked at each other. They both spoke quietly, with their mouths almost closed. Anokhin had placed his weekly report inside his newspaper's classified advertising section, which he would leave on the bench when he departed. If the controller had written instructions for him, Anokhin would find them in his dead-drop, a chink between two bricks in the wall of a mausoleum in the Russian Orthodox cemetery.

The controller – whose name Anokhin did not know – gave him instructions for yet another tawdry affair, a setup for sexual blackmail of a German diplomat.

"He will arrive Wednesday, and we have paid the desk clerk to put him in room 310. At two o'clock Wednesday morning, you will open the door on the loading dock and admit two of our men, then take them to room 308. They will need two hours to install the peepholes for the spy cameras and the wires for the recording equipment. Stay with them during that time in case they need something."

Anokhin grunted his assent.

"This will be our last meeting," the man continued. "Your new controller will meet you next week, same place. He'll also feed the pigeons, but with pistachios rather than peanuts. That's how you'll identify him. Don't worry about identifying yourself, he'll know you."

Anokhin grunted again. This would be his third controller change in three years.

The controller threw the last of his nuts to the pigeons and started to stand but then remembered something.

"Oh," he said. "I regret to tell you that your mother has died."

Anokhin started to turn towards the controller, then remembered that was forbidden.

"Please," he said from the side of his mouth, "please let me go to Moscow for her funeral."

"No, Citizen Anokhin, that won't be possible. You were told that you might have the opportunity to visit your family, but only if you did exceptional work. As your work is barely satisfactory, your request is denied."

MOSCOW, 1980

My attitude toward Leonid's stories had changed. At the beginning, I'd resisted when he wanted to tell me about Trotsky.
But he was giving me the Soviet history I'd been denied, and
I wanted to hear more, to know what had been hidden from
me, to know what I'd hidden from myself.

"After the Civil War," Leonid told me, "I had a choice. The
higher-ups in the Cheka liked me. They sent me through the
Frunze military academy in 1921 and told me I had a career
working for the Cheka inside the Soviet Union if I wanted it. I
thought about it – promotion would be faster that way. That's
what Sudoplatov did, and he passed me in rank although he
was younger than me. Or I could work undercover in the foreign services, which is what I chose. I'm good at languages, and I knew fewer people would be breathing down my
neck. As things turned out, it was the right choice. Yezhov
killed off half the NKVD in his purges. Plenty of those worked
abroad, but working at home was worse. You either were shot
as a traitor or you were forced to execute your brother officers, men you knew were blameless. And the collectivization
campaign that started in 1929 was the NKVD's work. Same
thing that I'd done while extracting grain from the peasants
in 1919, but on a much larger scale. It lasted three years with
maybe 12 million dead, most in the Ukraine. And then there
was setting up and running the camps. Working inside the
country was mostly boring, depressing, soul-killing. Besides,
I'd seen a little of the West during the Polish war. Everything
was cleaner, the women looked better, and I liked the food.
And if Poland seemed better than home, imagine Paris when
I finally got there."

Leonid, always the survivor, saw Soviet history as a novel
with himself at the center. But now I was the one who wanted to see the bigger picture, and I pulled him away from his
story toward our country's history, toward Stalin and Trotsky.

"What happened?" I asked. "How did Trotsky become the
devil while Stalin became God?"

"We – you, your mother, your sister, and I – were sent to
China and then back to Moscow for two years in April of 1927.
It was toward the end of Trotsky's fall," Leonid said. "I watched

it happen, not that I had any inside information. I hadn't seen Trotsky in the seven years since I left his train. And of course, no one asked my opinion on who should be top dog. I was a loyal party man, and I just followed orders, kept my head down, and tried to advance my career.

"On the street, people still saw Trotsky as Lenin's right-hand man for a long time. And at first, no one, even at the top, saw it coming – not Trotsky's fall, not Stalin's rise. Stalin kept himself in the shadows, and the others in the Politburo were the ones who had the glamor jobs. Trotsky was the commissar of the Red Army, the man who'd managed the October Revolution and then had won the Civil War. Zinoviev was party chief in Leningrad and the head of the International, which included all the Communist parties worldwide. Kamenev was party chief in Moscow and the leading Marxist theoretician, and Bukharin ran press and propaganda. And Stalin? He was the bureaucrat who did the jobs nobody else wanted to do. He was Commissar of Nationalities, which doesn't sound like much, does it? But half the country wasn't Russian – Turkmen, Azerbaijanis, Tartars, Armenians, Tadzhiks, Buriats, Yakuts... They knew no more about Marx than they did about Einstein. The others on the Politburo were European intellectuals, mostly Jews who considered Asiatics to be a lower form of life. Stalin was a Georgian and understood how Asiatics thought – blood feuds and loyalty to a chief. He convinced Lenin to organize the Soviet Union as a federation of supposedly autonomous nations, each with its own Party Secretary. No one else cared, so Stalin appointed all the Party Secretaries. Lenin set up a Workers' and Peasants' Inspectorate to make sure things were efficient and were corruption-free. Boring, right? Everyone was happy when Stalin offered to manage it, but that let him stick his nose anywhere he wanted.

"He handled all the details so well that Lenin gave him the most boring job of all: General Secretary of the Party. The Politburo was the group that made policy decisions, the Orgburo carried them out, and it was left to Stalin, the General Secretary, to handle the paperwork. He prepared the agendas for the Politburo meetings, produced the necessary documents, and oversaw communications between the Politburo and the Orgburo. And he kept the Party membership lists. At the end of the Civil War, the Party had 400,000 members – too many, Lenin thought. Get rid of the careerists, the uncommitted members, he told Stalin. Stalin kept those who backed him and removed the ones who didn't. I don't think he planned to be a dictator, at least not at first. He was good at bureaucracy, and he took the jobs no one else wanted. He never pushed himself forward, just did his jobs and did them well.

"Everyone worshipped and imitated Lenin, Stalin included. Zinoviev and Kamenev even took on Lenin's handwriting. The only one who didn't idolize Lenin was Trotsky, who admired him but treated him as a human being.

"By the end of 1921, Lenin's health was failing. No one could imagine him gone, but an assassin's bullet and thirty years of exile, revolution, and war had taken their toll. He had bad headaches. The doctors told him to take a couple of days off whenever the attacks came, and that helped for a while, but he couldn't stop working, and the headaches would start up again. The doctors sent him to the countryside with his secretaries, his sisters, and his wife. He was told to limit work to two hours a day. He tried to make Trotsky his number two who would run things in his absence, but Trotsky turned him down. He said the Russian people wouldn't accept a Jew.

"Lenin had his first stroke in May. The Politburo just bickered without him, but Stalin's organizations, his General Secretariat and his Inspectorate, kept clicking. Trotsky tried to disband them, but the rest of the Politburo refused; Lenin had put Stalin in charge, and besides, somebody needed to do all that work. Without Lenin looking over his shoulder, Stalin ran things his way and put his men in all the key jobs.

"Trotsky was visiting Lenin regularly but not making a big thing of it. Stalin visited Lenin and wrote a *Pravda* article that displayed his adoration. And then Lenin recovered! He returned to work, and he didn't like what he found. Everywhere he looked, he saw Stalin's Secretariat. He couldn't get his own orders carried out. He issued them, and they disappeared in Stalin's bureaucratic swamp.

"Lenin had a second stroke in December. He knew he was on his last legs, and he worried that the party would split into factions. He dictated his political testament to his wife,

Krupskaya. The two most capable men, he said, were Trotsky and Stalin. Now when this was finally read after his death, it surprised everyone – not that he had named Trotsky, who everyone knew was brilliant, but that he had said that of Stalin, the bureaucrat. But then Lenin waffled and didn't appoint either one as his successor. He said that he worried about both, saying Stalin had taken too much power and might not use it wisely, and that Trotsky was the most capable but was conceited and politically inept.

"A month later, Lenin thought better and amended his still unread will. He said that Stalin was too rude and unpleasant to be General Secretary. That wasn't published; only his secretaries and Krupskaya saw the document until after his death. In March, Lenin wrote Stalin a letter breaking off all personal contact, and he planned to attack Stalin at the Party Congress that April. Stalin saw what was coming and published adoring tributes to Lenin and made friends wherever he could. Luck was on his side. When the Congress opened, Lenin was too sick to travel.

"Lenin was dying, and Trotsky looked likely to be his successor, so Zinoviev, Kamenev, and Stalin got together to block him. Zinoviev, who was popular and was a good orator, was the front man; Kamenev was the strategist; and Stalin, once again, was the bureaucrat who did all the work. Together, they could swing Politburo votes their way, and that made Trotsky and his men "Oppositionists." Trotsky demanded democracy within the Party – the right to bring his proposals to the Central Committee – for which Kamenev and Zinoviev wanted him arrested.

Stalin was more moderate, saying we're all friends here, good Communists, we'll work this out. That was always his way. He'd let someone else take a hard line while he'd be the calming voice. What was striking about Stalin was that nothing was striking. He was modest – no womanizing, no heavy drinking. He lived with his wife in what had been servants' quarters in the Kremlin. He was friendly, even to Trotsky, especially to Trotsky. Sudoplatov was a security officer assigned to both the Politburo and the Central Committee. He told me Trotsky was the first to arrive at one of the Politburo meetings. He was sitting at the table when Kamenev and

Zinoviev came in and sat down with barely a nod to him. Then Stalin entered, shook Trotsky's hand, asked about his family. And Stalin was that way with everyone. Sudoplatov told me he'd see Stalin in the corner of a stairway, puffing on his pipe, listening for an hour to some Central Committee hack too unimportant for Trotsky to notice. Meanwhile, Stalin controlled the Party lists, and he quietly expelled many of Trotsky's supporters and promoted his men.

"Lenin died in January 1924. Kamenev had a plaster death mask made, but it was too horrible to show anyone; the last stroke had bugged Lenin's eyes almost out of his head. Trotsky was off at a health spa in the Caucasus and didn't return for the funeral. He claimed Stalin sent him a telegram with the wrong date for the ceremony, told him stay where you are, you'll never get back in time. But missing the funeral shows just how politically hopeless Trotsky was. He could have commandeered a train and run it flat out to Moscow. That sums it up: Trotsky sitting in a sulfur bath while Stalin stood by the bier reading his oath of allegiance to Lenin. Lenin would have hated that suck-up oath and the whole cult of himself. But Stalin, who had been a seminarian, understood what the nation needed – a Communist saint. Krupskaya, Lenin's wife, wanted her husband buried, but Stalin had the nation's top scientists mummify him and put him on display in Red Square. Even today, Lenin looks better dead than he ever did alive.

"The next big fight was within the Comintern, the organization of Communist parties from around the world. The Comintern was full of Trotsky's supporters: Trotsky was preaching world revolution, and Stalin was for consolidating socialism in one country, the Soviet Union. But Zinoviev swung the Comintern over to the triumvirate's side. The foreign parties were living off Soviet money, and Zinoviev controlled the purse strings. He convinced the national parties to demote or expel Trotsky's supporters. The Comintern issued a proclamation condemning Trotsky's Opposition.

"Lenin's testament was finally read out before the Central Committee in May, four months after his death. Stalin looked small and miserable as he listened. The cult of Lenin, which he had used to his benefit, cut both ways. It seemed like a sacrilege to go against Lenin's will, so Stalin's career was on the line. But Zinoviev and Kamenev were still worried about Trotsky and weren't about to ditch Stalin. They both spoke in Stalin's favor, saying Lenin's fears about Stalin's rudeness were groundless – just look how friendly and accommodating he had become. Krupskaya wanted the will published, but Kamenev convinced the Central Committee to suppress it because publication would only confuse the nation at a difficult time. Krupskaya hated Stalin, and he returned the feeling. He told her that if she didn't stop criticizing him, he would get Lenin a new widow."

MOSCOW, 1980

We took a lunch break. I'd brought egg sandwiches for both of us. I ate mine while Leonid ignored his and smoked, impatient to get on with it. It was easier to do things his way. He took up where he'd left off:

"What was Trotsky doing? Not enough. He thought that speeches, writing, and logic would win the day. He published an article recalling that Zinoviev and Kamenev had opposed Lenin in the October Revolution. But that didn't touch Stalin, who had supported Lenin at that time. And Stalin spoke out in support of his partners and said that while Trotsky had fought well in the Revolution, he'd done nothing special – this about the man Lenin had put in charge when he went back to Finland. Zinoviev published all Lenin's anti-Trotsky quotes from the time before Trotsky had joined the Bolsheviks. The Leninist cult was going full swing, and that put Trotsky on record as opposing Lenin. And most damning of all, the wrong people, the never-give-up Socialist Revolutionaries and Mensheviks, now supported Trotsky. When he walked through the streets, they cheered him.

"Trotsky was forced to resign as Commissar of the Red Army in January 1925. The Army's officers had all fought under him in the Civil War, and he might have pulled off a coup, but he never considered it. He was a straight Party man; he would win there or not at all. Trotsky continued to speak out, not in public but in Politburo and Central Committee meetings. He would argue his case, but he accepted Party decisions once made. Zinoviev demanded that he publicly admit that he had been wrong about everything, which Trotsky refused to do. Zinoviev wanted him kicked off the Politburo, but Stalin stood for moderation, for common sense, for safety first. He defended Trotsky, kept him in the Politburo.

"Right after the Civil War, when the economy had been a disaster, Lenin had allowed some capitalist activity – small factories, retail shops, grain traders – and encouraged private farmers. Trotsky had opposed that. He'd argued for collectivized farms – not by force – but he figured peasants would join voluntarily once they saw how much better their lives would be with farm machinery, communal kitchens, childcare, and so on. But Lenin insisted, and Trotsky went along. After Lenin's death, the economy came up again in the Politburo. Trotsky argued again for state-owned industry and collective farms. Bukharin was for private industry and farms. Stalin waited, watched, and straddled the middle.

"Zinoviev and Kamenev at last realized that Stalin, not Trotsky, was the danger and switched sides, went over to Trotsky and his Oppositionists. Krupskaya went with them. They called themselves 'The Leftist Opposition.' If they'd moved a year earlier, they might have had a chance. But it was too late. Stalin swung to the right and allied with Bukharin. He controlled the press, and he used it – now *he* was the one bringing up Zinoviev's and Kamenev's timidity in the 1917 Revolution, calling them the 'strikebreakers of October.' And he had the votes. He had packed the Central Committee with his up-and-comers and the Politburo with his toadies.

"This was also the time of the Chinese fiasco, in which you and I played a small part; you brought me my revolver. Everyone knew China was Stalin's fault – he had backed Chiang, and then Chiang slaughtered half the Chinese Communists. Trotsky said, 'I warned you.' That only made Stalin more determined to get rid of him. The worst enemy is the one who has been proven right.

"And then Trotsky did the unforgivable. In front of the Central Committee, he pointed his finger at Stalin and called him 'the gravedigger of the revolution.' Stalin stormed out of the room. Zinoviev was appalled: 'Why did you say that? Stalin won't forgive you or your family until the third or fourth generation!'

"He was right, of course. The NKVD eventually killed all four of Trotsky's children or hounded them to their deaths, and the gang that I sent to kill Trotsky in Mexico, led by that idiot painter David Siqueiros, even wounded his fourteen-year-old grandson.

"Trotsky was expelled from the Politburo the day after he pointed his finger at Stalin. Zinoviev and Kamenev followed shortly thereafter.

"Trotsky's Opposition was holding meetings for his supporters, and during my temporary stay in Moscow, I was in charge of the NKVD men infiltrating them. Going to Trotsky's meetings was risky. I sent someone else to the meetings where I knew he'd be speaking. I couldn't afford to have him recognize me. He might have called me out by name and embraced me!

"The meetings were usually in some worker's apartment. The students and workers would crowd into two rooms and Trotsky or Kamenev or Zinoviev would speak from the doorway between the rooms. Maybe 20,000 in total attended those meetings, and my men got most of their names. At first, the Central Committee let the meetings go ahead, but when they started to swell, they sent us in to break them up with clubs. Not in uniform though – we dressed as angry workers."

Personal loyalty meant nothing to Leonid, I knew. And the Party members who survived those years were like him. Husbands abandoned wives, and men who had been the closest of friends turned on each other. When the Party – which was coming to mean Stalin – changed its position, they changed instantly, without a thought. And sometimes even that wasn't enough. I could never have lived that way. And others suffered much worse than me. I had my father and stepfather as protectors.

Leonid continued: "1927 was the tenth anniversary of the Revolution, and half the world's Communists were coming to Russia to celebrate, two Mexican painters among them. I'd been given a list of foreigners who were to be monitored, so I had my eye on them even then, but I got to know them better ten years later: Diego Rivera and David Siqueiros.

"The radio and press were accusing Trotsky of treason, and that must have galled him. He knew what he'd done for the Revolution. The Opposition carried its own signs in the crowds and marches. Nothing overtly against Stalin, but everyone knew what the signs meant: 'Let us turn our fire against the right' and 'Let us carry out Lenin's will.' We in the NKVD were prepared for them. One of my men fired a warning shot at Trotsky's car, and another, who was dressed as a drunken fireman, jumped on the car's running board and put his ax through the window.

"Central Committee members were speaking to the crowd from the backs of trucks. Trotsky had balls, I'll give him that. He just drove up to the trucks and got out of his smashed-up car. Some idiot police captain recognized him as important, saluted him, and helped him up onto the back of an empty truck. No one had told the captain that Trotsky was on the shit list. I showed up just as Trotsky started to speak. I could see what was happening; everyone was ditching the other speakers and listening to Trotsky. I thought fast. Stopping Trotsky from speaking was only going to make him look good, and I couldn't force the crowd to go back and listen to the official speakers. I did the best I could. I told all the other speakers to climb up on Trotsky's truck and speak at once. It worked only to a degree. The crowd booed the official speakers and cheered Trotsky."

I sat through all of that without interrupting. Leonid was different in some way. He wasn't his usual mocking self.

I probed. "You cared for Trotsky, didn't you? You hoped he would win out."

Leonid started to argue, then stopped. He was more reflective than I'd seen him.

"Trotsky had helped me, and Stalin was a man to be feared, not loved. But what I wanted, who I liked, didn't matter. I was a Party man, and by the time Trotsky and his Opposition collapsed in 1928, Stalin *was* the party. Although he denied it, Trotsky tried to split the Party, so Stalin was right to exile him. And when he continued as a splitter, I did what was right. I had my orders, and I removed him."

Interesting, I thought. Leonid's euphemism "removed." Even forty years later, he didn't want to say "murdered."

MOSCOW, 1929

The day I saw Irina. I was nine years old. My sister, Svetlana, was dressing her dolls, and I was sitting at the kitchen table with my homework. My assignment was to compose a letter to Comrade Stalin. I pledged my life to the Revolution and thanked Stalin for his kindness, his selfless labor, and his wise leadership. All my homework was like that. Even the arithmetic problems were designed to teach a lesson: if a plot of land produced 523 kilos of grain before collectivization and 1,282 kilos after, what was the increase due to Communism?

The telephone rang, and Mama answered. It was Uncle Leonid, and I was surprised because he almost never called during the day. He kept late hours at the office and was rarely home for dinner. He would sometimes call Mama if he would not come home at all, but not always even then. The telephone call was short.

Mama kept asking questions: "Where are we going? When?"

I could tell she wasn't getting any answers. Leonid must have hung up, because she didn't say goodbye, just put the receiver down and turned to speak to us.

"Zoya, Svetlana, Leonid has a new assignment in a foreign country, and we will be joining him! It will be an adventure!"

Her smile was forced; I imagine that she had mixed feelings, that she was worried about the unknown but was relieved not to be left behind.

I asked her the same questions that she had asked Leonid, "Where are we going? When?"

These were questions for which she didn't have answers other than "I don't know" and "Soon, Leonid will tell us – we need to pack."

His assignment was a state secret, not to be shared with his family. Only later, after our ship had left from Sebastopol, did he tell us that we would be living in Turkey, in Istanbul. We didn't ask why we were with him, but I understand now. We were part of his cover, as I had been his cover on that Chinese train when I was five years old. Officially, he was a Soviet trade officer assigned to the Istanbul consulate.

Leonid had told Mama to shop for what we would need, so she took us to a store where she had privileges because of Leonid's rank. It was on the Arbat, the second story of a nondescript building that had no windows facing the street and no signs. We were just stepping back onto the Arbat with our bags when I saw Irina.

Irina and her mother were about to enter the metro station. I hadn't seen her since her family had disappeared from Harbin four years earlier, but I recognized her immediately – the same soulful eyes and oval face.

Before I could speak, she saw me and called out, "Zoya!"

Both our mothers turned. Mine smiled and stepped forward, but Irina's mother froze. Then, her face twisted in anger and fear, she grabbed Irina by the arm and pulled her into the station. I tried to follow, calling Irina's name. I heard her calling mine, her voice fading into silence as she descended on the station's escalator.

My mother held me back, and I understand now. While my mother didn't know why Irina's mother had acted that way – Leonid would have told her nothing about sending the hotel's doorman to his arrest – I'm sure she knew it had something to do with Leonid. That sort of thing must have happened to Mama more than once.

I wouldn't see Irina again for fifty years.

MOSCOW, 1980

If a stranger had been watching a silent film of Leonid speaking about Trotsky's downfall, he might have thought him deranged; Leonid's expression and bearing shifted that abruptly. One moment he would be admiring, then contemptuous, then laughing, then pitying. At times even loving.

"Stalin was finished being genial," Leonid said. "Things came to a head after all the foreign Communists left at the end of the celebration. Trotsky had no illusions. He predicted that he, Zinoviev, and Kamenev would be kicked off the Central Committee, and they were. That meant they were evicted from their Kremlin apartments because only Central Committee members could live there. Trotsky gave the NKVD a scare though. He left the Kremlin in the middle of the night and couldn't be found. For all anyone knew, he'd left the country. Stalin was furious, and everyone in the NKVD was frantic. Trotsky showed up a day later.

"The 15th Party Congress met with 1,600 delegates, not one of them from the Opposition. Trotsky said he would accept the Party's decisions, and that he would keep silent if he were ordered to do so, but he refused to recant what he'd already said and written. As he left the hall, delegates threw inkpots at him, threw his own books at his head shouting, 'No one reads your trash, but it's still useful for knocking you down!'

"Stalin wasn't sure enough of his place in 1927 to know what to do with Trotsky, who was too proud and too smart to grovel. If Stalin put him on trial, or if he had him mysteriously assassinated, he would make him a martyr. Better to hide him. He exiled him to Alma Ata in the Caucasus, near the Chinese border. Trotsky had expected Siberia, but Stalin rejected that. Siberia was where the tsar had exiled *his* political enemies. Besides, other Oppositionists were being sent to Siberia, and Stalin wanted Trotsky isolated.

"On the scheduled morning, Trotsky and his family waited for the NKVD. And waited. At two o'clock, there was a curt telephone call, no explanation, saying that the departure was delayed two days. The explanation arrived an hour later from a friend: 'I went to the train station to see you off. A thousand people blocked the tracks, and someone was driving a car with a huge portrait of you, Lev. There were rumors that they had you in shackles and that you were already on the train, so the crowd tried to storm the train. The NKVD troops beat them, threatened them with live fire. You still have friends here.'

"The two-day delay was another lie. At eight o'clock the next morning, an NKVD major with five soldiers behind him pounded on the door. (I heard all this from the major over drinks some years later).

"'A change of plans,' he told Trotsky's wife. 'You will be leaving today. Now, in fact. Please go to the car waiting by the door. Your luggage and boxes will follow.'

"Trotsky, still in his dressing gown, came out from his bedroom. 'Comrade Major,' he said, 'as you can see, none of us has prepared for the day. We will need an hour. Please have your men wait outside.'

"The major told me that he considered that for a moment, then waved his men out. As the last one passed, Trotsky called out to him, 'Kishkin!'

"The man was weeping. He turned toward Trotsky but couldn't face him. Kishkin was a sergeant from the Red 100, the soldiers on Trotsky's armored train.

"'Forgive me, Lev Davidovich,' Kishkin sobbed.

"The major, who hadn't expected this, told me that he grabbed Kishkin and shoved him out the door ahead of him, shouting at Trotsky 'One hour, no more!'

"When they returned an hour later, Trotsky was not to be seen, but the major heard him dictating some treatise to his son behind a locked door.

"'Kishkin! Break the door down!'

"Kishkin, sobbing, smashed the door. 'Forgive me Comrade Trotsky!' Kishkin cried. 'Shoot me!'

"'No one's shooting you, Kishkin,' Trotsky said. 'You're only doing your job.'

"When the major ordered Trotsky to leave for the car, he refused to go. The major told the other soldiers – not Kishkin, he'd given up on him – to muscle Trotsky out the door and down the stairs.

"Trotsky's sons, Lyova and Sergei, shouted to the neighbors, 'Look what they're doing! Carrying Comrade Trotsky away!'

"People turned away or shut their windows.

"The soldiers pushed Trotsky's sons into the back seat with Trotsky, put his wife in the front seat, and the major wedged himself into the back seat as well. Trotsky's son Sergei tried to jump out from the other side. The driver turned and grabbed him by the collar, and Sergei threw a punch that split the driver's lip.

"As the driver started to return the blow, the major shouted, 'Stop!' He didn't want any bruises when he delivered the family to the train.

"Trotsky demanded that his secretaries accompany him, but the major forbade it. Syermuks and Poznansky (the secretaries who'd tutored me on the armored train during the Civil War), bought tickets and traveled as private passengers at the back of the same train, and the major told me he missed that, or he would have arrested them.

"It was a nine-day trip to Frunze, the end of the rail line. When they arrived, they had a night in the station hotel before taking a bus overland to Alma Ata. The major escorted Trotsky to his room and was surprised to see one of Trotsky's secretaries leaving a room that he was sharing with the other. That was the end of the journey for those two. Both died in the camps.

"The Revolution had changed Alma Ata very little. No sewers, no electricity, no running water, and endemic malaria, leprosy, and cholera. Packs of rabid dogs howled in the streets. When spring came, Trotsky rented a peasant's house with a view of the mountains. The family harvested fruit, made preserves, hunted, fished, and relaxed a little. It wasn't a bad time for them, the major told me.

"After Stalin expelled Trotsky, he no longer needed Bukharin. He quickly dropped his rightist agenda and implemented Trotsky's leftist plans for industrialization and collectivization, naturally without giving Trotsky credit. The peasants resisted collectivization and buried grain and even took up arms in some areas. The Party sent 25,000 young Communists to the countryside to 'requisition food,' and they did the job more brutally than I'd ever done. The peasants rebelled, and many of the requisitioners were found by the roadside with their skulls split or their throats cut. The Party's reaction to that was brutal – millions executed or starved to death.

"Stalin went after Trotsky's supporters. The NKVD arrested them, sent their children to orphanages, executed some, and scattered the rest across Siberia and Central Asia. Trotsky wrote hundreds of letters trying to preserve the Opposition. Stalin cut off his mail, but Oppositionists still made pilgrimages to visit him in Alma Ata – internal exile wasn't isolating Trotsky.

"Stalin then made a mistake. He was still afraid to make Trotsky a martyr by killing him or putting him on trial, so he decided to expel him from the Soviet Union. He had a hard time getting any country to take him. Britain, Germany, and France all refused. What government would want a Communist revolutionary who called for its overthrow? But Kemal Ataturk, the leader of the new Turkish Republic, accepted. He and Stalin were on good terms. Stalin had sent Ataturk arms when he'd needed them, and Ataturk wanted to return the favor. In January 1929, Trotsky was given 24 hours to pack. The family was put on a train to Odessa, then onto an empty boat – named the *Ilyich*, after Lenin – for Istanbul. And I was summoned to the office of Menzhinsky, the NKVD head, and given my assignment: Go to Istanbul and keep an eye on Trotsky."

2

MOSCOW, 1931

Irina gazed across the river from their apartment, high in the new Shalobkova Residential District. It was like being a hawk; all of Moscow was open to her. There was the Kremlin with its domes, and there was the Lubyanka, where her mother worked. Mother had come home one night a month ago, all excited.

"I've been promoted! I'll be a stenographer for the NKVD's Second Deputy, Comrade Genrikh Yagoda. We're moving!"

"What about your old boss?" Irina asked.

She hadn't asked about him since her grandmother died, but maybe he would leave her mother alone now.

"Comrade Yagoda has transferred him to Kamchatka to head our office there."

Good, Irina thought. If only Papa could come home, life would be perfect.

❖❖❖

Irina took piano lessons each Monday at the Gnesin School of Music. Her teacher, Evgenia Fabionovna Gnesina could play all of Chopin's etudes from memory, while Irina was still struggling through easy minuets from Bach's "Anna Magdalena" notebook.

Whenever she held an eighth note too long, her teacher would snap at her, "You're not counting! If you don't count, you might as well close the music and stop playing."

All of her students rudely called her only "Evgenia" (not to her face of course) to differentiate her from her famous younger sister, Elena, who ran the school and grabbed all the best students for herself, leaving Evgenia with the mediocre and talentless – like Irina. Irina milked Evgenia's resentment. Each week, she went to the library and scoured the classical music press so that she could greet her teacher with, "Evgenia Fabionovna, I see your sister has won yet another prize. You must be so proud of her."

Her teacher's spring and autumn recitals, compulsory performances for all her students, were torture for Irina. Evgenia set the program using some rubric of her own combining age, difficulty of the piece, and the performer's skill. A recital program might begin with a cute five-year-old picking out "Twinkle, Twinkle Little Star," and advance through terrified older students in rough age and talent order, to Evgenia's favorite – sixteen-year-old Anatoly – playing Rachmaninoff's Piano Concerto No. 2, and ending with Evgenia herself, graciously agreeing after much pleading to play her Chopin etudes. Irina knew she wasn't talented at piano, but it was humiliating to be scheduled to play between two seven-year-olds, well before the other mediocre students her age. So, when Evgenia's daughter met Irina at the door to tell her mother was ill and her lesson would need to be postponed, she shouldered her bag and headed home with a smile.

She was about to enter their apartment when she heard a man's voice from within. She froze, remembering the coat on the chair, the weekly "special time" visits by her mother's interrogator. But her mother had said that he was now in Kamchatka! She listened for a moment. The man was laughing, relaxed, but she couldn't quite make out his words. Then, a woman's voice, softer than his, words indistinguishable, but it was her mother's. She couldn't just stand there by the door. She ran down the hall and hid in the cleaner's closet, peeking through a crack. She waited for almost an hour, all the time choking on solvent fumes.

Finally, the apartment door opened, and a tall man with an ugly pencil mustache, wearing a wrinkled military uniform without any emblems or badges, stepped into the hall. He looked very satisfied with himself, Irina thought. As he waited for the lift, he smiled as he adjusted his cap in front of a mirror and muttered something that Irina didn't altogether catch – a man's name and "Kamchatka."

Deep down, Irina knew this about her mother: that she loved only Irina's father, and that whatever she'd had to do, she done for her family. What would be the point of confronting her? Five minutes after the man she'd seen had left, Irina entered the apartment without a word.

A few days later, his photograph in *Pravda* confirmed her suspicion – Genrikh Yagoda, her mother's new boss.

❖❖❖

"I have exciting news, Irina! Comrade Yagoda has been put in charge of a top-secret project, and he's asked me to help him! Sit down, I'll explain."

How top-secret could it be, Irina thought, if she's allowed to explain it to me? Her mother pulled Irina's geography textbook from the shelf and opened to a map of northeastern Russia and the Scandinavian Peninsula.

"Suppose a ship captain was bringing timber from Archangel or Murmansk to Leningrad? How would he go?"

Irina looked at the map for a minute. "It wouldn't be far by train, but he couldn't take his ship there without going around, north of Norway, past Copenhagen, into the Baltic, past Helsinki."

"Very good, Irina! But suppose there were a canal that connected the White Sea to the Baltic."

"Much shorter," Irina nodded obediently.

Her mother triumphantly opened her satchel and produced a document with official stamps that laid out the route of the proposed canal.

"And that's what we'll do! It will be a direct connection! Ships will travel only a quarter the distance that they do now, and our warships will be able to travel quickly between the two seas entirely on our territory. It will be our canal, even grander than the capitalists' Panama and Suez canals. And we'll be part of it. We'll move to Medvezhyegorsk on the shore of Lake Onega, the canal's administrative center."

How could her mother parrot this propaganda?

MOSCOW, 1931

Mama, Svetlana, and I lived with Leonid in Istanbul for two years. I learned Turkish in the streets and German, my first academic foreign language, at school. It wasn't until 1951, when Leonid was first imprisoned, that I considered this sequence of events: Trotsky was expelled from the Soviet Union to Turkey in 1929, just before we arrived there; Trotsky's house burned in 1931; and Leonid was suddenly recalled to Moscow immediately after the fire.

When we returned to Moscow from Istanbul, Leonid must have already been promoted to a senior rank in the NKVD, because we were given an apartment in Government House, an enormous, just completed building on the Moscow River embankment. Important Party members lived there: political officials (Khrushchev, Beria), soldiers (Tukhachevsky, Zhukov), the hero-worker Stakhanov (often drunk and sprawled on a bench in the courtyard), prominent artists, writers, and scientists. And many ranking NKVD officers, including Leonid.

The building had a cinema, a theater, and shops that sold luxury food and clothing. There was almost no reason to leave, although chauffeured cars waited at the entrance. I didn't understand how exceptional our life was. I assumed that Communism had fulfilled its promise, that every Soviet citizen had what we had. I later asked Leonid how he and the other Government House residents justified the way we had lived.

"Simple," he said. "We, the vanguard of the Revolution, had sacrificed everything. We'd been exiled and imprisoned, had won the Civil War, had worked like dogs. It was only fair that we should also be the first to share Communism's material benefits. Soon, we thought, our way of life would be available to all."

I was eleven years old when we returned to Moscow. All my classmates had spent the past year in the Pioneers, and they had earned badges and medals that I didn't have. But I worked hard and caught up. I did everything the Pioneer handbook told me to do. I even set up an "atheist's corner" in our apartment with anti-religious pamphlets and pictures.

When I caught Leonid and Mama laughing at my shrine, I lectured them on every Communist's duty. I became a Pioneer group leader, and in my last year I was invited to the Artek summer camp in the Crimea, where I learned to sail. From nowhere, the Pioneer songs still pop into my head:

Then forward you workers, freedom awaits you,
O'er all the world on the land and the sea.
On with the fight for the cause of humanity.
March, march you toilers and the world shall be free.

I'm flipping through my box of family photos from back then. I wasn't what most people would call pretty – fat cheeks and a too-big mouth – and I certainly wasn't thin, but I look strong and confident. And I was popular. I organized dances and group hikes, and the boys all pursued me, which didn't interest me much.

I was soon changing in so many ways. I was both embarrassed by and proud of my new breasts. And I was suddenly angry about everything. I'd come into the apartment without greeting anyone and go right to my room and shut the door. I was nasty to Mama; because she was always there, she was an easy mark. My rudeness hurt her, which I found more satisfying than Leonid's reaction, which was reciprocated anger.

I'd confront Mama: "Why are Papa and Leonid gone for months at a time and we don't know where they are? Is that normal?" and "Why don't they ever tell us what they've done on those trips? Do they tell you? Do you even care?"

She, of course, didn't know any more than I did.

I attended a special school staffed by the best teachers. I was at the top of my class in academics, but it was sports that I lived for. I was a star in track, volleyball, basketball, swimming, far better than any other girl and as good as the best of the boys.

Leonid and Mama didn't care about sports, but Papa, when he was in Moscow, encouraged me. He timed my running and swimming with his stopwatch, and he watched my games whenever he could. We spent more time together in my early teen years than at any other time in my life. Mama didn't like that so much, which pleased me.

My best friend was Vera Gayibova. We shared everything. We gossiped about the girls in our class, speculated about the boys, and we practiced kissing techniques on each other.

One day on the schoolyard she told me that she'd learned about sex: "The man lifts up your nightgown and sticks his thing into you and squirts some stuff inside. You have to do it or you won't have any babies."

We agreed that it was most horrible thing and that we'd never do it even to make babies. We sometimes were friendly with Stalin's son, Vassily, who was short and red-haired. We didn't share everything with Vassily because he was a boy – no sex talk, no kissing – but we did feel sorry for him. Vassily didn't have a happy childhood. His father either bullied him or ignored him, he told us, and his mother often shut herself in her room, where he could hear her weeping.

Vassily's mother shot herself when we were twelve years old. Leonid told me never to mention it to anyone at school, and all the other children must have been told the same, because they said nothing. The newspaper said she'd died from a sudden illness. After his mother's funeral, I took his hand and told him how sorry I was. The other students looked away. Vassily wanted to be my boyfriend, but Leonid had warned me not to get too close to him, so I told him no. Looking back, I realize how good that advice was. After his mother's death, Vera and I didn't see as much of Vassily.

When I was twelve, I found a slim book of poems on my mother's bookshelf. The title was *Evening*, and the author was Anna Akhmatova. I loved the poems, and I shared them with Vera. I can still recite many of them from memory:

> *He gently touched my evening dress*
> *And said: "I am a loyal friend!"*
> *And yet the contact of his hand*
> *Felt nothing like a true caress.*

The poems were mostly about unrequited love. They moved me in ways that only a twelve-year-old can be moved. I thought I understood them, but when I read them now, I realize how little I did understand. In intense, emotional voices, Vera and I read them to each other, over and over. I asked Mama about the book. She smiled and told me that she'd loved it too. She was a young girl in 1912 when an uncle gave it to her for her birthday. I asked her to give me more of Akhmatova's poetry for my birthday, which was coming soon.

A few days later, she apologized. Leonid had told her that Akhmatova was no longer being published because the Party had decided that her poems were bourgeois and academic. But Mama let me keep the book, and Vera and I treasured it. Vera found a picture of Akhmatova – I don't know where – that she carried around in her wallet. Akhmatova was beautiful – high cheekbones, a strong nose, and great oval eyes – everything I lacked. Vera and I wrote imitative love poems to unknown future lovers. Poems about raindrops on the windowpane on a spring evening and the tears at our parting. I'm looking for them now, but they seem to be gone. At some point, I must have destroyed them out of embarrassment.

MEDVEZHYEGORSK, JANUARY 1932

"You'll like it here, Irina. Give it time. I know Medvezhyegorsk isn't Moscow, and I'm sure you miss your school friends, but we're making history here. Try to make new friends."

Irina nodded doubtfully and headed off for her first day of school. Her mother had told her to go to Comrade Arefyeva's seventh-grade classroom on the second floor. On the stair landing, two boys cursed each other and traded punches. She followed the girl ahead of her, stepping past the boys as quickly as possible. Comrade Arefyeva, a muscular, tight-lipped woman, beckoned to her as she entered the room.

"You're Irina?" She pointed toward a front-row desk. "Sit with Masha. We don't have enough books or desks to go around." And then she gave Irina a long, threatening look. "Do what I tell you, hear me? Do what I say and we'll have no problems."

The wall-clock told her that it was five minutes before class was to start. Irina remembered what her mother had said about making new friends. She asked Masha, the girl with dirty fingernails and greasy hair with whom she was forced to share a desk, about her father.

"He works at the Solovki corrective labor camp."

"And your mother?"

"My mother died," Masha said.

"I'm so sorry. How did she die?" As soon as those words passed her lips, Masha's expression made her want to take them back.

"What a nosy bitch you are! My father beat her to death with the fireplace poker. More questions? Why are we here in this trash-pit town? He served his three years in the camp, and now he's a guard there, that's why."

A boy with a patchy scalp in the desk behind theirs, who was sprawled with his legs in the aisle, snickered, "Go Masha!"

Masha didn't turn her head, but she muttered, "Shut up, Vania!" and jabbed his calf with a steel-nib pen.

He yelped. Arefyeva turned and started to walk toward them but stopped when the buzzer rang. She gave Vania the same death stare she'd given Irina earlier.

The school day had begun.

Arefyeva barked out: "Multiplication tables! Sevens table!"

The class began droning the table as if it were a religious chant. "Seven times one is seven, seven times two is fourteen, seven times three is twenty-one, ..."

Arefyeva patrolled the aisles, slapping a triangular architect's ruler against her palm every few seconds, glancing left and right at each student. Physical punishment of students was prohibited, Irina knew, but Arefyeva must not have been informed. When Vania whispered something filthy into Masha's ear, Arefyeva pretended not to notice. But when she was just behind him on her next patrol down his aisle, she gave him a hard crack across his ringwormed scalp with the ruler. He hadn't seen it coming, and she didn't even slow her step as she passed him.

"Foulmouthed pig," she said in a conversational tone.

Just so he would know what he was being punished for, Irina thought.

Irina didn't tell her mother about any of that. What was the point?

After a year in Medvezhyegorsk, Irina was miserable. She left school each day as quickly as possible and waited for her mother at the administrative offices, where she'd lose herself in reading Pushkin or Tolstoy. She had no interest in the canal's construction, and the scrawny, filthy laborers who sometimes appeared in the offices disgusted her. And worst of all, they hadn't received letters from Papa since they'd arrived. Mama had asked the NKVD officer, but he didn't know anything and wasn't much interested.

"Maybe it's because you moved and the letters are going wherever you were." But he still accepted their monthly letter to him, which Mama saw as a good sign.

Yagoda spent most of his time in Moscow, but his visits to the canal site terrified his staff. Irina, who sat in the hallway each afternoon, could sense the panic among the staff the week before he arrived. Her mother explained it to her. He would arrive with a team of accountants and interrogators, and they might summon anyone at any time, day or night, and demand detailed reports on every aspect of the canal's construction. Each visit was followed by demotions and even arrests of under-performers. As Yagoda's personal stenographer, her mother told her, she had to be available at short notice whenever he was there, so she wouldn't be home some nights.

Irina was twelve, the New Year's celebration was approaching, and her mother insisted that she go with her to the staff's New Year party.

"I don't want to go! No one else my age will be there. I'll just sit there with nothing to do!"

"Bring a book if you like, but you're going."

She was partway through *War and Peace* for the third time, so she sat at her mother's table with the book ostentatiously open. But the party wasn't as bad as she had feared. Yagoda was in Moscow, so the staff was relaxed. The dance band was good – waltzes interspersed with traditional songs like "Kalinka" and "Kazachok" and tangos from South America.

Her mother had made Irina a party dress and fixed her hair, but Irina kept her face in the book, determined to hold onto her resentment. She noticed that none of the young men in the room asked her mother to dance; only the oldest grandfathers, aged beyond any romantic suspicion, had the nerve to do so. One of them sat at their table, as perhaps he'd been instructed to do. Then a much younger man with tight, wavy hair, carrying a stack of shellac phonograph records in brown paper sleeves, joined their table to sit between Irina and the grandpa. Her mother smiled when he sat down.

"Good evening, Leopold. Let me introduce you to Irina, my daughter. Irina, this is Leopold Yakovlevich Teplitsky, a well-known pianist and conductor. Leopold, what do you think of the band tonight?"

"The trombone player is good," he said. Despite her intentions to have no fun, Irina looked up from her book. Teplitsky smiled at her.

"What are you reading?" he asked. "*War and Peace*, is it?" He glanced at the text. "Natasha's first ball! Wonderful, isn't it? She thinks no one will find her attractive, and by the end of the evening, every man in the room wants to dance with her."

The bandleader announced a fifteen-minute break, and

Teplitsky carried his disks to the phonograph and played five of them, one after the other without breaks or announcements. The music was beautiful, Irina thought, although unlike anything she'd heard before. She glanced at her mother, who looked nervous and unhappy as the music played.

When the band came back to the stage, Teplitsky returned to his seat and glanced toward Irina's mother. Rather than speak to her, he turned to Irina.

"I'm not sure what you know of American jazz music, Irina. Our Commissar of Culture and Education, Comrade Lunacharsky, sent me to America in 1926 to learn about the proletarian music 'jazz' that was popular there and to bring back whatever I could."

The grandpa had cupped his ear and was trying to follow whatever Teplitsky was saying. When Irina had tried to speak to him earlier, she'd found him completely deaf.

"I spent a year there, mostly in Philadelphia. Why Philadelphia, you might ask, why not New Orleans or New York? Because Comrade Lunacharsky had met a man who had told him that Philadelphia was the center of American jazz. At any rate, I played in many jazz clubs and bars, met many jazz musicians, and I returned with all that I could manage – scores, phonograph records, arrangements, instruments. Comrade Lunacharsky was happy with me.

"I started the Leningrad Jazz Orchestra, although it was difficult to explain the ideas of improvisation and syncopation to our classically trained musicians. They wanted to play scores exactly as written. Eventually, however, I managed to have some success, and our music became popular.

"Then the esteemed Maxim Gorky, a favorite writer of our stalwart leader Comrade Stalin, wrote that jazz was not proletarian music but 'a rattling, howling and screaming like the clamor of a metal pig.' And Comrade Lunacharsky, my former champion and benefactor, saw the error of his ways and agreed with Comrade Gorky, calling jazz 'sonic idiocy in the bourgeois-capitalist world.'

"As the man who had introduced jazz into Leningrad, I was charged and appropriately convicted of espionage and sentenced to two years at hard labor at the Solovetsky labor camp, from which I was released three months ago. I've learned from my errors and corrective experience. I'm now painting the clerical offices of the canal project while I await permission to return to Leningrad.

"So why, you might ask, am I playing jazz records at this dance? Am I insane? Am I anti-Soviet? Of course not. More careful analysis by our Marxist-Leninist music experts has established the fact that there are two types of jazz: authentic proletarian jazz as played by exploited American Negroes, and imitative salon jazz, as played by exploiting white capitalist Americans. The latter, of course, is not jazz at all, but a cruel parody of it. The five records I played tonight were by Duke Ellington's orchestra, and Mr. Ellington is an authentic Negro." To prove the fact, he pulled a publicity photo of Duke Ellington from his jacket pocket.

Irina burst out laughing. She watched Teplitsky as he glanced at her mother's relieved face.

He stood, bowed slightly to Irina, and said, "Irina Borisovna, may I have the honor of this dance?"

The band struck up Tchaikovsky's "Waltz of the Flowers," and, as he wheeled her across the floor, Irina knew exactly how Natasha Rostov must have felt at her first ball.

On Monday after school, Irina walked through the halls of the administrative building until she found Leopold Teplitsky up on a ladder, brush in hand, painting the cornice molding of an office.

Before she could speak, he broke in, "Irina! I'd hoped we could speak before I leave. If you've nothing better to do with your afternoons, would you like to join me in painting? Go right now to the Maintenance Office and ask for a permission slip. I've already told them about you. The office director said that voluntary labor for the state is always welcome."

Over the next two weeks, her conversations with Teplitsky taught her a great deal about the canal, her government, and her mother. If they were painting where someone might hear, they could say nothing. But there were several afternoons when they worked in a new wing that was unoccupied.

It was the last day before Teplitsky's release, and Irina still wasn't sure who he was, who he was to her mother, who she was to him. She started with her suspicions.

"You're a famous conductor. Why are you interested in me?"

Teplitsky spoke in a low voice, and he kept his eye on the door to the wing. "Because of my friendship with your mother."

Every man seemed to want to be her mother's friend. She didn't answer, just dipped her brush and continued painting a closet door.

"We *are* friends, Irina, your mother and I. But not the kind of friends that might worry you," Teplitsky said. "My own romantic inclinations are toward men, not women. Comrade Yagoda knows my predilections, which is why my friendship with your mother has been tolerated. Ask your mother to explain if any of that confuses you."

Irina had heard of men like that, but she'd never met one before. She thought about it for a moment. She didn't know what two men might do romantically, but as long as he wasn't after either her mother or her, it didn't matter.

"How did you become friends?"

"'Friend' is a word that has many meanings. The gospels are out of fashion right now, but I'll paraphrase: 'Greater love hath no man than this, that a man risks arrest for his friends.' Your mother and I have that sort of friendship."

"What did you do for her?"

"Ask her. She can tell you."

"What did she do for you?"

"She got me out of here. I'd met her at a reception when my orchestra played in Moscow two years ago. We chatted, liked each other, and that was it. When jazz suddenly became anti-Soviet and I was arrested, she followed my case in the newspapers. Then when "authentic" jazz was approved a few months ago, she went to Yagoda and suggested he could prove he was up to date on the Party line on music by releasing me. She had the form all ready for him to sign. You can say there's no risk in that, but if jazz is banned again, and Yagoda's enemies blame him for releasing me, he'll remember who gave him that paper. So, your mother's my friend. And you're her daughter, so you're my friend too."

Irina was quiet for several minutes.

"Why does my mother come home talking like a Communist?" she asked.

"We all have a shell we show the outside world. If you don't do that, you won't survive. It's hard for everyone, but much harder for your mother. By day, she works for the NKVD, where she transcribes lies and murderous plans. Along with everyone else, she prattles on there in Soviet-speak: she worships Stalin, she pretends enthusiasm for the canal and other Soviet idiocies. And then each afternoon she comes home to you, and it's difficult for her to switch on and off like an electric light. If she's open with you, she must reconstruct her entire shell the next morning. Think of her life: her husband is an enemy of the people, and the only reason for her employment at the Lubyanka is her extraordinary beauty, which she curses each morning at the mirror. But without that beauty, she'd be in a camp and you'd be in an orphanage. She'll never speak of this to your father, of course, and she's told me that you're aware of her problems and that she appreciates your pretended ignorance."

"What was it like to be a prisoner?"

"Have you looked at the starving, dirty wrecks that sweep the streets here?"

Irina felt sudden shame in the pit of her stomach, shame for the disgust she'd felt whenever she'd passed them.

"Sweeping streets in Medvezhyegorsk a very good job for a prisoner," Teplitsky said, "and before your mother got me freed, I would have given anything to have such a job.

"You can't see much of the construction from Medvezhyegorsk. The worst occurs far from here where the prisoners work. They dredge marshes, fell timber, blast rock faces, dig the canal, build locks, with no consideration for age or health. When I first arrived in March, the guards marched my convoy 30 kilometers from Medvezhyegorsk to Povenets. After stealing all our warm clothes, the guards dumped us in the forest. No barracks – we had to dig our own shelters with the few tools we'd been given.

"You've seen the slogan on the office walls here: 'Build quickly, sturdily, cheaply. Less metal, less concrete, more lumber, not a single kopeck of foreign currency.' What's the cheapest way to build? The Egyptians figured that out four thousand years ago – slaves! And that's why the NKVD was put in charge of the canal. Thousands were imprisoned during the collectivization campaign, so why not use them as slave labor? No need to spend much on food, warm clothing, or shelter. If they die, finding replacements is easy. If you run out, just arrest more.

"The canal is a joke. Prisoner-engineers designed it, most of whom had been convicted of anti-Soviet sabotage – funny, isn't that? I know several engineers who were arrested just because the NKVD needed them for the canal and didn't want to pay their salaries. The engineers are treated a little better than the workers because they're harder to replace. The canal is close to completion, and one engineer told me that they've used 100,000 slave-workers, and that a quarter of those have died. They're dying out there right now.

"Stalin handed Yagoda a schedule and budget, and Yagoda knows Stalin well. If he misses on either time or money, he's a dead man. There's a 70-meter level difference in water levels between the two ends of the canal and the engineers calculated that they'd need 19 locks to match them up. No sane engineer would build a lock without looking at the soil. Yagoda told the engineers he didn't have money for soil surveys, it would take too long anyway, just build the goddamn locks. Who was going to argue with Yagoda? Remember the phrase from the slogan, 'Less metal, less concrete, more lumber'? We're surrounded by forests, and the NKVD's slaves can fell as many trees as you like and mill them into logs. And so, the engineers designed the locks using wood rather than concrete, even though they knew they'll all rot and fail within a few years."

"Won't Stalin punish Yagoda then?"

"Maybe. But in Yagoda's world, a few years is an eternity. Who knows where Stalin or Yagoda will be then? Besides, Yagoda's cheated on the canal in other ways. He'll finish on time and on budget, but the canal will be worthless – you'll see. Before the canal opens, there will be endless publicity. The place is already swarming with photographers and filmmakers, and Yagoda humbly asked Stalin for permission to name it the "Stalin White Sea Canal." Stalin won't be able to blame Yagoda without looking bad himself, and Yagoda will likely get a medal rather than a bullet in the back of his neck. But one thing about Stalin, he never forgets."

Teplitsky stopped himself. "I'm sorry, I got carried away, I shouldn't be telling you all this. Please never speak of this, even to your mother. You asked what it was like being a prisoner. It was hell. If you have any way to slip any of the prisoners food or money, please do so, but be careful. Don't get caught. I don't know what you think of me, but I know how I think of you – as the younger sister I never had. I'll miss you and your mother when I leave. But after I'm gone, forget my name and never speak of me, and I'll try to forget yours until we meet again in better times."

Irina arrived home weeping, and her mother was waiting to embrace her.

"We'll miss him, Irina."

"Mama, he told me that you got him freed."

"True enough, but it wasn't much, and it's dangerous to speak of such things."

"I asked what he did for you, and he told me to ask you."

"He did something wonderful for both of us. He has news of your father."

"Mr. Teplitsky found Papa? Where is he?"

"Well, he doesn't know that. He found where he *was* two years ago, in Istanbul, working as a doorman. Leopold has a friend who works in the same hotel. Look – his friend sent Leopold a picture of Papa from the staff New Year's Party!"

Papa and two other uniformed doormen stood in a stiff pose, glasses raised under a banner "Happy New Year 1931!"

"He looks sad, Mama."

"He does, Irina, and that's because he misses us. But he also looks healthy, and that's the main thing."

"But where is he now? New Year's 1931 was just before we moved here, when we stopped getting his letters."

"Well, Leopold thinks Papa may have escaped! Leopold's friend didn't know Papa well, but he says he didn't show up for work one morning and that a Russian with a limp and a scar on his cheek was flashing money and asking questions about Papa. If he was dead, they wouldn't need to do that. If

Papa's on the run, it would be too dangerous for him to let us know where he was."

Anna sighed. "And now I have a great favor to ask, something you will hate doing."

How bad could anything be on this wonderful day?

"What, Mama?"

"The official opening of the canal will be in August. Stalin will come for an inspection tour in July, only two months from now. Everyone who works here will live in hell until then, and it's likely I won't see you much. So here's what you won't like: Yagoda sent for me this morning. He wants you to represent the children of Medvezhyegorsk when Stalin arrives. You're to give a short speech pledging every child's love and gratitude to him. Don't worry, you don't have to write the speech – Yagoda would never risk that – but you'll smile, curtsy, present him with flowers, look him in the eye, and say whatever you are told to say."

"No Mama! I can't! Why did you agree? How does Yagoda even know who I am?"

"He's never seen you. Believe me, I've been careful to keep things that way. But he does know I have a daughter. He thinks he's doing me a great favor, and I couldn't refuse. I have no choice in this, so you don't either. I'm sorry. This is our life under Stalin."

Stalin was to arrive by train that morning with Voroshilov and Kirov, two of his most abject toadies. Every detail, every second of his visit had been planned. An entire hotel had been constructed just for this day, so it was unlikely he would even visit the offices, but every sink and toilet had been scrubbed until it shone; any use of the toilets until after he left was strictly forbidden. And the rooms Irina had painted with Leopold two months earlier were painted again.

A director had been brought in from Leningrad's Marinsky Theater to coach the children's performance. They rehearsed in the main hall of the hotel – the backup site if the weather was bad – but it looked like the ceremony would take place in the square in front of the hotel. Irina stood in front of a hundred scrubbed children in pressed white gymnasium uniforms and

Pioneer scarves, precisely arranged in military formation.

The director was unhappy with Irina.

"No, no, your smile is false, and you don't smile at Stalin in any case! This is a man you adore, a man to whom you'd sacrifice your life! Don't smile, beam!"

Irina burst into tears, and her mother walked to her side and whispered into her ear, "Here's what you do: defocus your eyes so you won't see him clearly, and then pinch your arm until your eyes fill with tears. He'll like the tears. Then imagine that your father has returned."

"Much better!" the director said after Irina's next attempt.

Yagoda entered, completely unhinged, took one look at Irina and began shouting at her mother.

"Why is she so tall? She's supposed to be a little flower girl, and she's taller than he is. And why does she have breasts and an ass?" He wheeled on the director, "Who picked this girl?"

The director had the good sense not to remind him that it was he who had picked Irina.

"Comrade Yagoda," she said, "I've already solved the problems you've identified. Comrade Stalin will stand on a platform a full 20 cm higher than her level. And the dress and undergarments she will wear for the ceremony will take care of those other problems. She'll wear a strap brassiere that will flatten and spread her breasts, and her dress has a loose waist with a straight cut that will conceal her hips and derrière. We face the same problems every day in the theater."

Yagoda left the room without a word, and Irina heard him ranting at some poor soul down the hall.

"Comrade Stalin, father of us all, the children of Medvezhyegorsk welcome you. You are the sun who lights our morning and warms our day. You protect us from all enemies, both from within and without. Thank you for our happy childhood."

The first draft of Irina's speech had gone on for ten minutes, but the theater director had chopped it down to those few words.

"Enough," she said. "There's a long day ahead, and it will be hot out there."

Irina said her piece, curtsied, beamed at Stalin, and handed him the roses. He bent to kiss her cheek; he smelled of tobacco and bad teeth. I did it, Irina thought, it's over. He turned to Yagoda, Kirov, and Voroshilov, and they walked toward the pier and the steamship that would carry them along the canal. Kirov joked with Stalin, who was lighting his pipe, Voroshilov walked silently next to Kirov, and Yagoda walked a step behind, like a schoolboy who wasn't a member of the gang. He still looks nervous, Irina thought. The four of them walked up the gangplank to board. The porters carried baskets of fruit, cases of champagne, brandy, and vodka aboard. Why so much? Irina thought. There are only four of them.

The theater director smiled at her. "Wonderful job, Irina! I knew you could do it. Comrade Stalin must have been impressed, as he has invited you to join him on the canal trip. Come, you'll have to move quickly."

She grabbed Irina's wrist and began to tug her to the pier. "The boat's about to leave. Here – take the roses. He's left them behind."

What could she do? She looked for her mother but couldn't find her. She boarded.

Within an hour of leaving the dock, Irina realized it wasn't Stalin who'd invited her but Kirov.

"Come, sit with us!" he said and pulled her across his lap to a seat beside him at the drinks table, where she had only a few inches between him and the wall. He offered her champagne (which she refused) and slipped his hand under her bottom, saying, "What a big, fine girl you are!"

She squirmed and pushed his hand away, and ten minutes later the hand was there again.

Stalin chuckled at it, saying things like "Kirov never changes, does he boys?"

Yagoda pretended he didn't see and looked away. Voroshilov was the only man who came to her defense. The third time she twisted away, he said, "Knock it off, Kirov. She doesn't like what you're doing, and she's too young for it."

Kirov started to argue but then sat back with his leg still pressed against Irina's.

Stalin used affectionate nicknames with Kirov and Voroshilov but not with Yagoda; he was still not in the gang.

Stalin kidded them about mistakes and embarrassments from the past. "What was the name of that woman you kept in Tsaritsyn, Klim, the one I once mistook for a trained bear?"

But no one teased Stalin. Kirov was drunk, and as he drank more his praise for Stalin only became more effusive, things like, "Without you, where would we be?"

Yagoda kept silent.

The boat entered the canal at Povenets and stopped at the first lock. Irina wished she could go elsewhere, but Kirov had her trapped. She sensed a mood change. The men were moving from joking to business, and she knew she shouldn't be there. Instinctively, she crossed her arms on the tabletop and rested her head on them. As the water began to flow through the weirs, Stalin opened a papirosa and poured the spilled tobacco into his pipe, tamped, and lit it. All of that took a full minute, during which no one spoke. Irina slowed her breathing.

Stalin leaned back and said, "First, Comrade Yagoda, let me congratulate you on staying on budget and on time. Or at least close. You're two months late and 3 million rubles over, but what's that among friends?"

Irina thought that Voroshilov and Kirov laughed much louder than that little quip deserved. By the end of the day, she would learn that Stalin's henchmen considered any of his jokes a knee-slapper.

Irina continued to pretend sleep; she even allowed a little childish, convincing drool escape from the corner of her mouth onto the table, a bad habit her mother had tried to correct. The boat proceeded to the second lock, and the water level began to drop again.

"Maksim Gorky has agreed to edit a book on the canal," Stalin said. "We're celebrating it as the greatest achievement of our first five-year plan. Even the capitalists are astounded at what Communist planning and dedicated effort can achieve. Much of that is due to you, Yagoda."

Irina opened her eyelids a fraction, just enough to see that Yagoda's face had relaxed a bit, like a dog whose master had stopped beating him and instead scratched his ears.

"Thank you, Comrade Stalin," he said. "Nothing could have been accomplished without your unflagging support and instruction."

Stalin nodded his head in modest assent.

"Yagoda, When I return to Moscow, I'll address the Central Committee concerning the canal. Would you have time to assist me in preparing my speech?"

"Of course, Comrade Stalin. I am completely at your command."

"Let's start with the reasons for the canal, both commercial and military. Kirov, take notes if you don't mind." Kirov pulled a notepad and pen from his tunic pocket.

Irina peeked again. Yagoda looked nervous now, perhaps Stalin's surprising courtesy had something to do with that.

"Please, if you'd be so kind," Stalin said, "summarize both the commercial and military advantages of the I.V. Stalin White Sea – Baltic Sea Canal, to give it its formal name."

Irina wasn't sure what had changed, but Yagoda couldn't speak for a good ten seconds. He finally choked out the textbook answer: "To reduce commercial costs and shipping time between our northern ports and Leningrad, and to provide faster and more secure communication and passage between the Navy's Baltic and Northern fleets."

"Exactly," Stalin said. "Very good. Now to achieve that, our timber barges and warships would need to be able to pass through the canal and the locks. Just for the purpose of my speech, perhaps you could tell me what you know of that. How many of our naval ships, how many of our sea-going timber barges will be able to use the canal?"

Yagoda was completely unable to answer.

"Comrade Stalin, I know – I mean we can fix this problem soon – really, the engineers assure me –"

Stalin let him stammer for a good three minutes while Kirov shook his head and snickered and Voroshilov stared across the water.

"I see. You don't know the answers? These are simple questions," Stalin said in a reasonable voice. "Well, I did some research with the Naval Office before our trip, so I do know the answers. No warship bigger than a destroyer or submarine, and no sea-going timber barge can sail through this canal. Not one." And now his voice was louder. "Not a fucking one, you idiot. Your fucking canal is so shallow and narrow that it's useless. You have wasted two years and millions of rubles and have built a fucking toy canal, and you have had the nerve, the fucking nerve, to stick my name on it. I should have you shot."

So that's what Leopold had meant, Irina realized, when he said that Yagoda had cheated Stalin. He would meet the budget and schedule requirements by compromising on the canal's depth and width.

She heard Yagoda weeping.

"Forgive me, Comrade Stalin, I can fix this problem if you'll let me – "

"You won't be fixing shit, Yagoda. I won't have you shot because of the publicity. In fact, I'll give you an Order of Lenin for your achievements. Turn the boat around, I've seen enough."

Irina feigned sleep until the boat arrived at Medvezhyegorsk. One of the stewards shook her awake. The four men had left the table long ago, and they descended to the pier as the military band struck up the Internationale. Irina waited until they'd gone before she appeared at the rail, and her mother's terrified face relaxed when she saw her. Irina had been planning for the past hour.

She skipped childishly down the gangplank calling, "Mama, it was wonderful!"

And Anna responded immediately by embracing her. "Oh Irina, I'm so proud of you!"

That night Anna made Irina tell her what had happened, every second, every detail, over and over. Irina was confused; she'd thought her mother would be disgusted and angry over Kirov's groping. She was, but her fear was much bigger than her fury. She kept returning to Irina's pretended sleep.

"Are you sure they didn't think you were faking sleep? Did anyone see you when you peeked? Are you sure? Did Yagoda look at you strangely? Are you sure?"

"Mama, why is this so important? Are you angry?"

"I'm sorry, Irina, I'm just upset. Don't worry."

Irina thought for a moment. "Mama, if Yagoda thinks I overheard Stalin humiliate him, will he have us both killed?"

They planned it together. Anna went to work the next morning wearing her best blue dress. She waited until Yagoda was alone in his office and entered with a bouquet of red roses twice the size of the one that Irina had handed Stalin. She called him by the loving nickname she used only when they were alone – the name he'd told her his mother had called him.

"Genyosha, these flowers are from Irina and me. Thank you so much for what you did for her. It was the best day of her life, and of mine, too."

Yagoda leaned back in his chair.

"No problem, Anna," he said. "I'm glad I could do it. So she had a good time?"

"Of course she did, Genyosha. She's embarrassed though about falling asleep. She was so nervous that she hardly slept the night before."

"Did she say anything about Kirov?"

"She didn't seem to like him as much as you or Comrade Voroshilov. I'm embarrassed to say this, but she said she found him a little uncultured. I don't know why. She's just a little girl, and in the company of you and Comrade Stalin, anyone would suffer in comparison. As for Comrade Stalin, like the rest of us, she worships him. What would our cause be without him? And because of you, she had a day with him. A wonderful gift, one we'll both remember forever."

"You're welcome. Unfortunately, that must also be a farewell gift. As you know, Comrade Menzhinsky has been ill, and I have been forced to take on many of his duties, so I will be reorganizing my staff. But I've found a good position for you at Gosplan in the Electrification Office. Unfortunately, they insist that you must start on Monday, and I assured them you will be there. Thank you for your service." He stared at her speculatively. "And remember your oath to keep everything you have learned here secret."

Anna didn't speak for a moment, then wiped a false tear away and choked out, "That goes without saying, Comrade Yagoda. Thank you for the opportunity to serve you and our Party."

She turned and half-ran from the room, feigning heart-break. Neither she nor Irina ever saw Yagoda again.

MOSCOW, 1934

When I was fourteen years old, Sergei Kirov, an Old Bolshevik who had backed Stalin at every turn, was assassinated. Leonid came home as agitated as I'd ever seen him, muttering that there would be hell to pay. He was right, and the hell stretched over the next four years.

In the cinema that weekend, I watched the newsreel of Kirov's funeral. Stalin stood grim-faced by Kirov's casket and vowed to uncover the traitors behind his murder. Leonid told me later that Stalin was certain that Trotsky's followers were behind Kirov's death, and that they planned his own assassination as well. He ordered the NKVD chiefs, first Yagoda and then Yezhov, to root out the traitors in our midst. As things turned out, many of those traitors lived in our building, Government House.

The Great Purges began in August 1936, when Zinoviev and Kamenev, two of Lenin's oldest comrades, were put on trial. They stood in open court and confessed that Trotsky had ordered them to organize Kirov's assassination and to kill Stalin as well. Then they named others as accomplices, who were also arrested. The accomplices accused others during their interrogations, and so on. One confession could lead to a chain of hundreds of arrests. The less prominent simply disappeared, but the more important were put on public trial, and their confessions were even more alarming: they had spied for the Germans or Japanese or British, had poisoned water supplies, had wrecked trains. One after another they stood in the dock, showing no evidence of torture, and confessed to obscene crimes, all linked to Trotsky, who had somehow kept a vast network of saboteurs and spies within the very heart of the Party.

Almost every night, NKVD vans – "black marias" – pulled up in front of Government House, and boots echoed down the hallways. Would they pass by, or would they stop at our door? People prepared differently for arrest. When the knock came, some leaped from their windows or shot themselves at their kitchen tables. Leonid didn't plan to give up that easily; he packed a small bag with toiletries and clean underwear for the Lubyanka interrogation rooms.

Much later, Leonid told me what he'd heard from NKVD officers who made the arrests in our building. It was the same thing every night. The arrestee would first argue that the officer must have the wrong apartment. When the officer produced a warrant specifying the name and apartment number, the arrestee would blanch, would assure his wife that some mistake had been made, that he would clear things up and be back tomorrow. The fortunate ones returned in ten years, the less fortunate never did – a bullet to the head a few hours or days after they confessed. And they all confessed, and they all named others, who were arrested in turn.

Sometimes the NKVD would return the next day and arrest the wife. Older children were left behind to manage for themselves. If no relative stepped forward, small children were sent to an orphanage. If the wife was not arrested, she and the children were put out on the street with almost nothing; all their apartment's furnishings were the property of the state. Nearly every morning, I'd see women and children sitting on suitcases at the bus stop in front of Government House.

It was my job to prepare the family breakfast, so I was always the first awake. I had just set the table when I heard a knock at our door – a timid knock, certainly not an NKVD knock – nothing to be afraid of. I opened, and it was Vera. Her eyes were red and her hair a mess. She'd been weeping.

"My parents were arrested."

What was there to say? I embraced her. "Oh Vera, come in," I said, "I'll pour tea."

Even before I had Vera seated, Leonid was there in his dressing gown.

"Good morning to you, Vera. I'm sorry, but you can't be here. I must ask that you leave."

Vera burst into tears. Leonid took her arm and firmly guided her toward the door.

"What are you doing?" I shouted at him.

Vera had often been in our apartment, and Leonid had always been friendly to her.

He ignored me until he had her out the door, then turned to me and said, "You need to understand. We are all on trial, especially those of us who live in this building. And we are judged by the choices we make in friends. If Vera's parents are guilty of crimes, and you help Vera, that's evidence of your guilt. And if you're guilty, then I'm guilty. And if I'm guilty, you, your mother, and Svetlana will find yourselves sitting on your suitcases at the bus stop."

I shouted that he was monstrous and unfair, that Vera's parents were musicians, not spies, but Leonid was unmovable. Mama and Svetlana had come into the kitchen by then, and Leonid repeated everything he'd said to me and added this:

"Only family in the apartment unless I approve otherwise. And Zoya, I want to know the names of every one of your friends, both girls and boys. Especially boys." Romantic entanglements were apparently even more dangerous than friendships when it came to guilt.

I was sixteen years old. For the first time, I began to doubt. I still loved my country and believed in Communism, but I knew that something was wrong, although I couldn't have said what it was. I got up the nerve to ask Leonid whether all the people that were being arrested in our building were really spies and saboteurs. He thought for a while, and he didn't answer directly.

"You have to understand," he said. "It's not so much about the facts of individual guilt as it is about safeguarding the Revolution. There is a saying, 'When you chop wood, chips fly.' It may be that some of those arrested are only chips, but it is essential that we continue to chop wood. Now you must never speak of what I just told you."

And I didn't. I wasn't sure I understood what he'd said, but I did understand that silence was important.

I accused Leonid of being cruel and unfeeling, but he knew what he was doing. We survived. He left us in September 1936 (for the civil war in Spain, as I learned later, although he did not tell us that at the time.) He left just as Yezhov, a monster, became head of the NKVD and drove arrests to insane levels – more than half the men in Government House (and many of the women) were arrested, and their families were evicted. Leonid knew that he and his family would be safer if he were on foreign soil, so he left for Spain as quickly as he could.

The purges made school difficult. A student wouldn't show up one morning. If a teacher said that the student was out sick, we all relaxed, but if the teachers acted as if the student had never been there, we knew what had happened. A few of the students would whisper things at lunch – "Marina's father was arrested last night" – but Leonid had convinced me that I should keep my mouth shut, so I did.

Irina and Vera were my two great friendships. After Leonid pushed Vera out our door, I never saw her again.

MOSCOW, SEPTEMBER 1936

Irina listened by the janitor's door. Good, he was starting his supper. Her mother was out with Lena, an old friend from her Lubyanka days, so she could have an hour alone on the roof. Both the janitor and her mother had strictly forbidden her to go there (for different reasons – Mama because she worried for her safety, the janitor because he worried that she would damage the roof and cause leaks). She climbed the steep steps, wrestled open the rusted steel door, reached behind the chimney, removed a loose brick, and extracted the oil-cloth envelope that held the picture of her father in Istanbul.

Both she and her mother had spent hours with the photo the day Leopold had given it to them.

"A few more wrinkles," Mama had said. "but that's normal after five years."

Now it had been ten years, Irina thought. What does he look like now? Where is he? A few years ago, Leopold Teplitsky's friend said that someone thought they'd seen him in Bulgaria.

Her mother had wanted to destroy the snapshot. If the NKVD found it in their apartment, it would prove that they'd communicated illegally. But Irina pleaded that it was all she had of Papa, that burning it would be like killing him. She promised that she would bury it under a rock far from the apartment. Mama had never asked what she'd done with it, and Irina doubted that she would think the roof was "far from the apartment." But it comforted her to think that his photo was directly above her.

It was time to go. If Mama came home early, she would give her hell. One last look. She sometimes thought her mother was right. She'd gazed at it so many times she would still see every detail even if it disappeared completely. Why did she keep it? The answer was simple: Because it's Papa's picture.

She went downstairs and started her chemistry homework. The apartment was nothing like the fancy place Mama's first interrogator and Yagoda had supplied before they'd left for Medvezhyegorsk and the canal. She and Mama lived like ordinary Moscow citizens in one large room, with a communal kitchen and bathroom down the hall. That was enough for them: no lurking suitors, no "special times" when Irina had to stay away.

When Kirov was murdered, Irina remembered his hand groping her bottom, and she rejoiced. Her mother wasn't so sure. People at the NKVD were telling her how lucky she was to work somewhere else, that everyone at the Lubyanka was working 16-hour days investigating and documenting, that they were finding nests of Trotskyist spies at the very heart of the government. Then, just last month, Kamenev, Zinoviev, and fourteen other Old Bolsheviks were put on trial and confessed to horrible crimes. Just before the trial, the school library was closed "for renovations." It had reopened only this week; all the back copies of magazines and newspapers had disappeared, and every history book had been mutilated using razors and black ink.

When her mother came home on September 26, Irina saw the panic in her eyes.

"It's bad," she said. "My friend Lena's bought poison to kill herself if necessary. She says Yagoda's been demoted, been put in charge of Post and Telegraph – what a joke – and that Yezhov's been put in charge of the NKVD. I remember Yezhov – a worse bastard than even Yagoda. Lena says Yezhov immediately 'reorganized.' He sent Yagoda's deputies off to take charge in different provinces. He'll split them up and get them out of Moscow, then have them arrested on the trains and dragged back to the Lubyanka. He's building a case against Yagoda. He'll arrest anyone who worked for him. I don't know how much time I have."

Not much, as things turned out. Two NKVD officers came for them at two o'clock that morning, with a loud banging: "Open up, police, get dressed, come on!"

"Confess to nothing, sign nothing," her mother whispered. "Remember, you're just a silly schoolgirl."

One policeman tossed their apartment, throwing all the books and papers into boxes. The other disappeared for a few minutes, then came down the stairs from the roof waving the oilcloth envelope with her father's photo.

"What's this, my lovely?"

"Mama, I'm so sorry," Irina gasped.

Her mother shook her head. "It doesn't matter," she whispered. "They don't punish you for what you've done, so evidence won't matter."

"No talking, downstairs!" They stuffed them into separate wire cages in a black van without windows. Irina felt as if she might choke in the foul, hot air. Four other women had already been loaded into other cages, but they waited two hours more until the van was full. The van lurched forward, and after a few minutes, Mama whispered "Lubyanka." She'd recognized the turns. They were being taken to the NKVD headquarters where she'd worked, into a central courtyard. They could see nothing, but after two hours of listening to shouted curses and weeping, it was their turn.

The van's doors opened, "Get up! Out now! Move it!" The guards pushed them into a single file, "Look straight ahead! That means you, cow! No talking!" Irina couldn't see her mother.

Shortly after dawn, a guard pushed Irina toward a door. When she turned to look back for her mother, she stumbled and bloodied her knee. He yanked her up and pulled her through the door, then down the corridor to a room where a woman in uniform sat smoking behind a table while other policewomen processed women prisoners in various stages of dress.

A policewoman barked at Irina, "Undress! All clothes!" She inspected every orifice with a flashlight. "Hiding money? Jewelry? Drugs? Tell me now, no punishment!" She took her time. "Bend over! Spread buttocks! Wider! Again!" When she inspected Irina's vagina, she turned to the woman behind the table, laughing, "Still a virgin, look! How long will that last?"

They sprayed Irina with some horrible chemical, fished her clothes from a disinfecting box and threw them back at her, less shoelaces and her belt. After she had dressed, a different male guard escorted her through the photography and fingerprint rooms. Finally, hours later, he shoved her into an isolation cell.

They left her there for three days. There were no windows, a single electric bulb burned constantly, tasteless bread and tea were passed through the door in the morning, the same bread and disgusting soup in the evenings. On the fourth morning, a guard took her to an interrogator.

Irina was terrified that he would beat her – she'd heard screams in the middle of the night – but he was businesslike.

"Please sit," he said. "I have a few questions." He pulled a form from a desk drawer and began interviewing her.

"Full name? Date of birth?"

She worried when he asked questions about her father. "Occupation? Present location?"

She told him that he was a hotel doorman, that she didn't know his present location, she hadn't heard from him in over two years, and that she thought he was dead. To her relief, he wrote that down without asking further questions. He continued working though his form for another hour, going through her school history and record in the Pioneers.

In the same bureaucratic tone, he then asked, "When the traitor Yagoda handed you the bouquet of poisoned roses with instructions to kill Comrades Stalin, Kirov, and Voroshilov, what was your response?"

Irina was dumbfounded. The interrogator continued for three more hours, asking for details of the boat trip: who handled the flowers, did the roses have thorns, were there paper roses among the real roes, did they have any strange chemical odors, did any of the three intended victims feel ill.

Then he left for lunch and another interrogator entered, this one much ruder, louder, more threatening. Later, when she talked to other prisoners, she learned the name for it – the "conveyer belt" – a standard NKVD technique.

She was interrogated for 36 hours by different officers. An older woman, plump and grandmotherly, was sympathetic and said she would get everything fixed if she would only tell the truth. A man screamed at her, called her a traitorous whore as he sprayed spittle across her face. She would fall asleep for a few seconds, and the guard at the door would prod her awake with his rifle butt. Every interrogator asked her about the roses.

Finally, Irina screamed back, "I was thirteen years old! How stupid would a traitor have to be to recruit a child for a complicated murder plot? And if the roses were poisoned, why am I still alive?"

The interrogator thought for a minute. "Perhaps the traitor Yagoda gave you an antidote."

"Did he give one to Comrades Stalin and Voroshilov? They're alive too!"

She was moved to a different cell, identical to the first, and left there for what seemed to be days, maybe weeks, as she lost all sense of time. Then she was summoned for another interrogation, again by the same businesslike man with whom she'd begun. He didn't bring up the poisoned roses plot; perhaps they'd given up on that, Irina thought, because it was too ridiculous even for them.

Instead, he said, "Even if you've done nothing yourself, I'm sure you've witnessed crimes, and your failure to report them is itself a crime. People visited your mother, perhaps important people, and you heard what they talked about."

He meant Yagoda, Irina knew. "My mother always sent me out when she had visitors, and I never heard anything."

He kept up that line of questioning for several sessions, but Irina stuck to her story. Between sessions, they left her, sometimes for days, in her cell. She wasn't beaten, but every night she heard others screaming, and she wasn't allowed to sleep or even lie down the night before an interrogation.

Then her interrogator started a session differently. He looked relaxed, the way a workman does when a job's done and he's cleaning his tools.

"Your mother has confessed to everything, so we no longer need your testimony as to her visitors. But you must have heard or seen something at your school or friends' houses. Tell me about those things, and I'll let you see your mother."

She didn't fully understand then, but she did later. Interrogators, like all other Soviet workers, had quotas, in their case quotas for developing new cases. No interrogation was complete until the prisoner implicated others.

He wants a lie, and he'll let me see mother if I give him one, Irina thought. She told him that a teacher at her school, an unpleasant man who stared at her breasts and graded harshly, had made a joke about Comrade Stalin. The interrogator pulled yet another form from his drawer and asked for details: teacher's name, date, location, which class, the joke itself.

Irina stumbled on the last one. "I don't remember the joke."

The interrogator opened another drawer and handed her

a list of numbered anti-Stalin jokes.

"Was it one of these?"

Irina was too exhausted to even glance at the list.

"Number three," she said.

He nodded and filled in the final piece of information, then pushed the buzzer to summon a uniformed woman typist. While they waited, the interrogator offered Irina tea, and she accepted.

The typist returned with the typed accusation against the teacher. The interrogator skimmed it and passed it and his fountain pen to Irina, saying, "Sign at the bottom, initial all other pages."

God forgive me, Irina thought. I'm ruining this teacher's life so I can see my mother. But she signed.

"Send in the mother," the interrogator told the typist, who handed him more stacks of papers and left with Irina's signed accusation.

Anna must have been nearby, because a guard escorted her in only minutes later. Irina gasped. Was this her beautiful mother, so thin and sallow? She'd lost 15 kilos, had black pouches enter her eyes, and her hair was white and patchy.

"Please sit," the interrogator said.

Her mother's pain showed as she lowered herself into chair next to Irina at the steel table.

"Irina, I will explain," he said. "Your mother has confessed to accepting bribes: your fancy apartment and her position as the traitor Yagoda's aide. She has been duly convicted of the crime of wrecking under Soviet law, Article 58-7, and she has been sentenced to ten years labor in internal exile, although she could have received the death penalty for that crime. That lenient sentence was at my recommendation. The judicial troika is often influenced by interrogators' recommendations, and I may or may not make a similar recommendation in your case."

He gave Irina a stern look and continued. "You were the objective beneficiary of those crimes, so you are guilty too, although I consider your age to be a mitigating factor. Furthermore, the fingerprints on the photograph of your father are proof that you are guilty of illegal correspondence with an enemy agent outside the borders of the Soviet Union, which is punishable by death if the troika so decides. I have prepared a confession for you, which your mother has read. If you sign it, I will recommend that you receive only a two-year sentence, and that you and your mother be assigned to the same corrective-labor camp."

Irina looked at her mother; she nodded, and Irina signed.

SOLOVKI CORRECTIVE LABOR CAMP, 1936

The interrogator was an honorable man, as interrogators go. Irina received a two-year sentence, and both she and her mother were sent together to Solovki, the oldest of the camps, the camp that Leopold Teplitsky had survived, the one from which prisoners had worked on the White Sea Canal.

Nothing in the camps, Irina and Anna were to learn, goes as quickly as one might think. They were bounced from one prison to the next, from the Lubyanka to Butyrka Prison to Vladimir Prison, all in Moscow, sometimes sharing a cell, sometimes separated. Some prisons were stricter than others, some had worse food or better food, and some were dirtier or cleaner. But they were all prisons. They were in Vladimir for almost a month before the authorities organized a train to the transit camp at Kem on the mainland, from which they would leave for Solovetsky Island in the White Sea, where the Solovki camp was located. They left Vladimir on February 15 and rode in unheated cattle cars, sixty women in their car. Irina and her mother wrapped themselves in blankets and their overcoats and huddled in a corner. Perhaps the authorities had waited for the weather to improve. Only three in their car died on the four-day trip, and Irina was sure they all would have frozen if they'd travelled mid-January.

Teplitsky had told them about Solovki: "There's a transit prison on the mainland at Kem, but the main camp is on Solovetsky Island, 60 km away in the middle of the White Sea. Even in summer the water's so frigid that escape would be impossible even for the strongest swimmer, although a few have died trying. The Bolsheviks turned an old monastery on Solovetsky Island into a prison after the Civil War. The monks didn't like being thrown out, so they burned the wooden buildings, which were still smoldering when the first of the White prisoners arrived. It was mostly politicals at first – Whites, SRs, Mensheviks – but by the time I got there, more and more criminals."

Irina peered between the boards of their car as the train entered Kem Prison, where it was met by separate squads of male and female guards. Strange, Irina had noticed, how prudish the regime was. In the course of their duties, male guards never saw female prisoners unclothed or searched their bodies. Rape of a woman prisoner was severely punished, or so she had heard – not because anyone worried about the prisoners but because, if allowed, it would destroy all discipline among the guards. Voluntary prostitution by female prisoners was something else, of course, forbidden but tolerated.

The train pulled to a halt, and two uniformed women flung the sliding door aside and threw a cattle ramp against the car. Irina, Anna, and others who could still walk stumbled down. Irina looked back; soldiers tossed the three dead women onto a cart.

A guard slammed her truncheon into Irina's back. "Turn around, eyes straight ahead!"

A woman sergeant marched them into a clearing in the forest. "Welcome to Solovki, ladies. Why not take off your hats and coats? You think you're leaving anytime soon? That's right, everything off!"

She stood them at attention, stripped to the skin. Two women collapsed in the first hour, and the guards tied them to trees. That, Irina later learned, was the winter introduction to Solovki. In the summer, they also stripped the prisoners, then left them standing immobile for the clouds of mosquitos. Any complaints about "the rights of Soviet prisoners" was met with a beating and a single phrase that would be etched into Irina's memory for the rest of her life: "There is no Soviet power here, only Solovki power!"

Long after sundown, the sergeant allowed them to dress and find a bunk for the night. The next morning, they were on the boat to the Island. In a warmer month, in a different century, Irina thought, this trip to Solovetsky would have been beautiful. Twenty years ago, before the Revolution, it had been a holy place.

They'd received good advice from a trustee at Vladimir: "Being in the same camp doesn't mean you're living in the same building. You'll need to bribe someone, and you can do it from here if you like. Do you have money? Friends on the outside who can pay?'

They only had Leopold, and Mama gave her his name and address in Leningrad.

"I'm not allowed to write to him. We're not related."

"Doesn't matter. Either he's your friend or he's not. We have time. I'll send someone to him; if he gives her 50 rubles, you'll be in the same hut in Solovki."

The sergeant marched them through the women's camp, consulting a clipboard to assign prisoners to huts. Leopold hadn't forgotten them; Anna and Irina were in the same hut.

They soon understood the system: the huts were not run by the guards but by the women criminals – prostitutes, thieves, and murderers who stole the prisoners' clothing and boots, who demanded part of their food in 'taxes', and some of whom made direct sexual demands, especially to young girls like Irina. Anna suffered several beatings when she interfered. Meanwhile, the male guards kept trying to get the younger women off alone. That was easier to resist, because the administration punished rape by guards.

One guard, Viktor, kept making moon-faces at Irina. He was a young peasant who'd joined the NKVD for the pay and uniform; now he was stuck on this godforsaken island, bored and lonely. He was stupid, but not cruel. Irina talked with Anna, and she advised her to take up with him. He would protect her from the women and the other guards, she said, and would give her food and warm clothing. Anna had whored with Yagoda to save the two of them, and Irina whored with Viktor for the same reason.

You think there are things you'll never do, Irina thought, but you're wrong. When you're hungry, when your mother is hungry, when you need protection, you'll do what you need to do, and you'll do it without much thought.

Viktor wasn't so bad. He was no sadist, and while his sexual appetite was large, he was easily and quickly satisfied. The most important thing, her mother told Irina, was to avoid pregnancy. Some women prisoners sought it out because pregnant women were given time off before and after the birth, they received better rations, and the guards were forbidden to beat them. But both Irina and Anna knew Irina wouldn't be able to stand being separated from her child, which is what would happen. And sometimes, when workers were needed, the authorities forced women to have abortions, and some died from that. And typhus epidemics hit the camp every few months, killing many children. Mama explained the times when Irina would be most fertile, and Irina told Viktor he couldn't come near her then. To his credit, he complied. Meanwhile, he was bringing food – sugar, butter, bread, scraps from the guards' mess – which Irina shared with her mother and traded with other prisoners for warm clothing. Because she was a guard's woman, the criminals left her alone. And Viktor got her a job in the kitchen and Anna one in the laundry, so they weren't working outside.

MOSCOW, 1939

After Leonid left for Spain, my mother worked for the NKVD in the Gulag department. I'm not exactly sure what she did, some sort of economist. There were arrests every night in Government House, and I saw how afraid she was. She took me into the kitchen, turned on the water tap full blast, and pointed to where she'd hidden warm clothes in the cupboard. She showed me a sweater pocket where she'd put the address of a cousin who lived in the country, and she whispered that I should take Svetlana and live there if she were arrested. But Mama was spared, and we somehow all made it through those terrible years.

Meanwhile, I had normal teenage problems. I was never confident with boys. Mama told me that the thing to do was to smile at them, to laugh at their jokes and flatter them, but I saw where that had gotten her. I was in no hurry for romance, and I wasn't interested in fooling around in cloakrooms.

When I graduated from gymnasium in 1939 at age nineteen, I thought I might be ready to give men a try. I took up with Vassily Minayev, a classmate and a fellow athlete, a fast sprinter, considered a catch by other girls. He was good-looking, and his father, who worked for the NKVD technical services, provided him with western clothes. People noticed us wherever we went, and I was young and vulnerable enough to like that. Vassily had joined the army after leaving school. Because of his family history and his army service, my mother approved of him, and I'm sure she consulted Leonid by mail.

Vassily was pushing me; he proposed marriage, but I hesitated. I sensed something wasn't right with him, and I should have listened to my doubts.

Because he was a newly commissioned officer, he was transferred from one training school to another, and we would go months without seeing one another. He came home on leave, and he took me to a party where he knew everyone, and I knew no one. He introduced me as his wife. Now "wife" meant something different in the Soviet Union than it did abroad: In the early days after the Revolution, Communists would often marry without any ceremony, although that was less common by 1939. Leonid's "marriages" were of that sort, and I didn't want to be that kind of wife. I hadn't even accepted Vassily's marriage proposal, so I didn't like being introduced that way. I was happy if he wanted to call me his girlfriend, but nothing more.

I danced with several men at the party, and Vassily didn't like it. He grabbed my arm and pulled me out the door and took me to my apartment in Government House. No one was there but the two of us; Leonid was in Spain, and Mama and Svetlana were at a friend's dacha. Vassily took his army service pistol from his pocket, slammed it on the table and told me that if I didn't agree to marry him, he'd shoot himself.

It's difficult to explain why I took that as evidence of his great love rather than as proof of his insanity. We were married on September 6, 1940 in my father's Moscow apartment. Leonid missed the ceremony; it was two weeks after he'd managed the liquidation of Trotsky, although none of us knew about that until later.

Vassily drank non-stop at the wedding reception. When I danced with other men, he glowered at me. Pavel Sudoplatov, Leonid's friend (and boss in the NKVD at that time, although I also didn't know that) sat next to me with his arm around my shoulders and reminisced about my childhood. Vassily staggered over to us and insulted him. My stepmother, Lisa, ordered a car to take Vassily and me to our hotel before he got himself into real trouble. Sudoplatov was not someone to have as an enemy.

Vassily got rough in the car. He held my arms and shook me but didn't strike me. It was an NKVD car, and I could see that the driver was watching closely in the mirror. Lisa or Sudoplatov had almost certainly instructed him to intervene if he raised his hand to me.

The car was still moving when Vassily shouted, "You whore, you'd fuck anybody," threw the door open, and tumbled into the street.

The next morning, his disgusted father delivered him to our door. That was my wedding night.

That should have been the end of it, but Vassily moved in with us at Government House. We were of course eventually intimate, but during sex, his unhappiness became even clearer. There were no preliminaries. His eyes would shut tight, and his jerky thrusts brought him to a quick finish.

Mama and Svetlana despised him. He drank at all hours, and when Leonid's old friends visited – men who'd known me as a child – he became angry and jealous when they kissed my cheek. Mama told me to leave him, but I wasn't ready to admit failure. Perseverance had worked well in academics and sports, but it didn't serve as well in love.

Sudoplatov appointed Vassily as one of his aides – probably at Leonid's instigation to get him as far from me as possible – and sent him to Vladivostok in the Far East. Vassily begged me to go with him, promised that he would change, swore that he would stop drinking entirely. There would be no more jealousy.

I was pregnant. I'd decided to have an abortion, but both Vassily and Mama pleaded with me to keep the baby. Mama wanted me to have the baby in Moscow with her help. Vassily wanted me to have the baby in Vladivostok with him. I chose him.

As always happens with men like Vassily, nothing changed. I remember one night in January, thirty degrees of frost. Vassily was stumbling drunk, lurking behind the trash cans outside our barracks to catch my imaginary lovers, attacking soldiers who walked by. The military police arrested him, and his commander told him that he would be court-martialed if it happened again.

Tatiana was born June 2, 1941. I was nursing her by the window of our single room in the ramshackle army barracks outside Vladivostok when I heard drunken boots in the hallway. Vassily slammed the door open and upset the table, knocking a metal chair to the floor. Tatyana cried when I pulled my breast away. He shouted that I was a whore, that he would kill me and the sons of bitches I whored with, and he raised his hand as if to strike me, but I didn't flinch – he'd threatened many times but never carried through. He flopped facedown onto the bed. His muddy boots soiled the blankets, and he was snoring within seconds. Once I'd settled Tatiana, I rolled him onto the floor. I visited the Army travel office the next morning to request tickets to Moscow to take Tatiana home but was told that would require Vassily's approval – approval that he would never grant. I was desperate.

But when the Germans invaded on June 22, 1941, a date etched in every Soviet citizen's memory, all dependents were instructed to leave army bases immediately. In a way, the Germans saved me. As an officer's wife with a newborn, I was granted a seat on a packed train to Moscow.

On the ten-day trip home, I had time to contemplate my mistakes. Why had I chosen a man like Vassily? I'd known what he was like before I married him. And why didn't Papa or Mama or Leonid warn me? Twenty years later a Czech friend, a Western-trained psychologist, told me that young women with unreliable fathers often choose abusive, controlling men. I had to laugh at that: no one was less reliable than an NKVD agent, and I had one for a father and another for a stepfather.

Leonid was back in Moscow by then, but he wasn't living with us. The Germans were only a few kilometers from the city, and he and Sudoplatov were organizing saboteurs who would stay behind if Moscow had to be evacuated. I moved back into Government House with Mama, Svetlana, and Tatiana.

SOLOVKI CORRECTIVE LABOR CAMP, 1939

In early 1939, after two years in the camp, Irina's sentence was completed. Now that meant nothing because sentences were often extended. One woman who'd arrived with a two-year sentence when the prison opened in 1923 was still there. But Irina was released. In some ways, nothing much changed. Irina was not allowed to leave Solovetsky, not that she would have left while her mother was there. She married Viktor, and they were given a small hut because he had been promoted to sergeant. She still didn't want his child, but she couldn't tell him that. She douched with vinegar every night and hoped for the best. It worked for the time left on the island.

In August 1939, the orders came down: Solovetsky was to be closed. No reason was given, but the rumor was that the war with the Finns was going badly, and the island was too close to Finland. The prisoners would all be sent elsewhere, and the staff would be sent back to the mainland to Medvezhyegorsk, where Irina and Anna had lived during the construction of the canal. They were to be separated.

Irina was desperate, but there was nothing she could do. The healthy prisoners, including her mother, were loaded onto a boat and sent to the east. The ones who were sickly were put on a separate barge, which Irina heard was sunk a few miles away. A year later, she received a mailed notice that her mother had died of pneumonia.

MOSCOW, 1941

The first days of the war were terrifying. Desperate for news, we all crowded around the black speakers mounted on poles in the streets. We recognized disasters even when the announcer tried to hide them – news of "fierce fighting around Minsk" and then nothing in the next days, and we knew that Minsk had fallen. Stalin didn't speak to the nation for two weeks after the invasion, which worried everyone. But at least the war brought an end to the purges. No more NKVD boot-steps in the hallways of Government House at night, because resisting the invaders took all our energy, and no one had time to invent imaginary enemies.

I dragged myself through life. I was deadened emotionally after my disastrous marriage, and all I cared about was my baby Tatiana. I left her in a crèche each morning and worked twelve-hour days translating captured German documents. Then a metro ride to the crèche to nurse Tatiana, then volunteer work until midnight; I dug tank traps, spotted planes, fought fires, whatever was needed. The crèche's director announced that all children, including infants, would soon be evacuated to the east. Because my translations for the NKVD were essential work, I knew that I wouldn't be allowed to accompany Tatiana. Moscow might fall to the Germans, my child would be taken from me, and I'd failed at marriage. I wept, but I kept working.

I remember November 6, 1941, the eve of the twenty-fourth anniversary of the Revolution. Despite the dangers – no, *because* of the dangers – Stalin refused to cancel the celebration of the Revolution. The reception was to begin in an hour, and I was among the volunteers who carried chairs from the Gorky Street theaters to the Mayakovsky underground station, the city's deepest, where the deputies would be safe from German bombs and shells. I've always considered Mayakovsky to be our most beautiful station. Others are more ornate, but I love the way that its marble arches and domes repeat and stretch into the distance along the platform. As I straightened a row of chairs, I heard the screech of another arriving train, its seats removed and replaced by buffet tables. The deputies and Comrade Stalin could safely toast the Revolution here, I thought, but our soldiers would have a harder time of it. They would parade through Red Square tomorrow, then make a U-turn on Gorky Street and march straight to the Moscow front. Our army was so poorly equipped that many of the soldiers would not even have rifles. "Seize your weapons from the enemy" was what they were told.

Leonid had been absent for five years, and I'd heard that he had returned a month earlier. I was furious with him. He hadn't even come by to see his family at our – no, *his* – apartment at Government House. I'd heard that he was living at the Metropol Hotel, and that he had brought a tall Spanish woman back with him. That was bad enough, but then I heard that he'd sent the woman's son to Moscow *four years earlier* as a child refugee from the Spanish Civil War. He'd been with that woman for four years and hadn't written to tell my mother.

I heard his voice behind me calling, "Zoya!" I turned, and he opened his arms to embrace me. He'd come to the reception in full dress uniform. I didn't want his touch or kiss; I pushed back against his rows of medals. As we separated, I saw a new medal, the Order of Lenin. Its red enamel and gold leaped out at me.

"What did you do to earn that?" I asked. I was too angry to greet him.

"Awards aren't for specific deeds, Zoya. You know that. Especially in the NKVD."

That might be the official line, but he hadn't been given the Order of Lenin because he'd put in extra hours at the office. I'd had no word of where he'd been the last five years, but I suddenly understood. A four-line notice had appeared in *Pravda* a year earlier: Trotsky had been killed in Mexico by a "disillusioned follower."

"You eliminated Trotsky?" I said.

He didn't say yes, but he didn't deny it. He just smiled and trusted me to keep quiet.

"And this Spanish woman, who is she?" I said.

"Caridad Mercader. She also received the Order of Lenin."

I considered that. The woman must also have been involved in killing Trotsky.

"Is she your new wife?"

"Zoya, I'm not stupid. She's dedicated, she's fearless, and she's crazy. Crazy is not what I need in a woman."

As Stalin approached the rostrum, the apparatchiks, Leonid among them, applauded for what must have been fifteen minutes. It was as if they were in some contest to see who could clap the longest and hardest – their hands must have ached the next morning. Stalin's speech, which he repeated publicly the next day, wasn't the usual propaganda. Nothing about socialism or Marxism. Instead, he recalled heroic generals from Russian history and the Red Army's victories in the Civil War, when fourteen nations invaded us (Stalin did not mention the Red Army's leader at that time, Trotsky).

It was years before Leonid told me much about Caridad Mercader and her son Ramón. He developed a deep friendship with Ramón that went beyond the usual professional relationship. Leonid told me that he had driven a tank across the front, presenting a target to distract enemy gunners while Ramón's patrol snuck back across the lines. I don't know what Leonid did or didn't do with Caridad, but his bond with Ramón was absolute.

We volunteers waited for the speeches to end so that we could put everything away; no one invited us to the buffet, not even for leftovers. I returned home close to midnight. Fireworks exploded over Red Square, but no one was celebrating; the German advance seemed unstoppable. I was exhausted, and all I wanted to do was sleep.

The notice arrived in the morning mail, and the red-ink stamp on the envelope frightened me. I knew what was inside. It was an order to deliver Tatiana at noon on November 15 to the Savyolovsky railroad station for evacuation to the east. That morning, as I packed her diapers and warm clothing, she crawled a few feet across the floor for the first time. It broke my heart. The nurses and caregivers at the train station were kind, but they couldn't give the parents much time to say goodbye. That was just as well; more time would have only meant more pain. Mothers and fathers wept as they gave up their children and babies, and older children bawled as the caregivers herded them onto the train.

December of 1941 brought our first great victory, when we pushed the Germans back from the suburbs of Moscow. In June of 1942, I received notice that Tatiana would be returned to me. At the train station, mothers and fathers wept again but from joy, and children with their arms outstretched streaked across the platform to their parents. I worried that I wouldn't recognize Tatiana, but of course I did, although her mop of blonde hair had turned to dark ringlets, and she was walking! A woman who had cared for her told me what a wonderful, happy child she'd been. I thanked her for all she'd done, but I was jealous of the months she'd spent with my baby. It should have been me.

By the spring of 1943, we knew we would prevail against our enemies (although it would require two more years and millions more lives). But England and America were still only watching from the sidelines. Oh, they sent us supplies, and they bombed German cities, but we were the ones fighting and dying. Many of us suspected that our so-called Allies were only waiting for the Germans to weaken us before they would join with the remnants of the Nazis and invade us (although that was said only in whispers). We demanded a second front – an American-British invasion of France that would force the Germans to pull troops from the East.

Stalin, Roosevelt, and Churchill agreed to meet in Tehran in November 1943. I was appointed to be a lead interpreter and a hostess, and once again I was separated from Tatiana, although it was much easier knowing that my mother was caring for her in our home. My selection astounded me: although I was an excellent English interpreter, I was only twenty-three years old. I'm more cynical now, and I understand my appointment. I would be interpreting for Comrade Stalin and for our foreign secretary, Comrade Molotov, and my family's connections with the NKVD guaranteed my discretion. And my age didn't hurt. Men are lonely at such conferences. I was young, genial, and moderately attractive, and I was told to keep my ears open over drinks in the evenings. Nothing more than that, although I've talked with other interpreters who were ordered to go further. My father's and stepfather's NKVD rank spared me that degradation.

I married again just before the conference, and I proved

that I'd learned nothing about men. Indirectly, Comrade Molotov shared some of the blame, because his foreign office had a problem with my appointment to Tehran. All female interpreters posted overseas had to be married. The NKVD assigned Nikolai Skvortsov, one of its junior officers, to be my pretend husband. I'd had a crush on him when I was a young girl – he'd been my Pioneer leader. It was to be only a paper marriage, to be dissolved once the conference was over, but Skvortsov talked me into making it official.

Today I feel only pity for my first husband, jealous Vassily. He at least cared for me in his twisted way, but Skvortsov married me out of ambition because he saw me as his passport to promotion within the NKVD. He even bragged to his friends that he wouldn't have to support my daughter because her grandfathers would take care of her. Saying that was a mistake. It got back to my father, who confronted him and told me what he was up to. My second marriage was even shorter than my first. Why was I so eager to do what men asked of me? Today, I can barely remember Skvortsov's face.

The Tehran conference was to be held in the Soviet Embassy, and I was posted there a month before the starting date. President Roosevelt was in poor health, and the American Embassy was miles away. It would have been a security risk for him to cross the city in an automobile twice a day, so we invited him and his aides to stay in our Embassy. While I was outfitting the Americans' rooms with cut flowers and fruit bowls, I kept bumping into electricians stringing wires and re-plastering the walls. I knew enough not to ask questions when they told me they were improving the lighting.

The night before the conference was to begin, the American delegation hadn't yet arrived. Comrade Molotov instructed me to call the military airfield, and Admiral Leahy, the senior American military leader, came to the phone. Yes, he said, the President had arrived, but he would be spending the first night at the American embassy. Comrade Molotov sat next to me, trying to understand my English.

I gave him the admiral's message, and he began to shout, "What the hell do you think you are doing? Who the hell are you anyway?"

He called me a "dumb bitch" and things even more

objectionable, and he warned me that it would be my head if
Roosevelt didn't show up the next morning. Admiral Leahy was
still on the phone, and I could only hope he didn't understand
Russian. Admiral Leahy and General Marshall arrived a few
hours later to smooth things over, and the president did stay
with us beginning the next morning. He looked drawn and
unwell.

I was posted at the security gate before the conference's
start. There wasn't much to do there, and I challenged two of
the guards to a foot race; I'd been a champion runner in school.
We picked out a tree to run toward and began sprinting. When
we were almost there, a figure stepped out from behind a tree –
Comrade Beria, the NKVD director. There was a security agent
behind almost every tree, but we'd picked the worst one. We
all went back to work quickly.

I was surprised at how old and small Comrade Stalin was.
He appeared young and vigorous in posters and films, but
he was in fact a short, pockmarked old man. He didn't speak
much during the conference, but I watched him; he listened
to everything. He arrived last at every meeting. Churchill
and Roosevelt had already been seated for one session when
I realized that notepads weren't in place. I was rushing down
the marble steps with my arms full, and I turned the corner
and smashed into someone's shoulder. A collarless white
tunic – Stalin. I froze. I thought the security guards might
shoot me on the spot. But Comrade Voroshilov, the Defense
Minister, smiled and winked at me.

Churchill presented a sword to Stalin as a tribute to the de-
fenders of Stalingrad. Stalin kissed the scabbard and passed
it to an aide, who grasped it by the sword grip and dropped
the scabbard to the floor with a terrible clang. I was glad I
hadn't done that.

I was so busy organizing that I did less interpreting than I
would have liked. I was there for one session, however, when
Stalin proposed executing 50,000 German officers to destroy
their officer class. Roosevelt acted as if Stalin had told a joke.
He smiled and said, "Maybe 49,000 would be enough."

Churchill, however, was outraged and denounced the
cold-blooded execution of soldiers who fought for their
country." He stormed out of the room, but Stalin brought

him back and assured him that he was only joking. I'm sure that Churchill didn't believe him, although he did return to the table. Knowing what I know now, that Stalin ordered the execution of 20,000 Polish officers at Katyn Wood to destroy *their* officer class, I believe that he was dead serious. (My father has been accused of organizing the massacre at Katyn Wood, but I don't believe that. Sudoplatov, who has read the NKVD files on those events, assures me that he wasn't involved.)

After the conference ended, the NKVD asked me to stay on as a liaison to the American troops in Iran. As one of the few Allied women there, I received a lot of attention. One of the American officers told me I was a pinup girl. I didn't know what that meant, but he showed me pictures of American movie stars. He handled censoring mail, and he told me that American soldiers were mailing photographs of me home. They must have been desperate; I looked nothing like their Rita Hayworth. Like many, that American officer wanted more from me. But I'd seen what happened to Russians who were too friendly with foreigners, and I reported every conversation that I had with the Americans and British to the embassy's NKVD officer. Living with Leonid had taught me that much.

After Tehran, I served at the Yalta and Potsdam conferences. Roosevelt looked terrible at the Yalta Conference; he was to die two months later. Truman took over, and I translated for him at the Potsdam Conference, which was after the victory over Germany and just before our entry into the war against Japan. The Americans had their atomic bomb ready. They'd shared its development with the British, but they'd told us nothing.

As Stalin and Truman were walking out at the end of the final session, Truman leaned toward Stalin and spoke so quietly that I had to ask him to repeat himself. He was trying to be casual, and he offhandedly said that the Americans had a "new weapon of unusually destructive force." He looked nervous, like a schoolboy admitting something he should have confessed earlier.

Stalin just smiled and replied, "I hope you will put it to good use." He knew all about it, and so did I. I'd spent the past two months translating the American atomic bomb secrets.

Just after the Yalta Conference, I received a summons to the NKVD's central office at the Lubyanka for an appointment at ten o'clock the next morning. That was enough to make anyone nervous. I reported to the main desk in the lobby and was sent to the office of General Sudoplatov. That was reassuring – he was Leonid's friend, and if I'd been summoned to be arrested, he would not have been the one to interrogate me. But he was a very domineering man, and I did not like him.

I was told to wait in the hall, where I sat for an hour on a small chair. A tall, thin man with a long goatee (a grooming style that had become less popular after Trotsky's downfall) entered Sudoplatov's office. About fifteen minutes later, the secretary ushered me into the inner office, where Sudoplatov and the man with the goatee sat at a table. Sudoplatov greeted me by my first name (he had known me as a child) and then gave my name and patronymic to the man with the goatee, but he didn't introduce him to me.

Sudoplatov told me that I was being considered as a translator for scientific papers, and that this scientist would decide whether I was satisfactory. The scientist began to quiz me about physics and chemistry, which I had studied at an elementary level at gymnasium. I told him that I had done well in both subjects, but that I wasn't by any means a scientist. He was unhappy with that and was at the point of rejecting me.

Sudoplatov broke in. "Comrade Academician (he still did not say his name), I can vouch for this woman. She is highly intelligent and completely conversant with American English. You and your staff can teach her the science. What is most important is that our security services have confidence in her, which I cannot say of other translators you might select. It is your decision, but if you do not accept her, I have no one else to offer you."

After a long pause, the scientist nodded his acceptance and introduced himself to me as Academician Igor Vassilyevich Kurchatov.

I was never told that Kurchatov's assignment was to build an atomic bomb, but that became clear as I translated the documents. I divided my mind into two compartments. In the first compartment, I was a scientific translator who worked as quickly and accurately as possible without considering the subject of my translation. The second compartment was where the atomic bomb sat, and I kept the doors to that compartment closed even to myself. I never had a conversation with anyone, including Kurchatov, where I admitted that I knew what we were doing. After I finished the translations, I did not allow myself to remember or think about what I'd done. When I later read George Orwell's book, *1984*, it seemed that what I'd done was what he called "doublethink" – both knowing and not knowing simultaneously.

Translating the English was easy, but the technical terms! What was an "atomic pile"? I translated that as "a heap of atoms," and Kurchatov lectured me for fifteen minutes, told me to go read my physics books. Little by little, I learned. By the end, he told me I was making sense.

For security reasons, I met only with Kurchatov, not with other scientists on the project. The documents I translated came from what the Americans called their "Manhattan Project." I was translating a complicated memorandum where the author's name had (mistakenly, I'm certain) not been obscured. Klaus Fuchs (a German name, I noted, not an American name) described his plan for a trigger for the plutonium bomb. I knew of plans for a uranium bomb, but I knew nothing about plutonium. I went to my chemistry books; uranium was the last element in the periodic table, and I found no mention of an element named "plutonium," so I simply transliterated the English word and noted it as such. In the margins of Fuchs's memorandum, penciled notations in Russian referred to other documents. The handwriting seemed familiar: two different annotators, both of whose handwriting I seemed to recognize.

And then it came to me. My father and my stepmother, Lisa, had written the marginal notes. They never talked to me about their work on the bomb. No conscientious intelligence officer disclosed state secrets even to his family. But years later, after their deaths, I read that the two of them had been posted to America, where they managed Klaus Fuchs, the Rosenbergs, and our other agents who obtained the American secrets.

Comrade Beria was the overall director of our atomic bomb project, although I didn't know that at the time either. Our scientists have been accused of simply copying the American bombs. There is some truth in that; Beria and Stalin refused to allow any changes from the American plans because they wanted a Soviet bomb as quickly as possible. First, we would copy the Americans, then we would make improvements. But *our* project was run by *our* scientists, while the American bomb was mostly the work of German and Hungarian refugees from the Nazis. On August 29, 1949, we detonated our bomb, called "First Lightning," almost exactly four years after the Americans destroyed Hiroshima and Nagasaki. Only then did I allow myself to consider what I'd contributed. Our country had been threatened that entire time, because American warmongers continually called for the United States to destroy the Soviet Union before it developed its own bomb. (I've since learned that their President Eisenhower never considered such an attack. He said, "Defeating the Soviet Union is one thing. Then what do you do? Occupy it?" A wise man, Eisenhower.) We never intended to use the bomb, but it has kept us safe. I was proud of the small part I played, although I couldn't speak of it at the time.

But today, this last day of the Soviet Union, as I page through typescripts of Leonid's horrible monologues, I wonder whether any of it was worthwhile. My late friend Andrei Sakharov, who spent eighteen years designing our hydrogen bombs, was a dissident. He demanded human rights for our citizens, and he paid for it. They couldn't throw him out of the country as they did with Solzhenitsyn because he knew too much, so they sent him into internal exile for twenty years. But even he had no regrets about his military work. He believed that our nuclear weapons saved the world, that without the balance of terror between America and the Soviet Union, America would have used nuclear weapons in Korea and in its other wars. If so, what I did is worth something. But perhaps that's just rationalization. Did I just march along with everyone else doing whatever I was told?

MEDVEZHYEGORSK, DECEMBER 3, 1941

Irina awoke. "Shit, not again," she muttered to herself.

There was drunken shouting downstairs as the bar closed, and then the familiar sound of hobnailed boots banging against each wooden stair-tread as Katya led tonight's drunken customer to their room. A slurred, "I'll fuck you like you've never been fucked before," from just outside the door.

"I can't wait, honey" Katya whispered, "but quiet, don't wake my friend."

Katya fumbled with the lock. She must be drunker than usual, Irina thought, and he must have paid before they'd left the bar, because she pulled him directly toward her bed without further negotiation. Irina lifted a corner of her blanket. She'd been right – she'd recognized the drunk's voice – it was Milonov, a pompous ass and Medvezhyegorsk's deputy mayor, one of Katya's regulars. He'd dropped his pants around his boot-tops to expose a small, purplish dick half-hidden by his pendulous belly. Katya flopped sideways across her bed, legs spread, her red ballet shoes pointing left and right.

"Come on, lover," she cooed at him.

Still standing in his dirty boots, he pushed into her, and the bed creaked six times before Katya's faked moans finished him off.

He was still gasping when she said, "Time to go, honey."

"What! You ungrateful bitch, I buy you drinks all night, give you a can of smoked pork and three rubles, and you think you can throw me out? Maybe your friend will be more generous."

"Don't do that," Katya warned him.

His trousers still dropped, he shuffled across the room and collapsed across Irina's back. Irina was ready for him. When he tried to kiss her, she swiveled and slammed him across the bridge of his nose with an iron bar that she kept under her pillow. He screamed and held his face, blood spurting from the wound.

"Cunt! I'll kill you!"

He reached back to punch Irina but froze when he felt Katya's knife at his throat.

"Out, pig!" she hissed.

He tried to pull his pants up as he stood, but Katya wouldn't allow it. She pressed the knife closer and marched him through the door to the top of the stairs, then kicked his bare ass from behind. Between the vodka and his trousers-cinched ankles, he couldn't keep his balance. He crashed down the steps and lay moaning on the dirty ice for a full minute. Katya watched from the top of the stairs until he picked himself up.

"I'll make you pay for this!" he shouted up at her.

"No you won't, asshole," she yelled down at him. "If your wife found out what you've been up to, she'd cut your balls off, and besides, who will you report me to, the Finns?"

Katya locked the door, lit the Primus stove, and put out two cups for tea. "Sorry about that, Irina," she said.

"Don't worry about it," Irina said. "You're right, the Finns will take the town any day now. And when they do, I hope they'll hang him and every Red thug they find. We could give them a list of names if they need them. Most of them seem to be your customers." Katya laughed.

It was funny, Irina thought. A few years ago, she wouldn't have imagined being Katya's friend. Katya's a whore, a drunk, and Irina once watched her kill a man. But Irina had whored too – whored with Victor. And while she wasn't whoring at present, she was living off the money Katya made. So what if Katya's a drunk? She drinks because she couldn't bear letting those bastards touch her when she's sober. She's honest, and she's generous, and as far as killing somebody, Irina helped her drag the body into the forest. He deserved it – a rapist, and Katya stabbed him when she caught him raping their friend Albina, another whore. Why do men think whores deserve rape? And Katya understands her life because she'd done two years in Sokolniki too. They were more like sisters than friends. They'd shared the worst of Communism.

The rest of the town was in near panic when the Germans invaded on June 22, but they'd locked the door and had a private party, and they'd done the same again when the Finns invaded three days later. The Germans rolled through the Volga country, the Finns advanced through Karelia, and every Russian defeat brought a secret joy to both of them. Irina had prayed for the Finns to take Medvezhyegorsk – even the Germans if it came to that – but she had the sense to keep her mouth shut in public. When Katya was drunk, she spoke too freely, as she had tonight, yelling that taunt about the Finns down the steps. It was true that the Finns would soon take the town, but what if the Russians won the war and came back to Medvezhyegorsk to punish traitors? Irina had tried to warn her. When she was sober, Katya nodded and said she'd keep quiet, but she was seldom sober.

MOSCOW, 1944

Throughout the war, I visited wounded soldiers in the military hospital in Moscow. I would bring Tatiana with me. Just seeing her comforted the soldiers. I read newspapers, poems, and novels to them, or I just sat and visited. I read letters from mothers and sweethearts to men who'd been blinded, and I wrote letters for those who had lost arms or hands. It wasn't much, but it was something. Many women, young and old, were doing the same. Almost any female contact seemed to lift the soldiers' spirits.

I entered a hospital ward one Sunday evening and found a group of soldiers gathered around an imposing middle-aged woman. Her dress was almost a rag, but she wore a beautiful Turkish silk shawl, and she sat with her shoulders back and her head held high. Her face was gray, perhaps from illness. She was no longer slim, but I recognized her at once – the poet that Vera and I had loved, Anna Akhmatova. I'm paging through her collected poems now, remembering her voice, lilting and deep, as she read to the soldiers.

As quietly as possible, I moved to stand at the rear of her audience. She wasn't reading the girlish love poems that I remembered; she read what the soldiers needed, poems of our national struggle, poems of family, poems of hope. And then she read a poem that I doubt any of the soldiers understood – a poem about our government's suppression of her work.

Like a river I was turned off course
By the cruel and brutal epoch.
My life was counterfeited and it flowed
Into another channel past the other channel.
I never got to know my native shores.
Oh, just how many spectacles I missed,
The curtains rose without me
And, without me, fell. How many friends
Of mine, throughout my life, I never met
And just how many city skylines
Could have evoked my tears,
But I know just one city in the world,
And I can find it, blindfolded, in a dream.

How many poems I did not compose.
Their secret choir now encircles me
And one fine day, perhaps, it may just
Strangle me...
I know all the beginnings, all the ends,
And life after the end, and something else,
Which at the present time, I will not mention.
There is some other woman who has taken
The only place that I once used to claim,
And now she bears my lawful name,
Leaving an alias for me, with which,
I've done the best I could have hoped to do.
The grave I'll lay in will not be my own.
But there are times when wild gusts of spring
Or word arrangements in some casual book
Or someone's smile suddenly will draw
Me back into the life that did not happen.
In such a year this could have happened,
And in such – this: to travel, ponder, see,
And to recall, and enter a new love,
Like entering a mirror, with blunt awareness
Of treason and the wrinkle that did not exist
A day ago...
But if, from that life that I've lost,
I could have looked and seen my present life,
At last I'd know what envy truly is....

"The cruel and brutal epoch" was from Pushkin, I thought. What did she mean by that – our entire Soviet history? I was weeping as she finished, and she noticed me. I was at first too shy to speak to her and turned away, but when I looked again, she nodded at me. I introduced myself and asked if she would join me for a cup of tea.

The hospital cafeteria was cold and dirty, and it was crowded with visiting families. We carried our teacups to a quiet corner, and I pushed dirty dishes to one side of a table. I knew that she must have heard what I had to say many times, but I said it anyway: how much her poetry had meant to me as a young girl, and how disappointed I'd been when I was unable to find her poems in bookstores or libraries. And then I told her that my stepfather had told me that the Party had blocked publication because her work was considered bourgeois and academic, but that I certainly did not find it so.

She leaned toward me and asked, "What is your stepfather's work that he knows so much about why my poetry is banned?"

Since my childhood, I had been instructed never to discuss Leonid's work. But I didn't lie. "He is an NKVD officer."

She nodded and smiled from one side of her mouth. "I thought as much," she said. "Thank you for your honesty. And you, will you report the poem you just heard me read? Your stepfather and the NKVD would certainly not approve."

I answered without hesitation. "No, I won't."

She smiled again. "Well then," she said, "perhaps we will meet again. I'm waiting for permission to return to Leningrad. I'll read here every evening until then, and you are welcome to join me."

I listened to her read her poems for two months. Despite my family background (or perhaps because of my honesty in admitting it), she trusted me. In a flat, matter-of-fact manner, she told me a little of her terrible life. Her first husband, the poet Nikolai Gumilev, had been executed by the Bolsheviks in 1921.

"They killed him for nothing," she said. "A few days later I wrote this:

> *Terror fingers all things in the dark,*
> *Leads moonlight to the axe.*
> *There's an ominous knock behind the wall:*
> *A ghost, a thief or a rat."*

When I stupidly observed how different her current poetry was than the poems I'd read as a girl, she chuckled.

"Well, the situation has changed in the past thirty years," she said, "both for me and for Russia. There are more important things to write now than love poems. Besides, I no longer write much. Writing is much too dangerous. When the police knock at my door, I don't want a pile of manuscripts lying about. I compose poems, I memorize them, and then I burn them. My fellow poets and I read to each other in our homes, and we memorize each other's poetry. That way when a poet dies, the work does not die too."

I asked her whether she wasn't afraid of being arrested.

"Oh, I'm afraid," she said, "of course I am. But a poet's job is to tell the truth – verses that lie are evil, not poetry at all. Besides, others have suffered worse than I have. Mayakovsky shot himself when he realized that he wouldn't be able to write freely, and Mandelstam, my closest friend, died in the camps six years ago. But even after twenty years without a published poem, the NKVD knows that they would pay a price if they were to arrest me; many still remember me. So rather than arrest me, they arrest my son. He's in a camp in the north with a ten-year sentence. He's a hostage there, and his survival depends on my behavior. And so, I'm careful. But yes, I could be arrested, even executed as so many have been. I wrote a short poem about that:

> *For all the foolishness I've said*
> *The punishment is heavy,*
> *I could receive a pea of lead*
> *From the secretary."*

I laughed spontaneously, then looked around to make sure no one had heard. Stalin was the General Secretary of the Party, and jokes about Stalin could have terrible consequences. But during our visits to wounded soldiers, I never sensed that she was being watched. Perhaps visiting soldiers was an approved activity, so her watchers took their lunch break when she entered the hospital.

Akhmatova longed to return to her city, Leningrad. The Party gloried in our victory in Stalingrad, she told me, but it didn't speak of our humiliation in Leningrad. For 900 days, the city had been encircled and starved by the Germans. She despised Zhdanov, who had run Leningrad at the start of the war. Everyone in Leningrad knew what he'd done, she told me. He hadn't wanted to admit how ill-prepared the city was, so he had told Stalin and the Politburo that the warehouses were filled with food and supplies. In fact, the warehouses were empty, but because of Zhdanov's assurances, supply trains were sent elsewhere. More than a million Leningraders died of starvation during the siege. Pedestrians would drop dead on the sidewalk, and people would walk by their snow-covered bodies without looking.

She hadn't wanted to leave Leningrad, but the Party had evacuated prominent artists including her friend Shostakovich, who wrote his Leningrad Symphony in the east. I know that disturbing symphony well; its first movement has a jarring rhythm as the German tanks approach the city, and its final movement, which celebrates our victory (only anticipated when Shostakovich wrote the movement), is still unsettling.

Akhmatova said that she left Leningrad before the symphony's premiere, but that she had spoken to many who had attended. (Leonid once told me that he was the one who had flown the score into the city in a fighter plane.) The scarecrows of the Leningrad Radio Orchestra, their black evening clothes hanging limp on their wasted bodies and their shirt collars gaping around their chicken necks, performed. Many of the orchestra's members had already died, so musicians from the Red Army band filled in. The music would have been difficult even for a healthy orchestra. The brass and woodwinds sections had the hardest time – they no longer had the necessary wind – and the orchestra's conductor struggled to keep his arms up. But they somehow made it through to the end, and the audience stood and applauded for an hour. Those who had been turned away from the packed concert hall crowded the streets to listen on radio speakers, and our troops defending Leningrad listened by radio in their trenches. And some-one – Akhmatova wasn't sure who – dispatched night patrols into the no-man's-land between German and Soviet lines to point speakers toward the German trenches. Leonid told me that he'd interrogated German POWs and that they'd found the music terrifying.

She recited selections for me from a long poem in prog-ress, later titled *Requiem*; she feared that it would never be published. I have the poem's Prologue before me now:

Only the dead smiled back in those days,
Being at peace and safe from abuse,
Leningrad hung by the prison gates, dazed,

As an appendage without any use.

The convicts passed by in endless platoons,
Maddened by torment, disheartened,
The train whistles bellowed a saddening tune,
The song of definitive parting.

Stars of death cast their gazes between us,
Guiltless Russia ached to her roots,
Beneath the tires of black marias,
And the weight of blood-splattered boots.

I remembered the boots each night down the halls in front of our Government House apartment and the black marias – the police vans that had hauled away those who were arrested.

Before she left for Leningrad that May, I asked if I might write to her.

"Better not," she said. "It is at present impossible to say anything of meaning in a letter. But if you come to Leningrad, I would welcome your visit."

I'm ashamed to say that I never visited. I knew her apartment would be watched, and, unlike her, I was a coward.

In 1946, two years after Akhmatova had left Moscow, I opened *Pravda* to find an essay by the same Zhdanov who had left Leningrad so unprepared before the war. I thought that he was an odd choice as a literary critic. I doubted that he'd read a poem since his childhood nursery rhymes. He condemned Akhmatova as "half harlot, half nun" and accused her of poisoning the minds of Soviet youth. She was expelled from the Writers Union, which left her penniless. In 1949, her son was arrested again and given another ten-year sentence. In 1956, after Stalin's death, she was at last allowed to publish some lyrical poetry, but certainly not *Requiem*. We had to wait thirty years for that, and Akhmatova never saw it in print in Russia – she died in 1966.

My two months with Akhmatova changed me. When I was sixteen years old, I'd already known that all my arrested neighbors couldn't be spies and wreckers. But Leonid and my father had told me to trust the Party. The Revolution was threatened, they said, both from within and without, and our vigilance must be merciless. The guilt of an individual didn't matter. "When you chop wood, chips fly" – how many times had I heard that? I'd grown up with the Revolution and had received its benefits. I'd worn my Pioneer red scarf to its camps, I'd sung its songs, gone to its best schools, lived in luxury in its Government House, and traveled the world at its expense. I asked myself the question that had first come to me when Leonid had snatched *Red Cavalry* from my hands at age fifteen: if the Revolution had no place for Akhmatova or Babel, what was it worth?

MEDVEZHYEGORSK, JUNE 9, 1944

"Get out, Irina, or they'll kill you too!" Katya shouted. It was two o'clock in the afternoon, and Katya hadn't yet risen from bed.

Katya was almost always drunk now. Last night they'd heard steady low thunder to the south, but when she'd looked from the window, the skies were clear. A wounded Finn who'd come from the front explained it to her the next morning.

"Thunder? That's Russian guns and mortars crammed so close together and firing so fast that you can't hear individual rounds, only a dull roar. Our spotters say there are 3,000 of them, spaced every five meters. They're 150 kilometers from here, but you can still hear them when the wind's right."

Irina hadn't told Katya any of that.

Everyone knew that the Red Army would take Medvezhyegorsk within a few weeks. Russians who had studiously avoided any eye-contact with Katya while the Finns had run the city stared at her now, and some made throat-cutting or hangman's noose gestures. Irina hadn't whored with Finnish soldiers, but she'd shared a room with Katya, which might be enough for them to kill her too. Katya was right, it was time to go.

She packed her few things in a suitcase. "Katya, you should leave too. Go north into Finland."

"The Finns are keeping the roads clear for their retreat. They've posted signs, and they're shooting civilians they find on the roads."

"Go to the forests, then."

"Maybe they won't kill me," Katya said. "Maybe like in Italy, they'll only shave my head and beat me."

"This isn't Italy, Katya. Russians aren't that gentle."

On June 20, the Finns made a hurried withdrawal to their next defensive line, and the Red Army took Medvezhyegorsk. Irina had moved in with another building-cleaner she knew only slightly, Natalia, who lived a mile from town on what had been (and would soon be again) a collective farm. The rent to share her room was exorbitant, but Irina was happy to pay it. Natalia was less likely to denounce her, she thought, if she lost the rent money.

Natalia was ecstatic at the Red Army's return and was dressing for the celebration in the town center. Irina, afraid to show her face, pretended to share her enthusiasm. She stood on a ladder by the house's front door hanging the hammer-and-sickle red flag that she'd sewed from an old red dress and a few rags. Andrei, Natalia's two-year old son, hid behind the flag.

"Where did Andrei go?" Irina asked over and over, and Andrei pulled the flag back and laughed and laughed.

"You're sure you don't mind watching him, Irina? I could take Andrei with us."

"No, you go. Andrei has a runny nose, and I seem to be coming down with a cold too. We'll be fine here, and you need a break. You'll have more fun on your own."

Natalia returned after midnight, bubbling with patriotic joy and cheap vodka, and flopped into the armchair in front of the stove.

"You should have seen it, Irina, the town square is full of our soldiers. All the girls were kissing them, even married women and grandmothers. Our mayor and the other officials arrived about six o'clock on the first civilian train. The mayor gave a speech celebrating the partisans and all those who resisted the occupiers, and he promised there would be trials for the collaborators and black-market gougers. Everyone cheered at that!"

Natalia was none too bright, Irina thought. That should have made her nervous, because like almost everyone with access to meat and vegetables, she might be called a "black market gouger."

"Was the deputy mayor there?" she asked.

"Yes, he gave a speech too. But I didn't listen to much of that. I'd met a handsome corporal by then, and I never liked that fat jerk anyway. Who wants to listen to speeches when there are heroes to be had?" Natalia giggled.

"I'm glad that they'll punish the collaborators. We had too much of that. Did the mayor say when the trials would start?"

"Tomorrow, I think. He had four prosecutors lined up behind him."

"I'm glad you had a good time tonight, Natalia, you deserved it. And thank you so much for taking me in. I don't know what I would've done without you. I'm a little tired now, and I think I'll go to bed." Irina saw that her flattery was wasted; halfway through that sentence, Natalia had begun to snore.

Irina ran to the yard, hitched Natalia's pony to the farm cart and whipped the animal, driving as quickly as possible into town. She skirted the town square, where off-key drunken voices still accompanied a drunken regimental band's *Slavianka*, and headed for the house where she and Katya had lived. As quietly as possible, she climbed the stairs – the stairs that Katya had kicked the bare-assed deputy mayor down. The door was smashed in. Either Katya had fled on her own, or she'd been arrested. Irina headed for the town square on foot. Perhaps Kaya was hiding in an alley or hedgerow. She dodged groping soldiers, calling Katya's name softly whenever she felt it was safe.

The good citizens of Medvezhyegorsk hadn't waited for the trials. Three bodies, with "Informer" signs around their necks, hung from the second-floor balcony windows of the hotel. And one woman's body, whose shaved head was all the label she needed – a whore for the Fascist invaders. Her black tongue protruded from a face beaten beyond recognition. At first, Irina hoped it might be some other poor woman, but the red ballet shoe on her left foot shouted "Katya!"

3

MOSCOW, 1948

After the war, I worked as a translator for the NKVD. My supervisor called me into his office and told me that I would be sent to another site for some weeks.

When I asked where, for how long, what the job was, he snapped at me, "I don't know a damned thing. We're backed up with work here, and they pull you away from me with no notice. Don't ask questions, just show up tomorrow with your suitcase."

My mother told me not to worry, she would care for Tatiana. My co-workers were impressed (and given the times, I'm sure frightened) when a military car arrived to take me to an airbase outside Moscow, where an NKVD major met me; I was surprised that I deserved an escort of such high rank. He explained that he would take me to a secret research installation, where I would handle sensitive translations. He and I were the only passengers on a plane with its windows painted black, and when we landed, there were no signs identifying the military base. A woman NKVD lieutenant escorted me from the plane to an austere dormitory room; she told me that my supper and next morning's breakfast would be brought to me and that I was not to leave the room. It was a little like being in prison, I thought.

She met me again the next morning and walked me from my dormitory to a much larger building. We passed the obligatory busts of Lenin and Stalin in the lobby and climbed the stairs to a suite of offices. A second woman in NKVD uniform checked my papers and asked me to wait, and she offered me tea, a surprising courtesy. Her desk buzzer sounded a few minutes later, and she opened a door and held it for me. Academician Kurchatov, who had directed my translations of the American atomic bomb secrets, stood to greet me and invited me to sit.

We hadn't yet demonstrated our first Soviet atomic bomb at that time, and I knew no more about the progress of our efforts than any other Soviet citizens. I had never even been told officially that my earlier translations had anything to do with the bomb.

But Kurchatov tacitly acknowledged it in our conversation.

"Welcome Comrade Zarubina," he said. "Welcome to the Installation. That's what we call this place. I'm sorry for all the security, but it's necessary. It's important that our enemies don't know the location of our work. I can tell you that your earlier translations have been helpful to our efforts, and that we have more work for you. The Installation is short on office space, so I'll ask you to work from a table in the corner of the scientific library. I thought that might be best in any case, because the technical dictionaries you will need will be accessible there."

I thanked him for his confidence in me.

I began work the next morning. I picked up an English-language journal, *Bulletin of the Atomic Scientists*, that was shelved next to my table. It wasn't a technical journal, so I had no trouble understanding everything I read. I was shocked. The journal's editors and contributors were American scientists who had been involved in the development of the American atomic bomb, and they warned of the dangers of nuclear war. Why would America allow its scientists to identify themselves? And why allow them to speak this way?

I ate my meals with the NKVD guards, not the scientists. But I worked all day in the scientific library, where the scientists came and went. They weren't security-conscious at all, and they introduced themselves to me, so I knew all their names. I never began conversations about the project, but I couldn't help overhearing what they said to each other. I soon knew much more than I was supposed to.

The author's name had been blacked out on the first document I was given to translate, but I recognized him – Klaus Fuchs, the same scientist whose documents on the implosion mechanism for the plutonium bomb I had translated earlier. Fuchs was not a native English speaker, and his awkward Germanic constructions made him easy to spot.

In my earlier work for Kurchatov, I'd learned a fair amount of physics and chemistry. I soon realized that Fuchs's new document was not about an atomic bomb. It referred to a bomb called the "Super" that would be a hundred times more powerful than the atomic bomb. Its explosive force would not come from splitting atoms of the heaviest elements, uranium and plutonium, but rather from fusing different isotopes of hydrogen, the lightest element. The Super would contain an atomic bomb, but it would be used only as a trigger to heat and compress the hydrogen atoms and force them to fuse. I later overheard our scientists talking about the same bomb in the library.

Kurchatov must have been happy with my work, because he kept me at the Installation for several months despite my requests to return to Moscow to care for my seven-year-old daughter. A new scientist, a tall, shambling man with a shock of dark hair across his high forehead, passed me in the hallway one morning that June. Academician Tamm brought him to the library later that afternoon and introduced him to me as his most promising student – Andrei Sakharov.

Although Sakharov wore a wedding ring, I found him intensely attractive. And I believe he must have felt the same attraction, because he often visited the library to talk without even picking up any of the journals. If no one else was present, we conversed about life, poetry, and our families. But it never went further than that. He was a moral man who respected his wedding vows, and I did not want to be anyone's "other woman," certainly not after my two disastrous marriages.

Sakharov and I were talking in the library one morning when Academicians Landau and Leontovich entered. My table wasn't visible from the entrance; we broke off our conversation when we heard the door open, and they didn't notice us. They were engaged in a heated conversation., of which we heard every word.

Landau said, "Our government is a fascist regime, and it can't develop into anything decent. If it's unable to collapse in a peaceful way, then a third World War with all its horrors is inevitable."

Leontovich spoke over him. "Lev, there's still hope. When Stalin dies, we can return to the path of true socialism."

I couldn't let them continue. I coughed, and they broke off and left quickly. I was in a panic. If I didn't report their conversation, I would be guilty too.

But Sakharov reassured me. "Forget what you just heard," he said. "The rules are different here. Beria runs this project, and Tamm told me that he doesn't care about political reliability. He wants nuclear weapons, and Landau and Leontovich are delivering them. Tamm told me that in 1937 Landau was arrested for printing a leaflet that called Stalin's leadership of the Party a Fascist coup. That would be enough to get anyone else executed as a Trotskyist, but Beria pulled Landau out of prison when he saw the war coming. Here at the Installation you can say what you want if you're good enough. But you'd better be very good."

I didn't sleep well that night. What Landau had said was treason, and I couldn't agree with that. I still believed things could be fixed, as Leontovich had argued. But then I considered my neighbors' arrests and my time with Akhmatova. The Revolution had gone so far off track. Was Landau right? The next month, I left the Installation and returned to my privileged life in Moscow.

MOSCOW, 1981

I hosted my family's New Year's celebration at Leonid's apartment. It had to be there if Leonid was to attend. His balance was bad, and he'd fallen several times. I was setting the tables, and no one else had yet arrived. Leonid hunched in his armchair and stared at his shoes. He seemed pensive, not a common mood for him.

In a faint voice he said, "Zoya, can you come tomorrow? One last story."

I'd thought we were finished with his memories; our last session had been three months earlier. But I agreed. When I arrived the next morning, he looked like a man dressed for his own funeral. He'd spit-polished the shoes from his old NKVD dress uniform, and his pressed blue suit hung loosely on his withered frame. He struggled from his chair to greet me, and his account that day was unlike his earlier stories. It was less rehearsed, and I'm not sure that he was always aware that I was even in the room. He cursed often, something he rarely did in my presence unless he was angry. He drifted from presentation with ordered dates and facts to incoherence and then back again, and he told me things he'd done, brutal things and things with women, that he'd always been careful to conceal.

He waited until I was seated before he began.

"When Trotsky went to Mexico, I was in Spain where I was working under Alexander Orlov, who was the NKVD chief there. I arrived in September 1936, shortly after the Spanish Civil War began. Trotsky had called for Soviet support of the Spanish Republic, and Stalin couldn't let Trotsky appear more revolutionary than he was, so he sent airplanes, pilots, tanks, and 'advisors', which included Orlov and me. Stalin offered to safeguard the Spanish Republic's gold reserves, which would be used in part to buy Soviet arms for shipment to Spain. I had 7,800 crates of gold loaded onto a Russian steamer in the port of Cartagena, and Orlov told me what he'd heard Stalin had said: "The Spanish will no more see their gold again then they will see their own ears." That gold won me my Order of the Red Banner.

"If Stalin had had his way, the Communists would have

won the Civil War, and he would have had Spain under his control. But the last thing he wanted was a Spanish socialist government outside his control – a rival for leadership of the international left. Orlov and I were ordered to eliminate Trotskyist elements within the Republican leadership. In fact, there were few who cared about Trotsky, but by our definition, any leftist who wouldn't accept Communist discipline was a Trotskyist. That included the socialists and anarchists. We received some bad press, but less than you might think. I took Ernest Hemingway on a tour of one of our training camps. He first wrote that he loved the camp and us, although he later called us 'filthy swine,' and that skinny English socialist George Orwell said something similar. We did what we were ordered to do. It wasn't all one-sided though. We killed socialists and anarchists, and they killed us when they had the chance. We were just better at it.

"We arrested Andrés Nin and the rest of the anarchist leadership in Barcelona in June 1937, and Orlov put me in charge of their interrogations. We shot most of them at once – a bloody night; the executioners' hands must have ached from pulling triggers. But we put off shooting Nin because we wanted a confession that he was a German agent. We pressured him for days using the normal techniques. Nothing. I turned him over to Vidali and told him to get a confession one way or another. I had to leave the room – Vidali flayed the man alive. Nin held out, and he died before he confessed. I've never seen anyone like him.

"I was in Spain when I met the Mercader family. Three Communist sons – Pablo, Ramón, and Luis – and their Communist mother, Caridad. Luis, the youngest of the three, didn't count for much because he was only 14 years old at the time. And I met Pablo only a few times. Most of my dealings were with Caridad and with Ramón.

"I know you think that Caridad and I were lovers. She was a handsome woman, true enough, but I was always careful about sex with my agents. Sometimes sex is a way to bind an agent, to make her do what she would otherwise not. In Caridad's case that was not necessary. She was a fearless, dedicated Communist. Caridad's problem was that she was crazy, so sex with me would have been likely to make her even crazier and more difficult to control. Besides, I had no need for sex with Caridad. I had as many others as I wanted. Caridad and I traveled together after Ramón killed Trotsky, but sex just never came up between us. She didn't seem much interested in it. The woman never stopped talking about herself. By the end of my time with her, I didn't want to fuck her, I wanted to shoot her.

"I was interested in Ramón, not in his mother. I saw his potential as an agent. He was 23 years old and spoke Catalan, Castilian Spanish, and French without an accent. He was a captain in the Republican Army where he'd killed in hand-to-hand combat, and his movie-star looks meant that he could be effective with women should we need that. When he was wounded in the wrist, I visited him daily in the hospital and brought cigarettes and brandy. We'd drink and smoke, and within a week, I knew he was the one. It's always tricky recruiting a new agent. The usual way is to seduce little by little, the way one does with a difficult woman. That way, it's possible to stop halfway. Maybe the agent is willing to steal documents but not to kill, for example. But with Ramón there was no question. Like his mother, he was willing to do whatever the Party needed. I didn't yet know how I would use him, but I knew he would be important, maybe in going after Trotsky, which I could see looming in my future. I had him removed from the front and assigned as my personal aide.

"In the summer of 1937, I sent Ramón to Moscow for a new identity. He returned after two months as Jacques Mornard, Belgian businessman. They'd rehearsed him in the details of his Mornard family and personal life, provided him with Belgian clothing and luggage, and given him documents that were in good order.

"The first batch of the Moscow Trials – Kamenev and Zinoviev – began about then, which is why I'd been in a hurry to leave for Spain. It was safer to be out of the country. After the first trials, Stalin fired Yagoda and replaced him with Yezhov. One reason Stalin chose Yezhov, I think, was his height. Stalin was short, but next to Yezhov he looked like a giant. Yezhov arrested his old boss Yagoda and put him in the dock along with others of Stalin's old comrades-in-arms. Yezhov personally carried out Yagoda's death sentence by pounding him with a truncheon on the floor of a Lubyanka cell while screaming, 'Beat the dog! Beat the dog!' Yezhov liquidated almost all the remaining Old Bolsheviks, the high commands of the Army and Navy, and worst of all, half of the NKVD – the men and women who were his colleagues, the ones protecting the nation from foreign spies. Stalin finally called a stop because the purges were destroying the economy, the military, and the Party. But he let Yezhov dangle for some time after he replaced him with Beria, and I think he relished watching Yezhov struggle once he saw his end approaching. As a boy, Stalin must have enjoyed torturing small animals. Although it was safer for an NKVD officer to be working outside the country, many were recalled to Moscow for 'consultations' where they were interrogated and executed. And forced to accuse others; someone accused me of being an English spy, but I was spared, my guess is because the mission to kill Trotsky was already in the works.

"Orlov, my boss in Spain, was ordered to report to a Soviet ship in Antwerp. He saw what was coming and fled with his wife and daughter to America. He sent Stalin a letter, telling him that he'd sent unnamed attorneys documents that listed all our agents in the West, documents that described how we'd stolen the Spanish gold. He'd given the attorneys instructions to publish everything if he or his family come to harm. Why didn't everyone who was called back to Moscow do that? They'd seen their colleagues executed and should have seen what was coming. It's hard to explain. They believed in Communism and the brotherhood of the NKVD, believed that their willing return would prove their loyalty. Orlov was more cynical than the rest, and his blackmail worked. He died just a few years ago in his bed in Cleveland, Ohio.

"After Orlov fled, I was NKVD chief in Spain. Trotsky's son, Lev Sedova, was running the Trotskyist organization in Paris. Someone – maybe Orlov – sent an anonymous letter to Trotsky warning him that Mark Zborowski, his son's number-two in Paris, was an NKVD agent. Which was in fact the case. Trotsky's son wouldn't hear about it. He told Trotsky that the warning was a provocation. Soon after that, Trotsky's son died after an emergency appendectomy, a death for which some blamed me. Bullshit. The situation was perfect as it was, and his death could only disturb things. Zborowski already had all the mail and files, including the list of Trotskyist agents in Europe. So why would I kill Trotsky's son? Believe me, I grieved when I heard of his death. I would never remove an enemy as stupid as that. But things didn't work out too badly. Trotsky appointed Zborowski to take his son's place as editor of the *Bulletin of the Opposition* and head of the Paris Trotskyist office. The chief Trotskyist in Europe was then our man.

"The Moscow trials made Trotsky out as the source of all that went wrong in the Soviet Union. That was ludicrous, but it worked. Trotsky had been exiled a decade earlier and couldn't have harmed the Soviet Union had he tried, but he was a convenient Satan for the public. No one cared about Trotsky except Stalin, whose hatred was personal. Trotsky was the one who knew all his failings and lies, Trotsky had called him 'the gravedigger of the revolution,' so Stalin was hell-bent on his death. Although I hadn't yet been ordered to do so, I began to prepare for the assignment to kill him."

Leonid's agitation worried me. He refused to rest, but I made him drink some tea. He'd taken only a few sips before he began again.

"Trotsky arrived in Mexico in January of 1937. I wouldn't be there for another two years, but I followed his every move as best I could. He'd been pushed from one country to the next. In 1933, France had taken him in from Turkey, and he and his son published their anti-Stalin rag, The *Bulletin of the Opposition*, in Paris. When the French Communists negotiated to join the other parties of the left in the Popular Front, they insisted that Trotsky be deported.

"Norway took him at first, but then thought better. Why piss off their neighbor, the Soviet Union, over a washed-up revolutionary? They put him under house arrest, and it looked like he was finished. Norway would deport him to us unless some other country took him in. Then Mexico stepped up. What had happened was that Diego Rivera, that frog-faced fatboy painter, asked the Mexican president to offer Trotsky asylum. For Rivera, it was all about his image as a revolutionary artist. He called himself a Communist because that fit his image of himself, although he had no understanding of Marxism beyond 'Workers of the world, unite!'

"I'd first met Rivera in 1927 in Moscow at the tenth anniversary of the Revolution. Rivera was marching with a crowd of Trotsky's Oppositionists who managed to cross one corner of Red Square, and Trotsky tried to speak to them. Rivera, his belly hanging over his belt, pumped his fist and cheered him, '*Viva la revolúcion!*' Our men and the police attacked, and it turned into a real brawl. Rivera was supposed to paint a mural for the Moscow Red Army club, but I had him thrown out of the country as a Trotskyist. When he got back to Mexico, the local Communist Party elected him as its general secretary. Can you believe it?

"Besides his political idiocy, he was completely incompetent. He lost correspondence, squandered money, and made senseless proclamations. The Mexican Party threw him out a couple of years later, or rather, he threw himself out. He showed up at a Mexican Central Committee meeting, put a revolver on the table, and covered it with a handkerchief. Then he stood and put his hand on it as if he were swearing on a bible. 'I, Diego Rivera, General Secretary of the Mexican Communist Party, hereby expel myself.' Then he lifted the handkerchief, picked up the gun and waved it around pointing it at people before he smashed it into pieces. He'd made it out of clay.

"For Rivera, Communism was an outfit to wear, a game. He sent his wife, Frida Kahlo, to meet Trotsky's ship. Rivera couldn't make the trip himself because he was sick, probably from gorging himself on greasy Mexican slop.

"Trotsky and his wife Natalia arrived on a Norwegian tanker that anchored offshore in Tampico harbor in the middle of a forest of oil derricks. Trotsky knew Norway was cooperating with the NKVD, and he was sure he'd be killed the moment he stepped off the ship. He was right to be scared when he got to Mexico. If I'd been in his shoes, I'd have been shitting myself. He refused to leave, and the captain told him that he and his wife would be tied to chairs and carried if they wouldn't go on their own. Then a tug pulled alongside the tanker, and an American friend waved from its deck. The Trotskys boarded the tug and headed for the dock.

"Trotsky suspected we had men in the crowd of reporters and gawkers, and he wasn't wrong. Two Mexicans were hoping for a shot at him, one at the bottom of the gangplank when he left the boat and one where he would board his train. We used Mexicans so that killing him would look like a local affair, nothing that could be tied to the NKVD or Stalin. But Mexicans are notoriously trigger-happy and bad shots, and in my experience that's especially true of Mexican Communists. If I'd been in charge that day, I wouldn't have risked shooting him at the dock – give a Mexican a gun and he's likely to use it. Trotsky wasn't stupid. Once off the boat, he wedged himself between a Mexican general and Frida Kahlo. A bullet in the middle of Frida's single eyebrow wouldn't have been good press.

"I've seen the newsreels of his arrival. Trotsky dressed like he was playing golf – those funny pants that stop at the knees with long socks below. Mexican police, uniformed and plainclothes, were everywhere. It was just as well we didn't get Trotsky that day, because we put him to good use. He was the bogeyman at the Moscow trials, the saboteur Stalin blamed for every factory explosion, crop failure, typhus epidemic, and late train. And if we'd killed him then, I wouldn't have received my Order of Lenin because I wasn't there yet. Ramón's the man who killed Trotsky, but I ran the operation. My greatest achievement."

This, I realized, was the story Leonid had wanted to tell from the start; all the others had been preface. He was leaning forward in his chair, making sure that I got every word.

"Caridad Mercader, Ramón's mother, was in Tampico at the dock the day Trotsky arrived," Leonid said. "When someone shouted at her 'Bitch, you've come to prepare Trotsky's assassination,' she replied, 'Who knows?' That sort of loose talk disqualified her from being a good agent. She had no judgment, and she was principled but heartless. Her son Pablo was sent to a Republican Army punishment battalion for some minor offense – insubordination, drunk on duty, something like that, I'm not sure. Punishment battalions were placed at the point of an attack or used as a rear guard to cover a retreat, so being posted to one was close to a death sentence. I offered to have his sentence changed, but she refused, saying he'd deserved it. Pablo was run over by a tank.

"Trotsky announced the formation of the 'Fourth International,' an assembly of his followers from around the world. The first meeting was to be in Paris in September 1938, and Rudolf Klement, a German Trotskyist, was to be the secretary who would run things. Trotsky couldn't go himself because France wouldn't give him a visa. We grabbed Klement in July and held him until he wrote a letter to all the other Trotskyist leaders that he had broken with Trotsky because of Trotsky's support of fascism. Nobody believed the letter, everyone knew he had written it under torture. We shot Klement and hacked his body into pieces. Then we stuffed all the pieces but his head into a bag and threw them into the Seine. We left enough evidence so that his remains could be identified as a warning to the other Trotskyists.

"When Trotsky first arrived in Mexico, Diego Rivera let him use Frida's family house. Trotsky repaid Rivera by first fucking Frida and then firing Rivera from his position as secretary of the Mexican delegation to his new Fourth International. Rivera was completely incompetent, but you would have thought Trotsky wouldn't want to piss off the man responsible for his invitation to Mexico, the man in whose house he was living. Rivera threw him out, and Trotsky had to find somewhere else to live. American Trotskyists raised the money to buy another house, which Trotsky began fortifying against the attack he knew was coming.

"I wasn't in Mexico yet; I was still in Spain. I had once outranked Sudoplatov, but he was a better politician than I was, and Beria took a shine to him. After Beria took over as NKVD head from Yezhov, he made Sudoplatov deputy director of the Foreign Department, so he was my boss. Sudoplatov was a bureaucrat, but a good one. He would drop names – 'When I was speaking to Comrade Molotov the other day...' – but that didn't bother me. He told me to get ready to liquidate Trotsky, something I'd already started on. We already had agents within Trotsky's Paris organization, including Mark Zborowski and a maid in his Mexican house. But Orlon's defection complicated things because he knew all our agents. We needed an entirely new team.

"We couldn't allow Trotsky's death to be pinned on the Soviet Union. Sudoplatov told me to use Grigulevich and Vidali, who weren't Russian and had worked with me in Spain, as organizers and to keep a low profile myself. They were a real pair. I told you how they had skinned Andres Nin alive. After the war, Grigulevich was Costa Rican ambassador to Yugoslavia where he was assigned to kill Tito, although that mission was canceled after Stalin's death. He eventually became a historian and wrote 50-plus books about the Catholic Church. A complex man, Grigulevich. Vidali was more straightforward. He shot Julio Mella, ex-head of the Mexican Communist party, in what was either political or a lovers' quarrel or both. Nobody knew for sure, and believe me, you didn't want to ask Vidali too many questions.

"Anyway, the plan was that we'd have an agent inside Trotsky's compound who would open the gates to a gang of Mexicans, who would kill Trotsky and leave no trail to the NKVD. The fall-guy as leader of the attack would be David Siqueiros, a Mexican Communist and mural painter. As with Rivera, he'd been in Moscow in 1927. He was completely unreliable, so I never dealt with him directly, only through Grigulevich and Vidali. On the good side, he had led Mexican troops in the Spanish Civil War, so he knew firearms. And he saw himself as a revolutionary artist, so I knew he wouldn't refuse the job. But when our soldiers in Spain fought wearing rags, he wore skintight tailored uniforms and led men into battle wearing a purple and gold cape. He said, 'What's the point of being an artist if you can't design your own uniform?' He wanted to be famous, to be admired as a hero, and that's the last thing an agent should want. But everyone in Mexico knew he was crazy, so it might be credible that he had acted on his own when he was captured.

"I had other plans for Ramón: he would infiltrate the Trotsky household to obtain daily schedules and security arrangements, but he wouldn't be the man who would open the gates for Siqueiros's crew. Whoever did that would be known by the Mexican attackers who were captured, and they would give him up under interrogation. I didn't want to lose Ramón. He would be my backup if Siqueiros' attack failed, either as the assassin himself or as the man who could put Trotsky and the next assassin together.

"Sudoplatov and I went to Paris along with Grigulevich and Vidali in June 1938 to organize things. I sent Siqueiros to Paris and sent Ramón and Caridad there too, but I made sure Siqueiros traveled separately from the Mercaders. Siqueiros would know nothing about them, and they would know nothing about him. Sudoplatov returned to Moscow a few weeks later, and I ordered Grigulevich and Vidali back to Mexico with Siqueiros, telling them to keep him in check, to make sure he did nothing without orders, and not to get involved in recruiting his crew. I had little confidence in Siqueiros, but even if his attack failed, it would be a statement to the world that the Mexican Communists despised Trotsky. But Siqueiros did worry me. If he failed, I might be shot before I could try again.

"I stayed in Paris with Ramón and Caridad. I'd planned to use only Ramón in my backup operation, but I decided to involve his mother as well. She was a hard woman who would give her son the steel he would need to carry through. And if he got cold feet, I'd be able to read her. She was an open book.

"I spent two months training Ramón in elementary tradecraft: spotting surveillance, shaking a tail, communicating using dead letter drops, and so on. And in explaining Ramón's mission, which was not to kill Trotsky but to find a way into the household.

"You've heard of a 'honey trap' – a woman agent uses sex to get what she wants. Mata Hari didn't invent it. It goes back at least to Delilah giving Samson a haircut. One of Trotsky's secretaries, Hilda Ageloff, had a Trotskyist sister named Sylvia in New York. Sylvia had arms and legs like sticks, stringy hair, no tits or ass, sharp nose, thick eyeglasses. Ramón was good-looking, so he'd be the honey. Sylvia was planning to go to Paris as a translator at the founding meeting of Trotsky's Fourth International, and her sister's friend Ruby invited herself along. Ruby was our agent. They traveled second-class on the *Normandie*, practicing their schoolgirl French the whole way. In Paris, they conveniently bumped into Ramón, alias Jacques Mornard, a Belgian businessman with plenty of ready cash. Ruby said, 'Jacques, whatever are you doing in

Paris?' and one thing led to another. Sylvia and Ramón had a whirlwind courtship in the best nightclubs and restaurants. He had her pants off within the week. Sylvia returned to New York, and Ramón promised that he'd get there on business as soon as possible.

"Sudoplatov told me how Stalin gave him the order to eliminate Trotsky. Beria summoned Sudoplatov to his office, and the two of them took Beria's ZIL limousine to Stalin's Kremlin office. Sudoplatov told me he'd been there twice earlier, but that he was still weak in the knees when Stalin's secretary ushered them in. Stalin, dressed in his trademark white tunic, baggy pants, and knee-high boots, led them to a long table. He lit his pipe with a wooden match and asked Beria what he was doing about Trotsky, and Beria then suggested that Sudoplatov should be put in charge of killing him.

"Sudoplatov told me that Stalin looked straight at him, not at Beria. 'Get rid of Trotsky, and the whole Trotskyist organization will collapse. This effort has been handled badly, for which I blame those I entrusted with the assignment to liquidate him.' He had given the job earlier to Yezhov and Spiegelglas, both of whom had since been executed. Sudoplatov understood the threat. 'Within the year,' Stalin continued, still speaking to Sudoplatov. 'Spend whatever you need to and use whatever agents you think best. Report only to Comrade Beria.' The meeting was over.

"Beria and Sudoplatov returned to Beria's office, where Beria explained why Stalin was in a hurry. First, Trotsky had a book contract to write a biography of Stalin using the letters and archives he had taken with him into exile, so he couldn't be allowed to finish it. Second, Trotsky was no longer of any use. Stalin had ended the Moscow trials where Trotsky had played the bogeyman. But Stalin had a third reason that neither Beria nor Sudoplatov knew then: Stalin no longer worried that killing Trotsky would upset the international left. He was about to announce a pact with Nazi Germany, which meant that he would lose the soft leftists in any case. There'd be no cost to killing Trotsky.

"Sudoplatov told Beria that he wanted to bring me in as operational head in Mexico because I spoke Spanish. Beria agreed, and Sudoplatov ordered me to return to Moscow for consultations. Given what had happened to many other agents who had orders to return, I telephoned Sudoplatov before I went. I wanted to hear his voice because I knew Sudoplatov well. He reassured me. I arrived in Moscow a week later, and we sat in his office and talked over tea.

"Sudoplatov and I wrote up my plans to use Siqueiros and the Mercaders separately, and we took the document to Beria. Beria had his own crazy plan, which we had to listen to. He was a Georgian and wanted a plan that would involve Georgian exiles – 'Mingrelian princes' he called them – and, unbelievably, he wanted a plan that would involve Orlov! As politely as I could, I told him that I didn't know any Spanish-speaking Mingrelian princes in Mexico and that I thought working with Orlov would be difficult. He wouldn't want to meet with us because we would torture him until he revealed the names of the attorneys to whom he had given his documents. Beria muttered objections, but he finally accepted my plan.

"Beria was a strange man. Caridad Mercader, who met him later, said that, dressed in black wearing gold-rimmed glasses, he looked like a Jesuit. And while high party members could do pretty much what they wanted sexually, Beria carried it too far. He liked very young, very thin women, and he would spot one on a Moscow Street and send a driver to pick her up. Beria would have her that night, and the next day the driver would return her to the same spot with a bouquet of roses. Beria claimed it was all consensual, but what girl was going to refuse when a driver in an NKVD uniform told her to enter a ZIL limousine? What father, brother, husband, or mother was going to accuse the director of the NKVD of rape? The sex may have been technically consensual, but I heard that one of the girls was nine years old. I spent years in prison because they thought I was Beria's man, but the best that I can say of Beria is that Yezhov, his predecessor, was worse.

"I sent Ramón and Caridad to New York in late August so that Ramón could romance Sylvia. I had to deal with a Moscow Center fuckup. Someone had decided that Ramón needed yet another identity, even though Sylvia already knew him as Jacques Mornard, Belgian businessman. Moscow gave him a Canadian passport with the name 'Frank Jacson' – that's J-A-C-S-O-N, no K. I imagine Moscow Center thought no one would know how a French-Canadian accent sounded. But if he was supposed to be French-Canadian, why give him an English name? And if he needed an English name, why not spell it right? Sylvia of course wondered why he had a new name, and he had to explain the spelling at every border-crossing, hotel register, and ticket agency. Come to think of it, that might have been an advantage. No one would imagine an NKVD agent would travel under a name that stupid. I came up with a story for Ramón to tell Sylvia – that he was traveling under false papers to avoid the Belgian military draft. As it turned out, Sylvia was not a problem. She was so in love that he could have arrived calling himself 'Iosif Stalin' and she wouldn't have said a word.

"After New York, I sent Ramón to Mexico, supposedly working for an import-export company. Sylvia, desperate to see him, took sick leave from her job and joined him in Mexico on New Year's Day 1940. She was a trusted Trotskyist, and she visited Trotsky's house and offered to make herself useful as a secretary and translator. Ramón drove her to work in his Buick but never tried to enter the household. Sylvia talked about him to the Trotskys and to the guards, but they didn't see him as threatening the way they would have viewed an unknown Communist. Just another boring businessman."

Leonid's right arm was trembling. He wanted to go on, but I insisted that he take a break. I told him that if he wouldn't rest, I'd leave, and I made him another cup of tea and told him that if he would nap for an hour, we could continue. He took his shoes off and stretched out on the sofa, but he couldn't sleep. I put Debussy's *La Mer* on the phonograph at low volume, and it seemed to soothe him; the trembling stopped. He was watching the clock, and exactly an hour after I'd made him rest, he sat up and said it was time to continue.

He picked up where he'd left off. "If Siqueiros's attack on Trotsky's compound was to look spontaneous, we needed to motivate the Mexican left. The Mexican Communist Party got instructions from the Comintern and put 20,000 marchers in the streets shouting, 'Death to Trotsky!' Grigulevich and Vidali were with me by that time, and I told them to manage

Siqueiros's selection of men as best they could without being seen as running the show. As for myself, I was keeping
far away from Siqueiros. The man was impossible. He enlist-
ed his artist friends and some bums he had picked up on the
street for a few pesos, but no one with any experience. We
did have our man inside Trotsky's compound, Robert Harte,
an American who would open the gate. But he was weak, and
I knew he wouldn't stand up under questioning.

"The plan was simple, as it had to be with a crew like
Siqueiros's. Trotsky's house was in the shape of a 'T' with
Trotsky's bedroom in the middle of the T's stem. That room was
the target. There were guards inside the compound – mostly
American Trotskyists, few of whom had military experience –
and five Mexican policemen outside the walls. Two Mexican
girls, whose boyfriends were among the attackers, posed as
prostitutes working in the house across the street. The girls
made friends with the police; their mission was to get them
drunk the night of the attack. Some of our men would dress
as police, subdue the police guards, signal Harte to open the
gate, enter, and kill Trotsky. Simple enough, I thought.

"Siqueiros recruited twenty men – far more than could
be useful – and dressed some of them in police uniforms.
Grigulevich and Vidali accompanied them but tried to stay
inconspicuous so that they couldn't be identified in the police
questioning that would follow. I kept far away. Grigulevich
later told me that Siqueiros looked like something out of a
Marx Brothers movie, with a Pancho Villa fake mustache and
a police major's uniform that he'd had tailored for a better
fit. It was a moonless night, but Siqueiros wore dark glasses.
Already drunk and still clutching tequila bottles, the men
piled into four cars and headed for Trotsky's compound,
picking up a few more partygoers on the way.

"Most of the real policemen were drunk or passed out from
the party with the two girls, and the rest were fooled by the
police uniforms. They were tied up and gagged. Siqueiros
gave the knocking signal, Harte opened the main gate, and
all twenty of the attackers flooded in. None of the American
guards tried to stop them, and Siqueiros and his men
surrounded Trotsky's bedroom from all four sides. I blame
Grigulevich and Vidali for what happened next. One man –

not twenty – should have thrown a grenade into the bedroom to stun Trotsky, rushed in firing a machine gun, identified Trotsky's body, and put a final round into his forehead to make sure. That's standard practice for entering a hostile room, both in the infantry and in the NKVD. Instead, every single drunken Mexican blasted away through the walls and doors with everything he had, some of them with Thompson submachine guns with fifty-round drum clips.

"It's remarkable that the attackers didn't all kill each other, as they were firing directly through the bedroom from every angle. Someone did fire several rounds from a pistol into Trotsky's bed but didn't check to see that he was *in* the bed. Trotsky had rolled out of bed and was with his wife in the corner. No one thought to turn the lights on and look around. Despite all the noise and bullet holes, the only injury was a bullet wound to Trotsky's grandson's big toe; he was sleeping in the next room. The attackers were also supposed to burn the papers and archives that Trotsky was using to write his biography of Stalin. They failed at that too. Someone threw an incendiary bomb into his study, but it fizzled. Without checking to see whether they'd killed Trotsky or burned the papers – whether they'd accomplished anything – they left after they'd run out of ammunition, taking Robert Harte with them.

"I didn't know how bad it was until I read the newspapers the next morning. I sent a coded message to Sudoplatov, but it was delayed by the usual bungling at Moscow Center, so Stalin and Beria first heard about the failed attack from the TASS news agency, who had picked it up from the Western press. Sudoplatov and I were sure we were dead men. In a cable, I made no excuses. I admitted my guilt and threw myself on Stalin's and Beria's mercy, a quality for which they were not known. I did remind them that we had accomplished some things. Trotsky was blaming the attack on Stalin, but no one else believed that it was an NKVD operation because it had been so badly bungled. Given the number of bullet holes with no one even injured, the police thought it was a put-up job by Trotsky to win sympathy for his cause. They also suspected Rivera might have been involved. When the police came looking for him, the American movie actress Paulette Goddard put Rivera on the floor of her car and drove him to the American Embassy, where he received an entry visa to the United States after he agreed to act as their informant – a steadfast Communist, that Rivera. Goddard then took him to San Francisco, where he stayed for the next six months. I never understood why the most heartbreakingly beautiful women lined up to fuck that fat bastard.

"At first, the Mexican press followed the line that the attack was a fake. But then things started to go wrong. Siqueiros had disappeared, the police found the abandoned cars, and they traced one of the supposed prostitutes to an unemployed electrician who told them that Siqueiros had recruited him for the attack. And then the police found Robert Harte, or what was left of him. Grigulevich had shot him in the head, dug a hole in the basement of the farmhouse where they were hiding, poured lye on top of him, and filled the hole. He didn't use enough lye, and he didn't dig deep enough. The police dug where it smelled, and they found Harte's body and correctly assumed that he'd been an inside man and had opened the gate. Trotsky, on the other hand, believed in Harte and even put up a stone plaque in the garden of his compound. When I complained to Grigulevich about what he'd done with Harte, he answered, 'What was I supposed to do with him? Leave him to talk to the police? He was weak, and he could identify me.' Siqueiros couldn't be found and began to look very guilty, and the Mexican Communist Party disowned him. The poet Neruda smuggled Siqueiros out of the country. I told Moscow that while the attack had failed, it hadn't been worthless: the identified gunmen were Mexican artists, communists, and vagrants, all led by a single crazy painter – a spontaneous uprising with no evidence tying it to the NKVD.

"Sudoplatov told me that Beria screamed at him for half an hour, then asked him what should be done. Sudoplatov and I had already agreed that we wanted to shut down our entire network within Trotsky's organizations. We had too many people involved, some of whom might be double agents, and Orlov knew their names in any case. Beria argued against that – we had spent years building the network. But when the two of them called on Stalin, he was calm and asked Sudoplatov only one question: do you need the network to kill Trotsky? Sudoplatov assured him that we did not, that I had placed an assassin near Trotsky who was completely unknown to any-one within the network. That was Ramón. Stalin agreed with us. Trotsky's organization would collapse after his death, and we wouldn't need a network.

"Stalin's acceptance of my plan didn't ease my mind. I'd been given a second chance, but I knew I wouldn't get a third. And Sudoplatov had offered up Ramón as the assassin before I'd discussed it with Ramón, who thought his role was to in-filtrate Trotsky's household. I'd come to realize that Ramón was unsuitable as an assasin. He was moralistic and need-ed to believe in what he was doing. For me, it didn't matter whether Stalin or Trotsky was 'right.' Even Trotsky had once said that the Party was always right, and my job was to serve the Party; Stalin *was* the Party, and so I'd kill Trotsky if that's what he wanted. Ramón was brave. He had once killed a sen-try with a knife. But killing a soldier who is trying to kill you is one thing, while killing a 60-year-old man doddering around his study is another. The first is war, the second is murder. Ramón thought too much.

"I met with Ramón the day after Siqueiros's failure. I'd kept him separate from the Siqueiros group, so the attack was a surprise to him. I invited his mother to the meeting, figuring that he would be ashamed to refuse in her presence. I was solemn; I told him he would need to find a way to be alone with Trotsky inside his house, kill him silently without rais-ing an alarm, then calmly walk out into the street where a car would be waiting. Caridad glowed with pride, and Ramón re-peated what he had told me earlier – that he would do what-ever I asked.

"I'd already begun working him into Trotsky's household. At first, he'd driven Sylvia to work, nothing more. He'd chatted with the police outside the compound and with the American guards at the gate. He never tried to enter the house, but he was known as the boyfriend of Sylvia, and she was trusted. We had a stroke of luck that February. Alfred and Marguerite Rosmer, French Trotskyists, were Trotsky's guests in the compound. Sylvia knew Alfred from the meeting in Paris She invited the Rosmers to the apartment she shared with Ramón and introduced him to the Rosmers using his French-Canadian alias 'Frank Jacson.' The Rosmers then invited Sylvia and Mercader-Mornard-Jacson for a picnic in the country. Sylvia became part of our scheme, something I'm sure she's regretted ever since.

"I tried to keep Sylvia in Mexico by having Ramón pay her a salary to write meaningless articles for an imaginary periodical. I think she knew the payments were a sham but thought they were his way of keeping her close to him. But in March, she returned to her job in New York, which meant that Ramón stayed on in Mexico with no connection to the Trotsky household. But when Marguerite's husband Alfred underwent minor surgery, Ramón offered to drive her to and from the hospital, and he visited Alfred as well, bringing chocolates and flowers. Ramón became Marguerite's friend, and Marguerite was a friend of Natalia, Trotsky's wife. Ramón was almost one of the family.

"Four days after Siqueiros's bungled attack, Ramón entered the compound and met Trotsky for the first time. The Rosmers planned to leave Mexico for New York by ship from Veracruz, and Ramón told them he had business in Veracruz every couple of weeks and offered to drive them in his Buick. Natalia and one of Trotsky's typists decided to go with them in a second car. When Ramón arrived to pick up the Rosmers, he was invited into the compound for the first time. They were preparing for another attack like Siqueiros's – raising walls, installing steel shutters and doors and photoelectric alarms, none of which would protect Trotsky from Ramón. Ramón told me that Trotsky was in the courtyard, feeding his rabbits and chickens, and that he was surprised how ordinary Trotsky looked. He introduced himself as Frank, and Trotsky invited him to join them for breakfast while the Rosmers finished packing. Ramón had brought a toy glider for Trotsky's grandson, which went over well. Ramón was inside, and he was my only hope.

"They left for Veracruz in two cars. The second car, the one with the typist and Natalia, broke down two hours from Veracruz. They left the car in for repairs, and they all crowded into Ramón's Buick, which brought him still closer to Trotsky's wife. Although he claimed that he visited Veracruz every two weeks, Ramón had never been there and became hopelessly lost. Nobody asked questions; we were lucky that the typist had gone with Natalia rather than one of Trotsky's guards, who likely would have been suspicious.

"Ramón returned to Mexico City, where he dropped Natalia off at the Trotsky compound. He then drove the typist to the apartment she shared with two other American Trotskyists, Hank and Dorothy Schultz. With Sylvia in New York, Ramón had no excuse to return to the Trotsky compound, so he made friends with the Schultzes. He began dropping by every day or two, drinking coffee with Dorothy and playing with their two-year-old daughter. Then he did something stupid. He told them that he'd been close to Trotskyists in Paris and had even paid to publish an edition of the Trotskyist newspaper. I'm sure he got that idea from Caridad – involving her was my mistake. I'd hoped she would stabilize him, but I couldn't control her. Only she could have made up Ramón's stupid prattle about being a Trotskyist. I wanted Ramón known only as Sylvia's fiancé, but Caridad promoted him to professor of Marxist theory. His lie was stupid on its face: why would a businessman who claimed to find politics of no interest want to have anything to do with boring French Trotskyists, and why would he finance their newspaper? A few quick telegrams to Paris would have proved Ramón was a liar. But Hitler saved us. The Germans were storming through France, and all the French Trotskyists had gone into hiding or were already in concentration camps (including, unfortunately, our agent Mark Zborowski).

"The Schultzes' apartment became the gathering place for Trotsky's visiting American comrades. Ramón chauffeured them around the city, bought meals and drinks. He bragged about his business activities, said he was working for a war profiteer and had plenty of money. No one asked why he was so generous or had so much free time. And Ramón talked too much. He made things up on the spot when he would have done better to keep his mouth shut until he had rehearsed his stories with me. He told one story to one person, another story to another.

"I flinched when I heard Ramón call Trotsky what his acolytes called him – the 'Old Man'; he was beginning to see Trotsky as a person rather than a target. I sent Ramón to New York, partly so he could reunite with Sylvia and urge her to return to Mexico City, but mostly just to shut him up and to get him away from Caridad before he blew the game entirely. I told our agents in New York to calm him down and get him ready for what he would do. Ramón left his Buick with Trotsky's guards for their use, which made him still more popular.

"Ramón returned to Mexico at the end of June and called Sylvia in New York to say that he would be in Tampico for a week. I told him to go silent then, which I hoped would panic Sylvia into coming to Mexico. It worked. She sent one telegram after another, none of which he answered. Finally, at the end of July, he telegraphed Sylvia that he had been sick, and she wired back that she was coming to care for him. I sent a coded message to Sudoplatov. 'Everything is in order.'"

Leonid's arm was shaking badly by then, and he was drooling from the right side of his mouth. He kept dabbing at it with his handkerchief. He'd been talking nonstop for hours, and I told him that he needed another break, but he wouldn't hear of it.

"We're almost there!" he pleaded.

I let him continue. "Ramón had pretended to be sick, but by the time Sylvia arrived he was, with bad diarrhea and fevers. I think it was psychological. The day was approaching. Caridad was bursting with pride for her son, the hero, and Sylvia offered love and demanded love in return.

"Sylvia's return gave Ramón entry to Trotsky's compound. He picked her up at the airport and took her there for tea with the Trotskys and the guards. On my instructions, Ramón kept his mouth shut but nodded approvingly whenever Trotsky spoke. When someone asked Ramón whether he'd visited the Trotskyist headquarters when he'd been in New York, he shamefacedly said he'd been too involved with business, that his boss was starting a diamond-cutting operation with some Jewish emigres who'd smuggled uncut stones to New York from Holland. That confession, he told me, provoked a disapproving silence. But nobody said anything. Trotsky and his comrades saw Ramón as what Lenin called a 'useful idiot' – a sympathetic capitalist who was welcome because he bought drinks and supplied a car. No one questioned his Marxist beliefs because he was so clearly out of his depth. He was like a twelve-year-old at the dinner table trying to impress the adults. They tolerated him but paid no attention.

"Ramón and Sylvia were staying at the Hotel Montejo. Living with Sylvia was intolerable. He couldn't stand to be in the same room with her, much less make love to her. He snapped at her; she burst into tears – the usual behavior when love affairs go bad. And he was still sick, rushing for the commode every few minutes. He had always been slim, but he lost another five kilos and developed a tic in his left cheek. Things were going downhill, and Sylvia was threatening to return to New York, so I decided on August 17 as the day. I met with Ramón to plan.

"We needed a way to get Ramón and Trotsky alone in Trotsky's study. Ramón suggested that he write an article supporting Trotsky's views on the war and ask Trotsky for criticism. I was pretty sure this was Caridad's idea, and I didn't like Ramón pretending to be a Trotskyist. But given the situation as it was, this was not bad. Ramón told me he had already begun work on the article.

"We had to decide on a weapon. If Ramón was to walk out afterward, he would need to kill Trotsky silently – a knife, a club, something like that. Ramón was a mountain climber, and he showed me his climber's ice-axe, which would certainly be effective. It had a sharp spike on one end of the axe-head and a hatchet-style blade on the other. A blow to the head with either of them should kill a man instantly, the way a hammer drops a steer in an abattoir. But the axe-head was almost a foot long end-to-end, and the axe-handle was four feet. I told him a knife would be easier to conceal and use – just get behind Trotsky, grab his hair, pull his head back to expose the jugular, slash his throat deeply so that the airway was cut and he couldn't cry out, drop the knife, and walk out of the room. Ramón didn't like that; he said that Trotsky, despite his age, was physically strong and might be able to struggle and shout. Besides, he said, blood would spew from the severed artery and likely stain his clothing, making a surreptitious escape difficult. Ramón insisted on the ice-axe, said he could cut the handle of the ice-axe short and hide it under a raincoat over his arm. The guards no longer searched him, and he was sure he could bring it in. It was important that Ramón feel comfortable with the plan, so I gave in and agreed on the ice-axe. But if he could smuggle that axe past the guards, he could bring a knife as well, and he agreed to carry both.

"We discussed his escape. I told him that his mother and I would be waiting in a car around the corner. After he'd killed Trotsky, I told him to drop the knife and axe, sling the raincoat over his arm to hide the automatic pistol he would use if anyone tried to stop him, and walk calmly to the front gate. If anyone asked, he would say that he was going to his car to get some papers he had forgotten.

"Finally, we made backup plans for the possibility that he would be captured, either before or after killing Trotsky. I gave him a typed letter written in French, which he signed, and I told him to put it in his raincoat pocket. The letter painted him as a Trotskyist who had become disillusioned when Trotsky urged him to kill Stalin. Furthermore, Trotsky had told him to break with Sylvia, the woman he loved. I told him not to leave the letter behind; it was to be found on his person if he was seized. The goal was to turn blame for the killing away from the NKVD, but the letter's claims were a joke, and the letter itself was ungrammatical French and full of misspellings. More Moscow Center incompetence – I had nothing to do with it. I told him that if he was captured, he should say nothing: never admit you are Ramón Mercader, and never admit that you work for the NKVD.

"An ice-axe, a knife, and a gun – a fucking arsenal, all to kill one old man. I had loops and pockets sewn into the lining of his raincoat to hold the weapons, and I made sure they weren't visible when he slung the coat over his arm. We rehearsed the execution a hundred times. I would turn my back for a moment, Ramón would slide the ice-axe from its loop and swing it hard past the back of my head. Then he would drop the axe and knife, flip the safety on the pistol, throw the raincoat over his arm, and step out the door. The whole thing took less than ten seconds. I made him rehearse killing me with the knife, but I could see he was committed to the axe. It was less intimate, and he could kill Trotsky without touching him.

"As the day approached, Ramón was a man on fire. He

couldn't bear his mother's pride or Sylvia's lovesick questions about the future of their 'relationship.' She'd been reading Freud, and she asked Ramón psychological questions that made him want to punch her.

"The afternoon of August 17 was hot and sunny. Ramón parked in front of the compound and got out of the car awkwardly, hat on his head, an (unnecessary) raincoat carrying the weapons over his left arm, his briefcase in his right hand. Caridad and I watched from my car, parked a block away and across the street. Our luggage, tickets, and false papers were in the car's trunk.

"Ramón greeted the Mexican police outside the gate; he rang the bell and was admitted. Caridad was tense, as was I. We waited for Ramón to stroll out the gate and head for our car, or for a scream or a shout from inside – anything could happen. Caridad was muttering something under her breath, maybe the Catholic prayers she'd learned as a child from the Sacred Heart nuns. She tried to talk to me, but I shushed her. We needed to watch and concentrate. After only eleven minutes, the gate opened and Ramón stepped out, hat still on his head, raincoat on his arm, valise in his hand. But he didn't turn toward us. Instead, he got into his Buick and drove off.

"Caridad cursed, beat her hands against the dashboard, called Ramón a cowardly pig, spit that she was ashamed to be his mother, that he was a fucking rabbit not a man…. She was as heartless as when she had left her son Pablo in a punishment battalion. I slammed her head against the window and told her to shut her mouth. I drove her to her apartment and then went to meet Ramón at our safe house.

"He seemed dazed. He said that when he entered the compound, he found Trotsky feeding his rabbits in the courtyard, and he told him about the article he had written. The Old Man seemed irritated but invited him into the study. Trotsky held the door open for Ramón, then sat behind his desk. Ramón sat on the desk's edge, to Trotsky's left, which Ramón told me further irritated Trotsky. Trotsky's loaded automatic pistol lay on the desk. Ramón still had his hat on and the raincoat over his arm; he told me that he could tell that Trotsky found his behavior rude.

"Ramón paused. I pressed him, and he said that he'd felt

as though he, not Trotsky, was about to be struck, and that he froze. Trotsky read a few paragraphs of Ramón's article, skimmed the rest, looked up at Ramón and said the article was amateurish. He suggested some changes and told him to come back in a few days and he'd look at the next version. Trotsky stood up, held the door open, and Ramón left, ice-axe still hanging from the loop in his raincoat.

"I was sympathetic. I reminded him that he'd killed men before, that Trotsky was Communism's greatest enemy, and that I knew how dedicated he was to the cause. I told him that I knew he was no coward and that killing any man with whom he'd conversed and eaten was much more difficult than killing in battle. Once he had acted, however, he would be one of the Party's heroes.

"And then I explained my situation. I had failed with Siqueiros's attack, and if I failed again, I would be executed. He was the only one who could save me; Ramón sobbed like a schoolgirl and swore he could do what needed to be done.

"I stayed worried. I kept away from Ramón in case he was being followed by Trotsky's guards, but I put a man in the room next door to his at the Hotel Montejo to tell me how he was doing. Not well, was the report – not eating, not sleeping (the room lights were on all night), and furious arguments with Sylvia.

"Ramón and I agreed he would go back three days later, Tuesday, August 20, at five o'clock in the afternoon. Caridad and I were again in a car a block away. Construction workers swarmed over Trotsky's compound as Ramón pulled up in his Buick. Same drill – a clumsy exit from the car with hat and briefcase, his raincoat over his arm. I watched him through binoculars, and he looked terrible. He hadn't shaved in the three days since his last attempt on Trotsky, and he had dark bags under his eyes. He called up to one of the American guards at the top of the wall, 'Has Sylvia arrived yet?' and the guard shook his head to say she hadn't. The gate opened, and Ramón disappeared inside.

"We waited fourteen minutes – I was timing it. And then an endless scream. I started the car engine but waited. There were shouts, guards running along the tops of the walls. One yelled down to the police by the gate, 'Call an ambulance!' No

Ramón. I pulled away from the curb and slowly drove toward the highway to Veracruz, where the boat for Cuba awaited us.

"The story was in all the newspapers. Ramón struck Trotsky's head, but from the side. Perhaps Trotsky had seen the blow coming and turned. He used the broad end of the axe, and it pierced the skull and entered the brain, but didn't knock Trotsky unconscious. A tough old bastard. Trotsky screamed and struggled, and his guards subdued Ramón. Trotsky lived twenty-four hours, but there was no hope for him. Caridad beamed as she read one newspaper after another.

"Ramón refused to admit his identity, but Sylvia identified him as Jacques Mornard, a Belgian businessman. The police found the letter, which had 'NKVD' written all over it, and pressed him to admit he was a Soviet agent. He did exactly as I'd told him to do: keep your mouth shut, say nothing, never confess no matter what you are promised. I doubt the Mexican police are as effective as we are, but he later told me that they beat him every day for four years. He never talked.

"Caridad and I went from Veracruz to Havana, then after two months to New York with new identity papers. Then to California, where we sailed to Shanghai, then Vladivostok and the Trans-Siberian express to Moscow. Sudoplatov met us at the station. The President of the Soviet Union pinned the Order of Lenin on me and on Caridad, and the highest award, Hero of the Soviet Union, was promised for Ramón upon his release. Caridad was given an apartment in Moscow where she and her youngest son, Luis, would live. She did nothing there but drink coffee, knit, threaten to kill herself, and read detective novels. She drove poor Luis crazy."

I'd known that Leonid had managed Trotsky's murder, and I'd heard bits of the story from Ramón, but Leonid had never told me about it in any detail. Hearing it saddened me. He seemed to have been most concerned with his NKVD career. Perhaps that was human nature. The world changes and we ask only, "What does it mean for me?"

MOSCOW, 1951

Until Leonid's arrest, our family had eight good years. Leonid continued to advance within the NKVD, which occasionally changed its name without changing its purpose or methods. I translated atomic documents for Sudoplatov and Kurchatov, and I interpreted at the wartime conferences for Stalin and our foreign minister Comrade Molotov. After the war's end, I interpreted at the Nuremberg trials, where the top Nazis were in the dock. That was both a satisfying and a humbling experience. Our mission gathered in Berlin, and I saw what the American and British bombers had done to Germany. People were living like rats in the basements of bombed-out buildings. I've changed my outlook since then, but at that time I felt only a fierce joy that the Germans had been repaid at least in part for what they had done to us. We all hated them. In 1942, during the darkest days of the war, our poet Ilya Ehrenburg wrote this:

> The Germans are not human beings. Henceforth the word 'German' means to us the most terrible curse. From now on the word 'German' will trigger your rifle. We shall not speak anymore. We shall not get excited. We shall kill. If you have not killed at least one German a day, you have wasted that day. If you cannot kill your German with a bullet, kill him with your bayonet. If there is calm on your part of the front, if you are waiting for the fighting, kill a German before combThe at. If you leave a German alive, the German will hang a Russian and rape a Russian woman. If you kill one German, kill another – there is nothing more amusing for us than a heap of German corpses. Do not count days; do not count miles. Count only the number of Germans you have killed. Kill the German - this is your grandmother's prayer. Kill another German - this is what your children beseech you to do. Kill the German - this is the cry of your Russian earth. Do not waver. Do not let up. Kill.

No one argued with that. It's true that our soldiers raped thousands of German women and girls. Our men had spent the past two years advancing through our own lands, through cities and villages that the Germans had occupied. They saw what the Germans had done, rape and things worse than rape. Many of them passed through towns and villages where they'd lived, where they'd lost wives, mothers, and children to German murderers. When they crossed into Germany, they wanted revenge. And the German men were nowhere to be found. They were dead, or were fighting somewhere else, or had been taken prisoner. Some of our soldiers made the German women suffer for their nation's crimes. I've never discussed this with anyone outside the Soviet Union, not even Poles who suffered as much as we did at German hands. I don't justify rape – I've spent the last thirty years fighting for women's rights – but I still find it difficult to condemn our soldiers.

But I felt deep hatred for the Nazi leaders who were on trial at Nuremburg. They had the blood of fifty million people on their hands and had left Europe smashed. The trials were a joint Allied affair, so everything had to be agreed with the Americans, British, and French. I was present at many of those negotiations as an interpreter. In my opinion, and in the opinion of all of us in the USSR delegation, our Allies were far too lenient with the Germans. Only the top men and the worst of the killers were executed. If Stalin had had his way, every Nazi party member would have been shot without trial. Eight million of them. It would have been easy; we had the membership lists. At that time, I would have agreed with him. And no one of my generation has forgotten anything.

When the war ended, we all hoped for a little freedom – an end to boots in the hallway in the night and executions without trial. And at first, that seemed to be happening. But in the late 1940s, the Party started an "anti-cosmopolitan" campaign, which didn't touch our family at first. Anti-Semitism was forbidden, but if you didn't want to call a Jew a Jew, you called him a rootless cosmopolitan. Stalin was old and dependent on doctors. He looked around. Jews were everywhere. Jews were doctors, Jews were atomic scientists, Jews had capitalist relatives in the West, and the NKVD was full of Jews.

The very people who were supposed to cure and protect him were Jews. A round of anti-cosmopolitan purges uncovered a Jewish "Doctors' Plot" to kill Stalin and other Soviet leaders, and a Zionist plot within the NKVD leadership to do the same. Leonid was an NKVD major general. And a Jew.

I'd arranged to meet Leonid at the airport when he returned from an assignment in Estonia in 1951. I walked toward his plane, but it taxied into a far corner of the airport, where three black Zhiguli limousines waited. Leonid stepped from the plane, and I called his name. Two men had him by the arms, but he twisted and shouted over his shoulder, "Zoya, go home!"

The NKVD investigators arrived that night and stayed eleven hours. They went through all our books, and they seized my papers from the Tehran conference. One officer thought he'd found a treasure trove in photographs of me with Roosevelt and Churchill. My mother sobbed and didn't seem to understand what was happening. I was still translating secret material for the NKVD, and as soon as the investigative team left our apartment, I went to the Lubyanka and asked Sudoplatov, Leonid's friend, for advice.

He said, "You're at risk just by working here. You need to separate yourself from the NKVD. Go to the personnel department and write a request to be discharged."

I did.

Leonid and I supported seven family members. Suddenly he was in prison (or for all I knew, already shot), and I had no job and no salary. In a matter of days, we moved from well-off to dead broke. Our apartment was a perk of Leonid's position with the NKVD. We weren't evicted, but with Leonid in prison, we needed to pay rent.

Two days after Leonid's arrest, the doorbell rang. When I answered, I understood. I'd seen this film before. An attractive woman smiled and asked if she could come in. My mother was inside, still sobbing, so I stepped into the hall to talk. She said that her name was Muza, that she'd lived with Leonid in Spain, and that she was the mother of two children by him and hadn't heard from him since his trip to Tallinn. I told her that he'd been arrested. Her smile disappeared, and she said that she needed money. Another wife. What could I do? I gave her what I could. I was now responsible for ten family members, not seven.

We needed to know where Leonid was being held. That question couldn't be asked directly, because there was no central prison office open to the public. I knew what I had to do: I took a parcel of food, medicine, clothing, and tobacco to Butyrka prison and stood in line for hours. When my turn finally came, I stepped to the barred window and asked to leave my parcel for Leonid Eitingon. The woman wouldn't even look at me – I was a relative of a suspected enemy of the people. She flipped through a card index, said, "No such prisoner – package refused. Next in line!" There was nothing to do but try a different prison. On my third try, my package was refused at the Central Lubyanka prison but for a different reason – that the prisoner was not allowed to receive parcels, which meant that Leonid was there, that the interrogation was continuing, and that sentence had not yet been pronounced.

Other answers were also possible when one tried to leave a package. In the 1930s, during the worst of the purges, a parcel might be refused because the prisoner had been sentenced to "ten years imprisonment without right of correspondence." What that meant was that he or she had already been executed, although no one was sure of that at the time.

I was desperate for work and money. I was almost offered a job at the NKVD English-language school, but they refused me as a security risk. I, who had translated the American atomic bomb secrets, the most sensitive papers in the Soviet Union, was suddenly a security risk! And Leonid, of whom Stalin had said that not a hair on his head was to be touched, who had eliminated Trotsky, and who cared nothing at all about being a Jew, was suddenly a Zionist traitor. It was then that I lost all hope in Stalin. I had doubts before when people whom I believed to be innocent were arrested. Leonid had told me long ago, "When you chop wood, the chips fly." I'd once thought there was a certain logic to that, but now Leonid and I were chips.

I took a job at the Institute of Foreign Languages. The Dean there didn't care that I had a relative in prison. Many were in that situation. I taught English and gave private language lessons, and we managed to scrape by. Eighteen months later, on March 5, 1953, Stalin died. We were all in shock; he had run everything for almost thirty years. People wept in the streets as if they had lost their father. They cried, "What will become of us, what shall we do now?" Hundreds of thousands mobbed Red Square for his funeral, and hundreds were trampled to death. I expected I'd feel nothing, but I wept too and cursed myself for it.

Two weeks later, there was a knock at our door. Leonid, supported by two NKVD soldiers, held his Party card in front of his chest with both hands so we could see it. One of the soldiers held a cardboard box with his medals and citations, all of which had been returned. With Stalin dead, Lavrenty Beria, the chief of the NKVD, freed Leonid and others that he considered loyal to himself. Leonid was so weak he couldn't stand without help. He had lost 40 kilos in prison, and his bleeding ulcers had almost killed him. But he told me that despite the most rigorous interrogations, he had never confessed to anything. If he had, he would have been sentenced and executed. That was the game, and he knew it. All interrogations were supposed to end with a confession. Until that, interrogations continued.

Unlike me, Leonid wasn't disillusioned. He saw imprisonment and even possible execution as inevitable risks for an NKVD officer. After his release, he went to a hospital, where they fattened him up and returned him to Beria. He was back in the driver's seat, and I'm sure he turned the tables and punished the people who had imprisoned him. And my rehabilitation followed from his. I was offered reinstatement in the NKVD translation department at a higher position than the one I had left. I turned it down; I wanted nothing more to do with politics.

That was a good decision. Less than a year later, Beria was executed. After Stalin's death, there had been no single man in charge – leadership was supposedly shared among Beria, Khrushchev, Molotov, and Malenkov. But the other three were afraid of Beria, who led the NKVD and knew all their secrets. This is what Leonid told me: they ambushed Beria at a Politburo meeting. Khrushchev read a list of accusations, and Marshall Zhukov entered and arrested him. Beria was tried and convicted of treason and terrorism and was sentenced to death. As he was being taken to his execution, he fell to his knees and begged for mercy. They shoved a towel in his mouth and shot him.

I knew how horrible Beria was because I'd watched him up close. He liked to watch Hollywood movies late at night with the skinny young girls that he'd coerced into joining him at his Lubyanka offices, and I was summoned one night to provide simultaneous translation of a film. The girl couldn't have been older than fifteen, and she was trembling. I wanted to shout at her, "Get out of here!" but I didn't. I kept my head turned so I didn't have to look at him groping her and translated the film aloud. It may be the single thing I'm most ashamed of.

But Beria's execution was a disaster for Leonid, who had reported to him directly or indirectly since 1938. He and his boss Sudoplatov were seen as Beria's men, and both were arrested. If I'd accepted the translator's position that I was offered at the NKVD after Leonid was released, I would have been fired again.

Leonid told me about his second time in prison. He was philosophical. "Pavel Sudoplatov and I grew even closer in prison. I was interrogated in Butyrka prison, where my bleeding stomach ulcers flared up, and I was sent to the prison hospital. I was still under interrogation and was forbidden to speak to any other prisoner. But Pavel was in the next bed. He was on a hunger strike, so they'd knocked out his two front teeth and forced a tube down his throat to feed him. We whispered hello, but we didn't have much to say to each other; we'd both been arrested after Beria's execution and thought we were dead men. They might shoot Sudoplatov first, I thought, because he outranked me and was closer to Beria; on the other hand, they might shoot me first because I was a Jew. In the end, they didn't shoot either of us. Khrushchev and his friends wouldn't free us because we knew too much about what they'd done, but they kept us around because we might know things they didn't, or because they might want to reactivate our old agents in the West. Sudoplatov and I spent years together in Vladimir prison along with many other senior NKVD officers, and life there was tolerable."

MOSCOW, 1960

Leonid told me that had it not been for Caridad, Ramón would have served only four years in prison. The NKVD had bribed the Mexican prison officials: there was to be a jailbreak, Ramón and several others were to escape, and a waiting car would take him to freedom. But against all advice, Caridad went to Mexico and made a spectacle of herself. She pleaded histrionically for her son's freedom with everyone – the Mexican president, the head of the Mexican Communist Party, and any newspaper reporter who would talk to her. The publicity was too much, and the escape was called off. Ramón served another sixteen years.

In 1960, the Soviet Union still denied any responsibility for Trotsky's murder, so Czech diplomats met Ramón at the prison gate when he'd finished his term. When he eventually arrived in Moscow, his brother Luis and his mother went with Alexander Shelepin, the head of the NKVD, to the airport to greet Ramón. Luis told me that the first thing Ramón asked was, "Where's Leonid?" That was embarrassing for Shelepin because Leonid had spent the last six years in prison.

When I met Ramón, I could only pity him. I'd seen pictures of him as a young man. He was slim and handsome then, but twenty years of prison life had thickened his body. Our government gave him a good apartment, a car, and a pension, but he had no idea what to do with himself. He had his brother Luis and eventually he had Leonid, but no other friends. He didn't fit with the other Spanish Civil War refugees. They all knew he'd murdered Trotsky, and while none of them were Trotskyists, they wanted nothing to do with a cold-blooded killer. I went to several official receptions as Ramón's guest, and it was the same with Party officials. People knew what he had done; they saw his Hero of the Soviet Union medal on his lapel but turned away when he approached.

When Ramón arrived in Moscow in 1960, he brought his wife, Roquelia, a cabaret dancer. The Party had hired Roquelia for Ramón after his arrest; Mexican prisoners were allowed conjugal visits, and family members could bring food. Roquelia arrived with hot meals every day, she shared his bed on Saturday nights, and by the time of his release it had become a real marriage. But she despised Moscow; she never learned more than a few words of Russian, and she hated the food and the cold. She sat in their apartment all day with the heat cranked up to an unbearable level, she watched television that she couldn't understand, and she made unsatisfactory attempts to cook Mexican meals, complaining about the unavailability of peppers.

Ramón tried to free Leonid from prison. His medal gave him leverage, and he managed to get an appointment with Mikhail Suslov, a Politburo member, without specifying the reason. Suslov welcomed him into his office and thanked him for his service to the Party. But when Ramón began to plead for Leonid's release, Suslov's face froze. He shouted, "That man's fate has already been decided!" and threw Ramón out.

Khrushchev fell from power in 1964, and Leonid was released – but not rehabilitated. He wasn't given a permit to live in Moscow, so he skulked around the city, staying in different flats for a few nights each. He wasn't the same after prison. The way he fell on his food the first few weeks was impossible to watch. And he had illusions that he would be reinstated. He would take me into the street so that we could talk without risk of eavesdropping (no one cared), and he would say, "I know I could reactivate my agent networks. I'm ready to serve." His medals and his Party card were not returned.

Shelepin and I helped him get a Moscow residence permit, a small flat, and a job as a translator. My mother welcomed him home, but she was sick and bedridden. I told him he couldn't live with her. When she died two years later, Leonid returned to another wife, Yevgenia. But it was Ramón that he loved. The two of them would shuffle through the streets together, feeding pigeons in the park or sitting in a café playing dominoes. They smoked paparosi, drank tea or vodka, and repeated the same stories to each other, always in Catalan so that those around them wouldn't understand (no one cared).

Russians will join a queue without knowing what's for sale; whatever it is must be good or people wouldn't be lining up. But those who have the country's highest awards are privileged and can step to the head of any queue. The party had revoked Leonid's Order of Lenin, but Ramón still had his Hero of the Soviet Union medal. If shoes or sausage were for sale, Ramón would say, "It's time to put on my star," pin the metal to his lapel, and he and Leonid would step to the head of the line.

In the mid-1970s, Ramón collapsed with stomach pains. He suspected the security services had poisoned him to get him out of the way – that's how far his trust in the Soviet Union had slipped. He was rushed to the Kremlin clinic, where the doctors diagnosed stomach cancer. He and his wife were finished with Russia and requested permission to move someplace warmer. He wanted to return to Spain, but Franco was still in power, so that was out of the question.

The only Spanish-speaking Communist country was Cuba, and Castro welcomed him. Ramón died there in 1978, and his ashes were brought back to Russia. I sometimes visit his grave in Kuntsevo cemetery, where his tombstone reads "A Hero of the Soviet Union, Ramón Lopez." Even in death, the Soviet Union refused him his true name. After almost forty years, the Party still denied that its agent, Ramón Mercader, had assassinated Trotsky.

EAST BERLIN, 1968

I'd been permitted to travel outside the Soviet Union only once since the Nuremberg trials, for Yuri Gagarin's press tour. With Leonid in prison, I had a "relative imprisoned as an enemy of the people," so I didn't bother to apply for travel abroad. But after his release in 1964, I joined the World Peace Council and the Women's International Democratic Federation – two organizations that the Americans called "Communist fronts." I attended all the meetings, volunteered for the most boring subcommittees, and stood on cold street corners collecting signatures and coins for peace and women's rights. After a year as a dedicated worker, I was elected as a delegate to conferences in Helsinki, Paris, Berlin, Prague, and New York. I knew that I was being watched on those trips, so I didn't drink, and I stuck to the Party line. While I knew what Stalin had done inside the Soviet Union, I saw things differently in foreign affairs. So for the most part, I honestly believed the Party line – that the Americans were aggressors and that the Soviet Union wanted only peace. My attitude changed in 1968.

I was in East Berlin that August for a planning meeting for the 1969 World Peace Council assembly. Before the trip, the chairman of the Soviet delegation had instructed us to avoid conversations about Czechoslovakia. But that wasn't possible. The delegates from other countries talked about nothing else, only "the Prague Spring" and "socialism with a human face." The Soviet press ignored Czechoslovakia, but a young Czech delegate, Petra Dvořák, had brought newspapers and journals from Prague. I read them eagerly. On the morning of August 21, I was dressing to go downstairs for breakfast. I answered a knock on my hotel room door to find Petra in tears.

"Brezhnev sent tanks into Prague," she said. "The secret police are arresting everyone, and they're shipping our leaders to Moscow. I'm afraid they'll shoot them."

I didn't know what to say. This was the sort of thing Americans did with their Monroe Doctrine, I thought, invading Cuba and Mexico.

East Berlin radio was worthless. The announcer said something about "a united action by the socialist nations to prevent an imperialist coup in Czechoslovakia" and then moved to the football scores. But the West Berlin stations gave the Prague invasion continuous coverage. Petra and I took my portable radio down to breakfast, where we found that ten other delegates had also brought radios. An agitated apparatchik from the World Peace Council ordered us to turn them off, but no one paid him any attention. Some of us were angry, some were weeping, but no one felt obedient.

We all ignored the scheduled planning sessions and spent the day in the breakfast room scanning Western radio stations. The Germans among us, who were still dealing with their guilt from the war, didn't say much, but the Poles, Hungarians, Romanians, and Bulgarians were nearly as angry as the Czechs and Slovaks. The day before, we had all been comrades in the service of peace, but no longer. I could feel their fury.

"It's just like 30 years ago," someone snarled at me. "In 1938 the Germans invaded Prague, now it's the Russians." None of us in the Soviet delegation had the nerve to argue.

Petra didn't blame me personally, and she invited me for a walk that afternoon. Without a destination in mind, we walked west toward the Brandenburg gate. Soldiers blocked the approach to the gate, and behind it I could see the wall that separated East Berlin from West Berlin. Machine gun towers loomed every two hundred meters, and soldiers with automatic weapons patrolled the intervals.

Petra pointed toward the wall. "The official name isn't 'the Wall,'" she said, "it's the 'Anti-Fascist Protective Rampart,' built to keep spies, saboteurs, and drug dealers out of the German Democratic Republic. What do you think?"

"I don't know," I said. I was tired of conversations like that.

"Well," she said, "I'm sure that those machine guns are there for a reason. But I don't think anyone's been shot trying to escape from West Berlin to East Berlin."

I didn't reply. She pointed into the distance beyond the Brandenburg Gate.

"That's the Red Army Memorial," she said. "Typical Soviet planning – after the German surrender, the Red Army built it in the British zone by mistake, and now we can't get to it." An enormous statue of a helmeted Red Army soldier in his greatcoat, his rifle slung on his shoulder, stood atop a tall pillar in the memorial.

"You know what the Germans call that statue?" she said. She waited for my answer, which she didn't get. "He's the unknown rapist," she said.

Petra and I were friendly, and she didn't call me a fascist invader, but she was angry and was needling me. "If you don't believe in Communism," I said, "why are you here?"

"I'm here because this is the only game there is. I want a good job, I want to travel, and I need to be a Party member to do that."

We looked at the Wall in silence for a few minutes, and she said, "Your tanks won't end the resistance," she said. "The same thing will happen everywhere, even in your country. Have you read what Andrei Sakharov has written?"

That startled me. I hadn't seen Sakharov or heard from him since our brief time together at the Installation. He was a scientist, I thought, so what did he have to say about politics? I started to tell Petra that I knew Sakharov, but I stopped myself. My time at the Installation involved information that I'd sworn to keep secret.

"I have a copy of his essay," she told me, "When we get back to the hotel, you can read it."

We went to her room, and she fished around in the stack of newspapers and journals she'd showed me earlier. "Here it is!" She handed me an English-language document entitled "Reflections on Progress, Peaceful Coexistence, and Intellectual Freedom." I sat on Petra's bed and tried to read it while Petra chattered on.

"A physicist friend told me Sakharov is a famous scientist who invented your hydrogen bomb," she said. "He told me that the Soviet government gave him all sorts of awards – three times a Hero of Socialist Labor, a Lenin prize, and a Stalin prize back in the days when they still gave Stalin prizes. My friend says they don't know what to do with him."

"Where did you get this essay?" I asked.

"It was published in the West last month, and with our new freedom of the press, someone reprinted it in Czechoslovakia. You can keep if you like. I won't be taking it home through Czech customs after what's happened today. I heard that it's been circulating in *samizdat* in the Soviet Union for two months.

I'm surprised you didn't know about it."

I didn't tell her that I was too cautious to be part of the *samizdat* network, where carbon copies of suppressed works were passed from reader to reader.

"I think I heard something about it," I said.

I left Petra's room as quickly as I could and spent all night with Sakharov's essay. He was fearless. Unlike our World Peace Council, which saw problems only in the West, he had the courage to examine and criticize everything: the threat that nuclear war might destroy the planet, the attempts by the Soviet Union and America to control other nations, the wars in Vietnam and the Middle East, extreme poverty in the poorer nations, the threat from what we now call climate change, ecological pollution, Stalinism, the purges in the 1930s, the execution of millions by the NKVD, the Soviet forced labor camps, and the suppression of intellectual freedom. He was as honest as I remembered him, and he'd had the courage to put his name on the document. I thought of trying to contact him, but I knew that his mail and telephone would be watched. If I were identified as one of his correspondents, I wouldn't be allowed to travel.

I returned to Moscow, and I could smell fear in the streets. Did Prague mean that Stalin was being rehabilitated, that he was returning as if he'd never died? Khrushchev, for all his buffoonery, had let in a little air when he allowed Solzhenitsyn's *A Day in the Life of Ivan Denisovich* to be published. For the first time, people had been able to speak openly about the insanity of the purges and the sprawling network of forced-labor camps. But after Brezhnev and his gang pushed Khrushchev out in 1964, they slammed every window shut and banned all Solzhenitsyn's later works. We were all afraid of what might be next.

4

MOSCOW, 1981

By spring of 1981, Leonid was finished – chronic bleeding stomach ulcers and two heart attacks. It was time for him to die, and he knew it. He couldn't walk across a room without stumbling, and he was incontinent. His face showed his pain and humiliation, although he never complained. Despite everything, I loved him and knew I would miss him. My half-sister Svetlana, faithful as an unloved dog, cared for him in his last days. He was still dictating letters to Central Committee members, still trying to win his rehabilitation. They didn't give him what he wanted, but they did admit him to the Kremlin hospital, where he died. Perhaps a hundred attended his funeral, but I was the only speaker. His comrades from the Cheka shook my hand and apologized for their silence, said they wanted to "avoid complications." Like Leonid, they were dreaming; they were old men, and no one cared what they did or said.

Leonid was bitter at the end. He often talked of Ramón, who had died in Cuba three years earlier.

"Ramón was a believer," he said. "But I'm having second thoughts. After Ramón and I eliminated Trotsky, Beria beamed as the Order of Lenin was pinned on my chest. But in the end, what did it all get me? They shot Beria, and they took away my medals and my Party card. Our country's a shithouse."

He looked around the room and waved his hand. "It's like this apartment, leaking roof, broken plumbing, cracks in the walls, doors and windows that won't open or won't shut. We can build missiles, but we can't build an apartment. It's all shit. If there's an earthquake in Moscow, everything built after the Revolution will collapse. Communism is only propaganda now. No one believes. It's been a long slide: Lenin was a visionary; Stalin was a murderer but an iron-willed genius who brought us through the war; Khrushchev was a clown but at least tried to build socialism; Brezhnev is only a drunk, a corrupt, senile drunk. Who's next? I give us ten years at the outside. Then the next revolution."

❖ ❖ ❖

I thought that Trotsky's murder was the last of Leonid's secrets, but I was wrong. A month after he died, my telephone rang.

"It's Irina."

More than fifty years had passed since the day I'd seen her at the Arbat metro. The call was long-distance from her home in Medvezhyegorsk, far to the northeast. She wasn't talkative on the telephone. I thought she might be worried about the expensive call, but she wouldn't let me call her back. I invited her to stay with me in Moscow, and she arrived the next week.

I don't know what I'd expected. I remembered her as slim and lively, but the woman at my door looked older than the sixty years we both shared. She'd put herself together for the trip to Moscow. She'd ironed her best dress, and she'd had her hair done in a provincial permanent wave. But her body and face showed how hard her life had been. She was shapeless, and she'd trained herself to close her mouth when she spoke to hide the stainless-steel fillings in her remaining teeth. I welcomed her and invited her to sit. She limped as she crossed the room, and her varicose veins showed through her stockings. She was polite but closed; we didn't know how to speak to each other.

"I thank you for your kind invitation, Zoya Vassilyevna," she said as I poured tea. I told her about my daughter and asked about her family. That angered her. Her lips were pressed tight and her hands were clenched, and she said nothing.

"I'm sorry, Irina," I said. "Did I say something that offended you?"

"It's good that you have a family, Zoya. Your father and stepfather destroyed mine."

And then she told me the story I had not known, the story of her trip from Harbin to Moscow, of her father's arrest, of his life in Istanbul apart from his family, of her mother and her time in the camps. I listened carefully and didn't make excuses. I believe that I convinced her that I hadn't known what Leonid and my father had done, and she said she didn't blame me. But we are all marked with the sins of our fathers, and we both knew she couldn't forgive any of us. I filled her teacup and listened, no matter how painful. She turned away as she spoke, and her wrecked face blazed with anger. She had waited fifty years to tell me this.

"After the police arrested us at the train station," she said, "they took my mother away. They sent my grandmother and me to an open dormitory with other women and children. My mother rejoined us after about two weeks, and we were given a single room in a communal apartment in Moscow with four other families. Mama never spoke about her interrogation. What I suspect is that her interrogator became infatuated with her. She was released and given a clerical job at the Lubyanka, something that should have been impossible for the wife of an enemy of the people. I don't know that she granted her interrogator any favors, but if she did, she did it for me and for my grandmother, and I don't blame her for anything.

"Mama went to work each morning, I went to school, and Grandma kept the house. We received a letter from my father each month, and we were allowed to reply. All the letters were censored. We weren't allowed to know where he was living, and when he wrote about something as trivial as the weather, the censors obscured even that in dark ink. That was when you and I saw each other on the street in front of the Arbat metro station. My mother pulled me away from you. She blamed your family for what had been done to us." She stopped and looked me in the eye. I was weeping but kept quiet, afraid to interrupt her story."

After a few moments, she turned away and continued.

"My grandmother had several more strokes and died in 1928. That was hard for Mama and me because we were completely alone in Moscow. Mama's relatives were afraid to have anything to do with us; I heard Mama on the telephone, maybe speaking with her interrogator, pleading for permission for Papa to come to his mother's funeral, but he didn't come. Either the interrogator was unable to help her or he didn't even try. About 1930, our circumstances suddenly changed for the better. We were given a beautiful apartment across the river from the Lubyanka. I eventually realized the reason. My mother had come to the attention of General Genrikh Yagoda, then deputy chief of the NKVD. Mama was forty years old but still beautiful. I'm sure she wasn't Yagoda's only mistress – he had a reputation as a womanizer. Sometimes the telephone would ring, and my mother would send me out of the apartment. I once hid in the janitor's closet and watched Yagoda leave. Again, I don't blame Mama. What choice did she have? And whatever she did, she did for me. I know Mama loved only my father. And as I'll tell you, I too would become 'adaptable' in sexual matters."

Irina spent the day with me, and she spared me nothing. There were many things I might have said, but they all seem trivial.

"I'm sorry," was the best I could do. Neither of us spoke for a few minutes.

"And Viktor?" I asked.

"Oh yes, Viktor. He died in the war. I don't know much about him. He wrote letters, but I never answered. I still receive a small widow's pension, though."

"And you've lived in Medvezhyegorsk ever since?"

"Yes, why not? I was the daughter of two enemies of the state. I'm a convicted wrecker myself, so where was I going to go to better myself? Moscow? Leningrad? I had no internal passport, so I stayed where I was and worked as an office cleaner."

"No friends? No men?"

"I have friends, I'm human. Many women in Medvezhyegorsk have stories like mine. But no men. I was done with men after Viktor."

"And your father? Do you know how and where he died?"

"My father's not dead, he's in America, in New York. He's 92 years old and in good health."

She pulled a photograph from her bag. A tall, spare old man with a full head of hair braced himself on a cane against the wind that whipped his scarf. In the background, strong waves pounded against a beach. I recognized the face of Colonel Boris Anokhin, the kindly doorman in Harbin.

MOSCOW, 1981

I stared at the photo dumbfounded.

I managed to ask the inane question, "Why is he in New York?"

"Because he's been hiding from your stepfather all these years!" She spat that at me, then collected herself and continued in a carefully controlled voice. "If Eitingon had known where my father was, he would have killed him. He knew too much about Istanbul. I've only come to you now because Eitingon is finally dead. My father is in America, and he's afraid to return. I'm stuck in Russia and can't get out. He'll die soon, and we'll never see each other. I need your help."

That's why she had come to me – not to renew our friendship, as I had hoped. "What can I do?"

"You travel to the West. I see you in the newspapers; you're in Paris or somewhere else, at women's conferences, at peace meetings! Go to New York, speak with him, convince him things have changed here and that he can come home. Even I know that Brezhnev is not Stalin, that they're not going to shoot a ninety-year-old or throw him in the camps. But he's lived in hiding for fifty years, and he's afraid. He's survived by taking no risks."

I asked what she'd meant when she said that her father "knew too much about Istanbul," but all she'd say was "That's his story to tell."

She refused to give me his assumed name or his address. If I agreed to help, I should tell her before I went to New York. Once I was there, someone would contact me and arrange a meeting. When she stood to leave, I tried to embrace her. She endured it, but her shoulders were stiff. I had agreed to do things her way, so I began looking for a trip to New York.

The International Women's Conference was to be held in Nairobi in 1985. That was four years off, but planning sessions were already being scheduled. I called Tamara Goeubtsova, the Deputy Minister of Culture, whom I'd known for years. Arranging a trip to New York was easy – she was always inviting me to go on foreign missions. I usually declined because of family obligations, so she was happy to oblige. She put me down to attend a conference planning meeting to be held at the United Nations in November 1981, and I wrote to Irina to tell her the dates. Because she was almost as nervous about the KGB as her father was, I sent her a postcard and made it all gushy and excited: "Guess what, Irina? I'm going to New York!" and so on. I wrote that I'd send her more news (she would know that meant the name of my hotel) before I left. I had worked for the NKVD, but I'd never done anything surreptitious before. I felt a little like Klaus Fuchs, whose atomic bomb reports I'd translated, or like Stirlitz, the NKVD spy in Nazi Germany from our television series *17 Moments of Spring*. Or maybe I felt like Leonid.

I boarded an Aeroflot flight to New York's JFK Airport. I was the delegation head for the meeting, and two other women flew with me. Someone from our diplomatic staff would meet us at the airport, but I'd been asked to watch the other two on the plane. That was the way for Soviet citizens traveling to the West. We always had "minders." Behave badly – get drunk and loud in public, walk into a supermarket and exclaim, "There's nothing like this in Moscow," or get arrested for shoplifting – and you'd be sent back immediately and never allowed out again. Defect, and you'd never see your family again. I'd been on many foreign trips beginning with Tehran in 1943, and I knew that I was watched. I'm sure Anatoly Dobrynin, our long-time ambassador to Washington, had his minders too. Dodging mine would be a problem: how would I slip away and meet Irina's father?

It was a ten-hour flight to New York, and the other two women were too excited to sleep. One, whom I knew slightly, was reliable. She was matronly, about fifty years old, and talked of nothing but her grandchildren. I was surprised that the third woman had been allowed to go. She was in her early thirties and beautiful – wasp-waisted with long brown hair, and she was wearing a skirt that showed too much leg. She talked of nothing but clothing. It was her first time abroad, and I suspect some apparatchik had returned a favor by arranging her trip. With luck, the minders would focus on her and ignore me.

I tipped my seat back and pretended to sleep. I kept circling back to what Irina had said, that Leonid would have killed her father because "he knew too much about Istanbul." I hadn't known that her father had been in Istanbul until she'd told me of his arrest and exile. But I'd been in Istanbul with Leonid, Mama, and Svetlana between ages eleven and thirteen, and perhaps that was the time Irina meant. I'd loved Istanbul. Moscow was a world capitol but was drab, while Istanbul shone with colors. We had sailed there on a steamer from Sebastopol, and I'd never been at sea before. I remember our cabin with its porthole and two sets of bunk beds; Svetlana wanted a top bunk, but Leonid took one and I got the other because I was older. I stood at the rail with Leonid and let the spray hit my face. We crossed the Black Sea and entered the Bosporus at dawn. I remember exotic marble palaces on both sides, Europe to my right and Asia to my left. Leonid told me that the Turks had made their own revolution and had thrown out the caliph shortly after we had gotten rid of the tsar, but that while their revolution was good, it wasn't as good as ours, and that they would eventually need another one. When we docked, porters grabbed our bags and a driver from the Soviet consulate met us. We walked to the car through the fish market – scores of stalls selling every possible fish glistening on beds of green leaves, all the vendors shouting. As we drove to our apartment, I heard my first wailing call to prayer. We passed the Galata Tower, parked, and climbed four flights of stairs to a three-room apartment. Pastel borders were stenciled on the walls and ceilings. Instead of chairs in the parlor, we sat on rugs and floor cushions, and we had a view of the Bosporus from one window and of the Golden Horn from another.

At some point during my airplane reverie, I dozed off. I dreamed of minarets, fountains, sweet rice cakes.... And then I woke, remembering. It was shortly after we'd arrived in Istanbul. I was nine years old and playing with another girl in a public park, a slim, dark-haired girl who had made me think of Irina. A man on a park bench was reading a book. He wore ordinary clothes, not a doorman's uniform, but I was sure it was Irina's father. I'd been taught never to speak to strange men, but Irina's father wasn't a stranger, so I approached him. Before I could speak, he looked up from his book. He started; he recognized me, but he stood and walked off quickly without looking back. That evening I told my mother about the man, and she dismissed me with "People look like other people."

Irina's father had been in Istanbul when my family had been there, when Leonid had been watching Trotsky. What was the connection? What did her stepfather know "too much" about?

The embassy driver dropped us off at our not-very-nice hotel on 8th Avenue in Manhattan, a hotel typical of those used by the Soviet government for low-level delegates or interpreters. I'd been given the hotel's name before I left, so I'd been able to send Irina another chatty postcard with that information. I'd promised to send her a picture of the hotel with an "X" marking my window. An imposing, big-chested woman met us in the hotel's drab lobby. She, I knew, was our minder.

"Welcome, comrades," she said, "I've already taken care of registration. Here are your room keys."

The other two in our delegation – the matron and the beauty queen – were to share a room, but as the delegation head, I had a small room to myself! A good start. The minder instructed us to meet her in her room in an hour. As I showered and changed, I wondered how Irina's father would contact me; I knew he wouldn't trust the telephones.

I went to the minder's room for our briefing, and the room was a duplicate of mine – beige wallpaper, green carpet, chipped plastic-surfaced furniture with cigarette burns, bathroom with paper tape across the toilet bowl to prove it had been cleaned. I had to shuffle sideways to get around the bed. I'd never been in this hotel, but I'd stayed in this same type on other trips to America. The minder sat on the only chair, and the three of us lined up on her bed. The beauty queen, I could see, was disappointed. She had expected something more glamorous. This hotel might have been in Novosibirsk.

The minder went through the rules: back in the room by 11:00, always travel with another Soviet citizen, you may charge meals to your room but no alcohol or snacks, our car will take you to and from the UN each day, we have arranged a guided tour for Sunday, we have tickets for the New York Philharmonic on Tuesday evening, be aware that the FBI is watching you and listening to your phone calls…. I'd heard that speech on every trip. Then the minder passed out the expense envelopes – $18 in cash per day, $126 for the week, which was better than I'd seen on other trips. The matron beamed, and even the beauty queen brightened.

As the other two left, the minder asked me to stay behind.

"Zoya Vassilyevna," she said, "I know of your long service, and I apologize for subjecting you to all this. But for the other two, it is their first time abroad, and I want them to follow your example. I am worried about the young one, the one with the short dresses. Did she behave well on the plane?"

"No problems at all," I assured her. "But I'll let you know if she misbehaves."

Things couldn't be better. I'd been promoted to assistant minder.

I went to the lobby and bought a *New York Times* to brush up on my English. I was jet-lagged of course, and I thought it best to eat a light meal, so I took the newspaper to the coffee shop. I sat at the counter and ordered an omelet, and an old man took a seat one down from me. His suit was rumpled, which didn't fit the *Wall Street Journal* in his hand. He ordered only coffee and drank it quickly. When he asked for the check, his accent confirmed his origins – South Volga. He glanced at me meaningfully and left his carefully folded newspaper on the counter. Spy games, I thought. Irina's father had sent a friend as a messenger. I took the *Journal* and the *Times* back to my room.

I found a note inside his newspaper. In shaky Cyrillic script, it gave the address of a Ukrainian restaurant in Brighton Beach; below it, "Every day from 2:00 until 8:00." I had a subway map. The B subway train ran directly from my hotel to Brighton Beach, so that would be simple. But being absent from the conference and the minder would be harder. Perhaps I could have a headache on the day of our city tour or on the night at the symphony, but I had no experience with secret activity. Leonid would have found this easy, so I pretended to be Leonid.

Luck was with me. On the third night, the beauty queen disappeared with a man she had met in the hotel bar. The frantic minder banged on my door at midnight. She knew that if she lost one of her charges, she would find herself leading Intourist groups in Irkutsk. I calmed her, but when the car arrived to take us to the UN the next morning, the beauty queen was still missing. The minder had put off reporting her, which would make things all the worse if the woman had defected. When we returned to the hotel from the UN that afternoon, I took the minder aside.

"Listen," I said, "I'll go to the bars and nightclubs. I'll ask if they've seen her or if they know the man. I speak American English, so people won't know I'm Russian. You stay here and wait for her. But please realize that I will need to bend some rules. I'll look until I find her, even if it takes all night."

She wept in gratitude. "Thank you, Zoya Vassilyevna. Yes, you're too good, thank you so much."

I immediately left for the B train to Brighton Beach; the note had promised only that he would be there until eight o'clock.

I'll never understand why rich New York has the dirtiest, ugliest subway in the world, while poor Moscow's metro is like a chain of cathedrals. I stood the entire trip to Brighton Beach. I wasn't about to sit on *that* bench. Although as nervous as I was, it was easier to stand in any case.

I found the restaurant easily enough, but Irina's father was not to be seen. I took a table and ordered borscht and kvass, although it seemed silly to be dining on that in New York. After a few minutes, he entered and made his way toward me leaning on a cane. When he started to seat himself at the next table, I lost patience with his spy nonsense.

"Colonel Anokhin," I said, "I have come to meet you at some personal risk. I was sent by Irina. You are 92 years old, and you have but one hope of seeing her again, which is to trust me. Please sit at my table."

Addressing him as "Colonel Anokhin" changed something in him; I doubt he'd heard his real name, much less his rank, in years. His head was suddenly erect and his bearing military. He leaned his cane against my table and sat, then ordered borscht when the waitress came. We ate awkwardly without saying much.

"Is it possible that we could go to your apartment and talk more privately?" I asked.

"I don't live nearby," he said. "It's two subway trains connected by a bus."

He had organized our meeting in a Russian neighborhood but not in *his* Russian neighborhood. More spy games.

"I have money," I said. "We'll take a taxi."

I doubt he had ever splurged on a New York taxi. He started to argue, but I silenced him with "Remember how important this is." He opened his worn coin purse and paid our restaurant checks, and I didn't argue. When he tried to give the Sikh taxi driver his address, I stepped in to interpret. After forty years, he still spoke almost no English. The taxi ride was long, and he kept his eyes on the meter the entire trip, flinching with every tick. The fare was $12.40, which I imagined was what he spent on food for a week. We stopped in front of a two-domed Russian Orthodox Church in a run-down commercial neighborhood. The few people on the street were Black. I paid the driver and helped him out of the cab, and he led me to the back of the church and unlocked a door beneath an iron staircase.

"Here," he said, "this is where I live."

It was spare and clean: a concrete floor with a rug, a single bed, a bible on an end table by the bed, a kitchen table with two chairs, a wardrobe, and a bookcase covered with framed photographs – Irina must have sent him those through his friend.

"If you need the washroom, it's that way," he said and pointed toward a door that led to the boiler room.

He opened the radiator valve to warm the room, then filled the teakettle and put it on the electric hotplate. I kept my coat and took a seat at the table. When he had arranged tea, cups, sugar, rye bread, and pickles to his satisfaction, he took the seat across from me.

NEW YORK, 1981

We would have gotten nowhere if I'd waited for him to speak, so I began.

"Do you remember me? I was Irina's friend."

"I remember. In Harbin." He almost smiled.

"You know my family too. My father, my stepfather."

"Yes, I remember them well." The almost-smile disappeared.

"On the airplane flying here, I remembered seeing you in the park in Istanbul. You wouldn't speak to me."

"Yes. Your stepfather had me in his power then, and he wouldn't have wanted us to speak."

"Colonel Anokhin, I am here to do what Irina has asked of me: to help you return to Russia so you can spend your last years with her. I have the money to pay for your ticket, and I'm sure I can arrange the paperwork with the Soviet embassy. Irina has told me how my stepfather tricked you when you applied for a visa in Harbin fifty years ago. It won't be like that. Stalin has been dead almost thirty years, and no one is looking for you. You are an old man moving home to live with his daughter. It happens every day at the embassy. It's routine for them. Irina said you were afraid of my stepfather because of 'something that happened' in Istanbul, but she wouldn't tell me more than that. She said it was your story to tell, not hers. My stepfather, Leonid Eitingon, died last year, so he is no danger to you. I am trying to understand my family, and if you wish to tell me anything, I would be grateful. But you owe me nothing. I will do what I can for you and for Irina, whether you choose to speak of your past or you wish to keep silent."

He struggled not to weep – how lonely he must have been for the past fifty years. His voice broke as he spoke, slowly at first and then faster. He'd kept his story so long, and it burst out in a rush. I had to take his hand when I needed to interrupt with questions. He told me about Leonid tricking him into returning to Russia from Harbin, about the long train trip and his mother's illness, about his arrest, about his interrogation by my father, about his life as an NKVD informant in Istanbul.

"I wanted to be done with the Bolsheviks," he said. "I had no friends in Istanbul. Other Whites, men I'd served with in the hardest times, crossed the street to avoid me. They knew I wasn't to be trusted. I must be a spy, they knew, because I lived in Istanbul while my wife and daughter lived freely in Moscow. And they were right! My controller didn't bother infiltrating me into White organizations; he knew I would be worth nothing there. No, he made me into a pimp. I supplied hotel guests with prostitutes, women and men. I arranged for cameras and tape recorders, so he made me a blackmailer. I reported everything I heard, drunken conversations in the street or in the lobby, on what the maids told me about people in the wrong bedrooms. And I told my controller everything. I knew he staged some events to test me. I was an informer. I could have run, or I could have shot myself, but then Anna and Irina would have suffered. When my mother died, the Reds wouldn't let me bury her, and still I worked for them."

I shouldn't have asked then, but I did.

"What did my stepfather, Leonid Eitingon, have to do with you in Istanbul?"

I'd moved too quickly – Colonel Anokhin froze, mumbled something I didn't understand. I recovered as best I could.

"Please don't upset yourself, please tell me only what you want to tell. If it's not too much, perhaps you could tell me how you came to be living in a church basement in New York."

He relaxed; that question wasn't as threatening.

"I had to leave Istanbul immediately after the fire."

I wanted to ask "What fire? The fire in Trotsky's house on Prinkipo island?" But I didn't interrupt.

"I had only the clothes I was wearing and a few Turkish lire. I couldn't go to the Prinkipo ferry dock. Eitingon would be there with his pistol. Besides, I knew better than to go back to the hotel. The fishermen had small piers all around the island, and I paid a man with a boat who was going to Eskihisar, in the opposite direction, away from Istanbul. I didn't know Eskihisar, but I didn't think Eitingon would look there immediately.

"Eskihisar was a small port with a coaling station, and a few ships were in the harbor. I was lucky. A Bulgarian freighter was refueling, and I approached the captain. I had nothing to lose. Bulgarian and Russian are similar languages, and he spoke a little Russian. I made myself understood. I had no seaman's papers, but he didn't care. He needed a cook, and I worked my passage to Varna, a Bulgarian port on the Black Sea. No pay, but he sailed straight up the Bosporus without stopping in Istanbul. Once I was in Bulgaria, I felt a little safer. I shoveled coal for a year, saved enough to buy forged seaman's papers, signed on with a long-distance Italian freighter and jumped ship in New York. It was two years after the Istanbul fire. But I knew Eitingon still wanted me dead. I was the one who knew how he had failed in his mission in Istanbul.

"I was in America with no English, no papers, and no money. I couldn't go to the White Russian community. Every third man there would be an informer, just as I had been in Istanbul. Things were bad in America then. It was 1933, their Depression, and men were sleeping in parks and eating in soup kitchens. That's what I did too. I was in a Bowery soup line when I heard two men talking in Russian about a church being built in Brooklyn. If you worked there, they said, the priest would feed you. I asked for directions. That was how I came to this church, Holy Trinity.

"I walked here that night, across the bridge from the Bowery. It was warm, and I wrapped myself in a tarp that I found on the building site. I slept on the ground and woke at dawn, when I climbed into the half-excavated pit, picked up a shovel, and began to dig before anyone arrived. When the foreman showed up, my sweat showed that I had already been at work for an hour. They fed us well at noon, good Russian food provided by a rich believer. I worked the entire day and was the last to stop. The foreman gave me some leftover bread and fifty cents. He didn't pay the others.

"Same thing the next day and the day after. I worked dawn to sunset and slept on the building site. Do you remember Prince Myshkin in *The Idiot*? The simple believer, the holy fool? That's what I became. Eitingon was looking for an emigre colonel, not a fool. I'd stare into the bottom of the pit for five minutes without speaking, and I'd sing hymns while I worked. On the fourth day, the priest approached me. He knew that I had become his responsibility. He asked a rich believer to give me a bed in his garage and a little money. When the church was consecrated in 1935, I became its janitor and moved to this room. I've been here through four priests. Almost all the Russians have moved away, but they return from the suburbs on Sundays. The church continues.

"I started by pretending to be a believer, but pretending has made me one. I miss Irina, but I have a good life here. I have the church, my bible, and the people are kind to me. The priest pays me and lets me keep this room, even though I can't work the way I did. I still sweep the church, but he won't let me shovel snow or climb a ladder to clean the gutters. He hires a colored man for the heavy work."

Talking had relaxed him, so I gently turned him to the past. "Do you remember the day Trotsky arrived in Istanbul?"

"Remember? I was there! And so were half the Russians in Istanbul. It was cold, February 1929, I think, and we watched his ship steam in. The Ilyich, named for evil Lenin. Trotsky had led the Red Army in the Civil War, and we hated him for all we had suffered. Nothing but curses from the crowd around me. 'Shoot the swine!', 'Hang him!', and much worse. The Turkish police pushed us back at bayonet point. Trotsky's family and Stalin's secret policemen were the only passengers on the ship. Trotsky walked down the gangway and never turned his head. He and his wife disembarked, and the police rushed them to a car and drove them to the Soviet consulate, only a few blocks from the Pera, the hotel where I worked. He lived in the consulate for a month. I saw his wife and son on the street several times, but never him. Someone would have shot him – either a White or a Red pretending to be a White. Almost every Russian wanted him dead.

"After a month, he moved out of the consulate, first to a hotel, then to an apartment, then to a big house on Prinkipo, an island in the Sea of Marmara. You remember it. You went there for picnics with your family."

That startled me. "Yes, I remember," I said, "but how did you know about the picnics?"

"I was there too. I had met my controller in a park each week; then Eitingon showed up as my new controller. I remembered him, of course. Four years earlier, he had promised me that if I returned to Russia from Harbin, all would be forgiven. I started to speak about that, and he cut me off. 'We've never met.' Stared straight at me and said that, daring me to say otherwise. And after he became my controller, everything changed. No more blackmail with whores in the hotel. All he cared about was Trotsky. He sent me to Prinkipo on my days off from the hotel to learn what I could. He would sprawl on a blanket with you and the rest of your family, and I'd watch who came and went from Trotsky's house. I saw you picnicking with your family, and I remembered how you had played with Irina."

Colonel Anokhin's voice was stronger and more confident.

"Things went on that way for the summer and autumn of 1930," he said. "Eitingon picnicked on the grass with you and your family, while I did what he ordered. I watched the comings and goings at Trotsky's house and patrolled the island. I wasn't allowed to take notes. I had to memorize everything and write it down that night, then report to him. By the end of autumn, I could have walked the entire island blindfolded. Eitingon wanted to know everything – every house, street, gully, and cove. We knew the schedules and habits of Trotsky's bodyguards, of the iceman, of the grocery boy; I watched his wife and son come and go on the ferry to Istanbul, watched his neighbors. Nothing was too trivial. Europeans – mostly French and German – visited Trotsky and sometimes stayed a few days, but he never left the island. His only recreation was going out with an old Turkish fisherman on his boat. We spent several weeks investigating that man and his boat. I think that Eitingon considered drowning Trotsky in a boating accident, but he must have decided against it as too risky. We were not the only ones watching Trotsky. Turkish uniformed police, Turkish secret police, two German diplomats, and a few we never did identify swarmed over the island. Eitingon trained me to use a camera with a telescopic lens, and I planted my tripod in some bushes a few hundred yards away and took photos of the house from every angle. We spent less time on the island during winter, when neither vegetation nor visitors provided cover.

"In February 1931, Eitingon and I sat on the park bench by the mosque, and he made me what he called an offer, although I didn't have a choice.

"'I have a mission for you,' he said. 'Do this and succeed, and you'll be permitted to rejoin your wife and daughter in Moscow, or if you wish, they will be permitted to leave the Soviet Union and join you wherever you like. What I'm offering will be dangerous. There is a good chance you will die. If you die, I promise I'll protect your wife and daughter. You may have another reason to accept. You will avenge your White comrades. You will kill Trotsky.'

"Now I wasn't stupid enough to believe any of that. I knew that if I killed Trotsky, Eitingon wouldn't permit me to live. But if I refused, he'd kill me anyway, and there would be no protection for Anna and Irina. Without much hope, I pretended enthusiasm, and he laid out his plan.

"'We'll do it in the early hours of a Sunday,' he said. 'The guards change their shift at midnight, and the guard who takes over at the back of the house drinks on Saturday night. By three o'clock, he'll likely be asleep. Even if he's awake, I'll have no trouble eliminating him. We'll arrive on a small boat, just the two of us. You'll have a can of gasoline, a concussion grenade, and a pistol. I'll eliminate the guard and provide cover if you need it. You'll enter Trotsky's office quietly, spread the gasoline over the desk and carpets and into the file cabinets. Trotsky's bedroom is next door. If he hears you and comes out, you shoot him and put a final bullet through his brain. If he doesn't come out, you toss the grenade into his bedroom and immediately fire several rounds into his bed. Don't worry about his wife – just shoot. Again, put a final round in his skull. Return to the office, throw a match to the gasoline, and exit the way you came in. Then we run for it. Down the street a few hundred yards to the sea, where a different boat, a fast motor launch, will be waiting to take us to a freighter a few miles offshore. Within two weeks, you'll be with your wife and daughter.'"

"I knew he was lying, but what could I do? The plan was simple, but we rehearsed it for weeks.

"'You'll wear your own clothes, and you'll carry no identification' he told me. 'If you die, nothing can be traced to me. Dark sweater, dark trousers. Do you have a pistol? No? You used a Mauser in the war, right? You'll use that.'

"He drove me to a safe house in the country, about twenty kilometers from Istanbul on the Asian side of the Bosporus. I spent hours at target practice with the Mauser, then practiced endless simulations of entering the house, of spreading the gasoline around Trotsky's office, of shooting Trotsky when he entered the room, of shooting him in his bed if he did not. The Mauser had a 10-shot magazine, and Eitingon trained me to put eight shots into Trotsky's body and one bullet in his head, to keep one for an emergency.

"It wasn't hard to figure out Eitingon's real plan. My value to him was not as an assassin; there were many men, including Eitingon himself, who would have been much better choices for that. I was to be a dead assassin, shot by Trotsky or by Leonid or burned in the fire. It wouldn't take the Turkish police long to identify Boris Anokhin, a White Russian colonel and a doorman at the Pera Palace. Even if my body were burned beyond recognition, identification would be easy when I didn't show up for work the next morning. I doubted that the pistol Eitingon would hand me would even be loaded. Eitingon or one of his thugs would kill me as soon as I entered the house or more likely after I had spread the gasoline, would shoot Trotsky – and his wife and any guards who appeared on the scene– and would light the gasoline on the way out, leaving my carcass for the Turkish police.

"It all made sense. I could almost see the headline," he said.

TROTSKY KILLED, HOUSE BURNED!

EXILED RED ARMY COMMISSAR
ASSASSINATED ON TURKISH ISLAND
BY VENGEFUL WHITE RUSSIAN OFFICER

KILLER FOUND DEAD AT SCENE

NEW YORK, 1980

"What choice did I have?" Anokhin said. "I couldn't run for it, because Eitingon would make Anna and Irina pay. I decided that I would kill Eitingon instead of Trotsky on that night, and that I would need a loaded pistol. I was sure that the pistol that Eitingon would hand me would be unloaded, fired but not cleaned, as evidence that the gun had been used to kill Trotsky. I needed a loaded Mauser magazine that I could swap with the empty one between the time I left Eitingon and the time I entered Trotsky's house. Istanbul was awash with guns after the war, and I would have no problem buying magazines and ammunition for a Mauser. "Eitingon decided we would kill Trotsky the night of February 28 if the sky was overcast, which turned out to be the case. We left the Asian mainland about midnight in a small, sleek motorboat with an almost noiseless electric engine, just the two of us. Eitingon was sure of himself, and my guess is that he didn't want one of his thugs as a witness if things went wrong. He gave me a quick pat-down before he handed me a jerrycan of gasoline, but he held on to my Mauser, saying that he would give it to me when we landed. Eitingon wasn't stupid, and I expected that he would have anticipated my plan and would search me for ammunition. I worried about where to hide the bullets. Perhaps inside my stocking, or taped to the small of my back or even more private places. But I knew that Eitingon would find it wherever I hid it. Besides, I needed the ammunition to be somewhere I could get at it quickly and unobtrusively; he would be right behind me and watching me. I remembered the famous American writer Poe's story, The Purloined Letter. Always best to hide something in plain sight. I had applied tape to the magazines and stuck them to the back of my hand. I transferred then to the jerrycan when he handed it to me.

"Trotsky had a guard on the house roof, but his flashlight was too dim to reach as far as the water; the night was completely dark, with no moon visible and no lights in the house windows. The wind was strong and it masked what little noise our boat made. Eitingon cut the engine, and we glided under tree branches into a cove near the house. With his own Mauser drawn and pointed at me, he handed me my Mauser.

With my back to him, I sniffed the barrel of my gun. Just as I'd suspected, it had been fired and left uncleaned. He didn't search me for ammunition, and I soon found out why: he didn't think he needed to. I'd trained for hours shooting an old C96 Mauser, like the one I'd used in the war. That fired a 7.65 mm round, but he'd handed me a newer version of the gun, a 'Red 9' Mauser, which fired a 9-mm round. Even in the dark, I felt a large number '9' carved into the gun's wooden butt. Any 7.65 ammunition I'd brought was worthless."

For the first time since we'd met, Anokhin broke into a real smile. A triumphant smile.

"But I had him. I'd brought both ammunition types, two magazines, each loaded with 10 bullets, now both taped to the jerrycan.

"Eitingon gestured for me to leave the boat and climb to the house. He was only a few yards behind me, a pistol in one hand and a knife in the other, ready to silently kill the guard. I pretended to stumble to the ground. As I stood, I peeled the 9-mm magazine from the jerrycan and, as quietly as I could, I swapped it for the empty magazine that was in the gun. It was awkward to do so – I could have used a third hand – but I managed it. I then had a loaded pistol that Eitingon didn't know about. I thought of spinning and firing at him, but he had me in his sight, while I wasn't quite sure where he was. Besides, a pistol at 25 yards is inaccurate, and I was sure he was a better shot than I was. I continued toward the house. "Trotsky's household security was hopeless. No guard at the back, only the man on the roof who couldn't see the rear of the house. When the guard swung his flashlight away, I ran for the door. Eitingon was in the shrubbery somewhere behind me. He had gotten a key from one of his spies in Trotsky's household, and I opened the door and slipped inside. I left the door ajar so that I could exit quickly. Trotsky's study was through the door straight ahead, and the bedroom that he shared with his wife was just beyond that. I crouched and listened at the study door – nothing. I entered the study.

"I had a plan of sorts but it didn't amount to much. I wouldn't spread the gasoline and I wouldn't kill Trotsky. I'd just crouch in the study and wait. Eitingon couldn't just leave me there. I'd be captured, and I'd tell the police who had sent me. He would have to come after me. When he came through the door, I'd shoot him, run for the boat, and do my best to disappear. I crouched beside a file cabinet, aimed my gun at the door, and waited for Eitingon.

"Then the unexpected: the door to Trotsky's bedroom opened, and Trotsky appeared in his dressing gown. I recognized him at once – goatee, tortoise-shell eyeglasses, thick gray hair. He hadn't heard me, and he didn't notice me. When he switched on the light and turned toward his desk, he was a perfect target for a shot through the window.

"I shouted without thinking, 'Trotsky – get down!' He fell to the floor just as Eitingon fired three rounds through the window. Trotsky's cheek was pressed into the carpet. He twisted toward me and sputtered, 'Who are you?'

"But I had no time for him. Eitingon was at the door, scanning the room for me and for Trotsky. I fired twice, missing him, as well. He fired at me and backpedaled to the lawn. Trotsky shouted after him, 'Eitingon!' Then the grenade came through the window.

"Eitingon threw an incendiary grenade, one meant to start fires, not a fragmentation grenade meant to kill. He intended to ignite the gasoline that I was supposed to have spread. The grenade did start a fire, but nothing as intense as the one he expected. Trotsky's guards would soon arrive, so I ran for the door and then in the opposite direction Eitingon had taken. No more shots from Eitingon, he must have run for the boat. I've told you the rest already – the fisherman who took me to Eskihisar, the Bulgarian freighter, coming to New York, this church where we sit now.

"For the first few months, I looked over my shoulder. I expected Eitingon would have the whole NKVD after me, and that he would make Anna and Irina pay. I grieved for them, but I had no way to know their situation. But no one seemed to be after me. When I saw a newspaper account of the fire at Trotsky's house, it made no mention of arson or gunfire. Both the Turkish government and Trotsky, for their own reasons, must have wanted the fire to be accidental.

"I realized that if Eitingon wanted to kill me, he would need to do so himself. He'd taken a risk by involving me, and he couldn't let his bosses know that there was an unknown man somewhere in the world who knew about the failed mission. That also meant that Anna and Irina were likely safe too, at least for a time. He couldn't retaliate against them without raising questions about me. Eitingon and I spent almost fifty years in an uneasy truce. He would kill me personally if he could find me, but he couldn't involve the NKVD. And so long as I said nothing about that night, he would leave my wife and daughter untouched. It was Yezhov, not Eitingon, who sent them to the camps six years later.

"But one thing always puzzled me: Trotsky yelled 'Eitingon!' when he saw his face at the door. They must have known each other."

"They did," I said. "That was a secret my stepfather had to keep at all costs. He had been Trotsky's aide in the Civil War. Stalin would have had him killed for that."

I'd sworn to Leonid that I wouldn't tell his secret, but Colonel Anokhin deserved the truth.

NEW YORK, 1981

I left Colonel Anokhin's room the way I'd entered, through the janitor's door at the back. It was three o'clock in the morning, and the streets were deserted. I had no idea where I was, but I remembered that the taxi that had brought me had passed some lighted stores, and I wrapped my scarf tight across my mouth and pushed into a frigid wind in that direction. I found an all-night coffee shop and warmed myself there for a few minutes.

I asked the man at the counter where I might find a taxi, and he snorted, "No taxis around here even in the daytime. The A train's three blocks that way."

I took the subway – very lonely at that hour – and returned to my Manhattan hotel about five o'clock. I knocked on the minder's door.

She called, "A moment" in her heavily accented English. I'd woken her. She cracked the door open peeking over the chain but opened wide when she saw me. I was exhilarated after my night with Col. Anokhin, but I tried to appear suitably exhausted.

"I've been to every bar and nightclub," I told her, "but I haven't found her. It took forever. The bars don't close until four o'clock in the morning."

"Oh, thank you for all you've done for me, Zoya Vassilyevna. I'll never be able to repay your kindness. That tramp showed up a few hours ago; I called the embassy, and they've sent a woman who will guard her and put her on the next Aeroflot flight home. She'll never work professionally again, and she'll certainly never travel abroad. She'll be an example to the others."

I told the minder that I would need to catch a few hours of sleep and would miss the morning session, but that I'd join the conference in the afternoon. No argument from her; she said she would tell everyone I was sick.

I showered and slept for two hours, then called a friend at the Soviet embassy. I was casual; I told her that I had a friend who wanted to bring her ninety-year-old expatriate father home so that he could die in his native Russia.

"Bring him around," she said. "If he's ninety, we shouldn't

waste time."

I took a cab to Brooklyn, where I found Irina's father awake and sweeping the church. It took some convincing, but he finally agreed to go with me to the embassy. Everything went smoothly. My friend promised that she would expedite the application and would pay for the ticket from a fund the embassy kept to repatriate indigent citizens. I gave her the telephone number of the priest at the Brooklyn church, and she promised that she would contact him with the details. Irina's father would be in Moscow within two weeks. I sent him back to his Brooklyn church in a pre-paid taxi and went to the conference in Manhattan, where I dozed through the afternoon sessions.

I waited until I was back in Moscow to call Irina. I told her what I'd done, and she thanked me, but not warmly. When her father returned to the Soviet Union, she didn't invite me to join her in meeting him at the airport, she didn't answer my letters, and she cut my telephone calls short.

MOSCOW, 1991

Just a few weeks before the Soviet Union's collapse, Pavel Sudoplatov asked me to help him with his memoirs. He was my chief when I translated the American atomic bomb secrets, so I assumed he had questions about that. I took the metro to the address he gave me, a large apartment on Gorky Street – six spacious rooms in a building constructed before the Revolution. Like Leonid, Sudoplatov was imprisoned when Beria fell and wasn't rehabilitated when he was released after Khrushchev's ouster. He should have been as impoverished as Leonid had been, but things were changing rapidly in Russia in 1991. I asked myself, who was paying for his apartment?

A maid escorted me to Sudoplatov's study, where he and a male secretary were at work. Sudoplatov stood to welcome me and waved me to a chair in front of his antique French desk, all rococo curves and gilt paint. The maid served us tea, and Sudoplatov got to the point: he wanted confirmation that I had translated atomic secrets provided by Robert Oppenheimer, the head of the American atomic bomb design team during their Manhattan Project. Perhaps he thought that would increase sales of his memoirs.

I told him that I'd translated communications from Klaus Fuchs, Ted Hall, and others, but that I hadn't seen any communications from Oppenheimer, and that unless there was another translator of whom I was unaware, I doubted that any existed. He was disappointed, and for a moment I thought he would try to browbeat me into supporting his story, but he didn't.

We then made small talk for a while – or rather he spoke, and I listened, which was how almost all conversations with Sudoplatov went. He reminisced about Leonid, about their long service in the NKVD together, about all the difficult and dangerous missions they'd handled. Although I didn't say so, the way I remembered things was that Leonid did the dangerous work while Sudoplatov was in Moscow toadying up to Yagoda, Yezhov, Beria, or whoever was then on top of the NKVD. (Although considering the Purges, toadying in Moscow was perhaps more dangerous than fighting enemies abroad). Sudoplatov bragged about how he and Leonid had fought the fascists, anarchists, and Trotskyists in Spain; how they had eliminated Trotsky in Mexico; how they had supported our partisans behind the German lines; and how they had unjustly spent years together in prison. He didn't tell me what Leonid had told me – that Sudoplatov had doctored Leonid's file to remove all references to Trotsky, thereby saving Leonid's career and his life. If Sudoplatov didn't want to talk about that, I didn't either. But I did want to know more about what Leonid had done in Istanbul. And if Sudoplatov was writing his memoirs, he must no longer feel bound by the NKVD code of silence. I asked him what he knew about Leonid's mission to Istanbul between 1929 and 1931.

"I was there when the decision was made to send him," he said. "I wasn't Leonid's boss then. I was deputy to Menzhinsky, the head of the NKVD – then called the OGPU. He told me that Leonid was on his way for a meeting with him, and he explained things. We'd largely eliminated Trotsky's followers within the Soviet Union, but Trotsky was still a problem. He was in Istanbul, writing books and letters to foreign Communists, and he was publishing his *Bulletin of the Opposition*. He had somehow been allowed to take his archives with him, and he was quoting from Politburo and Central Committee minutes to smear Stalin. He was under the protection of Turkey's President Ataturk, who would react badly at any action we took against him on Turkish soil. We had our agents among Trotsky's servants, guards, and secretaries. We knew everything he was doing and read all his incoming and outgoing correspondence, but knowing was not enough. Trotsky was splitting the party, was calling Stalin a traitor and a gangster. He had to be stopped, but in some way that could not be traced to us.

"When Leonid arrived, the three of us spent several hours discussing Trotsky. I took notes as Menzhinsky gave Leonid these instructions:

"First and most important, nothing could be done that could be traced to the Soviet Union.

"Second, Trotsky's archives should be destroyed in a way that appeared accidental." Leonid suggested a fire, because the house on Prinkipo was old and wooden. A cooking fire, perhaps, or a log rolling from a fireplace in the middle of the

night. Menzhinsky just nodded; he would leave the details to
Leonid.

"Third, Trotsky should be eliminated, but only if his death
could, without any question, be blamed on natural causes or
accident." Leonid and Menzhinsky spent several hours discussing this. Their first idea was that Trotsky could die in the
same fire that burned his archive, but that seemed uncertain.
His family, bodyguards, and household staff would all try to
save him. Perhaps, Leonid suggested, Trotsky could be poisoned in a way that would seem to be heart failure. He was
known to have a bad heart. Too risky, Menzhinsky said. If
Trotsky were to suddenly die without explanation, the coro-
ner or Trotsky's followers would perform postmortem tests.
And even if a specific poison were not detected, the NKVD
would be suspected. There could be no ambiguity around his
death. Then Leonid suggested assassinating him but putting
the blame elsewhere. After all, we weren't the only ones who
would rejoice in his death; thousands of White exiles lived in
Istanbul and hated him.

"'I could organize it,' Leonid said. 'Trotsky dies and a dead
White is found with the murder weapon – no way to link us
to the death. Maybe the same White sets the fire that burns
Trotsky's archive.'

"Menzhinsky liked Leonid's plan, and he telephoned
Stalin, who wanted to hear more. Menzhinsky and Leonid left
for Stalin's Kremlin office, and I was not invited. But Leonid
later told me what happened. It was his second meeting with
Stalin, he said, although he doubted Stalin remembered the
first, at Tsaritsyn more than ten years earlier during the Civil
War. I told Leonid he was wrong about that, that Stalin never
forgot anything or anyone. The three of them sat at a table
in a room next to Stalin's office, and Menzhinsky presented
Leonid's plan, while Stalin listened attentively. At the end,
Stalin turned to Leonid and fixed him with the same unblinking
yellow stare as in their first meeting. As before, Leonid didn't
turn away.

"Stalin told him, 'You will of course adjust the details of
your plan to the local situation. The Party has confidence in
you and will remember what you achieve.'

"Which could of course be taken two ways. But Leonid

was always ready for a tough assignment. Some assignments worked well, some did not. That one did not, but Leonid survived it."

"What didn't go well?" I asked.

"Leonid managed the fire, but he set it himself, and it burned only a portion of the archive; Trotsky's son pulled most of the papers and files out onto the lawn. I think Leonid was wise to be cautious and to handle things himself. He told me that he decided that involving anyone else, especially a White exile, was too risky. What if the man talked to his friends or his family? The Turkish police also had informers in the White ranks, and both Menzhinsky and Stalin had impressed upon him that his absolute priority was that nothing he did could be traced to us. So, he burned the house on his own and waited for a better opportunity to kill Trotsky, which came nine years later in Mexico. We ordered Leonid back to Moscow immediately after the fire. You might remember that you left Istanbul in a hurry. Leonid was worried that he'd be blamed for his failure, but I convinced Menzhinsky, who convinced Stalin, that Leonid had done his best by being cautious, just as he'd been ordered."

Sudoplatov had bailed Leonid out yet again, although Leonid hadn't told him the truth – that he'd used Anokhin for the job. I thanked Sudoplatov for what he had told me, and he thanked me for my help with his memoirs. I left.

That was the last piece in the puzzle. I'd suspected something like that, but Sudoplatov had confirmed it. Leonid needed to kill Colonel Anokhin because Anokhin knew that he had bungled the fire and assassination, that he had involved an outsider, that the outsider had escaped, and that Leonid had lied to his superiors. If Anokhin had surfaced, Leonid would have been finished. He needed to kill Anokhin, but he had to do it on his own, without alerting anyone within the secret police of Anokhin's existence.

Leonid had spent the last seventeen years of his life pleading for a reversal of his conviction and for the return of his Party card and medals. It now seems likely that he will get what he wanted, ten years after his death, even after the disappearance of the Soviet Union. His appeal will be heard by the Russian Supreme Court, and I've been advised that it will almost certainly succeed. I broke a promise to Leonid when I told Colonel Anokhin that Leonid had been Trotsky's aide. But in my meeting with Sudoplatov, I feel that I settled my account with Leonid by telling Sudoplatov nothing about what happened in Turkey. Leonid's reputation within the security services – all he really cared about – will be preserved.

MOSCOW, DECEMBER 25, 1991

Ramón murdered Trotsky out of love. Ramón loved Leonid as a son loves his father, and by killing Trotsky, he saved Leonid. Leonid loved Ramón too, more than he loved his children, or me, or any of his wives. Leonid and Ramón spent almost every day together for eleven years, from Leonid's release from prison in 1964 until Ramón left for Cuba in 1975. They'd given their lives to Communism, and it had pushed them aside. Ramón died shunned, and Leonid died cast out. They still called themselves Communists, but none of us believed as we once had.

I met Sakharov again in 1987 at a demonstration in Sokolniki Park. Gorbachev's glasnost policy allowed protest meetings, so the police were out in force, but they didn't interfere. Sakharov remembered me when I introduced myself; his face lit up, and he introduced me to his wife, Yelena Bonner. I felt the tight bond between them.

He was older than when I'd known him of course, but he seemed more spent than aged. After the government had refused to allow his wife to go to London for medical treatments, he'd gone on two hunger strikes. His exhausted face showed the damage they'd done; he was to die two years later in 1989. After his 1968 essay (the one that Petra had given me in Berlin), he'd continued to press for human rights. Our newspapers vilified him, and his 1975 Nobel Peace Prize only made things worse. Our government's policy at that time was not to execute dissidents but to expel them. They had stripped Solzhenitsyn of his citizenship and put him on a plane to Sweden, but Sakharov knew too many military secrets for that. After he denounced the 1979 invasion of Afghanistan and called for a boycott of the 1980 Moscow Olympics, they isolated him and his wife in Gorki, a closed military city forbidden to foreigners, and kept them under constant police surveillance. I'd read all Sakharov's essays in public libraries during my travels to the West. Recently, under Gorbachev's glasnost, I've been able to buy his books, and I'm leafing through one now. His views changed over the years. He'd begun by believing that the Soviet Union was "a breakthrough into the future, a prototype for all countries."

He ended by comparing it to a cancer cell. "What kind of country is this," he asked, "cruel and without a soul, that destroys its best citizens and cynically breaks its own laws and international agreements?" I once thought I was in love with him, but I wouldn't have had the courage to share his life and struggle the way that Yelena Bonner did.

Irina's father died two years after he joined her in Russia, and Irina died last month. I never saw either of them again. Irina couldn't forgive my family for the harm it had done hers. For her, we personified Communism.

Today, the last day of the Soviet Union, I find myself humming the Internationale:

> *Arise, you prisoners of starvation!*
> *Arise, you wretched of the earth!*
> *…*
>
> *We want no condescending saviors*
> *To rule us from their judgment hall!*
>
> *…*

But that's what the Party was – a condescending savior that proclaimed its duty to rule in the name of the workers until we achieved "true socialism." Before he joined Lenin and the Bolsheviks, Trotsky predicted an inevitable cascade:–the Party would rule in the name of the workers, the Central Committee would rule in the name of the Party, the Politburo would rule in the name of the Central Committee, and a dictator would rule in the name of the Politburo. He was right. That's how we came to Stalin. But then Trotsky accepted the Bolshevik "truth." And a belief in absolute truth will justify anything – the Inquisition, the Crusades, Islamic jihad, Hitler's death camps, the Gulag, the Purges, anything. The Old Bolsheviks – Lenin, Trotsky, Stalin, even Khrushchev – believed their truth, believed that killing millions would bring us the brotherhood of man. The next generation, Brezhnev and his apparatchiks, wanted only "stability." No more purges, no more political executions, just their turn at the trough. Repression would still be needed, but nothing so brutal as in the past – vegetarian repression rather than cannibal repression. By the 1980s, when Gorbachev tried to remake Communism, twenty-five years of stagnation had drained all life from it. The structure had rotted, and Communism collapsed of its own weight.

Where did we go wrong? Some say that if Lenin had lived or if Trotsky, not Stalin, had prevailed, things would have been different. But Trotsky had it easy. When he wrote from exile, he was not accountable for the consequences of his policies, the very policies that Stalin took up, policies that killed millions. The peasants would have resisted collectivization under Trotsky as they did under Stalin, and Trotsky would have solved the problem as Stalin did – with blood and starvation. The Red Terror began in 1918 with Lenin, Sverdlov, and Trotsky, long before Stalin took power.

But our leaders couldn't have done it alone. On this last day of the Soviet Union, I'm looking at a studio portrait of myself, taken not too long ago. I'm smiling proudly – rows of medals cover my chest. I may not have murdered for the Communist dream, as Ramón, Leonid, and my father did, but I was there too.

HISTORICAL NOTES

Many novels begin with a notice something like this: "Any resemblance to characters living or dead is unintended." Not this one.

While the Anokhin family is fictional, many Soviet citizens shared their lives: irremediable divisions, blackmail, labor camps, death, internal or external exile.

The Eitingon family is a mixture of fact and fiction.

Mary Kay Widmers's *The Eitingons* and Inez Cope Jefferey's *Inside Russia: The Life and Times of Zoya Zarubina* allowed me to fill in details of Zoya's life. She translated the secrets of the Manhattan Project, and she interpreted at the wartime conferences and the Nuremberg trials, but I have no idea of her attitudes toward the Soviet experiment. I have her admiring Akhmatova and Babel, meeting with Sakharov at the hydrogen bomb development site, in Berlin during the invasion of Prague, all of which I have invented. I have omitted her third marriage, a happy one. I have no evidence that Zoya was involved in the Soviet hydrogen bomb development or that she ever met Akhmatova or Sakharov.

Leonid Eitingon managed Trotsky's murder, but many of the claims by my character Leonid are exaggerated or false – murdering the Romanovs, being Trotsky's aide, flying the score of Shostakovich's 7th symphony into Leningrad for its premiere, etc. I have made Leonid into the Zelig of Communism, which he was not.

Akhmatova was evacuated from Leningrad to Tashkent in the spring of 1942. She did not stop in Moscow upon her return, as I have it.

For almost all other characters, I have tried to follow the historical record as closely as possible.

The Soviet secret service changed its name (but not its methods) every few years. It began as the Cheka and ended as the KGB. Today's version in Russia is the FSB. Members still call themselves "Chekists", and for most of Leonid's time, it was the NKVD. I have restricted my usage to Cheka and NKVD, ignoring GPU, OGPU, NGVB, and MGB.

ACKNOWLEDGEMENTS

I want to offer thanks:

To my wife and editor, Ellen Coffey, who read countless manuscripts, always with the same advice: "Less history, more story."

To Yuri Slezkine, who welcomed me into his Soviet history classes at Berkeley.

To Caitlin Pulleyblank, Daniel Coffey, David Mattson, Richard Adler, George Lewinski, Richard Leskosky, Jonathan Omerman and Michael Whitt for reading earlier drafts.

To AgencyAxis for the book cover and interior design.

And finally to my publicist, Margaret Lawler.

Patrick Coffey spent most of his career in the design of instruments for chemical research, founding or co-founding a number of scientific instrument companies. In 2003, he began research into the history of chemistry as a Visiting Scholar at the University of California, Berkeley. *Live Not By Lies* is the culmination of his long fascination with the Soviet Union.

Patrick is also the author of *Cathedrals of Science* (Oxford University Press, 2008), a nonfiction examination of the rivalries that shaped modern chemistry. *Publishers Weekly* called it a "an engrossing, often somber history." *Chemistry World* called it "A gripping page-turning narrative that elegantly combines popular science with a serious history of science." That book was positively blurbed by two Nobel laureates.

CATHEDRALS OF SCIENCE
By Patrick Coffey
Awarded the 2008 PROSE prize as the year's best book on chemistry or physics.

"A graphic depiction of the personalities and rivalries that made modern chemistry."—*ISIS*

"A gripping page-turning narrative that elegantly combines popular science with a serious history of science." —*Chemistry World*

"The center of Patrick Coffey's remarkable story is the ultimate difficult genius, an American original, G. N. Lewis. Around him, in peace and war, move the men and women who have shaped our understanding of molecules and how they react. And they are hardly at peace with each other."—*Roald Hoffman, chemist, writer, and winner of the Nobel Prize in Chemistry*

"This superbly crafted book traces the intertwined careers of scientific Titans." —*Dudley Herschbach, winner of the Nobel Prize in Chemistry*

"Coffey excels at showing how chemistry developed both despite and because of personal rivalries in this complex and engaging tale." —*David Lindley, author of Uncertainty: Einstein, Heisenberg, Bohr, and the Struggle for the Soul of Science*

"This book is a joy to read." —*John Servos, Anson D. Morse Professor of History, Amherst College and author of Physical Chemistry in America*

"A history alive with brilliance and infused with human frailties. A compelling account of scientific revolution, tragedies, rivalries, and inspiration." —*Nancy Greenspan, author of The End of the Certain World: The Life and Science of Max Born*